THE SECRET LIVES OF SISTERS

LINDA KELSEY

The Secret
Lives of Sisters

HODDER

First published in Great Britain in 2008 by Hodder & Stoughton
An Hachette Livre UK company

First published in paperback in 2008

1

A CIP catalogue record for this title
is available from the British Library

ISBN 978 0 340 97659 3 (A format)
ISBN 978 0 340 93341 1 (B format)

Typeset in Plantin Light by Hewer Text UK Ltd, Edinburgh
Printed and bound by Clays Ltd, St Ives plc

Hodder & Stoughton policy is to use papers that are natural, renewable
and recyclable products and made from wood grown in sustainable
forests. The logging and manufacturing processes are expected to
conform to the environmental regulations of the country of origin.

Hodder & Stoughton Ltd
338 Euston Road
London NW1 3BH

www.hodder.co.uk

For Susan

Acknowledgements

Grateful acknowledgement is made for permission to reprint from the following copyrighted work:

'Résumé' by Dorothy Paker from *The Collected Dorothy Parker* (Gerald Duckworth & Co Ltd., 1973), copyright 1944 by Dorothy Parker, reprinted by permission of the publisher.

PART ONE

PART ONE

Chapter One

2007

Twenty years. I suppose it's quite a stretch for a woman in her prime to go without sex, or even a date worth recounting. And yet here I am, on the day of my daughter's wedding, after two decades of self-imposed purdah, sitting on the edge of my double bed in a silk dressing gown and feeling only mildly curious as to why I have no real desire to change the status quo.

I think, quite suddenly, of a sun-ripened, Mediterranean peach, succulent, oozing, irresistible. My darling Melissa. She flashes briefly into view through the half-open door of the en-suite bathroom. Then my thoughts come back to myself. Mother-of-the-bride. Successful businesswoman. And desiccated coconut, spooned from a tin. A wry smile widens my mouth. Because toasted and sprinkled on muffins, it occurs to me, even desiccated coconut tastes surprisingly good. Generally, you see, I know how to look on the bright side. And I've been so very busy all these years.

Today of all days, nothing must go wrong. And so far it hasn't. Three consecutive days of constant drizzle have given way to a glorious blue sky, punctuated by unthreatening cumulus mediocris. I've been committing clouds to memory lately. To help me deal with the stress of the wedding. Learning something new always alleviates my anxiety, even if I forget it all again within a week. One anxious moment I'll teach myself clouds. The next, the names of ten Pullitzer-prize-winning authors, perhaps. Or half a dozen Hungarian expressions. Like *köszönöm szépan*, which means *thank you very much*. The sheer effort and concentration needed works every time to distract me from being a 'worrywort' as my kids so love to call me. When I was little my family called me Mouse. Mouse. Worrywort. Not so much changes in fifty years.

I have no issue with these flat-based, billowing clouds and their cauliflower-like appearance. They're common in the summer months. Good-news clouds. Unlike cumulus congestus, the kind of bothersome clouds which are taller than they are wide and can cause brief downpours, cumulus mediocris have the advantage of being about equal in width and height. Result: no precipitation. A perfect, sunny day for my daughter's wedding. No rain, no pain. Hopefully.

David, of course, should have been here. To walk his beautiful daughter down the aisle, to give her away – as though children are ever ours to give. But David has been dead for almost twenty years. David, the father of my two children. Not my husband; we didn't believe in marriage. We believed in love. And like Gloria Steinem I had no desire to 'breed in captivity', as I saw it then. He died on 14 October 1987. It seemed ironic that he – and therefore I –

were felled just two nights before the Great Storm that felled 15 million trees. While the nation mourned for its trees, I mourned for David. The following Monday, US$500 billion were wiped off the Dow in a single day, and the London Stock Exchange followed suit. The nation mourned for its bank balance, and I mourned for David. In the wake of these more material disasters, it was as though David's death had been downgraded. Just one more tree destroyed. Just one more share plummeting. David dead.

Driving back down the M1 from Birmingham at midnight, after spending the day looking at potential warehouses for our burgeoning business and having dined with one of the landlords, David skidded out of control, went hurtling into the crash barrier, overturned and ended up upside down, facing the oncoming traffic. There was oil on the road; it was the oil that caused the skid. When the car finally came to a halt, it blew up, blowing David up with it. There was nothing much left to identify.

The Great Storm that followed was merely a soundtrack to my grief, a symphony of pain and anger conjured up by vengeful gods, as if they hadn't already created enough havoc. Huddled under the covers with my uncomprehending children, six-year-old Melissa and Charlie, three, not yet out of night-time nappies, the roar of the wind drowned out the sound of my sobs. 'This way, this way, come and get me,' I wanted to cry. I longed for a tree to come crashing through my window and annihilate me. All of us. If only we could all go together . . . be together again with David. But we couldn't. I had to save myself for my children. From the moment it happened I was in no doubt. I knew I had to survive for them. It wasn't a choice.

At the cemetery, where David was buried the day after Black Monday, trees on the perimeter had crashed onto gravestones, causing several to shatter and fragment. It added a grotesquely gothic dimension to the funeral. 'They've lost everything,' I heard a former college friend of David's whisper. Did he mean us, or some other family, whose investments had gone up in smoke? 'Have you heard how many trees came down in Kew?' some distant cousin of David's I'd never even met before asked the woman standing next to her, who I also didn't recognise. 'A third, they're saying up to a third of all the trees. An absolute tragedy.'

The storm, the financial crash, David's death – it felt like the Apocalypse had finally arrived. And in a way, for me, it had.

When David died, I kind of shut up shop, sexually speaking at least. The thing is I lost him before I'd had the time to fall out of love with him. That's cynical, I know, but we live in cynical times and I've seen more divorces than I've seen happy marriages. I'd met David only ten years earlier. Who's to say what I may have felt this much further down the line?

As my friend Janet so succinctly put it of her own husband: 'Dom was great for about a decade; the last ten years he's been a total pain in the ass, and if it hadn't been for the kids I'd have divorced him years ago. Think of all the happy memories I'd have had if he'd died instead of David.' As the words came out of her mouth, her hand flew to cover it. 'Jesus, did I really say that? Am I really such an oaf?'

'It's OK, Janet, it's really OK,' I replied. 'He's been dead so long I can handle it now.'

Janet has been my best buddy since childhood. She's never put a foot wrong as far as friendship is concerned. Sweet, loyal, steady Janet. We met on the first day of starting school, when we were five. She had a little beauty spot just above the corner of her mouth on the left-hand side. I had a matching one to the right of my mouth. Her birthday was the day after mine. We decided we were twins, separated at birth. Almost identical in height when we met, we seemed to grow at exactly the same pace as one another. And we both had dark brown hair, although mine was curly and hers straight. I never had to forgive Janet for saying – or doing – the wrong thing, because she never did anything to deliberately hurt me.

But no one knows how to behave in the face of death. What to say, how to compose their face when they offer you condolences, whether to talk about it endlessly, or not at all, whether to buck you up or leave you alone, when and whether to start fixing you up. I called a moratorium on men when David died. I could be a mother, I could be a breadwinner, I could even smile, but I couldn't do a man as well.

I don't dwell on this stuff all the time, not any more, but I suppose that weddings are the kind of occasions that bring all sorts of emotions sharply into focus.

Melissa, the about-to-be bride, thinks David and I must have been antediluvian in our attitudes to marriage. She doesn't remember a great deal about her father, and Charlie doesn't seem to remember him at all.

'What a reactionary pair of old hippies you and David were, missing out on all of this.'

'Revolutionary, I think you must mean,' I correct.

I'm leaning up against the doorway of the bathroom now. She's inside, draped in a towelling robe and with a towel turban on her head, applying moisturiser.

Melissa peers at a blemish on her cheek and touches it in a way I recognise.

'It's nothing, Melissa, don't even think about squeezing it. Unless, that is, you want to walk down the aisle with an approximation of a suppurating sore on your left cheek-bone.'

She gives the blemish a tiny little prod with her finger-nail, before turning the double-sided mirror around, away from the magnifying glass. 'All that living together without getting married, what was that about? What exactly was the point?'

'We didn't need a piece of paper to demonstrate our commitment. I was a feminist. Or at least I'd read the books.'

'But Mum, you're not even a proper widow. People just assume David was some bloke you used to hang out with and that you're a single mum by choice. It doesn't win the sympathy vote in the same way.'

'Where do you get your ideas from, Melissa? I don't want the sympathy vote. I never did. If there isn't a word for me, that's everyone else's problem, not mine.'

'So do you disapprove of my marrying Stefan?'

'It's not for me to approve or disapprove. I like him well enough and he makes you happy, which is what matters. But I'd rather have written you a cheque for twenty grand, which you could have put towards buying a flat that's bigger than my kitchen, than blow it on a lavish party that will be over in a matter of hours.'

'But if you couldn't have afforded it . . . if the market for Rampant Rabbits has suddenly dried up . . .'

'Melissa, my love, I never said I couldn't afford it. I can afford it. I'm a hugely successful businesswoman as all those Businesswoman of the Year awards on my mantelpiece and this lovely empty house will testify. I'm just trying to make a point.'

'But I don't know what your point is.'

'That a wedding is not a marriage. Look, it really doesn't matter – it's all going to be absolutely wonderful. It's just that I can't understand why big weddings, which were so quaintly old-fashioned a few years back, are now so very fashionable again.'

'Mum, I do wish you'd meet someone.'

'If I'd wanted to I probably would have done by now.'

'But why didn't you want to?'

'Too busy, I guess. With you two and the business. Too in love with the one that got away.'

Melissa walks over and enfolds me in terry towelling arms.

'Oh Mum, you're a true romantic, still pining after all these years. But you can't use the excuse of being too busy any more. Charlie and I aren't living at home, and you've got Cat and all these director people working in your company. What do they do all day long if not run things for you?'

'Look, you've made me cry,' I say, smiling weakly through watery eyes and drawing back from Melissa. 'My mascara's running and I haven't even seen you in your bridal gown yet. I'll be a wreck before the day is over. But to answer your question, I guess I've lost the knack, if ever I had it. And now I'm fifty-one. Who wants fifty-one when any man over the age of fifty himself can quite easily get forty-one, or even thirty-one?'

'But you're beautiful.'

'And you need to put your contact lenses in.'

The doorbell rings. It could be the hairdresser, the make-up artist, the photographer or the videographer. Or maybe all at once. Melissa has lined up a production team as efficiently as only a rising star in the competitive firmament of TV reality-show production would know how.

She's so very modern, my daughter. There's a fierceness about Melissa that sometimes scares me. Losing her father when she was so young could of course have something to do with it, making her tough before her time, and I suppose that to an extent she's inherited David's confidence, for which I'm grateful. Charlie's more like me, he can be quite meek, but physically he's the spitting image of his dad. Whenever I've said to Melissa, 'You sounded exactly like David when you said that,' or to Charlie, 'The way you walked into the room, you looked just like your father,' it seems to grate. I suppose you don't want to be defined by a dead person you hardly knew. So I hold back.

Melissa doesn't only know what she wants, she knows how to go about getting it. Stefan, the fiancé, is a high-flyer in TV himself, head of a fast-growing group of cable or satellite stations, I forget which, but I remember it's something to do with digital. It's TV you can watch on your watch, I think, or maybe it's on your mobile. I've not yet mugged up on twenty-first-century TV but it could be a good topic for my next anxious patch.

'Oh my God, Mum, he's clever, he's handsome, he's successful and s-o-o-o sexy,' Melissa enthused when she'd been seeing him for about three weeks. 'And his cooking is better than Jamie Oliver's.'

'Mmm, practically perfect,' I replied. 'He's also, I understand, forty-two, which is seventeen years older than you, and divorced with two teenagers.'

'Which means he'll be a great dad to our children when we have them.'

'Oh, so you're planning babies?'

'He's asked me to marry him.'

I tried to remain calm. 'But you've known him only three weeks.'

'So?'

'Can we just clear up one thing? You're telling me he'll be a great dad. Is this because he was a crap, absent dad first time around?'

'Exactly.'

'But where's the logic?'

'Well, because he was a crap dad first time around, he's determined to be brilliant next time. And of course he's completely over the whole drug thing.'

'And what drug thing might that be?'

'You know, the whole "how to score the next line of coke" thing. Everyone under thirty-five is doing it, but he's done it, and he's over it. Wouldn't touch the stuff again if it came free for life with freshly minted rolled-up fifties. Plus, he cooks so I don't have to.'

I wouldn't even have known how to start the conversation about Stefan's days as a junkie, so I focused on Melissa's cooking skills.

'Don't you want to? Don't you want to even learn how to?'

'Can't see any reason. How many thousands of meals have you cooked for us, and where did it get you?'

'Why did it have to get me anywhere? You had to eat and someone had to cook it. I enjoy cooking, it's calming and nurturing and loving and—'

'Whatever turns you on, Mum. I thought we were talking about me and Stefan. Did I mention he has loadsamoney? Or rather he would have if he hadn't had to give his bitch ex-wife half the house, pay all her bills because she's too lazy to work, as well as cough up two lots of school fees.'

'So if he still has half the house, how come he's moved out of rented accommodation and into your shoebox with you?'

'Well, he did have this habit, and he's still paying off his debts. Don't give me that look. He has been completely open and honest with me. Just like I'm being with you.'

Unlike Charlie, who tends to share only the most basic of information, Melissa barely burps without giving me a full account. There are things a parent just doesn't need to be told. I suppose she sees me as a friend and I should be grateful. I am grateful, and I adore her, but she constantly seeks my opinion, then gets furious when I give it. Though better this way than how it was with my mother.

Remembering this conversation, which took place at the time Melissa announced her engagement, I shiver at the thought of my beloved daughter marrying a debt-ridden former junkie with a demanding ex-wife and two surly teenage sons. Stefan is charming, amusing, smart, no question, but is he right for Melissa? And what in any case can I do about it? Precisely nada.

The doorbell rings again.

'Mum, will you get it? I can't go down like this.'

I pull my silk dressing gown tighter round me, walk over to the window and push up one of the slats in the wooden blinds to get a better view. There's a whole crowd down there! At least six of them, clutching camera cases and vanity cases and plastic carrier bags full of . . . stuff.

Behind them, coming up the pathway to the house, is an elderly woman in a thick, bean-green coat and clompy, laced black shoes – entirely unsuitable for this brilliantly sunny July day. From the upstairs window the woman appears to be short and squat in stature: a stubby, upright rectangle, no more than five foot tall, with heavy-set legs and arms straining at the seams of her coat. She's walking in a tottery sort of way with the aid of stick, shifting her weight from leg to leg in a motion that looks as though it's merely moving her from side to side rather than propelling her forwards towards the front door. But far from being fragile, her gait has a stubbornness to it, a gruff determination that marks her out as a survivor rather than a victim of the passing years. Her freshly permed hair, coiled like icing on the perimeter of a wedding cake, peeks out from under a headscarf.

I recognise the scarf, it's the one I bought her last Christmas from Hermès. I know it's insanity to buy such lavish presents for Mavis. She doesn't have a clue who or what Hermès is, and she'd be appalled if she knew how much it cost. But I do it every year. It's the kind of gift I might have bought for my own mother if she'd still been alive and it always gives me a particular satisfaction, treating Mavis as the equal she never was in our house.

I bang on the window enthusiastically and a half-dozen faces look up at me and start waving and grinning. Mavis shades her bifocals from the sun to look up, and a smile illuminates her powdery-pale face.

I wanted to send a car for her. Mavis, who lives in Essex these days, wouldn't hear of it. Despite the hip replacement, and despite the trembling in her hands, which could be the first stage of Parkinson's Disease, Mavis was determined to be at the wedding and adamant about getting the train in from Chelmsford to Liverpool Street, then taking the tube from there to Belsize Park, where we live.

I never did lose touch with Mavis. We were bound together in so very many ways.

'Mavis is here,' I call in the direction of the bathroom. 'Plus the director, cameraman, grip, gaffer, gofer, wardrobe mistress, stunt coordinator and goodness knows who else from your personal film-production team for the wedding of the year. Do you want Mavis up here with us, or shall I get her to wait down in the living room?'

'Why not bring her on up? The more the merrier. Bet she's gone overboard with the 4711 you bought her as her leaving present in 1966.'

I laugh. I don't think Melissa gets Mavis. I don't think she at all understands the bond between me and a maid who left our family home some forty years previously, and why I'm the only member of the family who continued to see her. There's no reason why she should understand; I've never properly explained. To do so would be like opening Pandora's box. And in my view, if the lid fits, you should keep it firmly shut.

Apart from me, and my children, and David before he died, no one has seen Mavis since she left when I was just ten years old. Well, she did meet my dad just once after she left, to make some arrangements. The truth is that I need Mavis as much as she needs me. Sometimes Mavis is the one person who can bring me back from the brink. How my sister Cat's going to react when she comes face to face with the woman she regards as her childhood tormentor is something I've mostly managed to avoid thinking about. I meant to warn Cat, I really did, but with all the excitement of the wedding preparations it must just have slipped my mind . . .

Chapter Two

The 1980s

The House of Hannah. I thought it had the right ring to it. Not cheap, not faddish or trendy, and definitely not sleazy.

David agreed. 'I like it. Sounds established before it's even off the starting blocks. And there's something you can trust about it as well. The product may be frivolous, but the name of the company tells you the business is anything but . . .'

I smiled at my lover, the man who'd made everything that had happened so far matter so much less. 'And with House of Hannah, I don't suppose the Dirty Mac Brigade will be beating a path to our door.'

'But surely,' he said, licking his lips mock-lasciviously, 'we wouldn't mind a few Dirty Macs. We do have to think of the bottom line.'

'You're impossible! I'm trying to launch a classy business here. If you want to throw pass-the-knickers parties with a glass of Babycham and a bunch of bored housewives, you've chosen the wrong girl. The House of Worth, the House of Chanel and all the other Paris salons, that's where I got my inspiration. I thought we should be a House of, too.'

'Yes, Hannah, my love, I quite agree, but let's not get carried away with ourselves. You're thinking about the great couturiers and I'm thinking about crotchless panties. And how I can't wait to see you in your very first pair. Come bit a closer, would you?'

We were sitting on the sofa, brainstorming. Or at least we were until David decided that we needed a sex break. We had sex breaks about as regularly as most workers had tea breaks at that point in our relationship. David had tangoed into my life and made me truly happy, perhaps for the first time.

I half-heartedly attempted resisting. 'But David, we're supposed to be working on the business plan . . .'

'This won't stop us. You know how inspired I get when your legs are wrapped around my neck.' It was impossible to reply. David was pulling my T-shirt over my head and I was effectively gagged.

'No more greying bras and big knicks for you, my girl,' he laughed, surveying my overwashed, understyled, once-white underwear. 'I see front ribbon fastenings and black-leather thongs.'

'Oh pleeease, David. How about a little decorum? All you do is lower the tone.'

'Forget the House of Hannah, Hannah. Let's call it the House of Harlots.'

'Or how about the House of Harpies?'

'Did you mean Herpes? Apparently there's a lot of it about.'

'You're disgusting.'

I was lying back on the sofa, laughing, lifting my bottom

to wriggle out of my jeans. 'How about handcuffs?' I suggested. 'Covered with real sable of course.'

'Whips. I love whips . . .'

'Oh yummy. I love walnut whips, too.'

David chose to ignore me. '. . . but only in the best-quality napa leather. I won't beat you too hard, at least not until you beg for it.'

'But I thought I was supposed to whip *you*. I thought you were a masochist. Now you tell me you're a sadist as well.'

'We clearly don't know one another as well as we thought.'

'Janet Reger, eat your heart out.' I giggled. 'There are two naughty new kids on the knickers block.'

'My twin peaks of perfection,' said David playfully as he cupped my now naked breasts in his hands, and his lips, feather-lightly, brushed over my nipples, making them hard and full of longing. 'We'll take a cast of your body and sculpt it, life-size, in bronze. It will stand in the lobby of company headquarters.'

'Could you just call the board meeting to a halt?' I requested breathlessly. 'There is some urgent other business I need to attend to.' I guided David inside me. How lucky I felt to have met the man who could fill all the empty places. I wanted to make love to him for the rest of my life.

I was in my third year of university when I met David. I was reading English. He was a bit of a boffin, having already graduated from Harvard Business School with an MBA. His first degree had been in languages, French and German, after which he'd worked for Deutsche Bank in Frankfurt for a couple of years. Instead of heading straight for the City or one of the big multinational corporations when he returned from the States, he had decided to teach for a while. My own university had just set up a business school, and David was perfectly placed not just to teach but to advise on course content. He had a dread of getting lost in a big organisation and believed himself to have an entrepreneurial streak. Although his goal was to set up in business on his own, he found he was a natural at teaching, and was happy to carry on with it until the right idea came along. He was still only twenty-seven when we met in 1977. Surprisingly, it turned out to be me, rather than him, who had the Big Idea. If I hadn't, I think he might still have been teaching when. . . . Well, I suppose if he'd still been teaching, he wouldn't have been driving back from Birmingham the night of. . . . This is pointless, but I still do it, twenty years on I still can't help myself

I must have picked up the business gene from my dad. From about the age of twelve, I used to go and work at his factory in Hackney in the holidays. He was trying as best he could to be a good father, and taking me to the factory didn't interfere with his social life.

We used to drive there in his big grey Jag with the leather seats and listen to Radio 4. My favourite job was packing. I loved it in the packing room, surrounded by boxes and dresses on rails that had already been sorted for orders and clipped together in bundles. Folding up the dresses neatly and putting them into cardboard boxes for postage to shops around the country had a pleasing certainty about it. You knew the outcome, not like when you learned something for an exam at school and didn't know whether or not you'd done well until the results came through. It was a job that demanded care, but not too much thinking. The packers were always nice to me, not just, I think, because I was the boss's daughter, but because I took my packing job seriously and didn't slack.

At lunchtime I'd go into my dad's office, which was separated off from the main stockroom. I'd help him do *The Times* crossword, or at least I'd try to. I hardly ever solved a clue, but I learned the principles of cryptic crosswords, and have remained hooked ever since. Like learning new facts by heart, doing a difficult crossword when I'm anxious is a fail-safe distraction.

We'd eat the ham and pickle sandwiches his secretary, Pat, had popped out to get. I think it was the ritual, the routine, that I craved and welcomed. It staved off, if only for a while, the confusion and chaos that had come to reign elsewhere in my life, in all our lives. Occasionally, while we were eating our sandwiches, someone would knock on the door to ask a question and my dad would give his opinion or tell them what to do. He had such an easy authority, and it made me proud that he was my dad.

The girls, as my dad called his seamstresses, sat at their sewing machines in long rows facing one another. In between them was the trough, where the discarded off-cuts of material would be thrown. The whirring of the machines and the constant chatter, punctuated by occasional bursts of shouting or laughter, made it seem a happy place. My dad would wander through, like a king greeting his public, stopping here and there to say something to one of the girls. There must have been about fifty of them, and he knew every one of them by name. He'd joke with them: 'That new boyfriend of yours, tell him if he doesn't treat you right he'll have me to deal with . . .' or 'Nice dress you're wearing. Would you mind coming into my office and taking it off so I can see how it's made?' And they'd banter back: 'Yes, Mr Saunders . . . No, Mr Saunders . . . Ooh, you are a one . . .'

'He's a real gent, your dad,' they'd say to me. 'Got an eye for the girls, that's for sure, but he'd never lay a hand on one of us.' 'Wouldn't mind if he did,' said the girl they all called Spotty because she always came to work wearing polka dots, and then everyone burst out laughing. I remembered how once my dad had said Mavis was better off working for us than working in a factory and I thought how very wrong he was. At least she would have had friends her own age, people who were what my parents called working class, people like her, instead of being the odd one out, not quite good enough to share a table with at supper.

I did sometimes hear the girls whispering about the situation at home. 'He must be lonely,' they said. 'So eligible,' they said. 'I wouldn't mind bagging myself someone as rich and handsome as him, even if he is twice my age,' said Spotty.

My dad had set up in the rag trade, as people used to call it then, shortly after the war, in the days when the average working girl or young housewife bought dresses rather than designer labels, and was desperate for anything new, stylish or not, after the privations of the war years.

'Anyone with more than a couple of brain cells could make a mint back then,' he insisted.

'But how, I want to know, how?' I'd badger him on the journey home from east London where the factory was, to north London where we lived.

'Well, you have to remember I was still in uniform. I was a major. It didn't just buy me respect, it bought me extra coupons from the Board of Trade to help me set up in business.'

'But what were the coupons for?'

My dad enjoyed telling stories. 'During the war, and for a few years after, when the war effort caused shortages from food to fabric, things had to be rationed. Otherwise the rich people, for example, might have bought up all the food while others might literally have starved. So the idea of coupons was to limit how much a person could get of everything from eggs to overcoats.'

'So was everything just free? The government gave you coupons for nothing?'

'And I thought you, Miss Mouse, were supposed to be the bright one in the family. No, of course none of it was free, you had to hand your coupon over to the shopkeeper along with your money. No coupon, no goods. Except on the black market, but we'll get to that.'

'So how did this help you to start up the business?'

'Well, I went along to the Board of Trade and got enough coupons to buy about two thousand yards of fabric. But before I bought the fabric I paid a visit to Oxford Street. I looked in all the dress shops at the different styles – there wasn't a great deal of variety at the time – and worked out which looked the most popular style from the number of shops it appeared in and how many of the same dress there were on the rails.'

'Tell me about the dress. Please tell me about the dress. I want you to tell me exactly what it looked like.' Business had taken on the aura of a magical world, not boring at all.

'OK, OK, let's take it nice and slowly, shall we? Now let me see . . . It had a crew neck and short sleeves, and it was a simple A-line shape with a pocket on either side at the front around hip level.'

'Yuk! Not exactly what Mum would call flattering.'

'It didn't really matter to me what it looked like, as long as it would sell. I wasn't trying to be Norman Hartnell, I was a businessman.'

'Would Mummy have worn it?' His eyes clouded for a moment, then he recovered himself and smiled.

'Your mother? Are you kidding? Mavis would have. Your mother was strictly a black-market sort of girl.'

'So how did *that* work?'

'Slowly, Mouse. We're getting there. I took the dress and the fabric to a small factory, had the dresses made up, sold them back down Oxford Street, and a business empire was born! Soon I had my own factory. Easy, I tell you; it was Easy Peasy, like that songbook you used to have. The black market, to answer your earlier question, was simply buying goods in addition to your rations. I'd managed to save up quite a bit during my time in India during the war. Ready cash and no documentation can get you a long way. Under-the-counter business was a way of life.'

'Are you a criminal, then?'

'In the strictest sense, yes. But look at all that employment I've created. I've boosted the economy and no harm done to anyone.'

'Would you let me come and work for you?'

'I thought that's exactly what you are doing.'

'I mean later, when I leave school.'

'I've been doing some thinking. You're smart, really smart. I'm not sure that university is going to do much for you in the long run, once you're married with kids, but you've got a brain and you might as well use it.'

'But I could come and work for you afterwards.'

'Out of the question. You can't run a business and a family at the same time.'

'I can't see why not.'

'That's because you're thirteen. University, yes. Taking over my business? Out of the question, young woman.'

In the sixties and seventies my dad's business really boomed. One day there was a picture on the front page of the *Daily Mirror* of Brigitte Bardot wearing a black and white op-art minidress; the next day my dad's company was selling an exact copy of it all along the King's Road.

You'd think Maurice, my dad, and David would have been made for one another. They weren't. I wasn't sure what made my dad more furious. The fact that we refused to get married, even after the children were born. Or David's business degree.

'Teaching! About bloody right for a boy with all those qualifications. Why doesn't anyone realise any more that the only way to learn about business is to work in one. No poncey MBA is going to show you how to do that. Harvard, shmarvard, if you ask me.'

I think that what Dad really wanted was for David to ask him for a job. But David didn't want a job with my dad – he could see my dad would only ever want to do things his way; and my dad was too proud to ask, in case David turned him down. Even when the business started to go downhill in the mid-1980s, and my dad was forced to sell it at a knock-down price, he was too pig-headed to ask for David's help. David could have introduced business systems, sourced factories abroad where the dresses could have been made cheaper to offset the pressure on margins in the UK retail trade. As Cat showed no sign of settling down with anyone, Dad's dynastic dreams about bringing sons-in-law into the business were just that. Dreams.

When Cat graduated from the London College of Fashion with a wow of a final-year degree show that had big-name manufacturers queuing to take her on, Dad could easily have persuaded her to design some cutting-edge collections for him. Instead, he sniffed, 'Cat's far too creative for my business. We're in the rag trade, not fashion. The last thing we need is a designer with too many ideas.'

It was partly chauvinism on my dad's part, partly a refusal to acknowledge that life – and business – was moving on.

David and I didn't always agree when we talked business, but we always sparked one another off, built on each other's ideas. The teasing and the joking and the joshing seemed to free our imaginations. My father thought we were doomed from the start.

'Number one: the only hands-on experience David's had as far as I'm aware is on his own dick,' he bellowed. When my dad was irate about something his whole personality seemed to change. He could go from City gent to East End barrow boy in an instant. 'Number two: I don't know how it happened, but I seem to have raised a daughter who is both a feminist and a mouse. All this new-fangled claptrap about job-sharing and maternity leave will bankrupt you before you've begun. And as if that's not bad enough, when anyone wants a pay rise you'll adopt your usual Mouse position and double their wages without a fight. Number three: if you want your marriage, or rather this ridiculous living-together relationship, to last, you need to spend as much time apart as possible. If you work together as well as eat together and sleep together, I guarantee you'll be separated before you start to show a profit. Not that I think this ridiculous knickers venture ever will show a profit. And then when you do split up, you're going to have to split the business too. How in hell are you going to handle that?'

There was never any use in fighting my dad. In any case, I had other influences in my life by then. One of them was called Helen Gurley Brown, the founder of *Cosmopolitan* magazine, which became my bible in the late 1970s. I was thrilled to discover that I wasn't the only Mouse in the universe. According to Helen Gurley Brown she, too, started as a mouse, as did countless other women. She had this theory about human mice, once describing herself as a mouseburger who, through patience, planning and never giving up, advanced in her chosen field and married the man of her dreams. So the two of us had something in common. She'd been a mouse, I still was. But even a mouse could make it if she really tried.

'Thanks for the encouragement, Dad,' was all I said. If you didn't have the right words to answer back, I'd discovered, the best thing was to keep quiet and then go off and do exactly as you pleased. I loathed any kind of confrontation.

He just laughed. 'Now don't misunderstand me, Hannah. I don't want you to think that I don't like David, because I do. And I'm not a philistine, I believe in education. If I didn't, I wouldn't have encouraged you to go to university. But I'd like David a whole lot more if he had the decency to put a ring on your finger and if he'd only realise that those letters after his name stand for Mean Bugger-All when it comes to business.'

It was 1980. I gave birth to My Big Idea the year before I gave birth to Melissa.

Despite the name of the company, I had no desire to be the front woman. My plan was to stay as much as possible behind the scenes. I knew I'd be comfortable sorting out marketing, production, personnel, while David would focus on finance and contracts and other admin. Cat, though she didn't know it yet, was going to be our public face. Extrovert and increasingly outrageous, Cat would be designer and PR extraordinaire. David wasn't so sure.

'She's so overbearing. It doesn't bother me, because I can give as good as I get. But you, you're like the incredible shrinking woman when you're in her presence.'

'But she's so creative.'

'So are you.'

'Not in the same way. I have ideas, but I couldn't design anything to save my life. And the thought of having my photo taken for a newspaper, or being interviewed on the radio – I know it's pathetic but I just can't do it.'

'I don't know what's the matter with you, Hannah. You're far more beautiful than Cat, so there's no question of who'd take the better picture. And you're far more articulate than Cat, so you'd be better at interviews as well.'

'David, you have to believe me, we really do need Cat. No Cat, no deal.'

'How come you're not the mouse with me? You're quite the dominatrix with poor old David.'

'I love you.'

'I love you back.'

The Big Idea was underwear. Subtly sexy underwear aimed at the new breed of power-dressing women who were just beginning to make waves in the business world. Women who went to work in navy or grey suits that gave nothing away, who had adopted the philosophy that the more serious they looked, the more likely they were to be taken seriously.

I'd seen the shoulders pads in *Dallas* and *Dynasty*, and had instantly understood why women fell in love with them. Not only did shoulder pads make your hips look slimmer, they made you look strong and in control. Big shoulders, big success, had become the career girl's mantra. I also knew, from my own inclinations and my observations of women around me, that women increasingly wanted not just jobs but careers which would free them from financial dependence on men. As women slowly amassed their own wealth, I concluded, they'd want to spend at least some of it on little luxuries for themselves.

If a woman needed to ape men in the workplace, she would need some kind of outlet for her femininity as well. Something that reminded her that beneath the tough exterior she was still essentially a woman. This flew in the face of orthodox feminism, but as a business proposition it was irresistible. If we could sell this idea in a subtle way, appealing to women's sensuality at the same time as countering the de-feminising effect of corporate culture, we'd be on to something. The guys wouldn't have a hint of what was going on underneath the pinstripe suiting; it would be a purely personal confidence booster, a way of playing the game required to get on, while introducing an invisible secret weapon . . . the sex siren within. I knew it was a smart idea. But just how smart it would turn out to be I could never have predicted.

Chapter Three

2007

The bride is not ready and I am beginning to sweat. Unless we leave in fifteen minutes we will be late. My face is turning from matte to shiny, and little damp patches are beginning to appear on the underarms of the devoré-silk vintage flapper dress I bought on eBay in a moment of mother-of-the-bride madness. I blame the photographer for the hold-up. Fresh from college she is anxious to leave no detail unrecorded. She has spent at least twenty minutes photographing Melissa's shoes. First in the box, nestled amongst tissue. Next in the box, but with the lid at a jaunty angle. After that out of the box, with the Jimmy Choo label clearly showing. Then from the back, from the side, from above. I hope we don't end up with an album full of wedding accessories and no bride. The same rigmarole for the dress. She feels compelled to photograph it on its hanger outside the cupboard, then lying on the bed like a shroud. Next the tiara is dangled from the dressing-table mirror, but 'it doesn't quite work', so it is repositioned on a plumped-up pillow on my bed. At last she turns her attention to the bride.

I consult my watch. 'Do we really need pictures of you in your rollers?' I ask Melissa, as the photographer squeals, 'Hold it just there, that's perfect,' and the stylist freezes in the middle of pinning a jumbo-sized roller into place.

'It's called reportage, Mum. I don't want a bunch of dreary line-ups.'

'And I thought that reportage was for covering wars, not weddings. Well, silly me. I wonder if the guests will blame the reportage when we arrive an hour late.'

The photographer is looking nervous. She'll probably take deliberately unflattering pictures of me now.

'It's a bride's prerogative to be late,' says Melissa.

'Yes, darling.'

Eventually Melissa's coiffure is done. Her thick, dark hair is piled in an up-do on top of her head, with trendy bed-head tendrils allowed to escape at the front and fall to her cream-puff shoulders.

'What about the tiara?' I ask.

'I'm off tiaras,' says Melissa firmly. 'They're such a cliché . . .'

'Since when exactly?'

'Since two minutes ago,' says Melissa, surveying the masterpiece that she is in the mirror.

'At least we'll have the photos.' I can't help but sound exasperated.

'Muuumm. . . .'

'Oh all right. Tiaras are yesterday's news. And it's only two hundred pounds' worth of Swarovski crystal,' I sigh.

Melissa plucks a small gardenia from her bridal bouquet and I hold my breath in the hope that the entire floral arrangement doesn't fall apart. She tucks the kidnapped bloom into her abundant up-do and of course she's right. It perfectly offsets her espresso-coloured hair.

With a complete lack of inhibition, despite the presence of the male videographer and the male make-up artist, Melissa stands, shrugs her robe from her shoulders and allows it to fall to the floor. She is wearing a cream satin strapless bra with matching briefs and suspender belt, decorated with chantilly lace, and a pair of silk stockings, all courtesy of the House of Hannah bridal range.

Paul, the videographer, makes a funny gurgling noise in his throat at the sight of her voluptuous, sexy-but-chaste form. I gasp too, not at her body, which I know well, but at her confidence.

'Horny, honey?' Melissa flashes Paul a smile, more dazzling even than usual thanks to a pre-nuptial regime of regularly applied teeth-bleaching preparation. 'It's the fact that the goods are forbidden, darling, isn't it, rather than the goods themselves? Does the trick every time.'

Paul is no slouch at sexual banter. 'I can see your card is marked on this particular day, sweetheart, but how about when you're home from the honeymoon? It would be an honour to give you a private screening of the wedding video.'

Melissa laughs and turns her attention to Igor, the make-up artist. He, too, is looking pop-eyed at the bride.

'Iggy, my love, I know it's not me, it's my underwear you're after. Just call my mum when this is over – some of her best customers are trannies.'

'Oh, how heavenly,' Igor replies. 'I don't suppose I could get a discount . . .' He looks hopefully at me from beneath his fluttering, false eyelashes.

'You've done such a great job with Melissa's make-up,' I say, trying to keep up with the conversation and ignore the fact that I am in a surreal re-enactment of *The Rocky Horror Show*. 'Anything you want from the collection is yours, anything at all, and all at cost.'

'You're an absolute angel! All of you, absolute angels.' Igor flicks his enormous blusher brush across Melissa's nose. '*Voilà*! You're done.'

Thank God Mavis decided to go downstairs and make herself a cup of tea while all this was going on. I'm not sure she could have coped. I'm not sure I can cope either.

'The dress, Melissa. Please, the dress.'

Charlie appears at the bedroom doorway.

'What's going on here? Bloody hell, Melissa, it looks like the set for a porn movie. Too much flesh, sister, too much flesh.'

'Thanks, bro, I love you, too. Actually, look at you, you scrub up extraordinarily well. I hardly recognise you.'

Igor eyes him up and down appreciatively.

Charlie, whose usual sartorial style is Camden Market grunge, grubby jeans and vintage rock-band-tour T-shirts, is wearing a black Giorgio Armani suit with a white shirt and black-and-white-striped tie. Paid for, of course, like everything else to do with this wedding, by me.

'You look so like . . .' I only just manage to stop myself from saying 'so like David at your age'.

'So like who?' Melissa chirps in cheerfully.

'Like a seriously stylish Mafiosi of course.'

'Thanks, Mum,' says Charlie, and I wonder if he's thanking me for the compliment or the fact that he knew exactly what was about to come out of my mouth before I stopped myself.

Charlie pulls a pair of dark sunglasses from his breast pocket and puts them on, running his fingers through his gelled hair, which usually flops forward to mask his entire face but on this occasion has been slicked back into near-submission.

'Wow,' says Melissa, 'you really are the perfect toy boy for my desperate single friends.'

'I don't do older women,' says Charlie sniffily. Does he 'do' women at all, I wonder. I've certainly never known him to have a girlfriend.

'Oh but you do,' I butt in, determined to ward off the fast-advancing chaos I can feel about to engulf us. 'Mavis is waiting downstairs in the kitchen. And you are going to go downstairs this very minute to put her into my car so you can drive her to the club. This minute, do you understand, before I . . . before I . . .'

'Now you're talking, Mum. When I said I don't do older women, I didn't mean Mavis. When it comes to older women Mavis is in a league of her own.'

'Careful, Charlie,' I say.

'It's all right, Mum, we all like Mavis, we really do. It will be a pleasure to escort her to the wedding. Right, I'm off.'

'Don't put her too near the front,' I call after him as he disappears from sight, thudding downstairs in the direction of his charge. Knowing Charlie, he'll plonk her right next to Cat.

It takes three of us to help Melissa into her Vera Wang strapless mermaid gown. It hugs her hourglass curves – her naturally pumped-up breasts, small waist, slightly visible mound of tummy and a bottom that bounces when she walks – like a second skin, before flaring dramatically just below the knee into a fan-tiered skirt that reaches to the floor and sweeps out behind her.

Melissa is so refreshingly unlike the fashionable catwalk skinnies in the magazines or any of her diet-obsessed girlfriends. She eats chocolate truffles and red meat and chunky chips with abandon and seems to enjoy having a body that appears to have been moulded in an altogether other era. Nothing would persuade Melissa into jeans or cargo pants or anything trendily androgynous. She's a late-fifties Vargas girl as drawn for the cover of *Playboy* magazine, but with an attitude honed by Girl Power. She dresses for her form in pencil skirts and high heels, clingy sweater dresses, or black polo necks cinched at the waist with a wide red patent belt. She adores the camp glamour of it all. In fact she'd be the perfect poster girl for the House of Hannah.

I've thought about it often, the great PR we'd get if the daughter of the founder of the company stripped off for the camera. Cat has tried to persuade me that in a post-feminist world in which even A-list actresses happily pose near-naked in glossy men's mags to publicise their latest movie, the taint of sleaze has virtually disappeared. But I've always held back. It's hypocritical, I know, but despite having made a fortune from peddling panties, I didn't want my daughter, my little girl, exposed in that way.

Puberty hit Melissa so early I was terrified for her. She didn't seem to mind and couldn't wait to prance around her bedroom in totally unsuitable new season samples from the House of Hannah catalogue, while I insisted on Marks & Spencer basics. As a young teenager Melissa had been way too full-blown for her pimpled peers. They seemed to visibly shrink in her presence, although I'm sure it was quite a different story after lights out under the protective cover of their duvets. Having frightened off all the boys her own age, from the age of fourteen Melissa always dated older men. Stefan was the latest in a long line of boyfriends almost old enough to be her father.

The shrinks would have had a field day. But it's too trite to assume that with no dad to call her own Melissa has spent her life searching for a father-figure. I tend to think that her attraction to older guys has more to do with her own early maturity and adolescent relationships than the fact that David died when she was six.

Charlie, three years Melissa's junior, is far more remote than his ambitious, self-assured sister. Although he doesn't appear to be unhappy, he seems – to me at least – to be on the edge of life, rather than in the thick of it. I know so little about him these days I sometimes feel like saying, 'I'm Hannah, pleased to meet you,' and taking our relationship from there, from the beginning. Not that it was like that at the beginning. From the age of three, when David died, to when he was twelve, Charlie and I did everything together.

I even taught myself to become a devotee of the Beautiful Game, which I secretly renamed the Hideous Game, buying a season ticket to the Arsenal, so he wouldn't miss out on football matches, boning up on all the players and driving to away matches around the country. We'd sing at the tops of our voices, play 'I spy', listen to tapes and make up quizzes, as we drove as far as Leeds or Southampton, however dreadful the weather. I enjoyed the drives we had together far more than the actual matches.

When the weather allowed it, I'd open the roof of my Golf Cabriolet and cruise down the motorway, the two of us singing even louder to compete with the noise of the wind and the traffic. After a match, Charlie would always curl up on the back seat and fall contentedly asleep. At home in the garden on Sundays I'd kick a ball around with him for hours, until he became old enough to realise I was rubbish. Then, when Charlie developed an obsession with cars and tractors and moving vehicles of any kind, I'd spend whole afternoons with him in Hamley's, drooling over miniature Ferraris and Porsches, while his sister happily played at the houses of her girlfriends. I'd constantly offer to invite round the kids from Charlie's school, but he'd always shrug and say, 'Maybe next weekend.' I seemed to be enough for him. Perhaps, subconsciously, I wanted to be enough for him, my quiet little man. Perhaps I tried too hard.

Melissa didn't appear to need me nearly as much as Charlie did, and yet she became the child who, as she grew older, grew closer.

Was I was more smothering than mothering when it came to Charlie? Perhaps. But what should you do when you're trying to be both a father and a mother to your child? And especially to a somewhat anxious child like Charlie. Or was it me who made him anxious? I could win awards for guilt.

I lost sight of Charlie when he was twelve, when he withdrew into himself, or at least away from me. That was when I felt the loss of David more acutely than ever. I used to lie awake in bed at night, asking myself how David might have responded when Charlie spent more and more time alone in his room with the door not tightly shut, but ajar, closed enough to signal that visitors were not especially welcome.

Melissa and Charlie, despite their diametrically opposed personalities, got on brilliantly. 'Don't be so much on his case all the time, Mum,' she'd tell me. 'He's all right. Leave him alone.' That, I thought, is probably what David would have said as well.

And then he met a boy at school, a boy called Tim, who seemed to be on his wavelength. And soon Tim was round at our place all the time. Tim played keyboard and said Charlie should learn to play the guitar. When Charlie asked for lessons, I was delighted. In fact the night he asked for lessons I went to bed and cried with relief. It seemed to me to be a sign, a positive omen. He may be separating from me, I thought, but perhaps I haven't ruined him after all. That's how it is when you don't have an opposite-sex parent to share things with. Every day I would ask myself if I was getting it wrong, and not know the answer. Two-parent families must ask themselves the same question, but at least it's a burden shared.

Shortly after Charlie took up lessons Tim announced to me that Charlie had natural talent. And he said it in front of Charlie, who beamed with pride. He needed someone other than his mother to tell him he was a good guy. After that there was a band, and he was always round at Tim's for band practice; and I felt lonelier, but better.

Charlie was never trouble. From infancy through adolescence he was always remarkably well behaved and studious, so I was shocked when he dropped out of a university course in psychology after just one year, and got himself various jobs in a record shop, in a bar, distributing flyers, none of which demanded his considerable brainpower.

Then one Sunday evening about six months ago, when he and I were sitting around with the weekend papers and a glass of wine, I noticed he was reading the Business section of *The Sunday Times*. Charlie had never shown the slightest interest in business before. And especially not in mine, which I suppose, at least when he was a teenager, was bound to be an embarrassment. And to a boy who lacked the social and sexual confidence of his older sister, I guess more embarrassing still.

'Thinking of becoming a mogul?' I asked, trying not to sound too hopeful, quietly praying that he might be thinking of doing something that involved more analytical thought than pulling pints.

'Actually I was thinking of coming to work for you. If you'd have me.'

My heart did a little flip.

'Are you serious?'

'Well, you said your website needs redesigning . . .'

Charlie had designed websites throughout his teens. He'd done one for the band, another for one of Melissa's boyfriends who'd been setting himself up as a freelance sports writer, and others for boys and even teachers at his school. And now he wanted to work for me! I was ecstatic.

'But I'm going to have to move out,' he continued. 'It's time, Mum . . .'

A kiss followed by a blow, but he was right, it was time.

So now, except for this one day, Melissa's wedding day, when the house is full of noise and people, I am alone. Rattling around in the house that David and I bought when Charlie was born. Like a solitary coin in a money box crying out for loose change to keep it company, this house needs more than me to make it into a home. And yet turning my back on this house, I've so often thought, would be like turning my back on David. Now I can see that something will have to be done.

In the meantime, I have to get Melissa down the stairs in one piece and into the vintage white Rolls-Royce that is to transport us to the private club near Westbourne Grove where the civil ceremony will take place.

There's quite a crowd waiting on the pavement to greet us. Summer tourists in family clumps, wielding cameras and thrilled to be about to witness a real-life English bride; passing Saturday shoppers clutching chic carrier bags with Paul Smith and Prada logos, curious to know if the celebration at this discreetly chic west London residence might turn out to be a celebrity wedding; and of course the wedding party guests themselves.

Cat always did stand out in a crowd. Quite deliberately. Even from behind, talking to another of the guests, she is unmistakable. Her height, five foot nine before you add the three-inch stiletto version of Roman sandals with fine leather straps that criss-cross up her slender legs; the short, chartreuse silk-jersey dress scooped alarmingly low at the back; the tattooed plumes of fire that snake up from the base of her bony spine; the long neck curved elegantly forward like a swan about to dip its beak in the water; hair in short, dyed, white-blonde spikes.

As the car draws up she turns, and instead of a look of warmth and delight at the arrival of the bride, the niece she adores, her face turns to a tableau of fury. The furrows on Cat's forehead, which haven't been seen in several years since her muscles were frozen with regular infusions of Botox, seem to have been freed from paralysis. Blood-red lips parted, teeth bared, she resembles a prairie dog about to attack.

Mavis. It has to be Mavis. Cat must have seen her. Surely, after all these years . . . But Cat is not great on forgiveness. Unlike me, a past master of repression, Cat wears her grudges on her sleeve. Surely Cat isn't going to make a scene. Not today.

As Melissa emerges from the car, the tourists and passers-by break into a small round of applause. Melissa glows and glistens like a Hollywood star on the red carpet at a premiere, turning in every direction so that her adoring public can all get a glimpse of her. The crowd is entranced.

'Breathtaking, darling. Simply breathtaking.' Cat is surveying Melissa with a smile that only momentarily masks her fury.

'You, too,' she says, turning to me. 'You look every bit the mother of the bride. An absolute flapper. But not, I hope, in a flap. Not with everything organised so perfectly, as usual.'

She leans forward and I proffer my cheek, which she ignores, her lips sweeping past towards my ear. 'How could you?' she hisses. 'How could you, you cow? . . . It's absolutely monstrous of you.'

I jerk back my head and whisper, 'Not now, Cat, please not now. You don't have to talk to her. You can simply ignore her. What's the big deal?'

'Abuse. That's what the big deal is. It's brought it all back, all of it.'

Melissa has turned round towards me.

'What is it, Mum? You look as though you've been slapped.'

'It's nothing, darling. I just suddenly felt a bit overwhelmed. I'm thinking that everyone needs to go in and sit down in the drawing room. We're already five minutes late. Cat, you need to go and sit down.'

'What's got into her?' asks Melissa as Cat stomps off. 'She was fine two seconds ago.'

'You know how mercurial Cat can be. Take no notice.'

Melissa has already forgotten the incident. I'm shaking inside.

'Where's the groom, Sas?' Melissa turns to her friend Saskia, lovely, normal, down-to-earth Saskia.

'Oh Stefan's been here ages. We made sure of that. He's already waiting in the drawing room so he doesn't get to see you before your grand entrance.'

The tourists and the shoppers drift away as the guests go inside. Saskia gathers the bottom of Melissa's train so she can make her way through the columned portico of Stefan's club, a favourite media hangout in an impressive eighteenth-century Robert Adam house. Commissioned originally as a private home, it was at the centre of a cocaine scandal a couple of years ago, when celebrities were spotted knocking back the stuff in the toilets by an undercover reporter for the *Sun*; but it has considerably cleaned up its act since and recently been granted a licence to conduct civil weddings.

As a venue, it's absolutely perfect. There's the panelled and gilded drawing room for the wedding ceremony, a courtyard and Long Gallery for the pre-dinner reception and a ballroom with vaulted ceiling and minstrels gallery for the dinner and dance. In the basement there's a wonderfully restored art deco lounge bar where Stefan's louche cronies will probably want to hang out until the small hours.

Now, standing in the lobby, it's just the three of us. Me, Melissa and Saskia. Charlie keeps darting back and forth from the drawing room to report on how the guests are settling themselves.

'Where did you put Mavis?' I ask him.

'The row behind Cat and the grandparents.'

'Don't tell me she's right behind Cat, please don't tell me that.'

'Well, actually, she will be. Mavis has been sitting there for ages and I put names on the seats for the family. Only Cat's wandering around talking to everyone and hadn't sat down yet last time I was in the room. Is there a problem?'

'There shouldn't be, but there is. . . .'

'Mum,' says Melissa, 'for just once in your life quit worrying about what Cat will think or what Cat will do.'

'And think about you instead?'

'Exactly. Me. Me. Me. Think only of me, your darling daughter and about-to-be bride.'

Melissa always warms my heart, with her paradoxical mix of ego and self-deprecation. She is so very much herself. Not like me. Not like David. But uniquely Melissa. I've written as much in my speech. The dreaded speech that's been worrying me for weeks.

I know I should put Cat to the back of my mind, but I can't quite manage it. There's no knowing what Cat might do. Cat will be able to feel Mavis's breath on the back of her neck if she sits where she's supposed to. Why does Cat do this to me? Why, despite our closeness and the love I feel for her, does she still have the ability to wind me up after all these years? And why hasn't she learned to curtail her capacity for creating mayhem out of molehills? I don't want to even have to think about this. Melissa, my daughter, is about to get married and the wedding ceremony is about to begin.

'Charlie, go and check one last time, would you? And if everything's in place, give the signal for the music to start.'

We make our way towards the back entrance to the drawing room as the opening bars of Ben E. King's 'Stand

By Me' ring out from inside. Charlie has swung open the door and stood back to let us through. Saskia fans out Melissa's dress from the back and the bride makes her entrance, clutching her gardenia pom-pom bouquet in two hands held at waist level. Melissa was adamant that I would walk her down the aisle, though there is barely room for the two of us side by side in the makeshift gangway that has been created between two sets of chairs.

Stay in the moment, I tell myself, stay in the moment. But as I look to left and right, bob my head slightly and smile at the guests all around, my mind is wandering, and I can't help my head filling with the image of a beach, a beach on which a little girl is running towards a man with outstretched arms, and the man is David, and the little girl is Melissa, and it is the summer of the year David died, on a beach in Norfolk, and as Melissa reaches him David scoops her up and swings her round and round and round and she screams with delight at the sensation of flying through the air with the wind whipping her hair and the sea salt causing her face and eyes to tingle.

'Stunning', 'gorgeous', 'absolutely A-list', 'a goddess'. The adjectives are flying in stage whispers around the room. Stefan has turned to look at his bride and his eyes are aglow as she reaches him. He loves her. Of that I have no doubt. I take my seat at the edge of the front row, next to my father. He is sitting stock-still and upright, retaining the bearing of a well-trained army officer. Next to my father, Cat, leaning far forward in her seat and almost folded over on herself, as if to escape as far from Mavis as possible. I look over my shoulder at Mavis. She nods and smiles approvingly.

The registrar is waiting for the music to finish before he begins the ceremony. I glance sideways again at my family. I note my father's double-breasted dark grey suit, with a fine blue pinstripe running through it. Immaculate, hardly worn I would imagine, but with shoulders just broad enough to betray its tailor-made origins of a couple of decades earlier. And the blue shirt, frayed slightly at the cuffs. An oversight, surely. But then his tie, too, not as it should be; neatly knotted for sure, but marked by a barely visible stain.

Cat, still bent forward to escape Mavis, with thin arms hanging limply at her sides and skin that adheres less tightly than before, looks vulnerable. A wave of sadness sweeps over me. My father, sliding into inevitable old age with its hallmarks of standards slipping and stains appearing. Cat, for ever beyond the possibility of motherhood now.

I won't cry, I won't cry, no I won't shed a tear
Just as long as you stand, stand by me

Surely, David, my love, I should be over you by now. The registrar clears his throat and the ceremony begins

The ceremony goes without a hitch. Melissa reads from Kahlil Gibran's *The Prophet*, a poem so aptly modern in its exaltation of spaces in togetherness, on filling each other's cup but not drinking from one cup, that it is hard to believe it was published in 1923. Stefan, unusually brief, echoes Melissa's message in the words of 'Eternity' by William

Blake, a man more unconventional for his time than even Gibran, despite writing more than a century earlier.

> *He who binds to himself a joy*
> *Does the winged life destroy;*
> *But he who kisses the joy as it flies*
> *Lives in eternity's sun rise.*

So much freedom these two seem determined to offer one another. Yet still they long to be wed. One day perhaps I'll figure it.

The ballroom is aglow with crystal chandeliers. A mass of white peonies, as lush and fleshy as the bride, form the centrepiece for each table. Cutlery glints against pristine white table linen in the glow of the silver candelabras. Thousands of bubbles rise and burst in champagne glasses. Heads are thrown back in laughter. The bride and groom are seated at the top table, surrounded by their friends.

I had always planned to get my speech over as early as possible so I could relax and enjoy the rest of the evening. So I will welcome the guests, and make the mother-of-the-bride speech, before food is served. The best man's speech and Stefan's response will follow after the main course. My stomach is in spasm. It's not just the fact of having to stand up and talk in front of 180 people, although that's nerve-racking enough. Since seeing the look of pure hatred on Cat's face outside the club, I have had a growing sense of dread.

As far as the speech is concerned, I've spent weeks honing it, and I think I've got it right. A good wedding speech is one that will make people laugh and possibly cry and doesn't last more than about eight minutes. I've picked anecdotes that illuminate Melissa's character and those that illustrate her achievements. I've tried to keep the wider audience in mind but I want Melissa to know I'm talking directly to her as well. I'm not big on public declarations of private feelings, but I want Melissa to be left in no doubt of the love and respect I have for her, and even the gratitude I feel for the solace and joy she – and Charlie – have given me. I will mention David, because I can't not mention him. I've memorised it, practised it, and have the whole thing written out in front of me – just in case. But the anxiety has been compounded by Cat, and instead of a mood of celebration I have a sense of profound unease, deep in the pit of my stomach.

Charlie, who is acting as MC for the evening, has called for quiet. He is inviting me up to the microphone and cheers and clapping having erupted spontaneously. Clutching my typewritten speech, I walk shakily to the microphone. I stand behind it and look around me, a smile fixed onto my face by fear. There is a tremor in my hand and the speech is shaking so violently the words in front of me are shifting in and out of focus. I survey the room.

My eyes scan the tables closest to the front. I see my father, smiling in my direction, clutching a whisky tumbler and swaying slightly in his seat. I'd primed the head waiter to offer him whisky as he never touches champagne, but I hadn't asked him to leave the bottle, which I could just make out, sitting on the table. I see Mavis, surrounded by my own friends, entirely out of place as usual, but not at all bothered by it, and with her attention fixed steadily on me.

I see a man enter through the double swing doors at the back of the room. He made it after all, I think with relief. Made it after all! I'm going quite mad. David is . . . David has been. . . . Hannah, for God's sake get a grip. Get a grip. And now my eyes alight on Cat. She's talking to the man next to her, deliberately ignoring the fact that I am about to speak. And then she turns to me, a sneer spreading slowly across her face, as if to say, *Cat's really got your tongue this time, hasn't she!*

I look at my opening words, though they're blurring in front of me. *Family and friends, first I would like to welcome* . . . And I clear my throat. And I try to speak. And I clear my throat again. But as has happened so many times before, although not for a very, very long time, nothing comes out. And the room in front of me is moving up and down, up and down, the floor is receding and rising up, the chandeliers are disappearing and reappearing. I clutch the microphone stand. I try once more to speak, and then everything goes black and I am gone.

PART TWO

Chapter Four

The 1950s

Hello, I'm Mouse. You become the labels you are given. Cat, my elder sister, had trouble spelling her name, which is how our parents came to shorten Catherine to Cat, a move designed to save embarrassment all round. Today you'd diagnose dyslexia in five minutes. Back on the cusp of the 1960s it was, 'Well, she's no genius, but she makes everyone laugh so she'll never be short of friends.' Label: Funny Girl. That was Cat – good for a laugh, but unlikely to win a Nobel Prize. I, on the other hand, was the family prodigy. 'Clever *and* pretty. What a combination,' everyone would say. 'But Hannah, you're as quiet as a mouse. If you know so much, why do you always keep it to yourself?' The favourite family jibe was, 'Cat got your tongue, has it?' And the double meaning was quite clear to me, even at the age of four. By the time I was five, I would happily have traded my dark, doe eyes and shiny black curls for Cat's ability to speak her mind without offending and reduce my father to helpless hysterics. She even made my mother laugh, sometimes. And that was quite an achievement. For years and years I really did think Cat had stolen my tongue, that somehow she had gobbled up my words before they could leave my mouth. Label: The Mouse. Laugh-a-minute, tongue-in-cheek Cat; silent, tongue-tied Hannah. Cat and Mouse. Even now. Even after fifty years.

I could be funny, too, but only silently, alone in my bed. I'd spend the time before falling off to sleep practising jokes and rehearsing witty one-liners. I even remember trying a joke in public one supper time . . . it was my first – and last. I must have been about seven. Lamb chops with mashed potatoes and mandarin jelly with cream were on the menu, which meant it was a Tuesday. Cat had stopped gabbling and there was a momentary silence. 'What sits at the bottom of the sea and is always anxious?' Three pairs of eyes – Cat's, my mother's and my father's – bored into me. 'No, I mean, like, what sits at the bottom of the sea biting its nails?' Cat gave an involuntary snort. Any second now the mashed potato she was shovelling into her mouth would splatter back out onto the plate as she failed to contain her laughter. Of course I was botching it, there was no other possibility.

'Be patient, Cat,' said Dad, as Cat's mirth began to rub off on him, and he swallowed hard to try to suppress the inevitable guffaw. I could feel myself reddening and a horrible clamminess in my hands.

'What does sit at the bottom of the sea feeling anxious and biting its nails?' Dad asked helpfully, to remind me of where I was.

'I know. I know,' chimed in Cat. 'A nervous wreck.' Mum and Dad clapped their hands in unison. Their eyes came alive. It was like someone had switched on the Christmas lights in Regent Street. The joke had been a good joke, a really good joke, but Cat had grabbed the punchline. Now it was Cat's joke. The tears gushed out of nowhere.

'Thank you for ruining everything, just like always,' I sobbed, jumping up, throwing my white linen napkin onto the table and running to the safety of the kitchen. I knew I'd done something terrible. I'd broken the Golden Rule of the Saunders household. I'd made a scene.

Cat of course was just as clever as me, cleverer in many ways, she simply got her letters mixed up and freaked out when it came to exams. No one knew about these things back then. So Cat wasn't especially encouraged to do well. And anyway, it didn't matter all that much for girls. Certainly no one in our family had ever been to university. Our dad was good at making money, and he assumed we'd find ourselves husbands who were good at making money too. They could even go into the family business if they were the right sort. He dreamed of a dynasty, but for that he thought he needed sons-in-law, since we girls were hardly likely to take on his mantle. Wrong, wrong, wrong. If only he'd known how things would turn out he might not have dismissed us quite so readily early on.

The problem was that Cat believed the publicity – she thought herself a bit stupid, and worked even harder to make people laugh, neglecting her studies altogether. 'I'm daft anyway, so why should I bother?' was how her thinking went. She loved to look in the full-length mirror inside her wardrobe and clown around, pulling ugly faces and contorting her long, gawky limbs into pretzel-like positions as she gave herself an out-loud pep talk.

'I'm daft but I'm funny. If you're funny you have lots of friends. People with lots of friends are lucky. Cat's a lucky girl, then, isn't she?'

How quickly the label attaches itself to the psyche. Making people laugh was Cat's territory, not mine. Any attempts to invade the realm of light entertainment where she ruled supreme must be immediately repelled.

At the age of three and a half I could read simple books with ease. I could do sums and recite multiplications up to the three times table. I was clever all right, not that there seemed to be much advantage to it. All that advanced knowledge, all that flash-card learning without the flash cards, was thanks to Mavis. No, of course Mavis wasn't my mother; no one in a family like ours would be saddled with a name like Mavis.

My mother's name was Eleanor. Dad was Maurice. Mavis was our maid. A less Victorian title might have been housekeeper. But I guess in our household my mum was supposed to be 'the keeper of the house', even though I never saw her do much keeping. This left Mavis to be the maid, as opposed to the daily, Dot, who was actually a twice-weekly and came to help Mavis clean our mock-Tudor mansion, which in any case wasn't a mansion but a five-bedroom house on the outer reaches of north London. Pretty grand by anyone's standards, but not actually a mansion.

Daily. What a nasty word that sounds now. Today Dot the daily might be called a cleaning lady or a cleaner – much more respectful. Certainly more PC. I can hardly believe how much everything has changed since my childhood. Life in the late 1950s must seem as alien to kids today as Victorian bustles and horse-drawn carriages did to me. And as for Mavis, our so-called maid, our very own Mrs Mop, Mavis was actually more of a nanny than anything else. Hence my supernatural reading and mathematical abilities. She'd sit with me for hours making numbers and letters seem like the most fun game in the world.

The funny thing is that although we were posh enough for a maid, we weren't actually posh enough for a nanny. The nanny bit was an unexpected bonus, beyond the call of duty. Mavis was already there when I was born. She cleaned, she cooked, she loved me. She was my best friend. I loved her. Cat loathed her, but only because she loathed Cat.

When my joke ended in humiliation and I ran to the safety of the kitchen, it was straight into Mavis's ample arms. 'There, there, sweetheart,' she said. 'Remember what I told you. Sticks and stones will break your bones . . .'

'. . . b-but words will never . . . hurt you . . .' I whimpered back, my voice half throttled by the proximity of my face to Mavis's tummy.

'Listen, pet, I'll make sure you get more mandarins in your jelly than Cat does. That'll get her back. She loves mandarins. Now go back to the dining room like nuffing ever 'appened.' I always took Mavis's advice.

★   ★   ★

I sat back down at the dining table. Barely audibly, I said, 'I'm fine now, thank you, and I'm sorry for the fuss,' which was, of course, a lie. I wasn't fine. And I wasn't sorry for the fuss. Conversation, between Cat and my father, resumed as normal. My mother, who was seated opposite me, allowed her fork to hover just above her plate, hardly ever putting food to mouth and staring into an area just above my head. I was tempted to turn around and see what fascinating things were going on behind me, but then I'd probably get told off for fidgeting. While Cat and my dad chattered, I stared at my mum staring over my head.

When the jelly arrived in individual bowls, along with Mavis and a large tray that had Velasquez's Rokeby Venus printed on it, I counted seven succulent segments – straight from the tin, not a trace of pith – in my portion. There were only two pieces in Cat's. Before Mavis left the room she winked at me. Now it was my turn to smile. Cat glowered, first at the bowl, then at me. Cat may have been good at speaking her mind, but not where Mavis was concerned. She was terrified of her. What scared me were things like the dolls in my cupboard, which I worried might come out and attack me in the middle of the night, like a gang of schoolgirl bullies, unless I locked them in and hid the key under my pillow. What scared Cat was Mavis. In Mavis's eyes I could do no wrong. In Mavis's eyes Cat did everything wrong. You would have thought my parents would have noticed. They didn't. Or for reasons of their own they chose not to.

The meal was over, bowls scraped almost clean. 'OK, my precious girls,' my dad said. 'Special Tuesday treat. You may now lick the plates.' That was what I most loved about my father. He was a strict disciplinarian, army major in the war and all that, but he loved to break the rules. Loved to shock.

'Oh Maurice, is that really necessary?' My mother knew it was pointless to object, but the words came out of their own accord, flat and with little inflection, carrying no conviction that her will might prevail. Cat and I punched the air with our fists. We *loved* licking the plate, especially on Tuesdays, when the last streaks of rich double cream were infused with the sweet-sharp citrus taste of mandarins. We knew what was coming next. THE WARNING! He breathed in deeply and wagged his index finger sternly. 'But if you ever, ever do this in company, I'm sending you both straight to boarding school. As far as table manners are concerned, licking the plate is the single worst crime you can ever commit. This is a family secret and it goes no further.' The fact that it had to be kept a secret from everyone, though not from Mavis of course, made it all the more exciting. Our faces were already in our bowls, our tongues lapping at the bottom and sides, like thirsty kittens. When we emerged, we each had a little smudge of cream at the end of our nose.

'Go and get cleaned up right now,' my mother said. 'Wash your hands and your faces and then you can go and watch *Dr Kildare*. You're not to touch anything on your way to the bathroom. Go on, the pair of you, you look like a couple of ragamuffins.' I liked the idea of Cat and I being a pair or a couple, of our matching in some way. I know that siblings often hate to be lumped together as though they have no personality of their own, but I was the opposite. I was always looking for things that would bind us, that would make Cat like me more.

My mother did manage a faint smile at the sight of the two of us with our cream-tipped noses, but it seemed to require the most enormous effort. She followed it with a sigh, one that suggested the smile and several whole sentences in a row had drained away all her energy. It made me think of a deflated balloon, not one you pop on purpose with a pin to make a loud bang, but one you blow up really big and then, instead of tying a knot, which is always really hard to do when you have small fingers, you let the air slowly release through your fingers until the balloon goes all sad and damp and shrivelled.

A bell sounded – muffled in tone, as though it were coming from under a cushion.

'No, it's all right, I'll go,' I said. 'Please,' I pleaded, 'let me go and tell her myself. I can wash my hands and face in there.'

The spell was broken, the remnants of carnival atmosphere vanished. 'For heaven's sake, Hannah, it's her job.' My dad was furious. And when he was mad he was scary. 'I put that bell under the carpet in a convenient position for my foot for good reason. So that Mavis can come and get the plates when we've finished. So that your mother doesn't have to get up. So we can all sit around the table together and eat our supper in civilised fashion.'

'But what's wrong with Mummy getting up? She's got legs, hasn't she?' I didn't shout this, as Cat would if she were angry. I said it quietly, with my head bowed towards my lap, muttering to myself like I'd seen old ladies do on the bus. Which didn't stop my dad from hearing me.

'One more remark like that and you will get a good hiding. Insolence is something I will not tolerate.'

My voice was tiny and tinny now. 'Please, Daddy, please.'

'Not another word, do you understand? You will *not* run into the kitchen again.' He banged the table with his fist. The spoon in his bowl did a little jump and crashed back down again.

I looked at my mother, and as I did so she averted her eyes.

'Mavis will have heard the bell,' my father continued, 'and she'll be on her way. Go and get cleaned up as your mother told you. NOW!'

Once again I felt the tears prick, but this time I wouldn't allow them out. It was horrible. Disgusting. Mavis was my friend, but she was treated like a slave. I sometimes wanted her to run away, like Eliza in *Uncle Tom's Cabin* did. But if Mavis did run away, then I'd be all on my own. Not really all on my own, but with everyone always ganging up on me that's what it would have felt like. And of course I knew that Mavis wasn't a slave. She was 'employed', as my father was constantly pointing out. She received a weekly wage and free board and lodging and had her own lovely (my parents' word, not mine) room next to my bedroom, with a view of the garden. A room full of furniture my parents no longer wanted and a threadbare carpet and curtains which had been left in the house by previous owners and which would have shamed my mother to death if they'd been in a room visitors ever saw.

I could never understand why Mavis didn't get herself a rich husband, someone who could rescue her from slavery, someone with whom she could go off and live happily ever after. They could buy a house nearby, then I could go and stay with them at weekends and in the holidays. Or she could come and babysit when my parents went out, which was often. I know she could be a bit grumpy, especially with Cat and Mummy, and I suppose a man might not want to marry you if you went around being grumpy a lot of the time. But then she was never, ever grumpy with me and, come to think of it, she was never grumpy with my dad either.

'You've got a soft spot for Mr Saunders, haven't you?' I heard Dot say to Mavis one morning when I was on half-term holiday and hanging around the house. They were having their mid-morning break in what we called the morning room, which was next to the kitchen. It was where we ate on Mavis's day or evenings off. That was another of the many millions of things that didn't make sense to me as a child. Why did we switch eating rooms just because Mavis was out? Surely my mother had the strength to push the dinner trolley from the kitchen to the dining room, which was only a few yards further, even though that was Mavis's job when she was around. Or Cat and I could have helped her if she needed it. Now I think that the real reason we always ate in the dining room, at one end of the highly polished mahogany table, was that my parents didn't want to hear Mavis banging and tutting in the kitchen, which she did quite a lot. Cat had perfected the art of imitating Mavis tutting. She would curl up her top lip to one side, then make her tongue spring away sharply from behind her top teeth. If it had been anyone else she was making fun of, I'd probably have laughed myself at her mean mimics. But when she was rude about Mavis I wanted to poke her eyes out.

Dot and Mavis were nattering over a cup of tea and munching on some shortbread biscuits. I'd come to ask Mavis if I could open a packet of Cadbury's chocolate fingers, which were my favourite. When Dot said that thing about Mavis having a soft spot for my dad Mavis started smoothing her apron down, over and over again, like she suddenly noticed it needed an iron.

'Haven't you got anything better to do than talk smutty nonsense?' Mavis replied. 'It's not me with the soft spot, Dot, it's you who's soft in the head.'

'All right, all right, no need to get shirty,' said Dot, changing the subject and muttering something about how the Vim she used to scour the bath brought her hands out in a rash. But Mavis was *very* shirty by the look of her. I thought it was all quite silly. Mavis, being rather plump, had lots of soft spots. Even her knees, which I'd seen when she lifted her skirt before bending down to scrub the floor, were soft and dimply. I wondered which of all her soft spots she reserved for my father. Perhaps it was her knees!

By the time I was seven, Mavis must have already been about twenty-seven; she looked a lot older than my mother, though she was actually about five years younger. She wasn't pretty at all, not like my mum, of whom I once heard the chap who delivered groceries to our back door say to his mate: 'She's so damn beautiful, that one, she could make a grown man weep.' 'Bit of an Ice Queen, if you ask me, mate,' his friend replied. 'But I reckon she'd thaw out right nicely if you rubbed her in the right places.' And one of them did that thing some of the stupid older boys in our school did when they saw a pretty girl, making a circle of their thumb and first finger and poking a finger from the other hand in and out of it. I didn't know what that was all about and I didn't care, but it seemed daft to me that you'd want to cry just because someone looked beautiful. You should be happy for them, I'd have thought.

As well as not being pretty, Mavis was a bit fat and a bit red in the face and her hair went all limp and stringy unless she washed it every other day, which she didn't. But I loved her, so I couldn't imagine why some rich man wouldn't sweep her off her feet, which is apparently what men are supposed to do.

My dad swept my mum off her feet. I know that for a fact because she told me that's how it happened, though you wouldn't think it if you saw them together. I mean they weren't all lovey-dovey like my friend Janet's parents were, always kissing and cuddling and making Janet and me feel a bit sick. They were just polite to one another, and a bit stiff like you'd be if you had to talk to a policeman or a doctor, which seemed strange considering they were married. At least they never shouted at one another. 'Your dad's got a lot to put up with,' Mavis said to me more than once. But it wasn't as though my mum made a fuss or anything. It was more like she wasn't there, even when she was, which I know is a bit hard for anyone who wasn't there themselves at the time to understand.

I didn't think Mavis needed to have someone handsome – well, not very anyway. He just had to come along and do that sweeping trick. Maybe while she was in the middle of doing a bit of sweeping herself, like on the porch at the front of the house, the man of her dreams (or rather my dreams) would walk by and spot her. He could run up to the house, grab Mavis's broom and sweep her off her feet there and then.

Mavis hadn't turned up in the dining room within a minute or so of my dad pressing the bell, so he pressed it again with his foot. Even as an adult I think of that bell and shudder. I was ashamed and embarrassed that we had a servant's bell. What made my parents think they were so la-di-da? Mavis was just as good as they were. She couldn't help being only half-able to read and write. Cat wasn't much better than Mavis in that respect. And being poor wasn't her fault either. Nor was it her fault that she said ' 'ere' instead of 'here' or ' 'em' instead of 'them'. It was how she was taught – or not taught, as my parents would say. What difference did any of it make? Mavis was Mavis and she was special. How I longed to gouge out the poisonous boil in the brown and beige patterned carpet, pull out the wire and hurl the offending object through the window.

Cat and I crossed the hallway to the downstairs toilet in silence. We shivered. It was always freezing in there, and when you sat on the loo you felt the back of your thighs were turning to ice. But I loved that little room. It had a round window, like the porthole on a ship. I used to sit on the toilet and imagine I was on a boat, in my cabin, looking out across an ocean of azure blue.

Cat ran the water in the sink. 'Go on, you go first,' she said, unusually charitable. I washed and dried. Then she washed and dried while I waited. Towel still in hand, she dabbed gently at the end of my nose. 'All spick and span,' she said, mimicking my mother who never loved us more than when we were scrubbed and polished and ready to go out in our shiny Startrite shoes. But there was a tenderness in Cat's touch as well, a tiny hint that we didn't have to be enemies, at least not all of the time. Despite the cold it felt cosy being in that little room together, just the two of us in our seaview cabin. At that moment I wanted to kiss my word-pinching, joke-filching, tongue-lashing, limelight-hogging older sister. But I didn't. 'We don't want to miss *Dr Kildare*, do we, dearest Mouse?' she said, the teasing edge working its way back into her voice. 'Especially as we all know you're madly in love with Richard Chamberlain.'

'I'm not,' I protested weakly, managing a feeble smile, and following her meekly into the living room. In the background I could hear the comforting clatter of dinner plates and the clang of cutlery as Mavis continued with her evening chores. I even heard Mavis making that tutting sound, and it made me smile again.

Chapter Five

Cat is putting on a show. She can't sing, she can't dance, she can't act. No one is prepared to tell her this except Mavis. And even Mavis doesn't say it directly. What Mavis does is make sly little digs. 'Better get the earplugs out, then,' she says, when Cat announces that there will be a matinee performance at 4 p.m. on Sunday. 'Fortunately Sunday's my day off and I won't have to listen to it.'

'Actually,' calls Cat over her shoulder as she flounces out the room, 'it's more of a fashion show. My very first catwalk show. And you, Mouse, are going to be the model.'

The minute Cat's out of the room, Mavis says, 'You're the one who ought to be putting on the show. She's a lump. And your voice! A proper little Judy Garland you are. Whereas Cat and her 'orrible catawool – it's enough to make the milk turn sour.'

I'm not sure Mavis has actually ever heard me sing. I like singing, but I hate anyone hearing me; and although I'm in the junior school choir, I generally mime, in case it doesn't come out properly. I suppose I wasn't bad as the Sugar Plum Fairy in the school panto version of *The Nutcracker*, but I only got that part because I refused to take on any role that involved speaking, and even then I threw up three times before I went on, I was so nervous. All I had to do was enter stage right, twirl twice, and exit stage left.

'Catawhatdidyousay?'

'Catawool. It's the noise a cat makes when it's cross, an 'orrible shrieking noise that puts your teeth on edge.'

'If your teeth were on the edge, they might fall out, mightn't they, and then you'd have to wear false ones, like the butcher?' It's so much easier chatting with Mavis than it is with anyone else.

'And if you had to buy a set of those dent-yours every time a cat-a-wooled,' I continue, 'then practically everyone would have them, and the people who make them would be very rich. And then Daddy would say that was a great idea for a business, and he'd probably open another factory, and it would sell dent-yours instead of dresses. Or maybe you could do a special offer and get free dent-yours with every dress. You know how he's always going on about new business ideas and having to keep the customer happy.'

'Too clever by half you are, young lady. Just like your dad. Bet you can't spell cat-a-wool.'

'Yes I can. C-a-t-a-w-o-o-l. See!'

'I'm sure you're right, you usually are. But let's look it up, just in case.' Mavis is absolutely tunnel-visioned in her mission to educate me.

It takes ages to find it in the dictionary, because we're looking in the wrong place.

'Maybe it's cat*er*wool,' I suggest after turning the pages backwards and forwards a dozen times.

Eventually we get there. 'Caterwaul! Look here. It's c-a-t-e-r-w-a-u-l.'

'Well, I never,' says Mavis.

'Well, I never, too,' I reply in my best high-and-mighty voice. Mavis musses the top of my hair, like she always does when she's in a cheerful mood.

Then my mother walks in. Something happens to Mavis's face. It reminds me of that soufflé Mavis made for one of my parents' dinner parties. For about two seconds after it came out of the oven it was all puffed up, just like it looked on the television when Fanny Cradock made one, but then it went sort of splat, and collapsed. Mavis was cross about that soufflé. 'Never 'appened to me before,' she grumbled. My mother acted like World War Three had broken out.

'Oh this is just a disaster. A complete and utter disaster. What will we do?'

'Lucky I made a trifle, too, then, isn't it?' Mavis had opened the fridge triumphantly.

My mother's hands did a funny kind of flutter in front of her face, which made me think of a butterfly flapping its wings. Then, putting one hand behind her head, she fiddled with the tiny tendrils of hair at the nape of her neck, the ones that had escaped from her early sixties up-do. Teasing wisps of hair seemed to quieten her. As she slowly recovered her composure I became transfixed by her beauty. She was wearing a simple, sleeveless black shift to just above her knees, with a triple-layered pearl choker and pearl earrings. A blonde version of Audrey Hepburn in *Breakfast at Tiffany's*.

'That does look absolutely . . . delicious,' she said, a little uncertainly. 'Perhaps not as impressive as a soufflé, but actually I rather prefer the taste of trifle, I think everyone does really. It's so . . . comforting. Don't you think so?' She looked at Mavis for reassurance, but Mavis wasn't offering any.

'And what about bowls? I think we should have bowls rather than plates for the trifle. If you wouldn't mind, Mavis.' Mavis raised her eyebrows, then headed towards the cupboard which housed the bowls, without objecting. Soundlessly she was objecting extremely loudly. I had already discovered that words played quite a small part in what people actually meant. Because I didn't say all that much myself most of the time, I was not just a good listener but a good watcher too. I knew at the time that body language counted for a lot; it just wasn't a phrase.

Mavis, as usual, had saved the day. What would Mummy do without Mavis? We were so lucky to have her. That thought made me feel nice and cosy inside my tummy.

So now I was watching Mavis's face cave in on itself like that disastrous soufflé and listening to my mother say, 'You know Mr Saunders and I are out for dinner tonight, Mavis?'

'Yes, you already told me.' When my mother's around, Mavis keeps conversation to a minimum. My eyes dart between the two women, wondering if they really hate one another or if this is how most people behave.

'I just wondered what you were thinking of making the girls for their tea.'

'Spaghetti Bolognese. Hannah loves it.'

'I hope Cat does, too,' says my mother, looking a bit unsure again, and I wonder why she doesn't know this sort of stuff. Even I know Cat doesn't like spaghetti Bolognese.

Last time we had it when my parents went out she just twirled the spaghetti round and round her fork while trying to scrape the meat bits off with her knife. She did attempt to eat it but I saw her almost gagging a couple of times, after which she gave up.

'Well, there's nothing else,' Mavis had said to Cat that night, 'so if you don't eat it you'll have to go to bed hungry.'

'I'll finish it if Cat doesn't want to,' I offered. 'It's delicious.'

Cat prodded at it one more time and as Mavis reached out across the table to grab the plate away, the fork Cat was holding dragged half the spaghetti in one direction as the plate went in another.

'You stupid, stupid girl,' Mavis shouted as the spaghetti and its sauce splattered the tablecloth like a Jackson Pollock painting and landed on Cat's lap. Cat looked down, helplessly.

'You know where the bin is, don't you? So what are you waiting for?' Cat fumbled around, trying to raise her skirt to make a kind of basket to stop the spaghetti falling onto the floor, then hobbled into the kitchen and over to the bin under the sink. It was a comical sight, but it didn't make me want to laugh. I could hear her making little grunting noises as she tried to tip the spaghetti from her skirt straight into the bin, but it must have been awkward having to take the lid off the bin first, and some bits must have missed and fallen onto the kitchen lino because I heard her give a little yelp.

'If you spill anything, make sure you clean it up before you come back in here,' shouted Mavis from the morning room.

'Should I go and help?' I asked.

Mavis shook her head. 'It's not your problem, it's hers. If she ate her dinner like a good girl this would never have happened. I'm fed up with the little minx.'

As usual, I felt like the rope in a game of tug-of-war. I did feel a bit sorry for Cat but I was also cross with her for spoiling my evening with Mavis.

A few minutes later, when Cat came back in, Mavis pointed out through the door and roared, 'Upstairs! Pyjamas. Teeth. Bed.' I looked from Cat to Mavis to Cat and back to Mavis. I didn't say a word. Cat disappeared, and I could hear her stomping angrily up the stairs.

'I'll get the mousse out of the fridge, Hannah. Would you like ice cream with it?'

'Yes please,' I whispered. I felt bad about Cat, I really did. But I so looked forward to the evenings when Mum and Dad were out and Mavis was in charge. Why should my evening be ruined as well as Cat's? I just wasn't going to let it happen.

'Shall we do the puzzle book?' I suggested.

'Good idea,' said Mavis. She went to the shelf above the fireplace and got down a pencil and a book of puzzles that came from W.H. Smith, a book which she'd bought for me from her own wages. She drew her chair up close to mine and the two of us settled down.

Later that night, I sneaked into Cat's room with a packet of Maltesers.

'Here,' I said, 'I got them from tuck at school, but then the bell rang and I didn't have time to eat them.'

'I hate her,' she said.

'If you tell Mummy and Daddy you hate her, they'll get rid of her. And then Mummy won't manage. How many times has Daddy told us about Mummy and her nerves and how we have to be sensitive to her situation and all that? And anyway, if Mavis leaves I'll run away from home and it will be all your fault.'

'Why's she always so mean to me?'

'She's not. You're just a fusspot. It's stupid not to like spaghetti Bolognese.'

'It's all right for you, she thinks your poos smell of eau de cologne.'

I giggled.

'Well, so what? Maybe they do.'

'They do not.'

'They do.'

'They do not. They're even smellier than mine.'

Cat opened the Maltesers and started lobbing them at me, one at a time. I ducked as best I could, picked them up and lobbed them back. They were getting runny and sticky, but it was fun and Cat and I were cracking up. And then she was picking up the melted Maltesers, and so was I, and we stuffed our mouths with them as fast as we could.

There'd be blue murder tomorrow when Mavis found Cat's sheets all smeared with chocolate, I thought, but I didn't suppose Cat would tell on me, because there wouldn't be any point. And it was so much fun that it was almost worth the trouble it was going to cause the next day. Which was easy for me to say because it wasn't me who was going to get into trouble. And it wasn't as though I knew Cat was going to start throwing Maltesers at me. I just didn't want her to have to go to sleep hungry. I was trying to be nice . . .

Cat may be the star of the show, but there's still plenty of work for me to do. There's furniture to move, under Cat's direction, costumes to sew, under Cat's direction, lines and songs to be rehearsed, with me having to play prompt. The show is going to start with a dance, followed by a couple of songs, followed by some poetry and jokes. And then the fashion show for which I am going to have to model. I'm also being forced to accompany Cat's singing on the piano with the help of the *Easy Peasy Songbook*. Cat has told me she expects me to use all fingers of both hands, but I'm only up to Grade 2 and it's not fair and my fingers are barely big enough to spread out for proper chords even if I could read them easily, which I can't. The trouble is Cat doesn't really try to sing along with the music, she races along like she's running for the bus and expects me to keep up with her, but she goes so fast it's impossible. I'd much prefer to go and play with my friend Janet than get involved in this boring old show but apparently I have to make up for Mavis's beastliness to Cat after the Maltesers' incident. When, the next morning before school, Mavis saw the dried-up chocolate bits on Cat's sheets and pillowcase she went berserk.

She called Cat 'a selfish little madam'. 'You're just like your mother,' she said. I knew that was meant to be hurtful, because of the way she said it. On the other hand, I thought that if any other person in the world had said it, you would suppose it was a compliment, and be expected to say thank you. A bit later, when Mavis was helping Cat with her plait, she yanked her hair and Cat flinched, and her eyes went quite watery, which got Mavis even crosser. I don't know if Mavis did it on purpose. Cat does have very unruly hair, according to my mother, so maybe Mavis was just having trouble getting the brush through it.

While all this was going on, our mother was in bed. I knew she must be awake because Mavis had already taken up the tray, the one with little legs so you don't have to balance it on your knees. She'd be sitting up in bed by now, in her baby-soft, lemony, crocheted bed jacket, eating breakfast. The tray would be laid, like it was every morning, with an embroidered cloth, a single pink carnation in a glass vase, triangles of toast in a silver holder – just like the ones they have in posh hotels, a pat of butter on an engraved glass dish and strawberry jam in a porcelain pot decorated with a blue and white pattern. There would be a small china teapot, a matching jug of milk and a sugar bowl with shiny silver tongs.

Our mother always had breakfast in bed, even on Sundays, Mavis's day off. On Sundays Cat and I were in charge. First of all Cat would rummage through the linen cupboard and find the little half-pinnies that Mavis wore if my parents had guests for dinner. They were white, a bit scratchy and nylon-y, but they had a frill round the edge and we thought they made us look like the Nippies who served us knickerbocker glories at Lyon's Tea House in

Piccadilly. I didn't want to be a Nippy, but I did want my dad to think I was nippy.

Cat would lay the tray, because she was the artist of the house, and I would carry, because Cat, as Mavis constantly reminded her, was all fingers and thumbs and might drop it. Cat would follow me up the stairs, trying to make me laugh so I'd have an accident. Everything would wobble like blancmange or Dot the daily's big bottom but I never once dropped the tray. When we got outside the bedroom, Cat would knock twice, and call, 'Room Service.' Mummy would be sitting there, propped up against the pillows, her blonde hair falling in soft waves to her shoulders, her face without lipstick or rouge porcelain-pale. I'd seen a film version of *The Lady of the Camellias*. Whenever I saw my mother sitting up in bed like that, I thought of Greta Garbo, as Camille, just before she died, all faded and frail but somehow lovelier-looking than when she was really well and dancing around the place with Armand.

'Hello, darlings,' my mother says on the morning of the concert. 'It's such a treat having you bring up my breakfast like this. I look forward to my breakfast on Sunday more than any other day of the week.'

I could just imagine the look on Mavis's face when she hands my mother the tray, the look of disapproval. But if my mother didn't like Mavis coming into her room with the tray and her if-looks-could-kill face, why didn't she ever come downstairs and have breakfast with us?'

'Mind if we sit on the bed with you?' Cat asks.

'That would be lovely, girls, but Mummy does have a bit of a headache this morning, so if you wouldn't mind, not too much noise.' Our mother often refers to herself in the third person.

The curtains are still half-drawn, and at eight o'clock on a winter's morning it's barely light outside, but my mother doesn't want the lights on, on account of her headache, so we arrange ourselves in the gloom on top of the blankets. It's a bit chilly and what we'd really like to do is wriggle under the covers and snuggle up all together and munch on bits of our mother's toast, especially as Dad has already gone off to play golf and it's a huge bed with loads of room. But Dad's side of the bed has already been made up, everything's neatly tucked in and folded back just right, and Mum would hate it if everything were messed up again. And if we did start sharing her breakfast, we might get crumbs all over the bedclothes and then Mum's headache would last for days and Dad would look all worried and we'd have to be on our best behaviour and walk around on tiptoes whispering all the time so as not to disturb her. So neither of us suggests actually getting into bed with our mother; we content ourselves with being slightly shivery on top of the blankets, and with watching her delicately nibbling her toast. I don't think my mother is very interested in food.

Despite the slight air of gloom, I love this room. I love to walk barefoot on the cream carpet with its thick, bouncy pile and to sit at my mother's dressing table, where I can view myself from all angles in the large, ornate, triple mirror. Once I've got the angle right, and can see my profile, I tap upwards under my chin with the backs of my fingers, like I've seen my mother do. If you do it every day about twenty times I think it stops you from going all crinkly when you're really old.

All down one side of the room, the side opposite the bed, are fitted cupboards. I had a snoop around once, when my parents were out, and Cat was watching telly, and Mavis was in her room, and I was bored. I found some really rude magazines on the shelf above where my dad hangs his suits and keeps things like boxes of tees and golf balls. The magazines had pictures of women with the biggest bosoms I'd ever seen and in some of the pictures there were two women, both without clothes and both with these enormous bosoms, and they were kissing one another and you could see their tongues. I knew right away I wasn't supposed to have seen these magazines, not ever, so I quickly put them back and never mentioned them to anyone. Not to Cat or Mavis or anyone.

To be honest I wasn't that bothered by it. I just thought it was a bit weird, and that as families went mine was a bit weirder than most. What interested me more than the yucky magazines were the cupboards themselves.

According to Mavis my mother had more cupboards than the Queen. All her clothes were covered with transparent plastic bags, and the clothes lined up according to colour, like a box of Caran d'Ache crayons. Even the pretty padded hangers, covered in flowered Liberty prints and handmade by Dot the daily, colour-matched the clothes. The previous Christmas Dot had made some smaller versions of the hangers for me and Cat. One each for our party dresses and one each for our favourite summer dresses, all in pink gingham.

I think we're what's called 'privileged'. We do seem to have an awful lot of people looking after us and looking after the house. I can't work out why my mother is always so tired and why she takes so long to get out of bed in the morning, and why she seems to come alive only on the nights when she puts on her make-up and her lovely dresses and her big diamond ring and goes out with my father.

The curtains in my parents' bedroom are made of heavy, Chinese silk and they reach from the ceiling to the floor. In fact they reach beyond the floor on purpose, my mother explained, ruching up against the carpet to create a sense of opulence, 'like you might find at the Ritz' is how she described it. I think my mother is very clever at things like that. I would think that curtains which ruche up against the floor would need to be shortened. Mavis thinks that, too, because they're a real nuisance when you have to vacuum. But I can see that my mother really does know about these things and I can see how Cat has got the same ability – to see how colours and patterns and objects and materials should be organised to make them look nice in a way I never could.

Mavis had said that if Cat wanted to buy material to make costumes with we should all go down to Berwick Street Market in Soho on Saturday morning. But for Cat an outing with Mavis was more torture than treat. She knew exactly how it would be. Me walking along Oxford Street hand in hand with Mavis and ooh-ing at aah-ing at all the shop windows, especially Selfridges, her trailing behind being ignored or maybe even losing us altogether in

Hamley's while she looked at dressing-up outfits and Mavis and I went off to see if any new games had been invented. So she begged our mother to come with us to look for materials instead of Mavis. Mum, to our surprise, agreed to take us on Saturday morning to John Lewis, as we urgently needed some new bits of school uniform. It would have been more fun to go to a market than fusty old John Lewis, but an outing was an outing,

Shopping trips are one of the few things I remember doing with my mother. Shopping, often. Playing? Having fun? Maybe I just don't have a very good memory.

I have to admit it: Cat is amazing. Between Saturday, after our morning shopping trip, and Sunday afternoon – with my help, which is probably more of a hindrance as I'm as bad at sewing as I am at being the centre of attention – she has got together about a dozen outfits, all of them completely brilliant. She got my dad to bring home these giant scissors from his factory and masses of crunchy brown paper. Then she started taking all these measurements, like from the back of my neck to my knee, around my waist, my shoulders from the neck, my arms, even my nose – but that was just a joke, she wasn't planning an entire outfit for my nose. And then she got me to measure her in the same way. Her nose was longer than mine, which I was pleased about, but so were her legs, which they should be because she's three years older, but she started calling me shorty, which I didn't like one bit. 'At least I don't look like a silly stick of spaghetti,' I said, more to myself than to her and she started jumping up and down and jabbing the huge scissors really close to my face, which was scary. 'Come on, little-legged Mouse,' she panted, a bit out of breath, 'we've got work to do.'

Next she started drawing out the outfits on the paper, to the right measurements, and then placing it on top of the fabric and cutting it carefully to size. It's not that difficult, I suppose, if you know what you're doing, but it's not how my mind works. I like thinking about words and how they sound and whether they might have started off in a different country and which country that might be. There are lots of words that come from Latin and also from Greek. I'm going to study Latin at school a bit later on, so hopefully I'll be able to work it out for myself rather than just guessing all the time.

I wonder why it is that when I wrap a tablecloth round me it looks like I've wrapped myself up in a tablecloth. But when Cat does the same it looks like something you'd see in the evening-dress section of the Harrods catalogue.

Cat says the outfits don't have to be well made or really neat as we're not wearing them to a party or anything, only for the show. Which is just as well because although I can work the sewing machine that's been moved from Mavis's room into mine for the weekend I can't make the lines straight.

Cat's going to dance a tarantella. So for that she needs a gypsy outfit and a tambourine and some of my mother's cast-off hoop earrings. Cat cuts a big circle of emerald-green felt for the skirt and a huge triangle for a shawl from some red shiny fabric. She's going to tie a scarf round her head, knotting it at the back of the neck.

Each outfit is painstakingly pieced together, from the 'prom' dress made of silk taffeta, like the ones they wear to graduation parties in American films about college kids, to be worn when Cat sings 'Ma, he's making eyes at me . . .', to a Charlie Chaplin outfit, for the jokes section, consisting of a pair of my dad's old trousers rolled up and held in at the waist with a big sash, plus an old white collarless shirt, a black waistcoat and a bowler hat that comes down over her eyes. The catwalk show is on the theme of Greek goddesses, with lots of one-shouldered numbers in slippery jersey material.

Cat will introduce each of the four catwalk outfits and I will parade up and down the red carpet that has been fashioned from some bolts of red cotton and which will run the length of the living room. It's all loads of work, and I don't even get time off to watch *Doctor Who*, which is my new most favourite television programme and which I like even more than *Doctor Kildare* or *Emergency Ward 10*, and it's not really fair, being bossed around by Cat all the time, but I don't dare say no to her. I don't know what would happen if I did say no, but just thinking about how Cat might explode makes me feel a bit dizzy and I'd rather get on with the job than feel dizzy all the time.

We're sent to bed around nine o'clock, but as soon as the house is quiet, Cat lollops into my room and we start to work again, me on the machine, Cat sewing by hand. We have to sew by torchlight because if we switched on the main light someone might see it and then we'd get found out and sent back to bed. After a while my eyes start to feel sore, but Cat says we just have to get on with it. We're not finished until 1 a.m. and I'm practically falling off my chair, but even then Cat says, 'You know, we're going to have to get up early tomorrow to get this done.'

No wonder I sometimes wish a crocodile would pass by our house and swallow her up. Then, just as I'm thinking she's the most hateful person in the world, she says, 'You've done a good job. A really good job. No way could I have got this together without you,' and I go kind of gooey, like the insides of posh dinner-party chocolates.

'Thank you, Cat. It's been really . . .' I hesitate, no longer sure what it's been. 'It's been really fun.'

At exactly 4 p.m. on Sunday afternoon, my parents file into the living room. My dad is beaming, my mother is looking a little bit concerned, probably about the fact that the furniture has been moved around. They have to hand me their tickets, which Cat has made herself and painted with a rather good picture of a dancing gypsy. One says Row A, Seat 1; the other Row A, Seat 2. My mother and father seat themselves on the sofa. This is my cue to move to the upright piano in the corner and bang it a few times, by way of announcing something is about to happen.

Cat flings open the door in her gypsy outfit as I rush from the piano to the record player. She stops in the doorway, so she is framed, as though in a photograph. She throws back her head, stretches her arms to full span so that one is pointing at an angle towards the top corner of the door, the other towards the bottom corner, in a perfect straight line, just like we've seen showgirls do on the television. Then she flies into the room to rapturous applause, shakes her tambourine, and whirls and whirls and hops and kicks to the sound of tarantella music wafting scratchily from the gramophone. My parents are laughing and cheering and my mother, for just a moment, looks not only beautiful but happy. Between the tarantella and the Charlie Chaplin, I return quietly to the piano, sit on the stool and stare down at the piano keys. I don't really mind that nobody even knows I'm here.

I wish I had those earplugs Mavis mentioned. I don't have the world's greatest voice myself but you'd have to be completely deaf not to realise just how dreadful Cat's voice is. Not that it really matters. Cat doesn't know what it is to be embarrassed, and she's so clearly enjoying herself that even when she shrieks 'Ma, he's making eyes at me' at the top of her voice and my mother's hands fly to her ears to protect them, Cat ploughs on, oblivious. I start playing the notes, but quickly give up as Cat's way ahead of me. And now all three of us are sitting with our hands over our ears, but even I'm laughing now, and when Cat finally plonks herself heavily on the floor, head to the carpet, arms outstretched, in a very, very inelegant imitation of a prima ballerina, we're all on our feet. 'It's a standing ovation!' says my dad. 'Look, everyone's standing.'

Cat, who's still curled up in a ball, lifts just her head and smiles. My dad walks towards her, hands her a tulip he's just grabbed from a vase on the coffee table, and bows really low, like you might to royalty.

Cat's up on her feet again, dripping with sweat.

'Mum, Dad, you just sit back and relax. Come on, Hannah, time to get changed for the fashion show.'

In the morning room, where the clothes are laid out, I am forced to strip down to my knickers. I step into a cerise silk-jersey, one-shoulder, toga-type thing, held together round the waist with a rope. Cat says it's the kind of outfit a Greek goddess might have worn to a disco.

'They didn't have discos in those days,' I say authoritatively.

'Shut up, know-all,' replies Cat.

I'm allowed to go barefoot, because that's what, according to Cat, Greek goddesses do. I know I must look ridiculous but I'm thinking that the sooner we get on with it, the sooner it will be over and I can go and finish my homework. Cat has splodged my lips with lipstick to match the dress and now she's thrust a jug that looks a bit like an urn, and a bunch of grapes from the fruit bowl at me.

'Here, take these.'

'What for?'

'To balance on your shoulder, dummy.'

'I can't manage both.'

'Of course you can. You hold the jug on your shoulder with one hand, and the grapes on the turned-over bit of your other hand.'

'It's called a palm.' Looking back, I think I could have won prizes for priggishness.

'I thought I told you to shut up. Just try to remember what I tell you. You need to stop right in the doorway. When I give the signal you walk down the catwalk, and past the sofa to the fireplace. You stop, turn round, walk back and out of the door to the kitchen. I'll follow to help you with outfit number two. Hurry up, they're waiting.'

'But don't I need one hand to hold the dress up? It's a bit long.'

'Of course not, dummy. It's supposed to trail, not flap around your ankles.'

Cat runs ahead and I walk nervously towards the lounge. The dress is a bit looser than it should be and certainly a bit too long, despite what Cat says. Like the curtains in my mother's bedroom, the dress may look more stylish if it trails a bit on the ground but the difference between this dress and the curtains is that no one has to walk down a catwalk wearing the curtains.

I make it to the doorway without mishap.

'Our first dress for the show –' Cat, posed with one hand resting on the shelf above the fireplace, is telling my parents – 'is made from silk jersey and drapes flatteringly across the body. Inspired by the Greek goddess of wine, whose name I can't pronounce—'

'Amphictyonis,' I say quietly, but no one seems to hear.

'– it can be made to order in time for the party season. Will the model please now step forward?'

I step tentatively onto the red carpet. So far so good, though my face is burning and I'm thinking it must be the same colour as the dress.

My mother is saying, 'Oh it's delicious. I simply have to have one.'

I take another tentative step and my foot catches the fabric at the front of the dress. I shake my foot away and continue my perilous journey. A few more steps and my foot catches again. I stumble and reach out for the coffee table to stop myself from falling. The urn plummets from my shoulder and shatters against the table. My mother screams as shards of clay pot zoom towards her like guided missiles. The cerise jersey has slid from my shoulder and sits on the floor around me like a puddle of blood. I'm standing naked except for a pair of white Marks & Spencer knickers. I don't cry. I don't say anything. I turn on my heels, run out of the room, up the stairs and into my bedroom. Slamming the door, I fling myself on to the eiderdown and bury my face in it, pounding one small fist against the pillow.

Some time later, it could have been minutes or hours, I really have no idea, there's a knock at the door. By now I'm sitting cross-legged on the coverlet, staring into dark space. The door opens and my mother, father and sister are standing there, not smiling.

'You ruined it,' says Cat.

'Ssh,' says my father. 'It wasn't her fault. It's all right, Hannah, it was an accident. These things happen . . .'

'That jug,' says my mother. 'It was a present, from my mother, for our third wedding anniversary.'

'I thought we'd agreed not to . . .' My father gives my mother a stern look, and reaches out to almost touch her on the shoulder. Then he seems to change his mind and withdraws it again.

'Come on, Hannah,' says Dad. 'Time for tea.'

I don't want tea. I don't want anything to do with any of them. I don't respond.

'Cat got your tongue again, has she?' says my father, his gentle tone turned quickly to one of exasperation.

I want to say, 'Just leave me alone.' I open my mouth but nothing comes out.

'It's enough, Hannah,' says my father. 'It's over. When you're ready, come downstairs and join us. I will not have you moping around for the rest of the day.'

They leave, quietly closing the door behind them.

I get up and go over to my little desk, switch on the table lamp and open the drawer. There's a small hand mirror in it. I look into the mirror and stick out my tongue. It's still there. I try to make the aaah sound the doctor asks you to make if you've got a sore throat, but still nothing comes. I can't speak! I feel like I'm locked in a room that's very small and I can't get out. I need help, but I can't call out for help. There are tears coming out of my eyes now, but no sound to go along with them. My voice! What's happened to it? Where has it gone?

Cat's got your tongue! Cat's got your tongue! Cat's got your tongue! I can hear the voices in my head, my mother's, my father's, Cat's, jeering at me over and over, whirring inside my head. I clap my hands to my ears, just like I did when Cat was singing, but the sound won't go away. I feel sick. I run to the bathroom and throw up in the toilet bowl. And then just as suddenly as they came the voices have disappeared and my own voice comes back. 'I want Mavis,' I weep, 'I want my Mavis.' I go back to my room and get into bed and wait.

At about six o'clock, a smiling Mavis puts her head around my door. I throw back the covers, leap up and rush towards the door. Pulling her by the hand – even though she hasn't got her coat off yet – I lead her back to the bed, patting the place where I want her to sit and hear my whole sad, sorry story.

'I couldn't speak, Mavis. My voice, it went completely.'

'Not completely, pet. You were just upset.'

'But Mavis, you don't understand. Nothing would come out. Absolutely nothing.'

'Cuddle time,' says Mavis.

We cuddle. And then we cuddle some more. And then when Mavis pulls back to see if I've had enough cuddling, I burrow myself into her again. Mavis is home. And everything's going to be all right.

Except life's not that simple. The next morning, Mavis gathers up all the clothes from Cat's show and using the shears my dad brought home from the factory snips them into hundreds of tiny pieces. She gathers them all up and then dumps them in the middle of Cat's bed. A present for when she gets home from school.

Cat's gone to a friend for tea, so I'm home before her, and Mavis leads me by the hand into Cat's bedroom so I can admire her handiwork. I gasp when I see what she's done and know immediately that Mavis has made a terrible mistake.

'That girl needs to know that she's not the centre of the universe. She deserves to be punished for upsetting you like that.'

'But you don't understand, Mavis, you really don't . . .'

'What don't I understand?'

'That they'll stand up for her. They always do. And that if they see you being beastly to Cat they'll send you away.'

'Oh no, they won't. They won't send me away. Not if they know which side their bread is buttered, they won't.'

'What's it got to do with bread and butter?'

'Forget the bread and butter. Downstairs I've got a nice piece of Victoria sponge waiting for you. Fresh-made today.'

Cake, as far as Mavis was concerned, was the answer to all life's problems. It was half-past four, my mother was having her afternoon rest, Cat wouldn't be back for at least an hour. So I had a whole hour, just me and Mavis and cake, before the fireworks would begin.

Cat got hysterical, which was to be expected. So hysterical that Mavis had to go and find a paper bag for her to breathe into. Once she got her breath back, she went barging into the room where my mum was having a siesta.

'What did she say?' I asked Cat later, silently praying that she hadn't promised to turn Mavis out of the house.

'What do you think she said?' said Cat angrily. 'What does always say?'

'I don't know,' I replied.

'Yes, you do. It never changes, does it? She said, "I'll ask your father to have words with Mavis." When I told her what Mavis had done, she just said we can always go and buy some more material from John Lewis. What's wrong with her? Why doesn't she see what's going on? Why doesn't she do anything about it? If only Mavis was out of the house everything would be all right. We could get another Mavis, a nice Mavis. But she'll never go. We're stuck with her for ever.'

I assume my father did have words, but Cat was right. She didn't get fired. For a couple of days after 'the incident' the silence in the house seemed to take on a sound of its own. The very absence of conversation assumed a texture and resonance akin to noise.

Mavis wouldn't talk to anyone except me and just nodded in response to instructions. My father kept looking at my mother over dinner, willing her to respond, but she appeared to be making a point of not looking back at him. Cat gave up bothering to amuse everyone and pulled accusing, bug-ugly faces at me whenever I caught her eye.

Slowly the stagnant air in the house lightened and retreated. My father suggested a weekend picnic. Cat came down to dinner wearing a dress fashioned from a black dustbin bag held together with safety pins and everyone laughed. And things returned to what passed for normal in our smart, suburban, happy family's home.

Chapter Six

Cat and I used to play the 'Who would you save?' game, although it was always Cat, not me, who instigated it.

'If you were in a lifeboat with the Queen and the Prime Minister, and you had to throw one overboard to save two of you, who would it be?' Cat asked.

'I'd save the Prime Minister. It's always "God save the Queen", never "God save the Prime Minister". So if I saved the Prime Minister, maybe God would still save the Queen.'

'Do you believe in God?'

'Maybe.'

'Like when?'

'If I tell you then it won't work.'

'What won't work?'

'My prayers won't work if I talk about them.'

'You're a bit pathetic you know, Mouse. A bit of a spaz . . .'

'What's it to you?'

'OK, Mouse, your turn.'

'If you were in a lifeboat with Mum and Dad, and you had to throw one overboard, who would it be?'

'Neither.'

'Then you'd all drown.'

'But I couldn't choose, it wasn't fair to ask me that.'

'That's the rule, though; you have to answer.'

'But it's stupid. It should be people we don't know.'

'Look, you started this game, not me. You have another turn, then.'

'If you were in a lifeboat with Mum and Mavis, and you had to throw one overboard to save two of you, who would it be?'

'I thought you said—'

'Yes, but you did one with people we know, so now I'm doing one.'

'And you wouldn't answer. Anyway, it's an easy one: Mavis.'

'Mavis?' Cat squawked incredulously.

'Yes, Mavis, because Mavis can swim and Mum can't.'

'That's cheating. The overboard one has to drown. So would it still be Mavis?'

'Yes, Mavis.'

'I don't believe you.'

'You don't have to.'

'Are you sure?'

'Of course I'm sure. Eleanor Marguerite Saunders is my mother, isn't she? I'd have to save her.'

'You see. No one wants to save Mavis. Not even you. No one on the entire planet would think she was worth saving.'

I was nine and I was getting really good at the business of lying. The truth was that if I was in a lifeboat with Mum, Dad, Cat and Mavis and three of the four had to go overboard, I'd still have saved Mavis. If you asked a grown-up who I should save it would probably be Cat they'd choose because she had her whole life ahead of her. That's what adults say when they read in the newspaper about a young person who's died. 'It's so sad, she had her whole life ahead of her.' I know it was only a game but it felt safer to tell a lie. I had a feeling that if I told the truth I'd be struck by lightning, or run down by a car, or shot by mistake walking past the bank when armed robbers were in the middle of a raid. Guilt wrapped itself round me as softly and easily as a velvet cloak.

What I understood was that you were supposed to love your mother more than your maid, if you had a maid, that is, which I knew most people didn't. It wasn't even that I didn't love my mother, I just didn't ever get to know her. No one knew her really, except perhaps my father, who treated her like she was the Baccarat crystal decanter in the sideboard in the dining room, so precious and so delicate she would shatter into a thousand pieces should you say boo to her when she wasn't expecting it. I thought of her more as a shadow or a ghost. Sometimes I used to think that she wasn't made up of flesh and blood at all, but that you could step right through her. She was never unkind to me in a way you could describe. She always wanted me to wrap up warm when I went out on a winter's day. She constantly steered me away from draughts whenever I was in her presence, and called the doctor if I so much as sneezed. She bought me lots of lovely clothes; my wardrobe was far more stuffed than those of most girls I knew. But interest in me, my studies or my friends she didn't even feign. Hugs, cuddles and proper kisses she didn't do. I could tell from the way her lips barely brushed my face when she greeted me, that she just didn't go in for that sort of thing.

It was different with Cat. Cat was such a spontaneous, touchy sort of person that my mother didn't really have any choice in the matter. She'd plant big, wet smackers on my mum's face, which my mother would discreetly wipe off with her handkerchief the moment Cat wasn't looking. Or Cat would come up to her from behind when she was sitting on the sofa, and fling her arms around my mother's neck. My mother would jump, but she'd allow Cat's arms to linger round her neck for a good few seconds before gently unravelling them.

Cat was natural, without inhibition, an irresistible force. With me and my mother it was like two animals sniffing one another out and both deciding simultaneously to retreat. And anyway I had Mavis on hand to give me all the affection I needed.

'I'm bored with this game,' said Cat.

'Me, too,' I replied.

It was always like this in those days. We didn't really play, we bickered. But I lived in hope that one day Cat would want me as her sister.

'Let's play darts.' My sister's idea.

'OK.'

We had this great dartboard in the playroom. Cat was always threatening to get her hands on some poison and then stab Mavis with one of the darts, but I didn't take her seriously.

'. . . But only till my friends get here. Suzie and Sandy are coming soon, then I want you to scram.'

'Why can't I stay?'

'Because we have important things to discuss and we don't want some bogey-nosed kid poking her bogey nose into our business.'

'Like sex, I suppose.'

'What do you know about sex, little Mouse?'

'More than you probably.'

Janet had told me all about sex, although not so much that I'd stopped believing babies were born out of your belly button. My mother had tried to tell me about sex. She asked me to sit at the end of her bed one morning while she was having breakfast because she wanted to have a little chat.

'I want to explain to you about the facts of life,' she said, without enthusiasm.

'What are they?'

'They're to do with how babies are made.'

'But I know all that stuff.'

'You do?' I saw the relief on my mother's face. My knowing already would save her the embarrassment of having to discuss it. 'You really are an old head on young shoulders, Hannah. Well, no need to go over old ground, then, is there?' She hesitated. 'But I do want you to know that if you really love someone it isn't all that awful after a while.'

'What, having babies?'

'Well, having babies can be awfully painful, but I meant the process you have to go through to make babies. You get used to it, I suppose.'

I longed to know more, from someone who'd really done it, like my mother, rather than Janet who just listened to what her mother told her and probably got half of it wrong by the time she got around to telling me about it. But my mum wasn't making it sound much like fun. In fact I decided there and then that I wasn't going to get married, not ever, that no way was I going to start expelling slimy aliens from my belly button, and I certainly wasn't going to engage in any activity – like jumping over the wooden horse in the gymnasium at school – that got only marginally less awful the more often you did it.

'Can I go now?' I asked.

My mother's head sank back gratefully on the pillow.

'You're a good girl, considering . . .' She tailed off.

Considering what, I wondered half-heartedly, as I slid off the lavender, satiny eiderdown. Having an enigmatic mother could be extremely tedious at times. Out on the landing. I could smell something almondy wafting up from the kitchen. I ran downstairs to find Mavis removing a whole tray of freshly baked macaroons from the oven. Cat said our father was nuts for macaroons. It was one of her little jokes.

If Cat, Suzie and Sandy were going to talk about sex, I could always play darts with Mavis. She wasn't as good at it as me, but unlike Cat she didn't get into a strop every time I beat her. Having Mavis in the house meant I always had someone to play with, so apart from Janet I didn't bother too much with other friends.

Our playroom was enormous, with a full-sized ping-pong table, and banquettes round the edge. The banquettes lifted up and inside we stored all our games and toys. Janet, who lived in a council house, liked to spend as much time as possible in our house; it was so much bigger and more exciting than hers.

'I wouldn't mind having weirdo parents if I could live in a place like this,' she said to me once, after we'd managed to bat the ball across the net two hundred and fifty times without missing a shot.

It was when I was in the playroom with Mavis that I tried broaching the subject of sex with her. 'That stuff you have to do to make babies,' I said to her, 'is it awful?'

'Depends who you do it with,' she laughed gruffly.

'Have you ever done it?'

Mavis shot me a look that seemed to carry some kind of warning. 'There are some questions, missy, that I'm not prepared to answer.'

'Would you like to have a baby?'

'Not if she's as much trouble as you,' she replied smiling, which wasn't really an answer at all. Then Mavis looked down at her feet and gave her head a little shake, as though something had popped into her mind that she wanted to get rid of. It made me wonder yet again if she had a secret boyfriend, a boyfriend she wanted to marry and have babies with.

'Hey, look, I've scored a bullseye. That's fifty points. Fifty points. Yippee!'

Mavis threw a dart. It hit the metal at the edge of the triple slot for the 7, and bounced off it, landing on the floor.

'Oh Mavis, that's a shame. You didn't score at all.' I genuinely wanted Mavis to do well, just not quite as well as me.

'You see,' she said. 'Darts is just like life. There are winners and there are losers. And you, my girl, will grow up to be a winner. I'll make sure of that.'

I was reading *The Diary of Anne Frank* for the third time when it happened. It was ten o'clock at night and I should have been asleep, but I was under the covers with the torch and the diary. I was up to the middle of 1944 and I'd just read the line 'When I write I can shake off all my cares,' which Anne wrote just a couple of months before the Secret Annexe, where she'd been hiding with her family, was exposed by the Nazis. To me, Anne was real. Not just a real person, but a real friend. I was sure that had we known one another, gone to the same school perhaps or met one day in the park, she would have become as good a friend as Janet.

Ours was not a shouty household. My parents never rowed with one another in front of us, and I never found out whether they argued out of earshot. The signs of disagreement between them were far more subtle. A particular look that passed between them, a change in tone of voice, a hardness behind my father's eyes, or one of my mother's sighs, sighs so quietly sad and melancholic that sometimes I wanted to go and stroke her gently, over and over, like she was a wounded kitten. Not that I ever did. Cat and I, on the other hand, rowed all the time. But that didn't count because sisters are allowed to have a go at one another; it's expected. Even so we reserved our shouting for our own quarters or the garden, because to shout within earshot of my mother was something we instinctively knew not to do.

It was more like loud whispering at first. I caught only fragments, disconnected words that made no sense. I heard the word 'Mavis' and then 'enough' and then 'cruelty'. Then the voices grew louder and more distinct, whole sentences travelling up the stairs and along the corridor and through the crack between my door and the floor and then up towards where I lay in bed.

My mother's voice was high-pitched and trembly. 'I can't take it any more, Maurice. You have to do something about her.'

Then my father, sombre and slow, like a judge or a headmaster. 'But there could be consequences, Eleanor. We have to consider Hannah.'

The voices were getting louder. My mother's more shrill. 'But we also have to think about Cat. And about me. Remember, in the beginning we got her for *me*. Not for Hannah. She's nothing less than a witch and I shall go quite mad if I have to put up with her in my house any longer.'

'You know I only want what's right for all of you.'

'You should have thought of that a long time ago. It's unbearable. Quite unbearable.'

I could picture my mother in her creamy satin dressing gown, looking beautiful and desperate. I imagined her clutching and pulling at my father's clothes, pleading with him. He would find it impossible to deny her.

I was holding my breath and praying, 'Dear God, please don't let it happen. Not now. I promise I'll be good. I'll love everybody the same – no, I'll love them all more. More than Mavis. And I'll love Cat, too, and I won't argue with her any more.' At that moment I really did believe that how much you loved someone was just a decision you made, like deciding to finish your homework before supper so you could watch television afterwards. I thought it could be that simple.

My father was talking again, trying to maintain control. 'Eleanor, you have to calm down. You'll wake the children. Perhaps you should take one of your pills.'

'I don't want one of my pills. They don't help. You have to get rid of her. Just get rid of her, that's all I ask. I'll be better, I promise. I'll manage. I'll find a way.'

Please, Daddy, I beg you, don't give in.

'But we got her precisely because you *couldn't* manage. You know, Eleanor dear, how difficult it is for you to manage.'

'If she doesn't leave . . . if she doesn't leave . . . I shall kill myself. And this time I'll succeed.'

It was as if the world had stopped. Nothing. Only silence. And going through my head: *What does she mean, 'I shall kill myself. And this time I'll succeed'?* I was twirling my fingers through my hair, over and over, round and round until my scalp hurt. Tighter and tighter until it felt the hair was parting with my head. I didn't care if it did. I would rather have been completely bald than have Mavis sent away.

And then my father's voice again. Softer now and full of reassurance. 'Of course, my dear. You're absolutely right. You've been through more than enough. I'll tell her in the morning. We'll make all the arrangements then. But we can't just cut her off, it wouldn't be right. We have to tread carefully. And I'm concerned you won't find it easy to cope without her.'

'Well, I certainly can't cope with her. My nerves are in pieces.'

'Then there's nothing more we can do now. I'm going to bed. Are you coming?'

'Not just yet. I think I'll stay down and read.'

'Eleanor, you're not thinking of having a drink, are you?'

'I don't drink, remember? I DO NOT DRINK. Sometimes I feel you're more of a jailer than a husband.'

'I only want to do what's right for you, my love. Tell me that you are sure this is what you want to do and—'

'After what Cat told me this afternoon . . . and after what she showed me . . .'

I felt my throat constricting as my recurring nightmare came back to me, cutting through the dark and flashing before my eyes. I could see Mavis sitting in a small fishing boat, being rowed further and further out to sea, further and further until a huge wave swept over the boat and Mavis disappeared, and then the water disappeared, too, and instead of the ocean I was standing in my garden looking out at a vast, sandy, empty desert. In my hand was a bucket of water, and floating on top of the water a photograph of me and Mavis, holding hands and smiling at the camera. As the water seeped into the photographic paper, the image seemed to smudge and fade until it disappeared altogether. My nightmare had become real and there was nothing I was going to be able to do about it. Mavis was about to disappear.

When the house was quiet, and all I could hear was the blood rushing inside my ears, I tiptoed quietly out of my room and walked along the corridor to where Mavis was probably fast asleep. I knocked quietly, but there was no response. I dared to knock slightly harder and I heard Mavis shifting herself under the bedclothes, disturbed but not awakened. So I crept in and over to her bed and shook her gently by the shoulder. 'Mavis, Mavis,' I whispered in her ear. 'You have to wake up. It's an emergency.'

Mavis, whose back was turned to me, rolled over and rubbed her eyes.

'What in God's name are you . . .? Say, pet, what's the matter? You're trembling – do you have a fever?'

'Listen to me, Mavis, we have to do something. Immediately. We have to run away.'

Mavis was fully awake now, sitting upright and motioning me to sit on the coverlet. 'Slowly now, luv. Tell me what's the matter. Are you ill?'

'Not ill, Mavis. Worse than that. They're going to send you away. In the morning. I heard them. And it's Cat's fault, she told them something. Something terrible that you did, but I don't believe her. She made it up. She made it up, didn't she? I hate her. I always hated her. I'll hate her for ever. I hate everybody except you.'

'Calm down now, sweetheart. Of course she made it up. But we do need to have a chat, you and I.'

'There's no time. We have to pack. I've got pounds and pounds in my piggy bank. We can go to a hotel. And we can look through my dad's pockets in the hall cupboard. There's bound to be some money in there. Once we're at the hotel we'll decide what to do next.'

'A hotel, eh? The Dorchester or the Savoy? Which would you prefer?' Mavis smiled.

'It's not funny, you have to believe me. Why are you trying to make jokes? They mean it. Daddy's going to do it in the morning.'

'Well, pet, perhaps it's time.'

'Time for what?' I answered in a quavery voice between sobs.

'Time for me to go. You don't need me now, not now that you're such a big girl. You're ten, it's time for you to stand on your own two feet a bit. Spend more time playing with Janet and the rest of the girls rather than boring old me. And before you know it you'll be having all the boys after you, and then you won't want me hanging around feeding you chocolate biscuits all the time.'

'Please don't leave me,' I begged. 'Please don't agree to go.'

'But if your dad chucks me out, I'm going to have to go. If I refuse he might call the police. He has the right. And you wouldn't want anything like that to happen, would you?'

'Prison? They wouldn't send you to prison, would they? Take you away in handcuffs in a black Maria, like they do on *Dixon of Dock Green*?'

For just a second or two it was beginning to sound all rather exciting. Then I remembered the reality.

'Listen, Mavis. You have to listen to me. If you really have to go, we can go together. I can pack now, and as soon as I hear Mum close her bedroom door we'll sneak out of the house. They won't even know we're gone until the morning and by then they won't know where to go looking for us.'

I was getting desperate. My sobs were growing louder, my nose was running, and I could hardly catch my breath.

'Come and snuggle up under the covers, Hannah. We'll sort something out, I promise we will.'

Mavis pulled back the sheets for me and then did something I knew my own mother would never do. She took me in her arms, smoothed my soggy, sweat-stained hair away from my face, wiped my tears and my nose with a tissue from beside her bed, and planted kiss after kiss on my forehead, until eventually I fell into an exhausted, dreamless sleep.

There was light filtering through the curtains when I awoke. Mavis was already dressed and was splashing her face at the basin in the corner of the room. My eyes felt tight and sore and I wanted to hide back under the bed clothes. For a moment I couldn't remember why I was in Mavis's room, then something in my sightline made me gasp. It was an open suitcase, half full.

'Mavis, you're already packing. Have they spoken to you yet?'

'No, luv, no one's up as yet, but I expect your dad soon will be.'

'But they might have changed their minds. Maybe I was having a nightmare. Maybe I dreamed it. Maybe I made a mistake.'

'From what you told me, I don't think so. And once your dad's mind is made up I've never known him to change it again.'

'But if I explain everything he might.'

'Explain? And what exactly do you think you might explain?'

'That I need you. That I have to have you here. That Cat is the biggest liar in the world. That she always tell lies.'

'And you really think they'll take your word against hers?'

'Well, why shouldn't they?'

'Because Cat's. . . . Well, it doesn't really matter what Cat is right now. What matters is that you understand that you'll be fine and I'll be fine and we'll get together lots and lots and that I'll always love you and be your friend. Be strong, sweet Hannah, be strong for your mate Mavis.'

'Where will you go?'

'To my brother's first, I expect. Then I'll get a job. A proper job in a factory. I'll never be a maid in anyone else's house, not after all the goings-on here.'

'A factory could be all right. My dad says that being a maid is better than working in a factory but he could be wrong, I suppose. I couldn't bear you to go to another family. You might find a girl to look after who you liked even more than you like me and then you'd forget all about me.'

'Not possible, pet.'

'Then I'd have to hate her as well as Cat and my parents.'

'You don't hate them, Hannah, not really.'

'I do. And I always will. Once you're gone it will be just me and Anne Frank in the house. I shan't talk to anyone else. Oh please don't go . . .' And then I started sobbing again.

A bell sounded. Not an alarm clock but another of those treacherous servant bells my father used to call Mavis. I looked at Mavis's clock on the bedside table: 6.45 and he was ringing the bell in his bedroom, a signal that he'd like his tea and biscuits and the newspaper if it had arrived on time. Even on a day like today, even on the worst day of my entire life, even on a day when he was going to throw the only person I loved out of the house for ever, my dad still had to have his tea and his biscuits delivered to him in his bedroom by the woman he was about to dismiss. No wonder I was angry enough to explode. Except that I didn't explode. I took all that rage and fury and hurt and kept it inside me, where it hammered at my heart, gnawed away at my bones, twisted my intestines, and finally robbed me of my voice.

For almost three weeks after Mavis left I couldn't utter a single word. This time Cat really had got my tongue. I wasn't refusing to speak as such, at least I don't think I was, although I did get some enjoyment from seeing the look of despair on my parents' faces when not a single word emitted from my mouth. Even Cat started offering bribes if I would only speak to her. I suppose it was nice to be wanted, when for so long I had felt mostly ignored. But still I couldn't speak and still I cried myself to sleep every night, silent tears rolling down my cheeks as I read and reread *Anne Frank's Diary* and looked at photos of me and Mavis together.

So when Cat said I could borrow her precious Beatles LP, *Please, Please Me*, I just shrugged and took it casually from the shelf. I knew perfectly well how much this album meant to her. She had stood with Suzie and Sandy for eight hours outside the Abbey Road studios where the Beatles had recorded it, just to get their autographs. She was rewarded with all four signatures and until this moment had never let me touch it, let alone listen to it when she was out of the room. Not speaking did, I have to say, have its advantages, but still I don't think I was doing it deliberately. It was scary to be trapped inside myself like that, storing up all that hatred for my parents and for Cat. And I was terrified that I might never be able to speak again.

At school the head teacher called my mum and dad in for a meeting and threatened to expel me, convinced I was just being manipulative and punishing my parents for having dismissed a servant of whom I was clearly fond. I did become the centre of attention for a while, both at home and at school, and it did occur to me that if Cat thought everything was going to be hunky-dory once Mavis was out of the house, it was my duty to Mavis to prove her wrong. At school the other girls suddenly found me fascinating. It seemed quite weird to me that when I was perfectly able to talk most of the girls couldn't be bothered with me. Now that I couldn't, they couldn't get enough of me. They even invented this new game for lunchtime where the whole class would sit in a giant circle on the grass and see how long they could keep quiet. The first to speak would have to leave the circle and the last one to speak, apart from me, who they realised wasn't about to say anything, would win.

It would only be about a minute before someone would start giggling, and once that happened the giggling would take hold like a virus, and then everyone would speak at once. Janet would always do quite well and last for ages, which was because she was my friend, and because she understood that I really couldn't speak. I would never have included her in my so-called punishment regime so she knew I wasn't faking; and because I wasn't faking she was determined to know what it felt like to be silent. I started writing notes to her instead of speaking, and if the teacher asked me a question in class I'd have to quickly scribble the answer on a piece of paper and hold it up.

My mother took me to the GP, who shone a light down my throat and asked me to say aah, which I sort of did, although it came out more as a breath that sounded like the sea than a proper aah. He couldn't detect any soreness or swelling when he felt the glands behind my ears and in my neck, and shook his head, mystified.

'Look, Hannah,' he said, 'if this is some kind of trick you're playing, I'm sure your parents know that you've been quite upset. But don't you think it's gone far enough now?'

I shook my head and the tears trickled down my face.

'I think,' he said, 'that perhaps Hannah should see a psychiatrist. It's very uncommon, I know, but there could be a psychological reason for her loss of voice.'

'I don't like psychiatrists,' said my mother. 'They mess with your head and make you worse.' I didn't know what she meant by *mess with your head*, but it didn't sound promising, and I shook my own head vigorously in protest.

'But I think we may need to investigate this further,' replied the doctor. 'I understand your reticence, but we don't want to let this continue much longer than it already has. It will probably be a good fortnight before you can see anyone, by which time, with any luck, the problem will have resolved itself.'

The problem did resolve itself. Two weeks and four days after Mavis left, on a Saturday morning around 11 a.m., my dad put me on the train for Chelmsford. It had been arranged that Mavis and I could spend the day together. She would meet me at the other end, and then escort me all the way home early in the evening, dropping me off outside our front door before returning to Chelmsford herself.

It was the first time I'd been on a train on my own. I was excited to be seeing Mavis and excited to be sitting with my nose pressed to the window, watching houses and chimneys and then trees and fields and cows whizzing by. The journey wasn't more than forty-five minutes from Liverpool Street. Mavis was on the platform waiting for me, and attached to a lead dangling from her hand was a gorgeous puppy.

I scampered down the steps from the train and ran along the platform towards Mavis.

'Hello, Mavis,' I shouted.

'Hello, Hannah.' She smiled. 'A pet for my pet. I thought you could name her yourself. And she'll be here every time you come to visit.'

'Oh she's so sweet, so sweet,' I said, crouching down and picking her up in my arms to let her lick my face. I'd always wanted a dog, but my dad said you should only have a dog if you lived in the country. My mother practically jumped out of her skin every time a dog went past on the opposite side of the street. I knew right away that she was a Cavalier King Charles Spaniel, with long flappy brown ears, a silky coat, waggy tail and dark, imploring eyes. 'I love her. Oh we're going to have such fun together.' Only then did I realise I had my voice back.

The appointment with the psychiatrist never took place. Cat and I never discussed Mavis again. And I never asked Cat about the bruises, not even after I started talking again. On the evening of the day of Mavis's departure, I had been at the basin brushing my teeth and Cat was behind me, luxuriating up to her neck in a bath full of bubbles. I could see her reflection in the bathroom mirror. She was in triumphant mood, smiling even to herself, and singing a Beatles medley. I was red-eyed and snotty-nosed from crying. I watched Cat dreamily pick up a pink foam sponge in the shape of a heart from the edge of the bath. Languorously raising one arm at a time, she sponged off the bubbles from her skin, starting at her wrists and working towards her shoulders. Even watching Cat through the reflection in the mirror, as the sponge passed her elbows and on to her upper arms, the bruises – purply blue against her white skin – were clearly visible. With arms still raised, Cat examined the bruises, swivelling her arms round from her shoulder joint, over and over again. I saw her lips purse and I could swear she was blowing little kisses at those blue bruises. But of course I could easily have been mistaken; she could just have been trying to dislodge some bubbles that had found their way into her mouth.

Chapter Seven

Mavis's departure created something of a power vacuum in the Saunders household. I didn't see it like that at the time of course; I was still only ten when she left. I simply viewed it as a great big empty hole that everyone else seemed busy trying to fill. Well, not my dad. I got the feeling that he was fed up with all of us and what he called our 'shenanigans'. Over the next couple of years my dad retreated into work and golf and a whole new hobby, gambling. Though whenever he did decide to make his presence felt, it was always memorable in some way.

My father was, like Cat, incredibly vivid. A room which he or Cat had entered would assume a bewitching brightness. He, I decided, glowed yellow. Cat, orange. My mother and, I feared, myself, made a room turn pale, less distinct. In the case of my mother, the palest of pale lavenders, or maybe eau de nil. She was far too beautiful to be invisible, but you could easily miss her. Once I came across the filmiest of spider webs, strung, like gossamer gauze, between the branches of a bush at the bottom of the garden, and unaccountably I thought of my mother. Me? There were people who thought I was pretty, too, as dark as my mother was fair. But when I tried to come up with a colour for myself, all I kept thinking of was tofu, colourless really. Like tofu, I could soak up and blend with whatever was around me. Take on the flavour of something else, but without having flavour or colour to call my own.

When my dad came home from the office, when he clanged on the door knocker proprietorially, to signal his arrival, even though he immediately afterwards put his own key in the lock, I would feel the tiniest frisson of excitement. It had become my job to pour his double Scotch. I suppose I've always enjoyed being useful and responsible, and this special task for my dad was something I treasured doing. I'd pour the whisky to exactly the point on the tumbler he liked it filled to. Then he'd inspect my work. 'Just a tad more,' or 'A tad less,' he used to say when I first became whisky-pourer-in-chief. 'A tad less' was tricky, as I had to pour whisky from the wide-mouthed tumbler back into the narrow-mouthed bottle without spilling any. But once I'd got the hang of it, he didn't need to correct me. I got it right every time. He drank his whisky neat. No ice. No water. It seemed a very manly thing to do.

In the beginning it was one double Scotch per evening. But over time, say two or three years, it's hard to remember exactly, the quantities increased. Even though it was never permitted to fill the glass above the designated level, I would generally be sent back for a refill, to pour another double. 'Same again, Mouse,' he'd say. 'The only person I trust to do a proper job of it.' And not so long after that he began having three doubles before dinner. I didn't really know if this was a lot or not. Even three doubles didn't amount to quite as much as a tumbler. And it wasn't as though his personality visibly changed when he drank. He didn't become aggressive like they did on *Coronation Street* when they'd had one too many pints. Nor did he go the other way and start being loud and jokey and thinking himself hysterically funny all the time, which was the other possibility if you got drunk. Or so I understood from my obsessive monitoring of the goings-on at the Rover's Return.

Since my dad was pretty funny completely sober, I couldn't tell the difference between drunk-funny and not-drunk funny, though you'd have to be able to take a joke against yourself to appreciate his humour. I'm not sure my mother ever did, but then she wasn't the type to laugh much at anything, least of all herself.

Our cocktail cabinet, which housed the whisky, was the real McCoy, burl walnut in the Queen Anne style with a mirrored, inside back wall, shelves of glass, and kitted out with crystal and bottles of expensive spirits. I adored this cabinet, this treasure trove full of glamorous, sophisticated, grown-up things.

My head was full of Hollywood images in those days and if you had asked me to draw a picture of my dad back then I would have drawn him in a dinner jacket (no matter that he mostly wore slacks and cashmere sweaters or a navy blazer and grey flannels). In my mind he was a suave film star who swirled spirits around glasses chinking with ice (and never mind either that he eschewed ice for himself), and was effortlessly witty and charming, ever ready to burst into a Cole Porter song. 'Well, Did You Evah', the song Bing and Frank sang in the *High Society*, was one of his favourites.

Apart from whisky, my dad was partial to Martinis, and whenever they had guests for dinner he'd mix what he called 'a mean Dean', his own invention, which he'd named after Dean Martin. Not that Dean Martin was his hero; my dad was a Frank Sinatra man, in absolute awe of what he called his 'timing'. He went on and on about his timing, never really mentioning his voice, which struck me as odd. But mean and Dean rhymed, making it a catchy name for a drink. I spent hours trying to come up with something that rhymed with Frank, and sounded good, but blank and dank and rank and stank would never make the grade. One morning, as I opened my eyes, it came to me. A Swanky Frankie. That would be a brilliant name for a cocktail. I couldn't wait to tell my dad, but when he came home that night and asked for his 'usual' I suddenly felt he'd think it silly, and kept it to myself. I was forever not saying things in case they sounded silly. Unlike Cat, who didn't care what came out of her mouth.

My dad's Martini specials were 99.9 per cent gin, or so he told us. 'The Martini, as the great wit H.L. Mencken has said, is the only American invention as perfect as the sonnet. You'd do well to remember that, girls.' The things he thought it important for us to know were incomprehensible to my mother. 'As for the right proportions of alcohol, you merely wave the dry vermouth over the gin.' I soon discovered the waving of the vermouth was a joke, you did actually have to add a bit.

After some brisk jiggling with ice in a chic fifties shaker my dad strained the liquor into classic, conical-shaped cocktail glasses. 'Add an olive, a twist of lemon peel and *voilà!* Go on, Cat, give it a go. Hannah, have a little taste. It'll do you good.' My mother's throat would emit a tiny squeak of protest as I took the sip that would set my own throat on fire and make Cat grasp hers as though she was being suffocated.

I haven't mentioned the key. The key to the cocktail cabinet that my dad kept on the same key ring as the key to the house. Whenever he wanted his whisky he'd hand me the tiny key. As soon as I'd poured, I had to lock the cabinet and hand him back the key. It was the ritual of unlocking and pouring and re-locking, and then going through the whole process all over again when he wanted refills that gave me a certain sense of importance in the Saunders household. Compared to having Mavis there, it wasn't much, I know, but it was something, and I clung to it.

Cat wasn't given the job because she was a klutz, whereas I was super-cautious and careful. Eager to please or insufferable goody-goody? Looking back, I can't quite decide. A bit of both I suspect. I wondered about that key, why on earth my dad bothered locking the cabinet, but I thought he probably wouldn't want to tell us. It was Cat who had the courage to ask the question.

'Dad, what's the point of the key? Are you frightened Hannah and I might steal the booze and get ourselves sloshed? Or Mummy perhaps?' The image of our mother drunk, lurching round the living room and laughing un-controllably and slurring her words was unimaginable. Cat and I giggled.

'I DO NOT DRINK. Tell the girls, Maurice, I DO NOT DRINK.' My mother was becoming agitated.

'Your mother does not drink. Your mother does not drink,' sniggered Dad in a poor imitation of a parrot.

'So why the key, then?' repeated Cat.

'"Theirs not to reason why, theirs but to do and die",' said my dad, successfully evading the question.

Cat sniffed. I could have told her he wouldn't give her a proper answer.

'Is that one of yours?' I asked. My dad adored famous quotations. He had one for every occasion so I suspected, like Mencken on Martinis, this must be one, too.

'Alfred, Lord Tennyson. "The Charge of the Light Brigade".'

'We must dooo, and we must diiiie,' said Cat theatrically, grabbing the grape scissors from the fruit bowl and pretend-plunging them into her heart. She and I started giggling again. 'Youuu tooo must diiiie,' she said, rushing at me with the scissors as I sprinted away from the cocktail cabinet, key still in hand, round the coffee table and out through the living-room door.

'Youuuu must diiiiiie,' Cat growled after me, gaining ground as I tripped and stumbled up the stairs. I ran panting into my room and kicked backwards against the door, which slammed to a close and then bounced straight back open again as Cat raced in after me and dived on top of me on the bed. Scrabbling to a sitting position, arms and legs flaying, and finally pinning me with her knees, 'Diiiiiiiiiiiiiie,' she growled again, raising the scissors above her head as if to plunge them into me from a great height.

'Mercy, mercy,' I cried, 'lest I wet the bed.'

'You deserve to diiiiiiiiiiiiiiiiiiiiiiiiiiiiiiiiiie.'

'Then I will wee-eth all over thee.'

And she collapsed on top of me again.

'Get off me, get off me,' I shrieked. 'Else I will wee-eth anyway.'

With a final theatrical flourish, Cat intoned, 'Theirs not to reason why, theirs but to wee and die,' and she rolled off me and off the bed and landed on the floor with a thud. The two of us were still heaving with laughter when my dad appeared in the doorway, whisky tumbler in hand, all hint of humour vanished. 'OK, girls, that's enough. When you've recovered your senses, your mother wants you downstairs for dinner. Hand me the key, Hannah, and I'll lock the cabinet for you. Two minutes. You've got two minutes.'

That's how it was with my dad. He'd goad us into a frenzy of excitement and then, when we were way out of control, before our exuberance had the chance to metabolise at its own pace, he put on the clamps. It may have been because of my mother. Dad was like a child himself. He'd play around and forget himself, but a quiet word from my mother, or a particular reproachful look, would bring him instantly back to earth, and we'd have to follow suit.

I suppose it was to be expected that Cat's power would grow now that Mavis was out of the way. For a while I really did want to hate Cat, but it didn't come altogether naturally, wasn't as easy to hate her as I thought it would be. I had to recognise that although, without Mavis on her tail, Cat had free range to lord it over me, to tell me what to do and when to do it, she was actually rather nicer – most of the time – than she'd ever been when Mavis was around. I wasn't sure if she felt a bit sorry for me or had decided that I wasn't quite as disgusting and despicable as she'd thought me in the past. Whatever the reason, things between Cat and me most definitely improved.

There was also a time, after Mavis left, when even my mother seemed to have perked up a bit. After Mavis we gave up on English maids and had Spanish or Portuguese ones instead. They kept pretty much to themselves and didn't really impinge on our lives. Cat and I mostly ignored them, and when my dad put his foot on the bell, I'd think of Mavis and feel almost glad that she wasn't around and at my parents' beck and call. The maids that followed Mavis weren't my friends, I made sure of that – partly I suppose out of loyalty to Mavis, partly because I couldn't see the point in getting too friendly with someone who probably wasn't going to hang around for long. And they didn't. My mother would check up on them all the time, sending things back to the laundry room for re-ironing, getting the beds made all over again because the hospital corners weren't as perfect as she wanted them, or the roast chicken would be on the dry side, and it was always Carmen or Maria rather than the chicken itself that was at fault.

Not surprisingly Carmen and Maria and Constanza and Ramona got fed up and left, and then my mother would get more headaches than normal and her eyes would get that scared look that freaked me out but also made me feel really angry and want to shout at her, which I didn't do. And then someone new would arrive and move into the room next to mine with her one suitcase and all her clothes

and knick-knacks and framed photos of her loved ones
from her home country, and I'd smile at the stranger and
say good morning, and how are you, and thank you and
goodnight, but I never bothered to find out about her or her
family or her life back in Spain or Portugal. 'Another one to
train in,' my mother would sigh. By saying nothing I was
complicit with my family's general lack of compassion. Not
once did I even stop to wonder if they might be lonely,
missing friends and family. Not once did I ask them
anything about themselves.

These women weren't *au pairs*, the latest trend in
domestic help, but proper old-fashioned maids. My parents preferred to choose middle-aged women with kids and
husbands back home, women who really needed the
money and would work hard and send most of their wages
to their families. They considered them more reliable than
the flighty 'nymphets of the north', as dad chose to label all
the blue-eyed blondes from Sweden and Denmark, not yet
out of their teens but queuing up for work and a chance to
bump into a Rolling Stone in Carnaby Street. But my
mother still chucked them out, our non-flighty, non-
nymphet maids, as regularly as last season's Chanel suit.
What did I care?

My mother's perking up involved her trying to get to
know me. But after so long of her not being at all interested
I found her questions both irritating and intrusive. Suddenly she was available to help me with my homework. I
didn't need help, but I wouldn't have minded reading my
compositions to someone, or talking about why Henry VIII
had so many wives, but I wasn't prepared to do it with her.

She's pretending, I kept thinking, she's only pretending to be interested. Like when she offered to play Scrabble or Monopoly with me. I felt she was putting on an act, and since I was at least as angry with her as I was with Cat, I'd always turn her down. 'No thanks, Mum,' I'd say, 'I'm up to this really exciting bit in my book and can't wait to find out what's going to happen,' or 'Actually I thought I'd ask Janet round so we can do our homework together,' or, mysteriously, 'I've got a letter to write.' The only person I ever had to write a letter to was Mavis, which my mum knew. It was my way of reminding her that I'd rather be with Mavis than I would with her, and that if she hadn't insisted my dad get rid of her she wouldn't have to be inviting me to join her in a game that I absolutely knew she didn't want to play.

I suppose it was rather easier to forget how beastly Cat could be because she could also be more fun than anyone else I'd ever met, including Janet. But my mum wasn't fun, she was just beautiful. And although beautiful wasn't much use to me, sometimes I found her spellbinding.

It was my mother's bedroom that still held the greatest magic for me. I'd graduated from a fascination with her wardrobes, to being mesmerised by watching her make up for her increasingly frequent nights out. She'd been through her pill-box hats and Oleg Cassini shifts phase, inspired by Jackie Onassis. Now, well into her thirties, she'd re-created herself as a true sixties dolly bird, and embraced her and my dad's thrice-weekly trips to the bright lights of the West End with a kind of manic zeal that belied her usually timorous approach to life. 'Oh we're off to the casino,' she'd say brightly. 'Your father is so popular, we get dinner for free.' It was years before I discovered that my parents' so-called free dinners were my dad's prize for losing so much money: the management's way of ensuring he'd be back for further punishment at the roulette tables. I don't think my mother realised it either.

She'd sit in front of her dressing-table mirror in a short, red and black Japanese kimono and heeled black marabou slippers, with a little plastic cape around her shoulders, tied at the front, to protect her from make-up spillages. Gazing into the mirror she'd sigh delicately, and then the elaborate ritual would begin. Jars of lotions and potions would be positioned in front of her in order of use and in strict alignment. 'First we have to cleanse . . . then tone . . . then moisturise,' she instructed, tapping a pearlised-pink manicured fingertip on each pot in turn. Her new three-step beauty programme was the result of a visit to the UK's first Clinique counter in 1968. I wondered if she'd gone into competition with Mavis, I thought meanly. Maybe here, at last, was something I could learn from her. Knowledge that Mavis, armed with her maths and English workbooks, and her skin prone to spots and redness, could never impart.

I wanted to resist showing an interest, to keep up the silent sneering and for her to know that she couldn't win me back this way, that I was going to carry on punishing her however hard she tried to make up for what she'd done. But just as Cat's full-throttle enthusiasms and vitality proved irresistible, so did my mother's fragile beauty. I was in awe, not of the person, not of anything as solid as that, but of her ethereality, her unreachable other-worldliness.

I suppose I did get the habit of paying attention to my skin from my mother, but I never got the hang of the make-up. Cat, in keeping with her artistic nature and willingness to experiment, and inspired by her tutorials in our mother's bedroom, became as passionate about make-up as she had been, since a small child, about clothes, wielding blusher brushes and mascara wands and lip-liner pencils like a true artist. She must have been fourteen or fifteen when she first came down to dinner one evening with the full works. My dad went ballistic, grabbing her by the wrist and dragging her upstairs to the bathroom where he pushed her head into the toilet bowl, not right in, but in just far enough that when he flushed the chain she was spattered with water. Then, pulling her up by her hair, he stood vigil while she scrubbed her face clean with soap and water.

'What do you think you are?' he'd shouted. 'Some kind of common little tart? You're far too young to wear make-up. Not a spot of it, you understand. Not until you're at least sixteen, and then only with my permission. You're still a child and you'd do well to remember it.' That evening over dinner Cat looked at him dry-eyed, and with such an air of defiance I thought he might lash out and hit her. But my dad was not a violent man, just a confusing, sometimes angry one. It was OK for Cat, and even me, to taste his whisky and his Martini, but we were way too young for some silly, painted-on eyelashes that every other kid Cat's age, and years younger, was drawing on daily. My parents may have hooked into the gambling and nightclub scene of the Swinging Sixties, but as far as their parenting style was concerned they were in a 1950s time warp. Or at least my dad was, and my mother just went along with it.

Having cleansed, toned and moisturised, my mother turned her attention to her hair. When the Pifco tongs were sufficiently hot, she'd painstakingly part her hair into sections. Clamp, roll, release. Clamp, roll, release. Section by section until perfect flicky symmetry was achieved around the perimeter. Next would come the application of panstick, dabbed and smoothed, over and over, to hide the blemishes she didn't have.

But it was the eyes that seemed to take for ever. Cat and I would sit cross-legged on the floor, one on either side of my mother's dressing-table stool, gazing up as if transfixed. First she'd dab her middle finger into a pot of white eye shadow, and brush it over her upper eyelids and under her brows. Then, with a fine brush, she'd dip into a pot of dark green shadow, like the green of her eyes, and trace a line along each of her eye sockets. After that came the false lashes, made from real mink she told us, followed by a hard, thin line of liquid eyeliner, precision-painted close to her upper lid. Kohl would be applied beneath her lower lashes and gently smudged. The mascara when it came to be put on to her lower lashes was built up layer after layer after layer, in tiny stroking movements of my mother's hand. The effect was hypnotic and I watched and watched until my own eyes began to lose their focus.

My mother's face was always pale. With a dusting of translucent powder it looked paler still. And then, with a final flourish of more panstick to drain the colour from her already preternaturally pale lips, my mother was born anew – a crying, walking, sleeping, talking, living doll, just like the old Cliff Richard song.

My mother's ministrations at the mirror might take as much as forty minutes. It was our time to be with her. Our special time all together. And it did feel special at the time. Only in retrospect would I rail at her selfishness, her self-absorption, her flutteriness. My mother had embraced the mini after seeing pictures of Jean Shrimpton in the papers. 'The Shrimp' had been photographed at the Melbourne Cup race meeting in Australia in 1965 wearing a short shift, and it was as if my mother felt some kind of kinship with her. Me and Anne Frank. My mother and Jean Shrimpton. She clipped her picture from the *Daily Express* and tucked it into the corner of her dressing-table mirror, for reference, where it stayed for several years. My mother had such patience for her appearance. Mostly she seemed either flustered or vacant, but when she was making up or dressing up she became quite calm and focused. Like an artist at work on a self-portrait.

Her skirts were pretty short for a mother, and just a bit embarrassing as far as I was concerned. More embarrassing still was my dad always going on about her legs, about them being totally gorgeous and 'up to her armpits', so I suppose she must have worn her skirts so short, at least in part, to please him. He talked about her legs as if they were separate entities, things that existed in their own right, quite apart from their owner. In fact he talked about them as though they were *his* legs, as though *he* owned them. 'Just look at my legs,' he'd say, when she walked into the room. All eyes would swivel to *her* legs, and I'd picture them striding towards him, on their own, without a torso attached. Cat seemed to have inherited my mother's legs in terms of length, though hers were straight-up-and-down skinny, rather than shapely like my mother's. My legs were a bit on the short side, and my knees were disgusting, really pudgy. Perhaps that's why I resented my mother and her short skirts; she looked so much better in them than I ever could.

After Dad took up gambling, the two of them went off to the casino at least twice a week. To places with names like the Curzon Club and Les Ambassadeurs. Places in May-fair, the ritziest part of town, where women wore real jewels that shimmered and sparkled, and revealed mounds of breasts and flashes of thigh and laughed easily, as though confidence were the most natural thing in the world. I'd actually witnessed this for myself. Several times we went with my parents, to take advantage of the free dinners. Watching at the entrance (we were not actually allowed inside the gaming room itself) and seeing those women and that jewellery, my eyes skimming the red and green baize as the croupiers scooped up chips or declared, 'Rien ne va plus,' as the roulette wheel whirred and the gamblers held their breath, the little ball bouncing around and around before landing on a single number that would make or break fortunes, I too felt my heart beat a little faster. My father would saunter between the roulette tables, playing more than one at once, casually issuing instructions to the croupiers whose eyes missed nothing.

My 1960s were spent on the sidelines. I was far too young to swing, but I vicariously lapped it up as I watched my parents dabble in whatever new and exciting thing the decade had to offer.

On Saturdays they would go to the Saddle Room, a nightclub in Park Lane, one of the first upmarket discotheques, where records rather than live music would be played. The next day, after a round of golf and fuelled by a few whiskies at the club – I could smell it on his breath as he entered the house, although to this day I honestly believe I never saw him less than fully in control of his actions – my father would regale us with stories of the celebrities and royalty they'd spotted, from the Beatles, who in their very early days would pop in to spin their latest disc, to King Hussein of Jordan and the racing driver Stirling Moss. One story, which my father related with glee, was to do with Helene Cordet, owner of the Saddle Room, who was alleged to have had a long-standing affair with her so-called close friend Prince Philip. Apparently Louise Cordet, daughter of Helene and a singer who'd had a couple of hits in the early sixties, was not Prince Philip's godchild, but his own child. Given my father's access to such salacious material, and his willingness to share it, it's not perhaps surprising that he seemed so glamorous.

The image was punctured only when he moved on from gossip to dancing. Back home from the clubhouse, he would invite us to watch as he performed catastrophic renditions of the Mashed Potato or the Hully Gully or the Funky Chicken, or whatever new dance craze had hit the nightclub scene the previous week. Then he'd try to teach us how to do it. The fact that he was a truly terrible dancer made the whole thing much funnier. My mother would spend most of Sunday in bed, recovering. Her bedroom was directly above the living room where the three of us would prance, wriggle and make a dreadful racket, but she never complained and neither did she ever offer to join in. Even when she finally came downstairs, often not until early evening, she said nothing about her version of the previous night's activities. Much as I often did with Cat, she left it to my dad to do the talking.

It was the late sixties by then, the gambling and the nightclubbing had been going on for several years. As my mother's flick-ups grew flickier and her skirts got shorter and her false eyelashes spikier, I got the distinct impression that she was trying to change herself in some essential way. Unlike Cat, who relished dressing up as an elaborate game, used it as an excuse to try out new facets of her already well-formed personality, and saw fashion as a means of creative expression, my mother seemed to be hiding behind her trendy new persona, wearing her Biba jersey dresses and Mary Quant op-art shifts and white PVC boots and elaborate make-up as a disguise, an attempt to become someone other than herself, to psych herself into being something she wasn't. I wanted it to work for her, because it occurred to me that if she *could* change herself, and for the better, perhaps I could change myself, too. Become less of a mouse.

But of course it couldn't work. It was an elaborate but essentially meaningless disguise. Her whole life was a disguise, as I discovered one day quite by accident.

★　　★　　★

Oh vodka's such a clever drink. You can't smell vodka because it's odourless. You can't see it because it's colourless. You can pour yourself a glass, add some ice, and call it a refreshing glass of water. You can half-fill a glass with it when no one's looking and top it up with tonic or lemonade, maybe mentioning in passing that you 'fancy something fizzy'. My mother didn't drink, so you'd never suspect. So once, that year of 1968 when I turned twelve, when I was feeling thirsty and saw one of my mother's glasses of water sitting half-empty on the kitchen worktop and was too lazy to reach up into the cupboard for a glass of my own, I picked up hers and had a sip. And it tasted funny. And it gave me that whoosh of heat sensation at the back of my throat that a sip of my dad's whisky gave me. So I had another sip, which didn't burn so much and felt really rather warm and pleasant. After that I knocked back the rest of what was in the glass and felt slightly floaty and pleased with myself. When I reached to put down the empty glass on the worktop I plonked it down clumsily, as though I'd slightly misjudged the distance between the surface and the glass in my hand. I thought the glass was about to shatter, but it didn't.

A moment later my mother walked in and asked distractedly, 'Where did I put my glass of water?'

'Oh I just finished it off,' I replied. 'It tasted really weird.'

'What did you say?' It annoyed me that my mother was always so distracted. Why couldn't she listen?

'I drank your water. Actually I think it must have been tonic water, and it must have been sitting here for ages because it was all flat and tasted sort of metallic. Look, I've got the glass here,' I said, picking it up again and heading for the fridge where we kept the Schweppes. 'I'll pour you some fresh.'

'How much was in that glass?' asked my mother, sounding suddenly alert.

'I've no idea,' I replied. 'Anyway what does it matter? I said I'd pour you some more.' My mother specialised in focusing on the irrelevant, the unimportant.

'Never, *ever* do that again,' my mother shouted at me, as if I'd committed some sort of terrible crime.

'But it's only a glass of tonic or something. What's the problem? What are you on about?' I wanted to scream, but even then I prided myself on my self-control.

'I'm not on about anything. You know you're not supposed to touch my things.'

You'd have thought I'd stolen one of her silk nighties and worn it for a sleepover at Janet's place.

'I thought I'd save on washing up,' I replied sullenly. My head felt a little fuzzy.

'And you know the rule about fizzy drinks.'

Yes, another of my father's rules. Fizzy drinks before dinner filled you up so you wouldn't eat your dinner properly. Fizzy drinks were full of sugar and would rot your teeth. Fizzy drinks were expensive and for special treats only.

'Are you feeling all right?' she asked, suddenly more concerned than cross.

'Of course I'm all right,' I replied sharply, although I was experiencing a funny whirring sensation inside my head.

'Then we'll forget about it,' she said, her voice softening. 'I didn't mean to shout.'

And then a picture popped into my brain. A picture of a key. The one my dad kept on his key ring with his keys to the house. And a locked cupboard. A very particular locked cupboard. And I looked at my mother and I knew. A fragment of conversation from an earlier time came clearly back to me, an argument that took place between my parents the night before Mavis was fired, while I was listening from my bedroom. 'I don't drink,' my mother had said. 'I DO NOT DRINK. Sometimes I feel you're more of a jailer than a husband.' And then the same thing, well almost, said again when Cat was larking around trying to imagine our mother drunk. Jailers. Keys. Locked cupboards. Not drinking. It was beginning to make sense. Despite the woozy feelings in my head, or perhaps because of the woozy feelings, I now understood. My thirsty mother had a secret. No one, especially my father, was supposed to know.

When I thought about it later I realised I rarely saw my mother without a glass of water to hand. On the kitchen table, on her dressing table, on the dining-room table. So simple a ruse. Only when my dad was around must she have poured a genuine glass of water. Or maybe not even then. Maybe he was as easily fooled by her trickery as me and Cat and she just did it in front of all of us. Laughing at us.

Flaunting it and yet somehow managing to keep it a secret. What was I going to do? Who was I going to tell?

My mother was looking at me funnily. She kept opening her mouth and moving towards me, as if she was on the verge of saying something, then changing her mind and turning her gaze in another direction.

'That tonic must have been standing there for ages,' she said, unable to let go of the topic.

Leave it out, Mum, I wanted to say. I do know what you're up to, you know.

'Whatever,' I replied dismissively. 'I promised I'd call Janet about the geography project. See you later.'

What I had in mind was to call Janet and tell her about my discovery. But when I went into the hallway to pick up the phone, I was conscious that my mum might be listening in, so I decided to save it up for when Janet and I would definitely be out of earshot. I rang Janet and told her I wanted to go and stay the night on Saturday.

'But your room's so much bigger and nicer than mine,' she replied. 'Why don't I come and stay with *you*?'

'You'll find out,' I replied mysteriously. 'Look it's important,' I said.

'OK, then, I'll ask my mum. She always feels bad that I stay with you all the time, so she'll be glad you're happy to stay in what she calls our "humble home". '

'Better a rumble home than a Rouse, I mean House of Rorrors, Horrors,' I whispered into the receiver, starting to snigger.

'Why are you speaking all funny?' asked Janet. 'Why have you gone all slurry?'

'I think I'm drunk,' I cackled.

'My God, Hannah, I think you are, too. What's going on over there, are you having a party?'

'Goodness no, young lady,' I said. 'We only drink water in this household. Ask your mum if I can stay on Saturday and call me back later.'

'Okey-doke.'

I put down the phone and ran cheerfully up the stairs. Now I was well and truly inebriated, for the first time in my life, I was quite unable to focus on the significance of my discovery. I lay on my bed, cupped my hands together behind my head and stared up at the ceiling, humming 'For Once in My Life' by Stevie Wonder, over and over again as the alcohol coursed through my veins and gave me the illusory sense that all was right with my world.

It was 1968. I was twelve, Cat fifteen. It was the year that Robert Kennedy and Dr Martin Luther King were both assassinated in the States. In Czechoslovakia the new communism 'with a human face' gave the Russians an excuse to march in with their tanks and put an end to the Prague Spring. In Paris, students sided with striking workers and rioted in the streets. I barely registered any of this. Something far more momentous was happening in the Saunders household. Cat and I were becoming friends.

It started with music and clothes. Cat had decided to educate me. She was toying with the idea of becoming a hippy and insisted we listen over and over to the Summer Of Love hit of the previous year, Scott McKenzie's 'San Francisco'. It wasn't the hippies' free-love philosophy she aspired to – that came just a little later – but the clothes they wore, and the idea of sporting flowers in her hair. Mods were so over by this time and since my mother had already cornered the ageing Dolly Bird look, and since no teenage girl aspires to look like her mother, Cat had to find a look of her own. I was still in short socks and not yet wrestling with such issues.

The contrast between wide-eyed Dolly Bird and Dippy Hippy was sufficiently extreme to tempt Cat into long, flowing skirts and to experiment with tie-dyeing T-shirts at home. The mess we created in the bathroom gave my mother major palpitations, but we always did clean up afterwards, or rather I did. Scouring the bath seemed a small price to pay Cat in exchange for a unique tie-dye T-shirt of my own created by my destined-for-designer-greatness sister.

That summer of 1968 we spent long hours in the garden plucking daisies from the lawn and threading them into garlands to wear in our hair. Then we'd go into Cat's bedroom and play 45s on her scratchy portable player. The fact that she invited me into her room, into her orbit, was enough to turn me traitor to Mavis. We never actually spoke of Mavis but sometimes I'd be really enjoying myself with Cat and I'd quite suddenly think of Mavis and feel that I wasn't supposed to be having fun in the company of Cat. I'd get this idea that I ought to stop right now what I was doing with Cat and leave the room. But I couldn't help myself having fun. And I couldn't leave. Cat wasn't only there, she was irresistible. She liked me! I was captivated.

The music she introduced me to was captivating, too. I'd been a Beatles fanatic and a follower of Stevie Wonder since the age of eight, but I was also still listening to *Junior Choice* on the radio, even though Cat used to laugh at me for it. I knew it was babyish, and that my attachment to 'Nellie the Elephant' and 'Ugly Duckling' and 'Jake the Peg' sung by Rolf Harris marked me out as a retard in Cat's eyes, but I was reluctant to let go of this programme that Mavis and I had shared every Saturday morning for so many years. I didn't want to put away childish things. Being a kid seemed complicated enough to me, being a grown-up even more of a pain. Except for the glamorous bits, like having one's own cocktail cabinet.

'Come upstairs and we'll listen to Fluff doing *Pick of the Pops*,' Cat suggested, quite out of the blue one Sunday afternoon.

'Who's Fluff?' I asked.

'Alan Freeman, you idiot. Don't you know anything? Look, are you coming or not?'

'Yes, please,' I replied. I felt like Cinderella must have felt when she received her invitation to the ball. And after that, as well as listening to *Pick of the Pops* we would watch *Top of the Pops* on TV together, every Thursday night. And even if Cat did go and call her friends immediately after to do an in-depth analysis of the week's hits and the fancia-bility rating of the latest band, at least I was no longer an outcast. In addition to which my musical tastes leapt into the present, making me feel less nerdy and naive. More, somehow, acceptable.

I'll never forget the music of 1968. 'The Dock of the Bay', Otis Redding. 'Light My Fire', the Doors. 'Mrs Robinson', Simon and Garfunkel. And our all-time sing-along favourite of that year, the Scaffold's 'Lily The Pink'.

Even today I remember the lyrics to those songs, every single word. That's because they became a kind of mantra. Whenever I thought about the other thing that happened, at the end of that year, I would sing those songs, preferably aloud, but silently if need be. And if I got one single word of one of those lyrics wrong, I would go straight back to the beginning of the whole medley and start over. It would keep my head full for hours; and I needed to keep it full because to empty my head at that particular point was too dangerous. That was the point when other things could rush in and fill up the space, things I couldn't, mustn't, allow in.

The only person I told about my mother's secret drinking when I first discovered it, was Janet. It was good to offload on her, but she didn't have any advice to offer me. To her we were already so exotic as a family, compared to how she saw her own boring brood, that this revelation was merely another exciting episode in the soap opera of our lives.

She dreamed of a life like mine. Servants, cocktails, casinos – the very words conjured up for Janet a world of unimaginable glamour. I longed for one like hers. Take-away fish and chips on Friday nights, and everyone hugger-mugger around the TV. What bliss.

If Janet came round to stay when my dad was in he'd always kiss her hand by way of greeting, with a loud smacking of his lips and an exaggerated sniff as he threw his head back afterwards, as if imbibing her irresistible fragrance.

'It's like I've walked into the pages of *Little Lord Fauntleroy*,' she trilled. 'Oh I do wish I could come and live with you.'

'For God's sake, Janet,' I replied frostily, 'can't you see it's all show? Believe me, I'm prepared to swap any time. But I can guarantee you'd soon be screaming to be let out.' It was the nearest I could get to being cross with her.

If I went to Janet's, her dad would gently pinch the end of my nose, wobble it slightly and say, 'Hello, best friend of Janet. Good to see you, girl.' I liked the way he made my nose tickle. And then Janet's mum would ask me questions and listen to the answers. I knew she was listening because she'd ask more questions in response to what I'd just said. After that she liked to squish up on the sofa between me and Janet and chat away about anything and everything.

'How lovely to see you, Janet,' my own mother said when Janet came round. And then she'd leave the room.

'Doesn't she look gorgeous?' Janet would sigh, in a near-faint, not even noticing my mother's complete lack of interest in her.

I did think of consulting Mavis about my mother and her drinking, but Mavis only ever had unkind things to say about my mother and that wasn't going to help at all at this point.

Now that Cat and I were getting closer, I felt that perhaps I could confide in her. I'd stayed awake for ages at night deliberating over whether it would be safe to tell Cat or whether she'd just go blurting it all out and create yet more turmoil, for which I might end up getting the blame. I wasn't even sure if my mother's secret drinking mattered all that much, although she and my father must have had a problem between them about it. My dad wouldn't have bothered with locking the cocktail-cabinet door if he hadn't wanted to keep my mother from drinking. Maybe she was frightened of him. Maybe she had reason to be.

'Cat, I need to talk to you,' I said. It was Sunday afternoon after *Pick of the Pops* and she was in an especially good mood because 'Hey Jude' had just made it to Number One, and because, at over seven minutes long, you could really get into singing along with it. Cat, unsurprisingly, was in love with John Lennon, the rebel. I had a crush on Paul, the baby-faced boy of the band.

'Then spill, I want to call Suzie and Sandy. There's so much to talk about. That song, apparently, although it's written by weedy Paul, is all about John Lennon leaving his wife for Yoko. It was going to be called "Hey Julian" originally.'

'Who's Julian?'

'John's son, dummy. Paul wrote it for Julian so Julian wouldn't mind so much about his dad. Oh never mind, I'm off.'

'Please, Cat . . .'

'I'm listening, Mouse. You have ten seconds, starting from now.'

'Mummy's an alcoholic.'

'A what?'

'An alcoholic. Well, she might be. That's what Janet thinks.'

'Are you nuts? She doesn't even drink.' At least I'd got her attention now.

'Well, she may not be an alcoholic, but she does drink. She drinks lots.'

'Yeah, gallons of the stuff. That really potent, turns-your-brains-to-mush stuff that comes out when you turn on the tap.'

'No, vodka.'

'You're kidding me.'

'I'm not, I'm serious.'

'And how, Detective Inspector Mouse, do you know all this?'

So I told her what had happened with me and her in the kitchen and how she'd lost her temper and then tried to cover it all up and make excuses and how I'd felt really peculiar and had to go and lie down because I was starting to feel dizzy.

Cat plonked herself down on the bed and cupped her faced with her hands.

'Bloody hell. This *is* serious.'

'You're not going to go rushing off and make a fuss, are you?' I pleaded, conscious of sounding somewhat pathetic and likely to get a blasting from Cat. 'I'm not sure what dad will do if he finds out.'

For once Cat couldn't think what to say. It seemed an age before she spoke.

'When did all this happen?'

I hesitated. 'A few weeks ago.' It was a couple of months, but I didn't want Cat to know how long I'd been keeping this from her.

'You should have told me immediately. She could have drunk herself to death by now.'

Typically overdramatic, I thought. For all we knew she'd been doing this for years.

'Sorry,' I replied.

'Look, I really do have speak to Suzie and Sandy. We'll sort this out later.'

'Are you going to tell them?'

'You mean like how you went blabbing straight to Janet? Of course I'm not. It would be all over school by tomorrow's mid-morning break.'

'But they're your friends, Cat. Can't you trust them?'

'You have so much still to learn, little Mouse. We'll talk again after supper. Now do me a favour and disappear.'

I was relieved that Cat had so quickly reverted to sounding like her normal self. Sarcastic. A bit mean. It was better than Cat rushing in and causing a rumpus without thinking it through first.

'We'll work something out, OK?' said Cat as I was leaving the room.

She didn't say 'I'll work something out', she said '*We'll* work something out'. She had acknowledged that we were in this together, as a team. My sister and I. A team. I could hardly believe it. I was seeing Mavis on Saturday. However tempted I felt, I wouldn't tell her about my mother and especially I wouldn't tell her about Cat and me becoming a team. I felt a slow smile spreading across my face. A great urge to sing and dance in every room of the house. Cat and I were a team! Like a tiny drop of dew evaporating on a leaf as the sun comes up, the business about my mother just melted clean away.

Chapter Eight

A bathroom used to be a hallowed place, a place of sanctuary. You only entered, when a grown-up was in there, if you were invited. My mother never invited us into her own private, en-suite bathroom with its chic, shag-pile grey carpet and a pink bath and sink and bidet, and shiny black splash-back tiles. A bidet was quite avant-garde in those days. As was the colour scheme. Avocado and peach were becoming all the rage. My mother didn't want her bathroom to look like everyone else's. Neither, we later understood, did she want prying eyes in her bathroom cabinet. Not that it would have occurred to Cat or me to look – what could there be of possible interest to either of us lurking behind the mirrored glass? After the vodka business though, prying – we called it spying, to give it an aura of cloak-and-dagger, to give us the sense of becoming proper detectives – became the norm.

What a different scenario from when Melissa and Charlie were growing up. They barged in on me with neither a knock nor a second thought, and I liked it that way, especially when they were little and one or other or both would perch on the side of the bath and chat about their day while I soaked, them already in their pyjamas, me winding down after a day of sales ledgers and sexy-knickers samples. Or winding down as much as is possible when you have two boisterous children scooping up bubbles from the bath and flicking them at your face. Life never stopped being worth living when David died. How could it when every day these two gave me something to feel grateful for?

When Cat and I were small, before the first buds of puberty appeared on Cat's chest – as a special treat on Mavis's day off, when she wasn't around to supervise – our father would sometimes come and get in the bath with us in our bathroom. At the appointed hour we would run the water to about halfway up the bath, and Cat and I would get in together, me at the uncomfortable end of course, with my back to the taps. Generally we'd bath separately, although using the same water, taking it in turns as to who would go first, with Cat always arguing that, as the elder, it should be her privilege. Neither of us wanted the second session, because by then the fresh, steamy water would have cooled to tepid and the soap would have left its marks on the surface of the water, forming a greasy scum that was hard to rinse off. I'm sure we had enough hot water for two baths, but there were certain things my dad regarded as wasteful, and a whole bath per child was one of them.

When Mavis was in charge Cat had no choice but to obey house rules. One day Cat could get in first, the next me. Sometimes I bagged the first slot two days in a row, thanks to Mavis's intervention on my behalf; Cat's indignation was ignored. But on days when Dad visited, sporting a pair of smart burgundy swimming trunks to preserve his modesty – and ours, I presume – there were no arguments. We couldn't wait to leap into the bath together and await the arrival of HAIRY MONSTER.

'Make way, girls,' he'd boom, as one big bushy leg after another loomed in front of our eyes, like a pair of giant tree trunks in an ancient forest. As he lowered himself into the bath, displacing the water and causing it to rise to ever more dangerously high levels, it would reach right up to my chin then splish over onto the bathroom floor. 'Eureka!' Cat and I would screech simultaneously.

'And your lesson for today . . .' grinned my dad. Cat would raise her eyebrows, not that boring old story again, but I never tired to hearing about a chap called Archimedes in Greece more than two thousand years ago, who got into a bath, flooded the floor much as my dad did, and made the incredible discovery in an instant about why some objects float and others sink. 'It's important to notice what's going on around you,' said my dad. 'That way you learn new things when you're least expecting to.'

Even though bath times with my dad were well and truly over by 1968, I was reminded of that remark after we found out about my mother and the vodka. He certainly hadn't noticed that.

'You'd better get the place cleaned up before your mother sees it,' Dad would say when he'd had enough, after we'd splashed and ducked his head under the water and made him blow bubbles and begged him not to get out just yet. As he stood in the bath we'd watch the water level drop back down again, and follow him out as he wrapped

himself in his towelling robe, wriggling out of his trunks
with his back to us, so we didn't get even the tiniest glimpse
of his private parts. I did try to sneak a look sometimes. I
was curious. What did he have that was so rude or dreadful
that he had to hide it? I'd never seen man or boy completely
naked, other than in pictures.

'Off you go, Mouse,' Cat would instruct. 'Get the mop
and a bucket.' So I would wrap myself in a towel and pad
downstairs, dripping and barefoot, to collect the necessary
equipment. It never occurred to me to bring up the mop
and bucket in advance. I liked things just the way they
were.

My parents' bathroom, unlike our utilitarian one with
linoleum on the floor, was just as I imagined a Hollywood
movie star's to be. It had 'his and hers' bathroom cabinets
and two sinks. Whatever women kept in their bathroom
cabinets or their dressing-table drawers was their own
business. The paraphernalia that accompanied woman-
hood was as much a mystery to my father as to any man of
his generation.

'I dread to think what you keep in there,' he'd say, when
my mother would complain about running out of space.
'My cabinet's three-quarters empty. You women are a
complete enigma. Aliens, the lot of you. Even with three in
the house I'm none the wiser.' She'd laugh, that barely-
there laugh of hers, and touch her hair in the special wispy
way that was both shy and coquettish.

Around the time of discovering my mother's secret drinking habit I started to think how odd it was that you can

share a home with people, sleep under the same roof, sit round a table together at mealtimes and still know practically nothing about them. It occurred to me that we were all as much foreigners to one another in lots of respects as the endless procession of maids who came and went. My mother had a secret life and therefore she was a stranger to me. Not that she and I had been exactly intimate before her little problem came to light. What struck me as even more peculiar was that I rather preferred what I saw as the new version of my mother. Although there was definitely something scary about it, at least now she had taken on some kind of personality. In my eyes it gave her a certain substance at last.

As far as my parents together were concerned, I'd always been on the lookout for some sort of special connection between them, like the one Janet's parents so obviously had. But if my dad didn't know about the drink, what else might there be that he didn't know about her? And vice versa. So perhaps they were strangers to one another, too.

As for what passed for intimacy between Cat and me and my dad, I even began to question that. There he was, bursting into our lives in all sorts of memorable ways, a bit like a circus performer enthralling his audience with his acrobatics, but then cartwheeling out of sight with equal suddenness. 'A larger-than-life character,' Mavis had once called him. 'A real dazzler.' That's what he did, our dad. He dazzled. He made us laugh until we cried. He meted out discipline and laid down laws. He swung effortlessly between breaking rules and making rules. But mostly he just dazzled. Dad was a brilliant showman, no more knowable, really, than my mother.

And then there was Cat, getting up to stuff that my parents didn't have a clue about. With boys. For all her inability to keep her mouth shut, a tendency to blurt whatever came into her head and make us all laugh with her outrageous pronouncements, she was scared of our father and his old-fashioned ideas about discipline and how women should behave. Not so scared as to abide by all his rules. Just scared enough to go to great lengths to cover her tracks.

Now that Cat and I were a team, I'd become her confidante. She had decided my sexual education was sorely lacking. We were sitting together on her bed.

'Rule number one: don't get pregnant.'

'I haven't even kissed a boy yet,' I replied, staring down at my short white socks and making mental connections. Why on earth would a boy want to kiss a girl who still dressed like a baby? Actually I had no desire to kiss a boy. Well, maybe Paul McCartney, but only because I knew it was quite impossible.

'No kissing? Now there's a surprise. But as dad would say, it's a slippery slope.'

'What is?'

'From kissing to pregnancy,' snorted Cat.

'You can't get pregnant from kissing. Even I know that.'

Things were happening to my body faster than I wanted and, unlike Cat had been, I was in no hurry to grow up. Recently I'd had my first period, which was a horrible shock, but no more a shock to me, I reasoned, than it must have been to any other girl. Then, after the first three months or so, it became pretty much routine. I didn't like the blood, or the twinges in my tummy, and I worried about the smell, and that others would be able to tell, but that wasn't really the issue. The physical side was just something to put up with. And now of course I'd finally twigged that babies didn't come from your belly button, but from your vagina. Which seemed no more or less horrific. What really got to me, and not in a good way, was the realisation that being an adult was likely to be a very complicated business. Look at my mother. Look at Mavis. Was either of them happy?

'So far you haven't told me anything I didn't know,' I said, trying to sound worldly-wise and sophisticated.

'OK, clever clogs. What do you know about blow jobs?'

'Blow jobs?'

'Yes. Going down.'

'Going down where?'

'Down *there*.'

'What are you on about?'

'What boys have. Down *there*.'

'You mean . . .' I was starting to feel uncomfortable.

'Yeah, willies . . . dicks . . . cocks.'

'Well, what about them?' Why did I get a funny, squirmy feeling when she said those words?

'Well, Mouse, if you don't want to get pregnant, that's what you do. They love it.'

'Sorry, Cat, but I'm not getting it.'

'You suck them off, Mouse. I'm the blow-job champion. Olympic gold medallist standard. I've done six and they're queuing up.'

'You mean . . .'

'You've gone all pale.'

'That's because I'm going to throw up.'

Cat licked her lips in a way that made my flesh feel all crawly.

'You know what they call me?'

'How could I? Don't tell me, OK? Don't tell me. I don't want to know. Let's change the subject.'

'They call me Little Blow Peep.'

That, at least, made me laugh. 'Please, Cat.'

'Please what, Mouse? I don't go the whole way. I'm going to wait until I'm at least sixteen. I'm a good girl,' she smirked. 'A virgin. Just like you.'

'But it's disgusting. Why would anyone want to do a thing like that? Why would a boy even want you to?'

'Think of it as a lovely lollipop and you'll soon get the hang of it.'

'I won't, I can promise you that. And anyway I think you're making it all up. It's just one of your stupid jokes.'

But somehow I knew it wasn't one of her jokes, and that she was telling me the truth.

'Have it your own way, Mouse.'

So that was Cat's secret life. Doing things with boys that my father would kill her for if he found out. If he could go that berserk when Cat played around with make-up, the repercussions for something like this didn't bear thinking about. I wouldn't even tell Janet about this. Far too dangerous.

So at least Cat and I were no longer strangers. On the one hand I was so happy that we were almost friends. But on the other, if becoming friends meant having to hear things about her pervy sex life, it had its disadvantages as well.

As for my own secret life, I wasn't getting up to anything worth reporting. But I did keep on having this terrible thought. A truly terrible thought that I couldn't get out of my head. I'd read in the *Daily Express* about an actress, a woman in her late thirties, who drank herself to death. Or rather drank so much that she fell off a sixteenth-floor balcony in a hotel in New York. And the terrible thought was this: If Mum drinks herself to death, might I be allowed to have Mavis back?

They were out. It was Ramona's evening off. Cat was old enough to babysit, so it was just the two us, alone. The perfect opportunity to search the place. The only equipment we needed was a cloth to wipe off incriminating fingermarks.

We took the stepladder from the cupboard under the stairs and dragged it between us up to my parents' bedroom. Cat, never one to miss an opportunity for shirking, was wearing one of her long hippy skirts. This ensured it would have to be me who climbed the ladder.

'Well, I'm the klutz, aren't I?' Cat launched in with an air of smug triumphalism. 'And you're famed throughout the land as Miss Dainty Dora, so it makes sense for you to brave the terrifying journey on your own. I mean, what would the old folk say if they came home and found me in a broken heap at the bottom of the ladder? I would hate to have to tell them that little Mouse had decided her mother was an alcoholic and had sent me scouting for evidence.'

I don't think we really understood the seriousness of what was going on. At twelve I was still young enough to want to turn it into a bit of an adventure. Like we were Darrell and Sally from *Malory Towers* or Anne and George from *The Famous Five*. Cat was busy being blasé.

'Oh it's all such a bore. How am I ever going to get to wear that fab crochet top for Suze's party on Saturday night if we don't hurry up? I haven't nearly finished knitting it yet. For goodness sake, Mouse, just get up that ladder, will you?'

Although I wasn't very fond of heights, and the old wooden ladder was a bit on the rickety side, even I could see that the journey posed no particular dangers. And now that Cat was so keen to include me in everything I found myself going out of my way to be accommodating.

'Please don't let go, that's all I ask.'

I scampered up as quickly as I could. When I reached high enough to open the cupboards at the top, I felt the ladder suddenly judder, as if a train had rumbled by right outside the window. My heart jolted and I let out a loud shriek. Screwing up my eyes and my shoulders, I looked round cautiously. Cat was standing at the bottom, laughing, and giving the ladder intermittent shakes with both hands.

'You asked me not to let go, and I haven't,' giggled Cat, giving the ladder another great shake. 'No need to freak out, babykins.'

'It isn't funny, Cat. It's really not funny. If you do that again I'll be the one to fall off and break my leg, and that will take just as much explaining as you breaking your leg.'

'For a mouse you're incredibly pompous. "Up your own arse" I think is the expression currently in vogue amongst the upper classes.' Cat seemed to have forgotten to be blasé about our detective work and was having a great deal of fun at my expense. I attempted ignoring her remarks and getting on with the job instead.

'Just hand me the torch so I can look to the back of the cupboard. You're the one who said you were in a hurry.'

'Shit,' said Cat. 'Shit, shit, shit, I left it downstairs.' And she skipped off, leaving me standing precariously atop an old ladder that didn't seem to have a firm grip at all on the shag-pile carpet.

I was feeling a bit clammy. To take my mind off the wobbly ladder I slowly and carefully opened the two doors in front of me. These built-in storage spaces above the hanging and shelf areas which housed my mother's clothes were designed to hold suitcases and other items she didn't need constant access to. With one hand still on the side of the ladder I used the other one to grab the handle of a large black-leather suitcase, starting to manoeuvre it out of the cupboard. The only way I could see to bring the case further out was to step down a rung and balance the case on my head. I thought of pictures I'd seen in the *National Geographic* of African women wearing baskets on their heads, and stood a little straighter and tried to elongate my neck. But to bring the suitcase to the floor I'd have to take both hands off the ladder, which looked quite impossible without losing my footing. Now I was really stuck. The ladder was wobbling, and I could neither haul the case over my head and let it fall to the ground nor shove it back inside the cupboard again because there was a little ridge or door catch in the way that prevented me from pushing it. I dared not move another inch without Cat there to hang on to the sides.

'Cat,' I called timorously, held rigid by the suitcase on my head, my voice disappearing into the cupboard. 'Please, Cat, come quickly.'

And that was when I realised the absurdity of what we were doing. Snooping into my mother's cupboards in search of vodka bottles. And so what if we did find them? What would it prove, other than what we already knew? Who would we tell? My head was beginning to hurt from the weight of the large leather suitcase. She's probably taking all this time on purpose, I thought bitterly, starting to hate Cat again for the first time in months. And then she was back, standing at the bottom of the ladder, but by this time there were tears running down my face. It wasn't just the suitcase and the fear of falling from the ladder, it was something bigger, but I couldn't find the words to articulate my emotions.

'What can you see? Tell me, what you can see.'

'I can't see anything, Cat,' I whimpered. 'I want to get down.' I wanted Cat to see I was really upset, that I meant it, and so I tried to swivel my head round a bit, beneath the weight of the case, to show her. As I did so Cat chose to shine the torch in my face, blinding me in both eyes. In a flash of panic, and using all my strength, I hauled the rest of the case from the cupboard with just too much energy. It slid past my head towards the floor at the exact same moment as I lost my footing and toppled backwards from the ladder with a scream, crushing Cat with the full weight of both me and the suitcase, the ladder a fraction of a second behind. She let out a terrifying wail, like a wounded elephant.

My God, I've killed her, I thought. I've killed my sister. My own head had bumped against the suitcase as I landed, but at least the impact of my fall had been cushioned, partly by the case, partly by Cat. The ladder, miraculously, had landed just to my side, hitting neither of us.

'Cat, Cat, are you all right?' She moaned.

I managed to haul the suitcase off her. I didn't know if I was hurt or not. She was lying flat on her back, breathing shallowly and blood was trickling from her nose and mouth.

'My arm . . . it's my arm.' We were both crying now.

'Cat, can you move?'

'No.'

'But you have to, we have to get you to bed, they mustn't find out.'

'But what about my arm?'

For the first time in our lives I found myself taking charge.

'Support the arm that hurts with the good one, and I'll help you up.'

I crouched down beside Cat. I could feel a rhythmical throbbing at the side of my forehead where a bump was beginning to form, but I knew I could disguise that with my fringe before my parents got home.

'OK now, slowly, very slowly.' I managed to help Cat into a sitting position. 'Now don't move. I'll get some stuff from the bathroom to wipe the blood.'

'But my arm . . .' Two drops of blood from Cat's nose plopped onto the cream carpet.

'Oh no, not the carpet.'

'It's me you should be worrying about, not the carpet.' Cat still had some spirit after all; maybe it wasn't as bad as it looked.

'But they'll see it. The stains, they'll see them.'

As I stood up I realised my ankle was hurting, in fact everything was hurting now, so I could only hobble rather than run into my mother's bathroom.

'What do I need?' I asked myself aloud, trying to keep a grip. 'OK, loo paper, cotton wool, TCP, a plaster for the cut on Cat's lip.'

Entering the hallowed bathroom, feeling shaky and bruised, I limped towards the loo to grab some paper. Returning to the basin, I caught sight of my flushed, tear-streaked face and the purple swelling on my forehead in the mirrored cabinet above it. There's bound to be everything I need in here, I thought, and I haven't time to go to our bathroom and get stuff from there. I can tidy a bit and cover up the evidence before she gets back.

But none of the things I was expecting were to be found. Yes, there were the usual lotions and potions, the body creams and the cosmetics and the bath oils and the nail-varnish remover and the hair rollers, but none of the emergency medical kit I'd been hoping for. Instead, there was bottle after bottle, and packet after packet, filled with pills I didn't recognise. Pills of so many different shapes and colours and sizes that for a moment I thought I'd opened the door on a tuck shop, full of delicious but forbidden sweets. What was all this stuff for? I scanned one shelf.

The names meant nothing to me. Librium. Valium. Imipramine hydrochloride. Nembutal. Seconal. Mandrax. Were they some kind of vitamins? Or was she suffering from some terrible terminal illness she hadn't told us about? Did this explain everything? My mother had a secret illness and she was saving us from having to share the burden of the worry. Protecting us after all. I so wanted this to be true, well, not the terminal bit, just the illness bit would do. But even as I was telling myself this new story, I wasn't convinced. Maybe I should try to remember the names and then go and look up all the pills in the medical dictionary in the school library, or maybe Cat would know at least what some of them were for. Not that now was the time to ask. I closed the cabinet carefully, wiped a small smear with a piece of the toilet paper and limped off to our own bathroom in search of supplies.

Mission not accomplished. There could be a hundred bottles of vodka still stashed away for all we knew.

Afterwards it occurred to me that my mother would never hide the vodka there because she'd never have the courage to climb the rickety ladder, which was the only way of reaching into the back of the cupboard.

I did manage to get the ladder back downstairs and back under the stairs, but I had to do it on my own because of Cat's arm. There was no way I was going to get the suitcase back up again, so I dragged it into my own room and hid it under the bed. They weren't going on holiday for ages, and in the meantime I'd think of something. I scrubbed at the bloodstain on the carpet for twenty minutes, which seemed to do the trick. My parents, when they eventually rolled up, would be unlikely to spot it, and by the morning it would be dry. The real problem would be explaining away Cat's arm.

'I'll just tell them I fell down the stairs,' she said.

We were sitting together side by side, on the top step of the staircase, when they walked through the front door at one o'clock in the morning. My mother's hair was all mussed and she was swaying slightly as she approached the stairs. My father's tie was hanging loose and the top two buttons of his shirt were undone.

'What the devil . . .' he said, squinting up at us from the hallway.

'I fell,' said Cat.

'She fell,' I said.

My dad decided to drive Cat to A and E.

'You shouldn't be driving,' said my mother. 'That's why we went to the Curzon by cab, so you could drink.'

'I'm perfectly all right,' he responded frostily. 'And in any case, how else do you think we're going to get there?'

It was agreed my mother would stay with me rather than go to the hospital because I was still too young to be left alone in the house. More than anything at that moment I wished she would offer to sit on the edge of my bed and hold my hand or stroke my forehead until I went to sleep.

What she did instead was say, 'This business with Cat has given me the most terrible headache. I need to take something for it, or I'll never get to sleep. Cat will be fine now, Hannah. Not to worry.'

She pecked me on the cheek and headed off towards her bedroom. Towards her bathroom, towards her bathroom cabinet, and to whichever of her magic pills would make her well again, if only for a few hours.

I lay in bed and pictured her standing there, picking out pills like she might a new pair of shoes.

Oh it's so hard to decide, they're all gorgeous. I think I'll try one of those pink ones first. It's so pretty. And maybe the blue. And I know the white's impractical, but it's also absolutely darling. Do you know what? I think I'll take the lot.

Yes, my mother was a shopaholic decades before it became fashionable. A shopaholic. An alcoholic. And, I now thought for the first time, perhaps a drugaholic, too, though I was sure that wasn't the right word for it.

I was still awake when first light filtered through the curtains. I was still awake when Cat arrived back just a little later, pale and exhausted-looking, her left arm in plaster up to her elbow.

The last thing she said to me before she closed my bedroom door was: 'There's nothing I can't do with one hand that I could do with two, and apart from that little cut my mouth at least is in perfect working order.' And then she winked at me. And that was when I decided I could handle the Little Blow Peep business, however much it made me want to throw up. Because the thing that made relationships special was secrets. Not the ones you held inside yourself, alone, but shared secrets. And now we shared so many of them. We were a proper unit now; not just any old sisters, but soul sisters, sisters under the skin, where it really mattered.

The good news was that I wasn't expected to go to school after the dramas of the night before. I finally went to sleep after Cat came home, and then I slept until noon. I dreamed of a suitcase filled with dismembered legs and arms sprinkled with brightly coloured Dolly Mixtures.

Chapter Nine

If my parents had ever actually seen the house that Mavis lived in, surely they would have banned me from going there. Her tiny Victorian workman's cottage sat right on the road. Literally on the road. There was no pavement, no pathway, not even a little porch. Just the steep road, and then the house at the edge of it. Buses went right by, and so did lorries, so that when you sat in the front room it was plunged into darkness on and off throughout the day. It was noisy, too. And, according to Mavis, a bit of a death trap. Further down the road there was a teeny strip of pavement, but then it petered out, and to get to Mavis's front door you had to hurl yourself at it when you were sure there wasn't any traffic coming.

If we misjudged our timing and Mavis was fumbling around for her keys and couldn't get them out of her bag in time, she'd shout, 'Backs to the wall!' and she'd scoop up Nostrils the dog and we'd have to flatten ourselves against the brickwork and the front window as the bus or lorry thundered past, honking its horn at us and creating a blast of wind that took our breath away and sent smoke billowing into our faces.

'That was a close shave, Mavis,' I'd shout, or 'Near thing, Mavis.'

'Sure was,' she'd reply cheerily. 'That lorry nearly had our guts for garters.'

And that's how the game would begin.

'We could have been dead as doornails.' Me shouting back, as another lorry trundled by.

'Or kicked the bucket.' Mavis starting to laugh.

'Or popped our clogs.' The longer it went on, the more fun it became.

'Or met our maker.' There was always a moment when Mavis would start wiping the tears from her eyes, tears caused by a mix of wind and smoke and laughter, as Nostrils continued to try to struggle out of her arms.

'Or bitten the dust.' Me.

'Or found ourselves six feet under.'

'Or given up the ghost.' Me.

'Or definitely done dancing.' Her.

'Upon the Stygian shore.'

'What the . . .'

I'd won! I'd been reading Greek myths again. No one could beat the Stygian shore.

'Got me stumped there, sweetheart. Let's go inside before we cop it.' Our throats were dry with laughter and pollution.

I named the game Death-Defying Definitions. Between visits I'd look up more euphemisms for dying in the school library. I'd send any new ones I'd discovered in one of my letters, and we'd both memorise as many as we could, then play the game whenever we had a hairy moment in the road outside Mavis's front door. Our repertoire grew and grew.

At first I thought it was wonderfully novel, doing what Cat called 'slumming it', Cat's pronouncement delivered in that special sneery way my sister reserved for all things to do with Mavis. It was certainly dark inside the small house, but Mavis had done her best to make it cheery; there was a brightly coloured oilcloth on the table with a dahlia pattern printed on it. Dahlias were Mavis's favourite flowers, and whenever I visited her in the late summer months I'd cut the biggest bunch I could manage from our garden, wrap the flowers in the previous day's newspaper and take them with me on the train.

There were several framed photos on top of an old wooden sideboard in Mavis's front room, mostly of me, or the two of us together, and one or two of her much older brother and sister-in-law. In one of the pictures her brother was in uniform.

'Pete was just a private,' said Mavis. 'Not like your dad, but then I suppose he didn't have your dad's education. Saw a lot of action though, more than your dad by all accounts. I'm not sure he's ever gotten over it.'

The sofa in Mavis's Parlour, as she jokingly called her front room, had a faded flower pattern that today would be regarded as the height of shabby chic, but at that time was simply shabby. It was worn away in places and a bright, knitted, home-made patchwork blanket – in day-glo orange and green and yellow – was thrown over the back of it to distract attention from the holes in the fabric. Mavis was a decent knitter. My teddy bear, Teddy, who I treasured and kept to hand down to my own kids, sported a Mavis original – a blue-and-white-striped knitted top, which Teddy wore under blue knitted dungarees.

Like the sofa, Mavis's carpet had been purchased at a rummage sale. Mavis loved rummage sales. The carpet was orange and brown geometrics, gave you vertigo just to look at it, but was in quite good condition. I reckoned it was probably something the original owners bought thinking it was trendy and modern, and then realised was a ghastly mistake. Although it was designed to be fitted in, there wasn't quite enough of it to reach the walls all round, so it just sat on top of the floorboards, more than a rug, less than a fitted carpet, over time curling up and fraying at the edges.

Behind the front room was the kitchen and at the end of the kitchen was a bath. That had been Mavis's main change to the house when she bought the place. There was still an outside toilet in the yard at the back, and there was nothing she could do about that, as there was no room for a proper bathroom, so she decided to have a bath plumbed in at the back of the kitchen.

I loved that house. It was like a doll's house compared to mine, a doll's house in need of repair, but with a coal fire in the grate that created a nice, cosy atmosphere. We always had a proper roast for lunch when I went there – chicken or beef or lamb, with roast potatoes and peas. Bread and butter pudding or fruit crumble to follow and a Victoria sponge or chocolate éclairs for tea.

The outside toilet was the only bit that freaked me out. It was a magnet for creepy-crawlies. In summer flies and wasps would swarm there. In autumn great big daddy-long-legs would dance across the timbered walls. In winter I had to put Mavis's coat on top of all my other clothes so I didn't freeze to death out there. I did manage to institute one modern innovation: to persuade Mavis to buy soft toilet tissue rather than the scratchy school-loo stuff she favoured.

I didn't enquire too much about Mavis's background. I knew she grew up on a farm, that her mother was dead and that her father had remarried and moved to Scotland. She'd lost touch with him. How horrible, I thought, to have no mother and a father who couldn't be bothered. Her brother and sister-in-law were the only people she regularly talked about, and sometimes we went to them for tea – I think she enjoyed showing me off. Certainly Pete and Mary, his wife, treated me like I was visiting royalty the first time I went to meet them. Mary baked Swiss rolls and shortbread biscuits, made mashed-egg sandwiches and put out her best china. I know it was her best china because Mavis told me so afterwards.

'Mavis never stops talking about you,' Mary smiled as she greeted us at the door. 'You're as pretty as she said, though you'll only need to be half as clever as she boasts to put us all to shame.'

I felt a bit embarrassed by her gushy greeting, then immediately felt cross with myself as I should have been able to see right away that she was only trying to be friendly.

'It's not often we get visitors from London,' she continued, as she led us into her lounge where the dining-room table was overflowing with food. 'We must seem like right hicks to you.'

I really didn't know what to reply, it wasn't as though London was very far away and although we might have been posher than her and Pete, we weren't that posh. So I said: 'Oh look, I can see right through from here into your back garden and it's full of dahlias. Just like we have in our garden.' I think that must have put her at her ease, because gardening is a great leveller and you can grow stuff whatever background you come from. I learned about levellers from my dad. Football if you were a man, horticulture, suitable for both sexes, and babies, but only if you were a woman. So after I mentioned the dahlias Mary looked a whole lot more relaxed and started chatting away as though I was just a normal girl rather than a member of the aristocracy.

Mostly though it was just Mavis and me. Our world was about the two of us. We didn't need other people. For entertainment we'd go into town and see a matinee movie. The films were often quite out of date, but I didn't mind. I remember going to see *To Kill a Mockingbird*. It made me cry, and at the same time I fell a bit in love with Gregory Peck. He was like a handsomer version of my dad. Afterwards we went and bought the book, and Mavis paid for it. When I look back, I realise that Mavis, even without much education, did far more to educate me than my own parents. She was always finding new ways – through games or films or books – of filling my head with ideas and information.

If there was no suitable film, we went to the shops. Or maybe a rummage sale. In the summer we stood outside the church and watched the weddings. Or Mavis would check out if there were any village fetes nearby, in Springfield or Danbury or Chelmer Village, and work out the buses so we could get there and back in time for me to catch my train if I wasn't staying over and sleeping on the sofa, which I was sometimes allowed to do. I loved the barrel races and the coconut shies and sometimes I'd buy jam that someone from the Townswomen's Guild had made. My dad would always make a point of telling me how delicious it was.

Mavis had a job in a factory by this time, working for Marconi on an assembly line – something to do with the cathode-ray tubes for television, which were vital components and the reason, she explained to me, that television was often referred to as 'the tube'.

There was one thing about Mavis I just didn't understand. She was younger than my mother, who dressed like a teenager, but she looked old enough to be my grandmother with her lumpiness, her old-fashioned clothes, her heavy shoes and short brown hair that was regularly cut but couldn't be described as having an actual style. She seemed to have stepped out of the 1940s as a middle-aged woman and stayed there.

'I'm surprised the council haven't come and pulled this house down,' said Mavis, when we were having one of our nice chats in her front room. 'Not that I'd want them to. It's mine, I own it, and that's saying something for someone who comes where I come from. Mind you, it only cost me eight-hundred quid; they practically had to give it away.'

'But isn't that quite a lot of money? How could you afford it?' I asked.

'Saved up, didn't I? Your dad offered me some money when I left, compensation he called it, but I wouldn't have none of it.'

'But you should have. I think we must be really rich.'

'Nobody pays me off, luv. And that's a lesson you need to learn. Never allow yourself to be paid off. You've got to stand on your own two feet. Rely on yourself.'

'I will, I promise.'

'I know you will. And whatever you do I'll be proud of you. I'm already proud of you.'

Mavis certainly knew how to make me feel good. It wasn't like stuff that people just say because they think it's polite or to butter you up. When Mavis said things like that, her face and eyes went kind of glowy. That wouldn't happen if you didn't mean it. She also used to say things that got stored away in my mind, like the thing about standing on your own two feet. It wasn't a feminist thing with her, like it became for me; it was because she didn't have anyone else to depend on. No man to support her and no family who would or could support her. For Mavis it was nothing to do with women's rights, it was about survival.

'You're a lucky girl, Hannah,' she told me, 'but sometimes luck runs out, and if it does you need to be prepared.'

Mavis never asked about the rest of the family, so I never brought them up, although she did refer to my dad occasionally. It was quite difficult at first, having to avoid even mentioning them, as I was still a kid and so much of my life involved them in one way or another that they were bound to crop up in natural conversation. It was the same when I went home after a visit to Mavis.

'Did you have a nice time, dear?' my mother asked.

'Yes, thank you,' I replied, and that was pretty much the end of it. Cat never even asked and my dad would say something along the lines of, 'Mavis all right, then?' and all I had to do was nod.

I started to think of my world as an old-fashioned apothecary's chest with dozens of different drawers contained within one large piece of furniture. Each small drawer, with its own small wooden knob for opening and closing it, contained a different secret, or if not a secret as such a bit of my life that needed to be kept separate from all the other bits. The way I saw it was that as long as each element was kept safe within its individual container, everything would be all right. I even started mentally labelling the drawers, with names like THINGS I DO WITH MAVIS and CAT'S ADVENTURES WITH BOYS and WATCHING MOTHER. There was one called THOUGHTS I KNOW I SHOULDN'T HAVE. That was the box that haunted me for . . . well, for ever I suppose.

Of course it wasn't my fault. Bad thoughts can't make bad things happen. I was twelve. I was old enough to know that. But knowing something and feeling it are entirely different things. These are some of the things that I felt, and went on feeling: if I hadn't filed that particular bad thought, the worst of bad thoughts, in my apothecary's chest, the scene I encountered that day in the bathroom might never have happened. If I had loved her a little more, it could all have been avoided. Even if loving her more wouldn't have helped, maybe if I'd been easier to love it wouldn't have happened. Maybe she did it to get away from me, the daughter she couldn't stand. To do such a terrible thing she must have been really hurting. If she was really hurting, I should have noticed. Also, I knew about the contents of her bathroom cabinet. So did Cat. We should have told our father right away, not just carried on spying and waiting. So even if my bad thoughts couldn't be responsible for what happened, my lack of action was.

But other feelings kept crowding in as well – not just the guilt, the horror and the shame of it – but a fury that frightened me more even than the actuality of what happened. An anger that made my head feel it was filling up with blood, blood that bubbled and swelled inside it until the only way to relieve the pressure would be for it to burst out of my scalp in dramatic cascades like water from a fountain. How dare she? How dare she do this to me? And to Cat. And to my father. How could she deliberately destroy our family? To carry her selfishness to such a degree that she would do this to us.

What happened was this. I came in from school. Cat, I knew, had gone to a friend. I called, 'Mum,' but there was no reply. We were between maids. Ramona had stormed off back to Spain – she couldn't take any more of my mother's criticism – and Carmen wasn't due to arrive until the next week. Although I wasn't really allowed to be alone in the house, my mother was a hopeless timekeeper – especially if she was out on one of her shopping jaunts

– and often got home well after me. I had a key and it didn't bother me at all. In fact I liked the feeling of being alone in our big empty house with no one to answer to. Going into our kitchen to make a glass of Nesquik, getting the biscuits from the cupboard, having some quiet time. I wouldn't have called myself a solitary child, it was just that being on my own didn't feel lonely.

I opened my satchel and put my books down on the table in the morning room, then I sat down to enjoy my drink and biscuits. There were French doors leading from the morning room into the back garden. Being November it was already dark outside and I could hear the gathering wind beating the branches of the near-leafless trees. The central heating was on and, having just come in from the cold, I could feel the heat turning my face from pale to pink. I was about to go and ring Janet, when I noticed a tiny bead of water on the table. Where did that come from, I wondered, then dismissed it from my mind. Even though we'd only seen one another an hour earlier, I felt like having a chat with Janet. So I left the morning room and went into the hallway.

'What's new, Janet?' I asked.

'What, since an hour ago?'

'Yeah . . .'

'Well, I met this amazing guy on the bus on the way home. He's in a band, he's really sexy and he gave me two tickets for a gig he's doing on Saturday.'

'Wow,' I said, 'are you telling me the truth?'

'Of course not, you idiot. And like we'd be allowed to go even if it was true. I came home and my mum had the startlingly original idea of asking me how my day was and that's the sum total of what's happened since we last spoke.'

'Well, at least your mum bothers to get home for you.'

'Out spending the family fortune again, is she?' giggled Janet.

'Did you know all the doormen in Bond Street bow when they see her?'

'Yeah, and if they saw my mum, they'd send her straight round to the tradesman's entrance at the back.'

'That's mean, your mum's lovely.'

'Lovely, yes, but fashion's just not her thing, you know . . . She thinks it's a plot to keep women in their place.'

'What place?'

'Don't ask me.'

Janet and I could go on like this for hours, but I suddenly got the urge to have another biscuit.

'Better be off,' I said. 'Call you later . . .'

'Sure dos,' Janet replied.

When I went back into the morning room I noticed there were more drips of water on the table. I looked up at the ceiling and spotted what looked like a small bulge. The whole of the downstairs had been redecorated only the year before and I'd watched the workmen carefully line the plaster on the ceiling with plain wallpaper, before painting it over in palest cream. I remembered my mother with the cream paint swatches spread out in front of her. They all looked pretty similar to me. Well, I could see that they were minimally different, that not one of the hundred or more paint swatches was exactly like any other, but I couldn't see that it would actually make any difference to the final look of the room. My mother disagreed.

'There wouldn't be so many variations on what is basically one colour unless it was important to the outcome,' said my mother.

I must have shrugged, because she continued, 'I wouldn't really expect you to get it, Hannah. You see the world in words. Like Cat, I see it in colours and patterns and textures and forms. It's a temperament thing.'

Cat had talked to me about tripping. About drugs that played games with your head and made you see the world in dizzying, dazzling, psychedelic hues. Cat hadn't actually taken LSD, or so she told me, but she seemed to know all about it. I wondered if LSD featured in my mother's pharmaceutical repertoire.

'I like that one,' I said, pointing randomly.

'Too eggy,' said my mother.

'What about that one?' I said, pointing again.

'Too clotted.'

At that point I had lost interest and left the room. But now, in the room again, and with the drips coming from the ceiling with increasing frequency, I began to feel somewhat alarmed. I knew my mother's bathroom was directly above. Maybe the toilet had overflowed, or she'd left a tap running when she went out.

I'd go and have a look upstairs in a minute, but it wasn't a big deal. My mother would be home soon and she'd have to ring my dad who would sort it out. So I finished my biscuit and my milk before going up to investigate.

As I climbed the stairs, half expecting to hear my mother's key in the lock behind me, I suddenly became uneasy. Water dripping through the ceiling wasn't normal. I looked at my watch. It was five-twenty and even allowing for lateness she should be home by now. As I neared the top of the stairs, something flipped in my brain and I broke into a run, launching myself at the door to my parents' bedroom. The bathroom was in the right-hand corner of the room and water was seeping out beneath the closed door into the bedroom.

They say that before someone has a heart attack, just moments before the physical symptoms begin to manifest themselves, it is quite typical to be overcome with a sense of doom, a premonition, if not of death then of something awful about to happen. Before even reaching the bathroom door, that's how I felt. I knew that my mother hadn't gone out leaving a tap running. She was far too fastidious and anxious to make that kind of mistake. I knew I should burst into the bathroom to see what was going on, but I stopped. I stopped and stood there, in a puddle of water, unable to turn the doorknob that would let me into the bathroom.

The water was pooling around me, spreading further into the bedroom. I watched it as it slowly journeyed across the floor.

You have to do something, Hannah, I told myself. You have to do something.

I gripped my trembling hand around the doorknob, but I'd lost the strength to turn it. It took the full force of both my hands to turn that knob.

And there she was. Lying on her back just under the water. There was blood everywhere, smeared on the basin, on the tiles and even on the carpet. There were bottles of pills scattered all over the place, in the basin, on the floor and one bobbing on top of the water in the bath. Some were opened, and the pills had spilled out. Some were still closed. And there was a razor blade, a single blade, embedded in the bar of soap on the edge of the bath. Like Excalibur. My mother must have placed it there, shortly after cutting her wrists and getting into a running bath, her brain bombarded with pills, the blood pouring out.

A kind of frigid calm came over me. I walked towards the bath, leaning over my dead mother to turn off the taps. Then I stepped back and gazed at her pale naked body, slightly parted lips, her fair hair fanning out in the water. I didn't see her as my mother. I thought of the pre-Raphaelite exhibition I'd been to on a school trip just months before. It had been my favourite painting in the whole of the exhibition – John Everett Millais's *Ophelia*, in which she floats downstream in a river, partially submerged, dead or drowning. I wondered if my mother, so influenced – unlike her younger daughter, or so she mistakenly thought – by images, had ever seen that painting herself. Whether it had inspired or affected her in some way.

How strangely the mind works. All this I considered as I stood there, staring dispassionately at my dead mother. And then I crumpled, sinking to the floor, curling up as small as I could, head on my knees, arms folded around my head to shield me from the sight of her, waiting, just waiting, for someone to arrive. That someone was Cat. Cat who screamed and screamed and screamed until her screaming brought me back to my senses, or near enough back to them to enable me to walk to the little table on my mother's side of the bed and to pick up the phone and ring my father, who was just leaving the office.

'Something's happened to Mummy,' I sobbed. 'Something terrible.' My father didn't ask what had happened. It was as if he knew. As if he had been waiting for it to happen all along.

I stayed sitting on the bed, looking at my lap and at my arms and legs, limp and quivering. Death-Defying Definitions, I thought. Popped her clogs. Met her maker. Kicked the bucket. So hilarious, such great fun. I knew that was one particular game Mavis and I would never play again.

Chapter Ten

'We should have told Dad about the pills right away,' I said to Cat.

'Well, we didn't,' said Cat. 'And anyway it wasn't the pills that killed her.'

'But if she hadn't taken the pills, then she might not have been crazy enough to cut herself.'

'Too late now, Mouse,' said Cat.

'But we might have been able to stop her. Which makes it our fault.'

'You can blame yourself if you want to, but what good will it do?'

'I'm not blaming myself, I'm just saying . . .'

'Well, don't just say. It's pointless. And telling Dad is pointless, too. It will just make him angrier than he already is.'

We got into the habit of arguing like this in the days after my mother's death. And Cat was right, our father did seem more angry than he was sorrowful. I was reminded of one of Mavis's sayings: 'Everyone has their own way of dealing with things, and you just have to let them get on with it.'

When the GP had come round to confirm our mother's death, Dad had fired off his fury like a machine-gun.

'You bastard, you bloody drug-pushing bastard,' he bellowed as soon as Dr Arkwright stepped into the hallway. He even gave him a couple of little pushes in the chest with the palm of his hand, nothing violent, more like a boxer warming up, practising his jabs. But the doctor still had to step back to stop himself losing his balance.

'Daaad,' I pleaded, to no avail.

Dr Arkwright was a mild-mannered man, close to sixty, I calculated. When I went to his surgery, he would peer over his reading glasses and smile at me.

'And what's the trouble, young lady?' he'd ask, addressing me directly rather than the adult who accompanied me. I liked that about him and the fact that he always wore a bow tie. In my opinion he was gentle and considerate and had as much time for his patients as they needed. He never seemed to be in any kind of hurry. Dr Arkwright was the only doctor Cat and I had ever known. He administered whatever vaccinations we needed, and if we had tonsillitis or chicken pox or measles, he'd always turn up for home visits with his leather doctor's bag and a friendly smile. A proper old-fashioned doctor, my dad had always called him in the past. Not at all how I imagined a drug-pusher.

'Now Mr Saunders,' said Dr Arkwright, adjusting his bow tie a little in response to my father's outburst, then continuing calmly as usual, as if malicious attacks from his patients were all in a day's work: 'I understand your grief and your anger, it's only natural in these tragic circumstances, but you have to give me time to explain myself. I'm shocked as well by what's happened. Certainly I was aware that your wife had – well, let us say that she had certain problems – but she didn't strike me as someone who would take her own life.'

'So why the cornucopia of pills? The veritable arsenal of pharmaceuticals that she kept in her medicine cabinet? Where the fuck did she get those from? Who are you anyway? Dr Arkwright or Dr Overdose?'

'Now, now, Mr Saunders, it is important that I see your wife and confirm the death. Afterwards, perhaps, we can come back downstairs and discuss these matters. Cat and Hannah, my dear girls, I am so very sorry for your loss.'

Cat and I were sitting on the sofa, nodding robotically.

'A little brandy wouldn't do the girls any harm at a time like this. What do you think, Mr Saunders?'

'They can help themselves if they want to. Go on, girls, the good doctor thinks you should get drunk. Then you can become alcoholics like your mother and then he can prescribe you lots of lovely pills in all your favourite colours.'

'Please, Mr Saunders, I understand, I really do, but this isn't helping the girls one bit. Think of the terrible shock *they've* had. And poor Hannah, being the one to find her. Look at the two of them, they're shivering. It's warm in here, the heating's on, and they're shivering. That, Mr Saunders, is a classic response to trauma and what they need is to be wrapped up in blankets and given a small drop of something. Is there no other family member or friend who could be here at this time? It's too much for you to have to deal with all on your own.'

The doctor's comment seemed to jolt my father back to reason, to the importance of keeping himself in check in front of us.

'I'm so sorry, pussycats,' he said. His face was ashen, his eyes blinking so quickly that they seemed to mirror my racing heart. 'I'm so . . . so . . . stunned, I suppose, that I don't know what I'm doing or saying at the moment. Try not to take any notice of me, I'm not thinking straight at all. Of course Dr Arkwright is right. I'll get you a couple of your mother's shawls from the hall cupboard and then I'll pour you something. Would the two of you like a little brandy?'

'Yes, please,' we said in unison, continuing to shiver.

'And to answer your question, Dr Arkwright, we really don't need anyone else here right now. I'm perfectly capable of looking after my children until we've sorted out some help.'

My father disappeared to find the shawls while we sat in silence. When he returned the shawls were bunched up in the crook of his neck, held in place with both hands. He turned his head to the side and down, burrowing his nose into the fabric as if to draw my mother's essence from the lingering perfume. Then he came over to the sofa and placed the shawls between us. Picking them up again, one at a time, he draped them around us by turn – first me, then Cat, depositing a kiss on the top of each of our heads as he completed his task. Then he opened the cocktail cabinet and poured a small amount of brandy from a decanter into two large balloons, before indicating to the doctor that he was ready to take him upstairs. I felt as though I were watching a dream sequence in slow motion. When he was gone, we warmed the glasses in the palms of our hands as we'd seen our father do so many times before, then swirled the liquor around the glass, allowing its vapours to escape up into our nostrils. And then we sat and sipped and shivered, and waited for the shawl and the brandy to do whatever they were supposed to do, and for our father to come back downstairs again.

When the two of them returned I noticed that the doctor looked almost as pale and upset as the rest of us.

'Have a seat, doctor,' said my father, pointing at an armchair. 'Wouldn't be surprised if you could handle a brandy yourself.'

'Normally I never accept a drink while on my rounds, but in this case I think I'll make an exception.' He smiled across at us, his eyes watery behind his spectacles. 'Now, do you want to have this discussion with the girls around, or would you rather we did it in private?'

'There are to be no more secrets between us now,' he said, turning to face us. 'They need to understand.' But even then I felt it was a ruse, just talk to make us feel better, that he was mouthing rather than meaning what he said. I sensed that secrets were woven into the fabric of our lives, and extracting them wasn't as simple as saying there were no longer to be any.

'That sounds like a good plan to me,' said Dr Arkwright. 'First of all the girls need to have something explained to them. Your mother was suffering from depression. Depression isn't just being sad or down in the dumps about something, it's a serious illness that requires medical treatment. Sometimes depression can be brought on by a sad event, like a bereavement, or ongoing stress, sometimes it's a chemical change that occurs in the brain, and sometimes a combination of all the things I've mentioned. There's a lot we don't know about depression, but we can try to help it with medication. I did prescribe an antidepressant for your mother, and a mild tranquilliser that I cautioned her to take only very occasionally. But most of those pills we found upstairs in the bathroom did not come from me. They are the kind of pills that can be got on street corners in the less salubrious areas, they get offered to revellers in nightclubs and sometimes can even be acquired on prescription from unscrupulous private doctors who demand large amounts of money and ask no questions. Your mother, I'm afraid, must have fallen prey to some pretty unsavoury characters.'

'She just wasn't there . . .' I muttered.

'What was that?' asked my father.

'It was like she was there but invisible at the same time.'

'You're talking rubbish.' Cat elbowed me in the ribs.

'The first time I met her,' said my dad, 'I thought she was the most exquisite creature I'd ever seen.'

'Bullshit, crap and bullshit,' exploded Cat, her voice louder and more shrill with each succeeding word. All of us swivelled to look at her.

'She was our mother, right? Our MOTHER. Why are you saying she was invisible or exquisite or any of that baloney? She was our mother. And she's dead. *Dead. Dead. Dead.* Killed herself because we weren't worth hanging around for. Isn't that the truth? None of us mattered to her enough for her to stay around. We just weren't worth it.' And she threw herself into the corner of the sofa, sobbing hysterically, as the rest of us continued to sip our brandies, politely, like we were at a vicar's tea party.

There was a coroner's report following an inquest. It was everything we expected. The vodka. The cocktail of pills. The deliberate self-mutilation with a razor blade, cutting a main artery, sending blood pumping round the bathroom.

During those early weeks I often got the feeling that we were all play-acting in an elaborate drama. Eventually it would be over and we'd return to normal, with my mother rising from the dead to take her final bow before the curtain fell and the audience erupted into spontaneous applause and cries of 'Bravo! Encore!'

Then there was also fear. Fear that made me startle at the smallest noise, that caused me to keep checking behind me as I walked to and from school, to make sure I wasn't being followed. I found myself shaking curtains and pillows and even the clothes I wore every day to be certain there were no spiders or wasps lurking in folds of fabric. But what made me most fearful of all was looking at my father.

In his grief he had become, to my twelve-year-old eyes, an old, old man. His body no longer filled his skin, his eyes were bloodshot, his flesh the grey of my school uniform. I barely recognised him, and I no longer had the job of pouring his whisky, which became a focus of my worry. He preferred to pour his own, larger and more frequently than I was used to. The cocktail cabinet was left unlocked, in silent rebuke to the family's failure to stop my mother drinking. He sat in his favourite armchair, not speaking, weaving the key through the fingers of his right hand, backwards and forwards, backwards and forwards, like a magician with a favourite card, endlessly weaving, faster and faster, until I wanted to scream: 'That key won't tell you anything. Look at *us*. Talk to *us*. We're not dead as well, you know.'

It terrified me, the way my father was behaving. Would we end up losing him, too? Our domestic arrangements were a shambles. Dot was off sick, suffering stress. The house was a mess, shoes and coats flung everywhere, washing overflowing in the linen basket, dirty plates piled high in the sink. Dot had helped to clear up the devastation in the bathroom, but even though my dad had cleaned away the worst of the blood before she arrived, afterwards she said her nerves couldn't take it. She'd definitely be back, but not for a bit. Couldn't bear the sight of us poor mites having to fend for ourselves and live with the memory of how our mother had killed herself.

'I won't ever have that old cow in my house again.' My dad practically spat the words out. 'She can't bear the sight of you suffering? If she can't bear for you to suffer, why the fuck doesn't she stay and help us? What are we supposed to do? Lily-livered bitch.'

'I don't suppose . . .' I said nervously, 'I don't suppose . . .'

'You don't suppose what?' said my father, impatiently. How I longed for him to be funny again and for his eyes to smile and sparkle.

'Well . . . well, I was thinking . . . Mavis. I mean, just for a bit . . . if she can fit it round her job, take time off or something.'

'Say, Hannah, that's a pretty smart idea. She could even come back . . .'

For a second everything seemed brighter.

'But no, of course not,' he continued. 'What am I thinking? Not long term, but maybe for a bit. I mean, the circumstances, they're exceptional.'

Cat let out a piercing scream, covering her ears as she did so. For a moment we'd forgotten she was there, and now she was Munch's famous painting come to life.

'If that woman even steps inside this house, I'm leaving home. Running away and not coming back again, not ever. Do you understand that, both of you? Is that what you were thinking, Hannah? You scheming cow. That with Mummy out of the way we could have Mavis back. Is that what you were hoping? That one day Mummy would kill herself and—'

Cat had voiced my most wicked thought. It was as though she could read my mind. But it had only ever been a thought, I hadn't meant it, I had never, ever wished my mother dead.

'That's enough, Cat,' said my father. 'Enough. Do you hear? Of course that's not what Hannah was thinking and it was cruel of you to say it. Apologise to your sister. Right now.'

'I won't apologise, and you can't make me. I'm sixteen soon. You can't make me.' And then she turned to me. 'I've always hated you, Hannah. Surely you know that.'

My father raised his hand, but instead of hitting Cat he let his hand rest, mid-air. He turned it over and over, and stared at it as if waiting for it to tell him something. Then he slowly raised his other hand and brought them both to cover his face, obscuring his features completely. He began to sob. For the first time since our mother died, our father was crying in front of us.

Cat turned and ran out of the room. I went to comfort my father. I touched his arm, tried to say the word 'Daddy', but it wouldn't come out. I looked up at him, but he didn't want to know, he turned his face away.

'I'm sorry, Hannah,' he said. 'Not now. We'll come up with something.'

I wanted to tell him I loved him, that I'd look after him, that we'd be all right, but I couldn't. Cat had made it happen again. The voices, taunting me. *Cat got your tongue. Cat got your tongue.* I felt the panic rise from my stomach. Not again! Not now. I couldn't deal with this. I needed Cat to be my friend, not my enemy. Who else did we have if not each other?

For want of knowing what else to do I walked into the kitchen, took a half-empty bottle of milk from the fridge and poured myself a glass. The milk, when I tasted it, was rancid. I drank it anyway, in great, heaving gulps and without pause. A pain in my stomach, a really bad pain, might be just what I needed. Then I could concentrate on that, rather than on the other pain, the pain that seemed to attacking me from all directions, threatening to engulf me. The rising bile of fear met the sour milk as it sank towards my stomach. I vomited all over the floor.

Before Cat's outburst, which was about a week after my mother killed herself, Cat and I had taken to sharing a bed at night. That very first night, I'd got into my own bed, clutched my teddy bear tightly to my chest, and started to recite the lyrics of the songs I'd learned that summer. I waited and waited – for an hour or maybe even two – listening out for signs that Cat was preparing herself for sleep. Maybe she'd send me away, but then again . . . Eventually I heard the faint but certain click of the light being switched off on Cat's bedside table. Then, still clutching Teddy, I walked towards her room, noticing her door had been left ajar rather than closed as it normally would be. I didn't knock, I simply walked in quietly, stood at the foot of Cat's bed and said, 'May I . . .?' Cat brought her arm out from under the blankets and patted the top of the coverlet.

'Hop in, little Mouse,' she said, and I did, it was so easy, and it felt so right. And after that I just turned up, didn't even have to ask, and we curled up together. Sometimes like spoons, our bodies moulding into one another. Sometimes face to face, so we could catch the warmth of each other's breath as our salt tears mingled on the pillow, uniting us as we'd never been united before.

The night of the Mavis explosion I knew it was pointless to go into Cat's room. That short phase, that brief respite, that moment when we were the sisters I'd always dreamed we could be, was over. She'd probably never allow me into her bed again. I went to my own bed as usual, silently recited the words from my mantra – 'Dock of the Bay', 'Mrs Robinson', 'Light My Fire', 'Lily the Pink' – every now and again trying, and failing, to say some words out loud.

I don't know how long I lay there, staring up at the ceiling, clutching Teddy, silently repeating lyrics to songs that had no real meaning for me. And then a chink of light, from the hallway, appeared at the edge of my door, and it grew larger and brighter as the door was opened and a figure appeared wearing a black and red kimono. I sat bolt upright. She was back! She'd come back! The red dragon against the black fabric was clearly visible. My mother was standing there in the doorway. I couldn't breathe. But then the apparition in the doorway said something.

'May I . . .?' she said quietly. And it was Cat's voice, and Cat's face, and Cat's body and I was saved. Only the kimono belonged to my mother. And I patted the coverlet, just as Cat had done for me, and the words came out easily.

'Hop in, Big Sister,' I said.

That night, as we curled up together, I thought about those separate drawers in my imaginary apothecary's chest. Could I really continue to have a drawer for my relationship with my sister, and another for my relationship with Mavis? Or would one of them have to go?

Ramona's replacement, Carmen, arrived the day after Cat's outburst, two days before my mother's funeral. Cat and I answered the door to her. She followed us into the kitchen, took one look at the devastation in front of her and started crossing herself and exclaiming loudly in Spanish: '*¡madre mia!* Where you *madre?*'

'Dead. *Muerte*,' I replied.

She crossed herself some more.

'*Mis niños pobres*. My poor children . . . How long? How much dead?'

'Very dead. Seven days,' said Cat.

And Carmen promptly burst into tears. It wasn't an auspicious beginning, but Carmen believed she had been sent by the good Lord to save us, and so she set about her tasks of cooking and cleaning and laundering and ironing with the passion of a zealot, as if her domestic mission was the one thing that would ensure her entry to heaven.

Our extended family certainly wasn't much use. My mother's parents lived in Switzerland. They'd gone there shortly after my parents had married because my grandfather had emphysema, and they hoped the clean mountain air would help. I knew my grandfather was now too frail to travel, but we were all shocked that my grandmother didn't even bother to make the trip for our mother's funeral. She and my father spoke on the phone; she said my grandfather was too ill to be left alone. I'd never met my grandmother. There had always been talk of trips to Switzerland to see them, but these trips never materialised. Either Grandpa wasn't well enough, or they had other visitors, or when they did finally deign to give us dates they always seemed to fall during term-time. We got gifts and cards on our birthdays and at Christmas, though. 'Guilt gifts,' my dad called them, which didn't at all bother me and Cat because who'd turn their nose up at a £25 voucher for Harrods, an absolute fortune in those days? All we had to do in return was send a nice thank you note, and remember to send cards on their own birthdays and anniversary.

It suited Cat and me just fine because it meant three trips a year to the magical toy department at Harrods – once on her birthday, once on mine, and once after Christmas. The only bit I didn't enjoy was the dressing up we had to do. We had these special navy suits when we were little – with Peter Pan collars and pleated skirts, which we wore with pale pink cardigans. They were made for us by a proper dressmaker, like miniature couture, and made us look more like the offspring of European royalty than the daughters of a businessman from Barnet, but it kept my mother happy. And afterwards we'd go out for tea, laden with green and gold carrier bags, and have hot chocolate and sandwiches with the crusts off at a posh Knightsbridge tea house.

Dad told us there'd been a bit of a falling-out with my mother's parents around the time I was born, but he never offered an explanation as to what the falling-out was about. As for my father's relatives, his dad was dead, his mother in a nursing home, his sister gone to live in Australia. Fortunately Cat and I were in no mood to have relatives fussing over us and feeling sorry for us.

'I hate it,' said Cat, 'when people do that special tilting-head thing to show they feel sorry for you. It makes them look mornonic.'

'Moronic, I think you mean,' I said gently. 'And when they speak in whispers rather than normal voices, in case a loud voice might upset you,' I added. 'As though you'll be just fine as long as their voice is quiet. As though you won't mind so much that your mother is dead as long as they talk to you in that special tone of voice.'

'Or when they hug you and hardly know you.'

'Especially when they have smelly breath.'

For some reason, this made Cat and me laugh. Even with our mother not yet buried there were moments when we could laugh. And once we started we couldn't stop.

'Did you hear about the suicidal twin?' spluttered Cat.

'Did I hear what about the suicidal twin?' I snorted.

'She killed her sister by mistake.'

The two of us fell onto the sofa, breathless with desperate laughter.

When we'd recovered. I turned to Cat and recited:

> *'Razors pain you;*
> *Rivers are damp;*
> *Acid stains you;*
> *And drugs cause cramp;*
> *Guns aren't lawful;*
> *Nooses give;*
> *Gas smells awful;*
> *You might as well live.'*

'Bloody hell, Mouse, that's proper poetry.'

'Dorothy Parker was a proper poet,' I said.

'What Dorothy? Dorothy as in *The Wizard of Oz*?' said Cat.

And that got me laughing even more. And even though Cat didn't know why it was so funny, she started up again, too. The racket alerted Carmen who appeared in the doorway of the living room.

'*Mis niños pobres*,' she said, not for the first time, shaking her head at us. 'You eat now,' she said. 'You feel better.'

That of course cracked us up again. We laughed and laughed until the tears came and we no longer knew – or even cared – if they were tears of laughter or of pain.

After the funeral, when everyone came back to our house for drinks and squares of tortilla prepared by Carmen, who in forty-eight hours since her arrival had proved herself indispensable, I skulked in corners eavesdropping:

'It's not as easy to kill yourself by cutting your wrists as you might think,' I heard a neighbour say.

'She did her homework apparently, cutting up from the wrist rather than across it,' replied her companion.

'How ghastly,' replied the other person, 'but how do you know?'

'Someone overheard Maurice talking about it. Oh what a mess. Those girls' lives are ruined.'

'Not that she was much of a mother anyway. Did you see the way she used to get herself up? Since that Mavis left, I reckon those two girls have been neglected.'

'Goodness knows how they'll turn out. Wild, I wouldn't be surprised.'

I couldn't bear it any longer, this being talked about and dissected. Predictions about how Cat and I would turn out being made by strangers. The whole thing was surreal. And it went on being surreal, for months and months, with only Carmen to give the household some semblance of order and routine.

Mavis didn't come to the funeral. She didn't even know what had happened until after the funeral was over as she didn't have a phone of her own. In the past, whenever me. I'm all right, really I am.' For reasons I didn't fully understand I wanted the conversation to end as quickly as possible. 'Look I'm sorry, but I have to go, Carmen's calling me for dinner.' Carmen wasn't calling me for dinner, but I was desperate to put down the phone.

There were many times I longed to cling to Mavis for comfort after what happened. To judge from my behaviour you'd have thought quite the opposite. I found myself drifting further and further away, avoiding going to see her and writing less frequently. Mavis had rushed off and got herself a phone, thinking we would cosy up for long chats on a regular basis now that my mother wasn't around. But I never once rang her in all those months following my mother's suicide, always leaving it to her to phone me, and then cutting the conversation short with whatever excuse came to hand.

Allowing myself to be loved by Mavis no longer seemed fair now that Cat didn't have a mother to love her. And now that it was Cat who mattered to me most it was important somehow that we were on an equal footing.

The one thing that could have brought Mavis and me together pulled us apart.

I kept Mavis at a distance for some years after my mother's death. I wasn't thinking of her, I was thinking of me. Somehow, despite the drama of our lives, I became a teenager, with teenage preoccupations. And what's more boring to a teenager than an adult who wants to take up your precious time going to rummage sales and having a natter over a nice piece of sponge cake?

Chapter Eleven

My father never remarried, never even came close to it as far as I was aware. His brightness was all burned out, never to return. It was as though my mother's silent reproachfulness, her hinted disapproval, which he mostly ignored when she was alive, hovered over him all the time now that she was gone. Was it grief or was it guilt? He didn't speak of his own feelings so I could only guess that guilt played the greater part, that he saw himself in some way responsible for her death.

What had happened, by mysterious alchemy, was that no sooner was my mother dead than he started to mythologise her. Nobody could match her beauty, he said, and on a strictly physical basis I could see that might be the case. But when he talked of my mother he talked as much of her 'inner beauty' as of her appearance, and it didn't ring at all true to me.

I was quite sure it wasn't my imagination that my parents' relationship was a cold and distant one. Being polite doesn't constitute love or even affection. There wasn't much point in canvassing Cat for her opinion, as she had gone the way of our father, elevating Eleanor to iconic status.

Sometimes the way they sang her praises made me wonder if we'd all shared a home with the same woman.

'Your mother was the most sensitive person you're ever likely to meet,' said my dad, over one of our rare suppers together. Mostly he had dinner at the casino.

Sensitive? More thin-skinned than sensitive I wanted to reply, not the same thing at all. Exposed and raw, like a flayed animal, perhaps. Sensitive to herself, oh yes. But to be truly sensitive, don't you have to be sensitive to others? Don't you have to know that topping yourself is not the kindest way to behave towards those to whom you have a responsibility? I was angry with her when she was alive and even angrier with her for dying.

I nodded, morosely, as if in complete agreement.

'And the most stylish woman on the planet, too,' added Cat, with wistful admiration. 'Wait till I design my first collection, I'm going to dedicate it to her. I'll make her famous and her name will appear in *Vogue* alongside mine, and in fashion magazines all over the world. *The Eleanor Collection*. Everyone will want an Eleanor. I'll get great big blow-up pictures of her and have them all over the studio.'

A little tremor went through me at the thought of our mother being turned into such a heroine, gazing down at us, larger than life, from the walls of Cat's studio, but at the same time I couldn't help smiling. Cat's certainty was so impressive, and I believed in Cat as much as she believed in herself. I wanted her to be a star. What I didn't want was for my dad and Cat to turn my mother, in death, into something she never was when she was alive.

And hadn't we – especially Cat – always made fun of my
mother's slavish attention to fashion, laughed at her
determination to be a sixties dolly bird, a mere Jean
Shrimpton replica, a model clone, rather than adapting
the look to suit her as an individual? If I died, would they
remember me as a lion rather than a mouse? Layer upon
layer of fantasy and self-deception.

History was being rewritten as we ate our supper and I
was powerless to stop it. Or at least powerless to stop it
unless I was willing to be branded heartless and unfeeling.
But of course I wasn't unfeeling. If anything, I was too full
of feeling. It's just that my feelings were the wrong sort of
feelings. They didn't coincide with those of my dad and
Cat.

Me, Cat and Maurice, gamely attempting to play happy
families around the morning-room table. We never sat in
the dining room once my mother was gone, my dad said it
was too formal, and too depressing. I wasn't surprised that
he preferred spending his evenings at the casino to being
confronted, nightly, by Eleanor's absence.

Cat was rarely around either. She had abandoned all
pretence at studying after clocking up just three O Levels,
and moving on to a sixth-form college where art was her
one A Level subject, a subject she devoured like a starving
man presented with a sudden feast, a subject at which she
was so naturally talented that no art school in the country
would want to turn her down. Whatever she turned her
hand to – oil painting, crayon drawings, screen-printing or
collage, the results were always daring and distinctive,
always full of colour and pattern and depth and texture.

Her teachers were impressed, but determined to slow her down. 'Think about what you do,' they implored her, 'and think about why you're doing it.'

Cat wasn't interested in their strait-jacket approach. She refused to be tamed by their criticism. Instead she went looking for inspiration from the Old Masters at the National Gallery and the costume galleries at the V & A as well as in the hippest markets and boutiques. She took me with her to Regent's Park to see the ducks, which I was happy to do. While I fed them with stale bread she gazed at their feathers, committing their kaleidoscopic colours to memory, as she did with the gradations of green of the leaves on the trees. Most of her clothes were junk-shop bargains, altered to fit and re-fashioned with added bits of fabric, new buttons, pockets in unlikely positions. At home Cat would knit, sew, crochet, paint – she was consumed by her own creativity.

Most nights she went to pubs and discos with friends, returning home extremely late or not at all. To me she seemed manic, buzzing, totally engaged, perhaps it helped her deal with her grief. Increasingly often my dad wasn't coming home either – so he no longer had any jurisdiction over Cat's nocturnal habits.

Although my father wanted to avoid commitment, he comforted himself with an endless stream of girlfriends, all of whom were nearer to Cat's age than his. Rather than subject them to our rudeness and disdain, he generally chose to sleep away. On the few occasions he did bring back one of his 'bints' for the night – it was Cat's idea to call

Dad adores blue-eyed blondes.

'Or the one before that,' I might add. Cat and I were well-rehearsed at this, although I recognised that we were being unnecessarily mean, and that the girls themselves had done nothing to deserve it other than to take a fancy to man old enough to be their father, and possibly rich enough to be their sugar-daddy.

Once Cat told a bint, 'It's bed only, I'm afraid. We don't do breakfast, do we, Hannah?' The girl in question had fled straight out of the house, leaving the door wide open and not even shouting a goodbye to my father, who was upstairs in the bathroom at the time. The bathroom had been re-modelled after my mother's suicide. It was wall-to-wall avocado now, and there was only one bathroom cabinet.

The worst occasion was when one of dad's girlfriends came down wearing my mother's red and black kimono.

One second Cat was sitting sedately at the table munch-ing cornflakes, the next she was throwing herself at the intruder like a cornered cat.

'Get it off, you bitch. You fucking bitch,' she screamed, trying to tear the robe from her body.

This particular girl – afterwards we discovered she did have a name, and that her name was Mandy – was more than a match for Cat. She pushed Cat away with a forceful shove and the fabric, to which Cat had been clinging, ripped, exposing Mandy's right nipple. Mandy, unfazed, narrowed her eyes, looking first at me then at Cat, with a contempt that mirrored our own of a few moments earlier.

'Sorry to offend your sensibilities, sweeties,' she said, 'but it was just sitting there, eyeing me up from the hook behind the bathroom door. No wonder your mother—'

I could see Cat was about to launch herself at Mandy again, so I grabbed her arm to hold her back.

Mandy sniffed. 'What a fucking nuthouse this is. Shame really. Maurice is quite sexy for an old guy. Tell you what, girls, I'll do you a favour . . .'

And in a single flicking motion of one hand she undid the belt of the kimono and shrugged it off her shoulders with the practised skill of a striptease artist, which perhaps she was. Standing stark naked in front of us she tossed her shoulder-length hair, turned her back and cutely rounded bottom on us, and marched out of the kitchen, buttocks bobbing, and back up the stairs.

Cat and I looked at one another, astonished . . . and impressed.

'Well, at least the bint has a bit of spunk,' said Cat after a long pause. 'I think I'll tell Dad that if she wants to come again we should buy a special visitors' robe. It did my head in seeing her in Mum's kimono, but I'd quite like to meet this one again.' Mandy never did come back and over time Dad brought home his girlfriends even less often.

We assumed, from the ceaseless stream of phone messages from girls with increasingly exotic names, that my father's sex life was busy and varied, but he was learning that sex away was less fraught than sex on home territory. It suited us. We didn't begrudge our father a sex life, we just didn't want it shoved in our faces.

Cat was becoming ever more outgoing and excitable. As soon as she turned sixteen she went off to a Marie Stopes clinic in Soho and got herself put on the Pill.

If the phone wasn't ringing for my dad, it was ringing for Cat. Suzie, Sandy and the rest of her girl gang remained fiercely loyal, but now there were always gravelly voiced boys calling as well. I never understood the way Cat felt about sex. I was as prim as she was promiscuous. As self-conscious as she was uninhibited.

'You need to read a bit less Jane Austen and a bit more Harold Robbins and Jacqueline Susann,' she told me. 'You're living way too far in the past. You need to loosen up, Mouse, tune in to your big sister. Let it all hang out.' But I was hooked on the idea of love as opposed to sex. The more I knew about sex, from Cat's graphic descriptions, the more grubby and unappealing it seemed. Something to be avoided rather than sought after. I did envy Cat's ability to have fun, but not her determination to open her legs at every possible opportunity.

Janet and I discussed Cat for hours, not because I brought her up all the time, but because Janet had become obsessed with her. Janet's view was that everyone knew Cat was a slut, and that was why she was so 'popular'.

in from of Janet.

Cat became more extrovert; I became more introspective. But who's to say who was handling my mother's death more successfully? For Cat, night time was the worst – the quiet, dead of night, when the effects of the cannabis she regularly smoked had drifted away, when the temporary anaesthetic of orgasm induced by sex with a stranger, had worn off. Even by the time she was eighteen, there were still many, many nights when she'd appear at my bedside as late as 3 or 4 a.m. and snuggle up to me for comfort. I got used to her sharp angles – her bony knees and elbows digging into my soft flesh. Her dope-scented breath, slowing and quietening as soon as she cuddled reassuringly close.

For me there wasn't so much a sensation of grief as a constant, low-grade anxiety. It manifested itself in an over-awareness of my body and its functions. I'd often find it hard to catch my breath and would have to remind myself to breathe properly, in and out, in and out, as though something I had once known instinctively how to do I had now forgotten. Sometimes I felt I was about to lose the hang of walking. Just one foot in front of the other,

Hannah, I'd tell myself. Just a step at a time. My balance would be affected, not to the extent that I might fall, but things that should have been in sharp focus would, for no apparent reason, start to sway in front of me, almost imperceptibly, but enough to throw me out of kilter, to make me aware that something wasn't quite as it should be. I never talked to anyone about this, and nor did I relate it in any way to my feelings about my mother. Only when David died, and those exact same symptoms returned, did I finally connect the two.

Janet and I, aged fifteen as Cat turned eighteen, were resolutely virgins. By then I'd lost count of the guys Cat had told me she'd slept with. That spring, before she was due to go to college to study fashion design, she went to Paris for three months, to stay with a distant cousin of ours who lived in the smart suburb of Neuilly-sur-Seine. I missed my sister then, with a sharp stab of loneliness that took me by surprise and pinched my heart, a sensation far more concrete than anything I'd felt while ostensibly mourning my mother.

I went out in search of stationery, something that I hoped would appeal to Cat's sense of style. After spending about two hours with Janet in the stationery department at Selfridges, while she patiently indulged my indecision until she could bear it no longer and gave me a five-minute deadline, I finally settled on some crisp pink gingham paper with matching envelopes. A little bit Barbie, a little bit whacky. And very Cat.

I knew that hoping Cat would respond to my letters was pointless. Cat drew, she didn't write. But I didn't care, I was determined to write to her anyway, several times a week. My life was pretty boring really, so I decided to make most of it up, and added in little jokes and sarcastic observations that I thought would make Cat laugh. It surprised me that I could be funny on paper in a way that I could never be in conversation, and I was hopeful that Cat would be amused. One day, after she'd been gone about six weeks, a postcard arrived. It was a picture of the Eiffel Tower, onto which Cat had drawn a stick person hanging off the edge near the top and brandishing a carrier bag which said 'I love Paris.' It was her first communication with me. I turned the card over from the picture to see what Cat had written. It was short and to the point:

> *Dear Mouse,*
>
> *Men so sexy even you'd get the hots. Clothes to die for. Sat next to Alain Delon at the Café de Flore, practically on his lap. He smiled at me, I swear. And gave me a light. Come quickly. Ten days minimum. Madeleine, the Wicked Witch, has finally given in to my nagging.*
>
> *Cat xxx*

My body felt lit up, illuminated from inside by dancing stars. So this is what happiness feels like, I thought. Since my mother's death, I had been effectively mummified, wrapped from head to toe in tight bandages that restricted my movements and my thoughts and the ability of light to reach and warm me. And now I'd been unwrapped, and set free. Underneath the bandages, to my surprise, I appeared to be healed, a fresh new layer of skin had formed, and I was ready to face the world – pink, shiny and optimistic.

I thought of Mavis then. I'd shut out the light and I'd shut out Mavis. I must have hurt her terribly. She must have felt the distance I'd created between us, must have noticed how the length of time between visits had grown, first from three weeks to four, then to five and six and more. After Paris, I'd make things right between us. Not that Mavis had shown any sign of disappointment. Quite the opposite in fact. She had said in so many ways that I needed to find my own destiny. She used expressions learned from her upbringing on a farm: 'Hannah, my girl, you must learn to plough your own furrow', or 'One day you will know how to till your own soil.'

Of course my father would agree for me to go to Paris, there was no reason for him not to. I could even time it to coincide with my sixteenth birthday in April. I was off to Paris to stay with my sister, who wanted me there. And not because she was miserable, but because she was having the time of her life, and wanted to share it with me.

Paris marked a turning point. It was my first trip abroad, my first time in an aeroplane, my first taste of freedom. Soaring above the clouds, my face glued to the window from the moment of take-off until we touched down on the runway forty-five minutes later at Le Bourget airport, I felt I was on the brink of something momentous, as though my life – my real life – was about to begin. It occurred to me that everything before had been a practice run, a not very successful practice run in which I tripped up and made mistakes at every turn. But now I was ready for the real thing, and it was tantalisingly close.

I was seduced by Paris before I'd even set foot in it. The mere mention of the Café de Flore on Cat's postcard or the thought of sipping *café au lait* at Les Deux Magots sent my head into a romantic spin. At the time I secretly harboured a desire to become a writer, so to be able to sit where Saint-Exupéry, Hemingway, Oscar Wilde and Simone de Beauvoir had discussed important matters of the day with their fellow writers and written in their notebooks, was reason enough to love Paris. My vision of Paris was a hotchpotch of images drawn from different eras. I thought of *Gigi*, the movie of Colette's story, and pictured in my mind the sidewalks beside the Bois de Boulogne with horse-drawn carriages. I remembered a black and white photographic image of the 1950s, taken in a typical Parisian square, in which a couple kissed uninhibitedly, oblivious to the pedestrians around them. I assumed everyone wore black polo necks and drank Pernod while smoking Gauloises out of blue packets in smoky dives.

Cat striding towards me in the arrivals hall painted a different picture altogether. My gawky grown-up sister, with her bendy-doll gait and outrageous outfit, turned heads all around her – looks that ranged from amusement and disapproval to open-mouthed admiration. Cat was wearing tiny hot-pants in day-glo pink with black opaque tights and over-the-knee purple suede boots. On her top half she wore a silky tight-fitting blouse with a purple and white floral print and huge bell sleeves. The big floppy-brimmed hat on her head undulated like a wave as she moved and the fringed tassels of her suede shoulder bag tickled her skinny thighs like feathers.

As my bird-of-paradise sibling stretched out her arms, and a broad grin bared her teeth between candy pink lips, I felt my excitement evaporate. What was I thinking? I was still a grey little Mouse. How idiotic of me to think that anything might have changed.

'Mouse, you look fabulous!' said Cat, drawing back from a hug and holding me at arms' length. 'I love the gypsy look and it so suits your dark hair and eyes.'

Cat, her old sarcastic self. I looked down despondently at my three-tiered peasant skirt, rope-heeled espadrilles and Romanian gypsy drawstring top with its black and red embroidery. I'd tried so hard to get my look together, and I'd made a fool of myself.

But then Cat said, 'Why the long face, Mouse? You do look fabulous, you know. I'm not having you on.' And somehow I knew she meant it and my mood lifted again.

'Oh Cat, I've so missed you.'

'Well, since you seem to have spent almost your entire time since I've been gone writing to me, I assumed you weren't exactly having a ball.'

'Is it really wonderful here, Cat? You certainly look like you've been having fun.'

'It's bliss, Mouse. Except for Madeleine the Wicked Witch, it's perfect. But I know exactly how to handle her, so there's no way she gets to cramp my style. Come on, *mon petit choux*, it's time I took you on the town.' She grabbed my bag from me with one hand, and said, 'We'll talk on the bus. I've *so* much to tell you.'

had paid her extremely generously for putting up Clar, and that the little envelope he asked me to hand to her when I arrived at her apartment contained a stash of notes to cover my stay as well.

Madeleine could only have been French. She was a tiny, doll-like little creature, no more than five foot two but with a perfect, neat figure, moulded, it seemed, from a scaled-down model of a life-sized woman. Her clothes were immaculate, but severe. She wore knee-length black or navy skirts with pale tights and low court shoes, teamed with a cream silky blouse. Her hair was cut in a short, silver bob with a thick fringe that sliced across her forehead, well above her eyebrows that had been plucked into a thin line, darkened with pencil. Her lips and nails were red.

She smelled of lemons, which suited her sharp tongue. 'You may not have a mother, but at least you have a father and a sister,' she told me. 'I have nothing and no one. No husband, no children, no siblings.' Madeleine gave the impression that the world had owed her a favour but had forgotten to give it to her. She had lived in Paris throughout the Nazi occupation of World War Two, and hinted at – without spelling out details – the privations from which she'd suffered. 'We barely had enough to eat; I had no new shoes for six years even though my feet hadn't yet stopped growing,' was as far as she was prepared to go.

Her dear brother had died on the very last day of the war, whether killed by the enemy or as a result of natural causes we never found out. It was Madeleine's way. She'd hint, but refuse to tell us the full story. Cat reckoned it was a power thing, that her holding out on us made her seem more interesting than she really was.

But she did a lot for Cat in her way. Staying with Madeleine was the equivalent of going to finishing school.

Madeleine worked in fashion for a large American buying house. It was her job to visit all the fashion houses in Paris as well as to go to the prêt-à-porter shows. She even secured a meeting with Karl Lagerfeld, or rather one of his senior assistants at Chloë, the couture house for which he was chief designer. While Madeleine and Cat were being shown around the atelier, Lagerfeld sashayed by and greeted Madeleine as though she were a friend, pecking her ostentatiously on both cheeks.

'I was so excited I almost wet my knickers,' recounted Cat. 'Karl Lagerfeld. Imagine. And when Madeleine told him that I wanted to be a designer he said that if I were to prove myself at college he'd consider taking me on either for a summer or even as an apprentice.

'And the shows. Oh God, the shows. Yves Saint Laurent, fab, fab, fab. Dior, far out. Kenzo, radical. Sonia Rykiel, *so* groovy. Sonia Rykiel is wild – she actually read out a poem as the soundtrack to her show – that was so cool, even though I didn't understand a word of it – and she has this amazing red hair, and all the seams of her knitwear are on the outside rather than the inside. Isn't that brilliant? Inside-out clothes. I'm going to dye my hair the same colour as hers when I get home – I'd do it here but Madeleine would kill me if I messed up her bathroom. You can help me do it, Mouse.'

I'd seen Cat this excited many times, but there was something new about it: it had an air of substance as well as hysteria. How lucky Cat is, I thought, to know what she wants to do and exactly how she's going to go about it.

'Sure I'll help dye your hair, but I don't suppose you could stop calling me Mouse and start calling me Hannah. Please, Cat.'

'But you are Mouse, Mouse. And I'm Cat. And together we're Cat and Mouse. We go together like Noddy and Big Ears, or Simon and Garfunkel or Bourne and Hollingsworth. It's what we are and it's never been any different. Why would you want to change it now?'

'I don't want to change it now, I've never wanted to be Mouse. And you can say we go together but at least Cat is your real name, whereas Mouse . . .'

'Look, I'll do a deal. I won't call you Mouse in front of other people, just when we're together. All right?'

'I don't see why—'

'It's as far as I'm prepared to go. I want to tell you about Kenzo. He's Japanese. He makes these incredible prints in these far-out colour combinations. He's a genius. He's got this boutique, Jungle Jap, we're going to go there together.

Yves Saint Laurent and Karl Lagerfeld are geniuses, too. Oh God, they're all geniuses. How am I ever going to be as good as them?'

The moment to discuss the future of my life as Mouse had passed. I was in Paris. The French for mouse was *la souris*. Somehow it sounded better in French.

'. . . So we'll go to Jungle Jap. And Galeries Lafayette. And Les Puces, the flea-market, really early in the morning. They've got all this vintage gear from the twenties, thirties and forties, and it's cheap, cheap, cheap. Oh yes, and Le Drugstore . . .'

'What drugs?'

'Fear not, Miss Goody Two-Shoes. It's not a place to buy drugs, though I wouldn't be surprised if you could. It's a kind of bar-cum-restaurant with shops and stuff. It's the best. It's kind of American but also kind of French. You just chill out there and have hamburgers and milkshakes and everyone's young and cool and there are so many boys to choose from. French students, American students, Germans, Swedes . . . Pick-up spot *numero uno*. We're going to have a ball—'

'Café de Flore,' I interrupted. 'And the Eiffel Tower and croissants and Notre Dame and steak with *frites* and Sacre Coeur and baguettes and the Louvre. And a boat along the Seine. And I want to see men selling onions wearing berets. Do they really exist other than on postcards?'

'*Mais oui, ma souris*, they do. And organ grinders. I shall be your guide. And I will cook you a steak with my very own hands. Madeleine taught me. You have to eat it *bleu*, which is blue which means rare. All red and bloody.'

I pretended to gag, but it really did sound disgusting.

'It's amazing, I'm telling you. And you eat it with a green salad with vinaigrette. Madeleine showed me how to make the dressing – oil and vinegar and a little mayonnaise and mustard and garlic and salt and pepper. She says the English don't have a clue when it comes to cooking. And you're going to eat *moules* and *escargots*.'

'Which are . . .'

'Mussels and snails.'

'I'm not.'

'You are. Even if I have to force-feed you. And I'll show you how to pick out the snails with a pin, and to mop up all the lovely garlicky butter they're served with. It's heaven here, you'll see.'

And it was. And I did eat *moules* and *escargots* and bloody steak, and after the first tentative taste I loved them all. And I did sit in cafés that great writers had sat in before me, and although I didn't spot any poets or film stars I could conjure them up quite easily. And the sun shone a lot of the time, and we sat on top of the Bateau Mouche together and went down the end of the boat to find a corner on our own so we could sing our own version of 'I Love Paris'.

'I love Paris in the springtime,' screeched Cat, and I replied, even more tunelessly, 'I love Paris all the year.'

And then together, 'Why on earth do I love Paris? Because I first kissed here.'

And it turned out to be true. I met him at Le Drugstore, just as Cat had predicted. He was French, he was a bit of a hippy with dark shoulder-length hair, and he was reading

English Literature at the Sorbonne. How could I not fall for a boy with such credentials?

Cat and I were sitting opposite one another having milkshakes in one of the booths and these two guys, both in sexy black-leather motorbike jackets, came over and one of them, pulling a Gauloise from a packet and placing it between full, sulky lips said, in meltingly melodic English, 'Do you 'ave a light?'

Cat and I both giggled, because we knew it was the corniest line possible and that if they smoked they'd have one of those cool Zippo lighters that everyone had and they were just trying to chat us up. And of course when Cat said she didn't have a light, which was just a way of testing them as she never went anywhere without fags and matches, surprise, surprise, out came a Zippo from a back pocket of a pair of faded Levis, by which time the guys were already sidling their bottoms into our booth.

Jean-Christophe, the one who asked for the light, and who seemed to have already chosen me, was studying English, and his friend, Michel, was also at the Sorbonne, studying classical music, but he played in a jazz band, too. They wanted us to go on to a movie. There was something about Jean-Christophe, with his silky hair and his earring and dark stubble and ban the bomb T-shirt and of course his French accent and leather jacket, that made me feel quite weak. This was an entirely new sensation to me. And because I was in Paris and everything seemed possible I wasn't quite as Mouse-like as usual. Or maybe I was, and it just wasn't very important for me to say much as I was pretty and I was English, and that's all I needed to be to make me a bit special in the eyes of a French boy on the make.

So Cat rang Madeleine and said we were going to a movie and we might be back late, and Madeleine said that unless we were home by 11 o'clock she'd lock the apartment door from the inside, and Cat told the boys that and they laughed. But in any case we had enough time for the cinema. The film was Bunuel's *The Discreet Charm of the Bourgeoisie*, a completely off-the-wall movie like nothing I'd ever seen before, having grown up an Odeon rather than an art-house girl. It seemed to be about a group of people trying to get together for a dinner party and weird things constantly thwarting their attempts, like the guests arriving while their hosts were making love in the garden. But I wasn't really concentrating anyway, because about five minutes after the film had started Jean-Christophe's arm had snaked its way around my shoulder. I turned to my left to see what Cat was up to, and she was already snogging. Five minutes later I was, too.

And even though I was going to be sixteen in two days time, this was my very first snog, and it was all right. Better than all right actually. And when Jean-Christophe put his hand on my thigh, over my gypsy skirt, and started bunching it up in his hand to get to the hem, so he could put his hand up my skirt, I wanted him to do it, but I stopped him, because I thought I should, even though I got the feeling that Michel's hand had gone well and truly past the hem of Cat's skirt a good twenty minutes earlier. And then I pulled back to look at the screen and saw what looked like a corpse lying on a table in a restaurant and I thought that what I was doing was a lot less disturbing and a lot more arousing than the film. And at some point, when Jean-Christophe tried his luck for what must have been the fourth time, I let him, and when his hand reached right between my legs, right to where my skin met my knickers, I involuntarily squeezed my thighs together and let him play with his fingers between my legs until my insides felt achy and full and swollen, and it was so good that I couldn't deal with it any more and pulled his hand away again. And then Jean-Christophe took my hand and placed it on his crotch, right over his penis, which was hard, and I could feel the heat of it, even through his jeans. I left my hand where he'd placed it, unmoving, as though it were frozen, but when he started to wriggle beneath me I quickly removed it again, and he must have realised it was about as far as I was prepared to go, because we went back to snogging and that was that until the lights came up.

As we were leaving the cinema, Cat whispered, 'You should see your mouth, Hannah. You look like you've been stung by a bee.'

That night, behind the curtain that cut the living room in Madeleine's apartment in two, in the part that housed the two narrow day-beds and doubled up as our sleeping quarters, Cat said, 'So what do you say, Mouse?'

And I replied, 'I say goodnight.' And I went to sleep with a smile on my face.

Our time together in Paris sped by. We wanted to be with Jean-Christophe and Michel as much as we could, so we did shops and galleries and sightseeing without them, then went to find them outside the university in rue Victor Cousin when they'd finished their studies for the day. There was nothing we could do about Madeleine's 11 p.m. curfew, and even Cat wasn't going to disregard her rules because Madeleine was quite capable of telling Cat to take the next plane home, but there were more than enough hours in between for us all to be together, to discover the smoky dives of my fantasies and for my crash-course in sexual education to be completed.

To reach Jean-Christophe and Michel's grungy eyrie at the top of a crumbly old house, which was tucked inside a courtyard that was invisible from the street, we had to take the metro from Odeon to Pigalle. Pigalle was the city's sleaze headquarters where jazz clubs, cinema houses showing porn, strip joints and hostess bars huddled together companionably and prostitutes roamed the streets with a swagger that suggested ownership of the very cobbles on which they walked.

The flat smelled of cigarettes and garlic and damp towels; paint and plaster were peeling off the walls, and some of it just lay in slabs on the floor, undisturbed, where it must have fallen months if not years before. Cinema posters of the *nouvelle vague*, from films like Truffaut's *Jules et Jim* and Jean-Luc Godard's *Alphaville*, – none of which, to J-C's horrified amazement, I'd seen – were half-pinned to the walls. Ashtrays, pilfered from cafés and slipped discreetly into the pockets of J-C's army surplus greatcoat, were piled high with cigarette stubs, and perched on the orange crates which doubled as a coffee table. Empty wine bottles stuffed with candles dripped wax amazed how easily and naturally I let it happen, how I had abandoned my prim propriety and was prepared to go all the way with the first boy to kiss me and in less than a week from when we first met. So when Jean-Christophe exclaimed, 'Merde!' just moments after he had broken through my virginity, I was too absorbed in the short, sharp stab of pain of entry and the general intensity of it to translate and realise that things weren't going to plan. Even when he withdrew suddenly just as I thought we were beginning, and even when I realised he had ejaculated inside me, which he had explained he wouldn't, I didn't really take it in. I was more concerned that I'd put J-C into a bad mood than anything else. So I suggested we light another joint and pretty soon he seemed to have forgotten all about the fact that he hadn't worn a condom and had come inside me; and we curled up together and stared at the ceiling until Cat poked her head around the curtain that divided us from one another, as in Madeleine's flat, and grinned, saying, 'Curfew time.'

The next day I went home to London and started writing letters, to Cat, but also now to Jean-Christophe.

He never replied, not once. And two weeks later, when my period was due, I didn't worry about it. I was far more concerned that J-C hadn't written. And it was another two weeks before the possibility of it even occurred to me. That I wasn't going to get my period. That I was in deep, deep trouble. That I was sixteen years old. And that I was going to have a baby.

Chapter Twelve

Maybe I was imagining it. Didn't I read somewhere that flying could play havoc with your menstrual cycle? And I'd been to Paris after all. It wasn't far, but it was flying. As for J-C he'd hardly been inside me for a minute. But then I wasn't completely stupid; I did know it's not about how long someone's been inside you, it's about what they leave behind. I'd always thought sex was a bad idea, I knew I didn't want – or need – it. Until, that is, Jean-Christophe turned up and it seemed so easy, so natural. And now look where it had got me. Then again, I told myself, it's not that unusual for girls to miss a period. I remembered the word for it: amenorrhoea – meaning absence of menstruation, from the Greek '*a*' meaning no, plus '*men*', month, and *rhoia*, flow. Literal translation: no monthly flow. Why couldn't I just shut up with the Greek? What was the bloody point? 'No monthly flow' meant 'yes several weeks pregnant.'

On the other hand I'd lost a bit of weight lately. Janet told me once that if you lost loads of weight, like skinny minny Sarah in our class did, you could stop getting your periods altogether. Girls were starting to talk about something called anorexia, an actual illness that made you think you were fat when you were thin and caused you to stop wanting to eat. Even to starve yourself to death. But I'd lost only a couple of pounds and I hadn't gone off my food although I had nearly thrown up once or twice when I tried to eat my breakfast before dashing off to school. Maybe I had anorexia.

Who was I trying to kid?

I made a decision. The decision was to wait. To wait until my next period was due and if it didn't come then I'd do something about it. I'd tell Janet. And then what? I was supposed to be revising for my O Levels. Every night I would come home determined to study to take my mind off the possibility that I might be . . . I couldn't even say the word to myself any longer. I stared at the books for hours and hours and hours, nothing sinking in, not even sure afterwards if it had been a maths book or a geography book that I'd had in front of me for all that time.

My father was at the casino most evenings. Carmen would prepare something for me to eat – delicious tortilla or paella or spicy fish stew. I'd push the food round my plate and barely touch it. One evening when my dad was in he said: 'You're looking a bit off-colour. Are you feeling all right?'

'Just a bit nervous about the exams,' I lied.

'Well, a bit less burning the midnight oil and a bit more sleep might be a good thing.'

'Yes, Dad, you're probably right.'

'And you need to eat properly. That's what Carmen's here for. We're lucky she's such a great cook. CAAR . . . MEN,' he roared, in the direction of the kitchen. Carmen instantly appeared in the doorway leading into the morning room, wiping her hands on her apron and fixing my father with her broadest smile, revealing two missing bottom teeth.

'Carmen, you need to feed Hannah up, you understand? You need to make her eat.'

'*Si, señor*, I try . . . She no good girl. I no understand no eat . . .'

'Are you missing your sister?' asked my dad more gently, turning back towards me.

'Yes, Dad, lots.'

'Look, I do know it's hard for you, it's hard for all of us, without your mother. We just have to try as best we can. And all things considered, I guess we're not doing too badly.'

'No, Dad, not too badly.' I reached across the table to take his hand, which was still wrapped around his fork.

'Do you speak to Mavis much these days?'

'Not as much as I used to and not as much as I should. It's just there's so much else going on.'

'Mavis always *adored* you, you know that,' he said, with such emphasis in his voice on the word *adored* that I realised he understood, that he was trying to acknowledge the depth of our special relationship. 'And aren't I right in thinking that you used to confide in her?'

'Always.'

'And now . . .?'

'Well, not really. But I'm sixteen. I'm supposed to know what I'm doing by now.' I managed a feeble little laugh, aware of the ridiculousness of that remark, given my current situation. My dad must have sensed my help-lessness.

'Oh my poor Hannah. Just because you lost your mother, you're not expected to be grown-up, not fully anyway, not just yet. Do you know what I need right now, Hannah?'

'A top-up?' I replied, eyeing his near-empty whisky tumbler.

'No, not a top-up, you silly girl, a cuddle. Come and sit on my lap like you used to.' He moved his chair back from the table to make room for me and I went over and sat on his lap. I put both arms around his neck and burrowed into it to stifle the sobs that racked my body.

'That's all right, my girl,' he said. 'A good cry is just what you needed.' He probably thought I was crying for my mother. And in a way perhaps I was. I stayed in that position for a long time, nestled into my father. Maurice was a big man with a big head and a big neck and big arms that made me feel tiny and protected.

'Dad,' I asked, when I'd calmed down sufficiently to speak, 'can you explain to me about Mavis?'

'Explain what?' he asked, suddenly defensive, as if I'd accused him of something.

'Like why Mummy hated her, and why, if she hated her, we kept her for so long.'

'Well, your mother was very fragile, particularly so both before and after you were born, and when you all got back from Switzerland she was quite emotionally exhausted so it made sense—'

to give the casino a night off. I've been winning so much money off them lately I should think they'd be quite relieved if I fail to turn up this evening.'

He smiled at me, but looked distracted. He's playing for time, I thought, working out what to say. For sixteen years no one had mentioned Switzerland, except in reference to my grandparents. Switzerland had slipped everyone's mind, just as it had slipped back in again now. I was going to get an answer about Switzerland, once he'd filled his whisky glass, once he'd had the chance to concoct a convincing story. But surely you don't forget something like that. It made no sense at all.

When Dad returned he was humming 'The Hills Are Alive With the Sound of Music' . . . I could feel myself being manipulated before he'd even begun to speak. He was working up to turning Switzerland into an amusing little anecdote . . .

'I can't believe we've never talked about Switzerland before,' said my dad, trying to be both casual and incredulous at the same time. 'It's where you were born. Surely you remember us telling . . .'

'Born! I don't believe it. Dad, don't you think I would remember something as big as that if you'd told me? I didn't even know I'd been to Switzerland, ever. We were always talking about going to visit Grandma and Grandpa, but it never happened. No one ever said I'd been there before, was actually *born* there . . .'

'But of course you were born there. Your mother went when she was pregnant with you, she went with Mavis . . .'

'With Mavis! This is getting more incredible by the second. Mavis has never mentioned it either. It's beginning to sound less *The Sound of Music* and more like *The Godfather*.'

'What do you mean, *The Godfather*?' grinned my father, looking pleased to have got onto more comfortable footing.

'I mean *omerta*, the Mafia oath of silence. All that swearing-to-secrecy stuff amongst the clan. Why didn't anyone ever tell me?'

'Don't make such a fuss,' said my dad, cross now. 'We couldn't exactly have told you when you were born, could we, and by the time you were old enough to understand, it just wasn't on our minds. It was irrelevant. You were born there, you came home. End of story.'

'But *why* was I born in Switzerland, Dad? Surely I deserve an explanation.'

'It's straightforward enough, darling. Your mother had had a difficult first pregnancy and birth with Cat, and her psychological as well as physical health were poor. So we thought it would be a good idea for her to spend a few months in Switzerland with her parents, relaxing in the mountain air. Plus, the hospitals and doctors there had such a good reputation. Cat wasn't yet at school, and I was working all hours to get the business going, so I couldn't give your mother any attention at all. There was no need for Mummy to be at home, not if it would be better for her health to be close to the mountains, and if she could be looked after for a while by her own mother. She missed her mother terribly. Mavis went to help with Cat and to bring you all back once Mummy was strong enough to travel after you were born.' He folded his arms and jerked his shoulders downwards decisively, in a way that suggested he'd successfully completed his story.

'But how come not even Cat has ever talked about it?'

'Because she was barely three, that's why. By the time you were old enough to talk about it together she would have forgotten she'd been there.'

It did all seem feasible, I supposed. Everything had always been about doing what was best for my mother. But I still couldn't understand why no one – not my mother, not my father, not Mavis, not Cat – had ever talked about it. And how come, if my mother missed her own mother so much, they never saw one another again after I was born?

We seemed to have exhausted the subject of Switzerland. I could tell my father had had enough. If I went on and on about it, he might move from irritation to anger, and I didn't want to ruin this rare moment of intimacy. Maybe Mavis would be more forthcoming. At least, unlike my dad, she'd actually been there when I was born. Switzerland would have to wait, though it would continue to play on my mind.

'But that doesn't explain why Mavis liked me so much and was always so horrible to Cat.'

'You know what Cat's like. She's what you girls would call a bit of a drama queen. I'm sure Mavis wasn't horrible to her, just a bit short-tempered sometimes. Cat's always blown up everything out of all proportion. And because you were so quiet and smart I suppose Mavis found you easier to handle. Cat and you are polar opposites, north and south. And that's why I'm a lucky man. I have two gorgeous daughters who are equally special but entirely different.'

He smiled and looked proud and I caught a glimpse of my dad as I remembered him, from before. Dad had stopped glowing a long time ago; the lines around his eyes and across his forehead were etched deeper, and his skin – beneath the golf tan – hinted at a greyish pallor, but he still had the ability to charm me into cheerfulness with his flashes of warmth and humour. His explanation was rubbish, but I had more important things to worry about.

Without knowing it, Dad had also got one thing sorted for me. He had reminded me how I used to confide in

Mavis. She was the one person I could always trust. Just because I'd become reluctant to be too close to her since Mum died, didn't mean that she couldn't still be trusted. If I didn't get my period in the next two days, when I was due again, I was going to call Mavis and go and see her. Of course I could talk to Mavis. Mavis would know what to do. She always had before. And Dad was right about something else as well. Even if he didn't know what was troubling me, he did know that I wasn't grown-up enough to handle it on my own.

My period didn't come. I gave it four more days from when it was due, then I rang Mavis.

'Mavis, it's me, Hannah.'

'I know it's you. Just because we haven't spoken for nearly two months doesn't mean I've forgotten the sound of your voice.'

'I'm sorry, Mavis, it's just . . .'

'No sorry, no excuses and no worries. You've been busy, what with Paris an' all. Nice postcard by the way. So how's the revision going?'

'Not so good.'

'I don't hear from you for two months and all I get is a "not so good" in a voice that makes it sound like the cat's died.' Cat's died? For a second I thought she was talking about Cat, some kind of sick joke. 'The cat hasn't died, has it?' she continued. I breathed a sigh of relief.

'Mavis, I don't have a cat.'

'My point exactly.'

'I need to see you.'

'Need or want?'

'Both actually. I know it's short notice, but are you by any chance free on Saturday?'

'Don't go all posh on me, girl. Short notice . . . any chance free? When was I ever not free to see you?'

'Sorry, Mavis, it's just . . .'

'I said it before, stop the sorry, will you? Are you coming to me, or me to you, me hiding round the corner at the bus stop as usual in case your sister spots me?'

I no longer found it funny when Mavis made sarcastic remarks about Cat, but I hadn't yet worked out a way of telling her. 'Cat's still in Paris, and me to you, please. Can I stay the night?'

'Nostrils and I will be honoured.'

'Oh how is Nostrils?' I asked, immediately cheered at the thought of lying on the old sofa with Nostrils curled up on top of me, and with me stroking her silky ears to lull us both into sleep.

'She's fine, but she's been missing you. Just like me. See you Saturday, then, usual time.'

I put down the phone and placed my hands on my tummy. I could swear it was growing. Mavis would know what to do.

'Hannah, you look bloody awful. What's going on? I hope you didn't overdo it on the frogs' legs.'

I smiled weakly. 'I didn't go near the frogs' legs actually. But I did kiss a frog, and unfortunately he didn't turn into a prince.'

'Frogs who fail to turn into princes is actually quite a pet subject of mine. You can tell me about it later. Nostrils wants to say hello to you.'

I bent down on the train platform and Nostrils leapt into my arms.

'So good to see you, Nostrils. And you, too, Mavis. I missed you.'

'Now don't you start going soppy on me. I know exactly how it works. You were too busy to give me the time of day. Then something happened to upset you. Then all of a sudden you needed good old Mavis again. I'm right, aren't I?'

'You're always right,' I smiled. 'But not so much of the old. I happen to know it's your birthday in three days' time, and you're going to be thirty-seven.' I had Mavis's present with me, a set of non-stick cake tins in four different sizes – she'd love them, I was sure. Mavis shrugged.

'I may only be thirty-seven but I'm still too old to find a decent husband and have those seven kids I was promising myself. Expect my eggs have all shrivelled up and died.'

The mention of kids made my stomach lurch, and a wave of nausea rose into my throat.

'Mavis, I feel a bit funny. I think I'm going to be sick.'

'You certainly do look a bit on the green side. We'll get you back to the house as quickly as we can and get you sorted.'

I had planned to wait at least until we were seated at the table in her front room with a cup of tea. To break my news gently, with a 'Mavis, there's something I have to tell you . . .' But at that very moment a young woman, hand in hand with a toddler, and sporting a huge bump that indicated she was about to pop another baby any minute, walked by on her way to the station exit, and the enormity of it all struck me with the force of a tornado.

I grabbed Mavis's arm. 'Mavis, listen to me. Mavis . . . I've got to tell you something. It can't wait another minute.' I didn't even care who could overhear us. I had to say it, and I had to say it now.

She looked at me, glanced momentarily away towards the pregnant woman with her toddler, and back at me again.

'Oh pet, you're not, are you?'

'I think so . . .' I was trembling now, all over, even as the sun shone directly down on us.

'How far gone?'

'I've missed two periods in a row.'

'I'll kill the bastard who . . .'

'But he wasn't a bastard, and it wasn't really his fault. Mavis, you've got to tell me what I'm going to do . . .'

'Oh Hannah, I never thought it would happen to you . . . not to my Hannah.' She stumbled backwards a step and for a fraction of a second, I thought she might fall over, but she caught her footing and grabbed on to the back of the bench right behind her, sitting down heavily. She stared out past me, across the railway tracks. I waited.

When she spoke it was to herself, not me. 'Cat I could understand, she was the one who I thought was set for trouble . . . She was always asking for trouble, that one, but not . . . I could kick myself, I should have . . .'

'Mavis, I . . . You . . . You can't blame yourself, that's ridiculous.'

Mavis seemed to suddenly remember I was there. 'It's all right, luv, we'll think of something. Come on now, we can't stay here on the platform all day.' Mavis hauled herself up as though she could barely carry her own weight. I was relieved she didn't even attempt to comfort me with any form of physical contact. She must have known I'd have fallen apart, right there on the platform, if she had.

Neither of us seemed to know what to say next. We headed silently for the exit. When we were clear of the station, Mavis finally put her arm around my waist. She was a good three inches smaller than me, and as I glanced down at the top of her head I noticed her light brown hair was tinged silver at the roots and I realised for the first time that Mavis wasn't, as I had always thought, totally without vanity. She did care about her appearance. She dyed her hair. How little I still knew about her. I had always assumed that men, children, fashion, looks, meant nothing to Mavis. At that moment I saw how foolish I'd been to think Mavis was so different from other women. Looking at those silver-grey roots made me feel overwhelmingly sad. Too late for a husband and seven children, she'd said jokingly. But had she really meant it as a joke? We were each lost in our own thoughts. Not a single word passed between us as we trudged slowly towards Mavis's house and up the hill to her front door.

'You have two options, Hannah,' said Mavis, revived, sensible again, her hands clutched around a mug of steaming tea. 'You have the baby or you have an abortion.'

you're lucky in that respect. All you need is a couple of doctors to agree that you're in no fit state mentally to have a baby and bob's your uncle, you can be rid of it, and back to life as normal the following day. If that's what you want . . .'

'Of course an abortion is not what I want, but anything else is just impossible. Mavis, will you help me? Will you come with me to the doctor? We don't even have to tell my dad, do we?'

Mavis sat up straighter, as if to garner strength. 'That's not a route I'm prepared to take, Hannah. Not telling your dad is not an option. If something were to go wrong and then he were to find out . . . It doesn't bear thinking about.'

'But he'll go mad, stark staring, loony psychotic. And with Mum dead, it could finish him off. It's ages since you saw him, but I'm telling you, he's all over the place since she's been gone. He pretends to be OK, and he has all these stupid girlfriends, none of whom are more than about twelve years old, but he doesn't light places up like he used to. Can't we just go and get it done, and not tell him anything? Please, Mavis, you have to listen to me. If he finds out he'll never forgive me, I'm sure of it. He'll think I've let him down. He'll take it personally, he'll, he'll . . .'

I looked at Mavis, but she didn't seem to be concentrating. She was watching lorries hurtling past the window.

'Please, Mavis,' I pleaded. 'Please listen to me.'

'I am listening, Hannah,' she replied, turning back to me again. 'But I'm thinking as well. How do you really feel about abortion? It's not a light thing to enter into.'

'Do you mean women's right to choose and all that?'

'Yes, the moral side, the right or wrong side, rather than the practical one.'

'Well, we had this debate in school, and nearly everyone said that if you wanted to have an abortion you should be able to and it was no one else's business. But I wasn't sure. I kept thinking that those cells would end up being a baby. Nothing to do with religion, I just kept thinking it might be wrong, it might be killing, and that we don't know and can't know. But that was then, before it happened to me. Now I don't care, I just want to get rid of it.'

'Hannah, there is another way.'

'Like what? That I tell Jean-Christophe and he asks me to marry him and I go and live in Paris happily ever after? Even if it were possible it's the last thing in the world I'd want. I don't want to ever see him again.'

'John Christopher whoever he is doesn't even come into it. But what I have to say is very serious, and you're going to have to think about it very carefully.'

'Of course I will, but I can't see that it will make any difference. I mean, I can't have a baby, I just can't.'

'What I said to you back on the platform about being thirty-seven and too old for babies and all that was true. But it's also true that I always wanted to have a baby of my own. And I would have had one at one point, but it didn't work out, and I didn't have a boyfriend who was going to stand by me and, well, never mind about that, but the fact is I'm single and childless and I'm not likely to meet anyone now, and even if I did it would probably be too late.'

Mavis wasn't making much sense; I didn't know what she was getting at. It wasn't like Mavis to go on about herself, and this wasn't about her anyway, it was about me, so I couldn't understand why was she doing this. The likelihood of my pregnancy – who was I kidding? I didn't need a test to know I was well and truly in the club – had obviously really got to her. It seemed to be reminding her of everything she didn't have. Perhaps that's what she was trying to tell me. Perhaps she'd had an abortion once and now regretted it.

'It's so unfair,' I said. 'You would love to have a baby and it would make everything in your life great. And I would hate to have a baby and it would completely ruin my life. It's all wrong. It's not fair.'

'Life rarely is . . .' said Mavis, tailing off again and gazing into the middle distance.

And then it struck me, with pure, crystal clarity.

'Oh my God . . . Oh my God . . . Mavis, I want to, I want to have . . .'

Mavis once again looked back at me. I felt she could read my thoughts. I could have sworn she knew exactly what I was thinking, and that what I was thinking she was thinking. But she wasn't going to be the first to say it. Neither of us could find the words. It was too immense. Too crazy. Too impossible . . .

'Mavis, I, I . . .'

'Yes, Hannah. : . . .'

'Mavis, you know how you looked after me as a child . . .'

'Not likely to forget, am I?' Mavis smiled, looking more like the Mavis who had all the answers, the Mavis who would sort everything out.

And then I found the words, the ones I'd never dared to speak before. 'You know I always thought you were more like a mother was supposed to be than my own mother . . .'

Mavis didn't seem to find this as momentous a declaration as I did. 'Well, that wasn't so hard given your mother's funny ways . . . but she couldn't help herself, you know.' For perhaps the first time Mavis was speaking of my mother without a note of criticism in her voice, with something approaching sympathy.

'Yes, but I always thought you'd make a wonderful mother, it's just I never knew you really wanted to be one . . .'

'Where's this going, pet?' She knew exactly where it was going, I was sure of that.

'Mavis, it's not like sixteen-year-olds don't have babies, is it? I mean, I wouldn't be the first. And I'd be scared stiff, especially about the pain, and growing fat and everyone talking about me, and the girls at school calling me a slut, even though they're all hypocrites and have slept with loads of boys and I've only done it once, but then, you see, the minute it was born you could just take it, you could adopt it, and it would be yours, and we'd never have to tell it that I was the mother. And hardly anyone need even know about it. You'd be the baby's mother and I could still see it when I came to visit, but it would be yours. And it would all work out because you'd be so much better as a mother than me. And I wouldn't have to have an abortion and you'd have a baby.'

'We're psychic us two, aren't we?' Mavis looked at me with moist eyes.

'Telepathic, more like it.' I smiled back.

And for a moment or two we both basked in the glorious simplicity of the solution. Mavis would be happy. And it would be me, Hannah, who'd waved my magic wand and made her dreams come true. It would be my gift, my thank you to Mavis for her kindness to me for all those years. It could work, it could really work. . . . And then I thought of my dad, and of Cat, and my friends, and school, and my teachers and I felt more exhausted than I had ever felt before.

'I think I need to lie down,' I said. My arms and legs felt so heavy I could barely carry myself the few steps from the chair to the sofa where I lay down on my side, curling up into a ball, with my knees hugged to my chest.

'Mavis,' I said, 'I need to know about Switzerland . . .' But I was asleep before I could get an answer.

The next thing I knew, Mavis was gently shaking my arm: 'You've been asleep for three hours, Hannah, and I'm worried if you sleep any longer you won't sleep at all tonight.'

In the moment between sleep and wakefulness I'd completely forgotten I was pregnant. I rubbed my eyes and was flooded with images of Cat and me in Paris, sashaying down the Champs-Elysées arm in arm, laughing at Madeleine's prim pronouncements, running in and out of clothes shops together, trying on dozens of things we had no intention of buying, sitting in cafés with Jean-Christophe and Michel, filled with those inner-achy stirrings of desire. I had never felt so happy or so free. Mavis's little front room slowly came into focus and I was jolted back to reality.

'Oh Mavis, I don't know what happened . . .'

'Exhaustion. That's what happened. We've got a lot of talking to do, you and me. Lunch went cold hours ago, but it shouldn't taste too bad. We'll eat and we'll talk. You need to get something down you. After all, there are two of you to feed now . . .'

Chapter Thirteen

On 15 January 1973, I gave birth to a healthy 61b 4oz boy. Mavis was with me throughout my labour, twelve hours, no complications, in the private wing of London's Middlesex Hospital, all expenses paid by my father. I had an epidural, so was relieved of the worst of the pain. Mavis and my dad had sorted out most of the adoption papers before Frank was born. Frank was Mavis's choice of name, because Frank was her baby. Frank Horton. Frank – nothing to do with me – Horton. Frank went straight onto the bottle; there was no point in breastfeeding a baby that wasn't going home with me, that wasn't mine.

I'd managed, somehow, almost from the moment our plan had been hatched, to convince myself that the baby belonged to Mavis. It was Mavis's baby and I was merely the vessel in which it grew. I had borrowed an image from the herbs I'd grown that same spring in little terracotta pots on our back terrace. I'd filled the pots with fresh compost and sprinkled the earth with parsley and tarragon and fennel seeds. Like those pink pots I was a necessary container to enable the seed inside me to flourish, but I was as little connected to what grew within me as those sprouting herbs were to the clay that surrounded them. It wasn't a very convincing argument, I know, but in the absence of a better one it helped for me to think of myself that way. As long as I visualised myself as a vast terracotta urn, a human-sized version of those pots, I could ignore the fact that my body was feeding as well as containing the thing that grew inside it.

There were other lies I told myself, too. Like I didn't care that J-C had never replied to those early letters I sent him on my return from Paris. After I knew, for sure, that I was pregnant, I stopped writing to him. I wiped the slate clean of him. Even if I'd thought, for that short, blissful period in Paris, that I was in love with him, the fact that I was carrying his baby killed both lust and love, replacing it at first with regret and ultimately indifference. I hoped the baby, boy or girl, wouldn't look like him, that there would be no traces of J-C in Mavis's baby. Even in my most private thoughts I would only allow myself to think of the baby as belonging to Mavis. If, even once, I uttered the words my and baby in the same breath, everything might change, and I couldn't afford for that to happen.

Mavis had been the one to tell my father. When I got home that Sunday night after telling her of my pregnancy, she had rung and arranged a meeting. They'd met the following Wednesday and talked things through. How long they'd spent together and what passed between them, I had no idea. When my father came home that Wednesday evening, I was sitting in the morning room, speaking aloud to myself in faltering French in preparation for my O Level oral the next day, trying to distract myself from the explosion that was sure to follow. I heard my father's key in the lock and felt I was about to faint.

I didn't go to greet him, I was paralysed on my seat. I heard him clear his throat, then the slight rustling of a jacket as he removed it and placed it on the coat stand in the hall. Then he went into the downstairs loo. After a minute or so I heard the flushing of the chain and the sound of running water. And then a door opening and closing and the sound of footsteps coming towards me. I held my breath.

He came into the morning room and still I didn't dare to move or even look up at him. I could see a pair of grey-flannel trousered legs in front of me as he pulled out a chair and brought it close to me. He sat down.

'Look at me, Hannah,' he said. 'Turn your chair towards mine.'

I shuffled my bottom and the chair in his direction, without properly getting up and still without looking up. I focused on his knees, directly opposite, close almost to touching. He shifted position, his knees brushed mine, and I shuddered.

'Give me your hands,' he said. I stretched out my arms and he took one of my hands in each of his.

'Look at me, Hannah,' he said. 'You have to look at me.'

My hands were shaking and still I couldn't look.

'I'm not angry, my darling. Not angry at all.'

My head shot up from its hanging position. So he wasn't going to try to kill me. He wasn't even going to hit me or scream at me. Not angry, he had said it himself.

It was safe to look at him. In his eyes I saw only pain and

compassion. I wanted him to close them and let me kiss his eyelids, kiss the pain away.

'I blame myself entirely, Hannah. You had no proper direction, no proper knowledge.'

I said nothing. First Mavis blamed herself. Now my father blamed himself. What about me? Wasn't I to blame?

'This wild idea of yours. Did it come from you or Mavis?'

'It came from both of us. It's as though we both thought of it at exactly the same moment.'

'That's what Mavis told me, too. It's still early days, Hannah. I know how to arrange a private abortion, it's an easy thing. No one would know anything about it. You could get back to your life, forget all about it. Enjoy yourself, as a teenager should.'

'I want Mavis to have the baby. She would give it all the love it needed.' I was surprised at the steely determination in my voice. For once not cowered or Mouse-like at all.

'You need to understand something, Hannah. Giving away a baby is no small thing. You may think it's nothing now, but you won't think that once it's born, once you see it as a living person. And you won't be able to take it back in ten years' time either. Once this baby belongs to Mavis, it's hers for life.'

'I know that, Dad. It's what I want.'

'You know that in your head,' sighed my dad, 'but I'm worried about your heart. About the consequences. Everything has consequences.'

'This baby means nothing to me,' I said coldly. 'What would I want with a baby? But to give a baby to Mavis, it would mean everything to her . . . it's what's right. All that time she cared for me.'

'If only your mother were alive . . .'

That was when I totally lost control.

'And what difference would that make?' I screamed, wresting my hands from his. 'She was useless. Useless, useless, useless.' I batted my arms like a bird, panicked by the small space in which it finds itself trapped, with nowhere to fly to. 'She didn't care about anyone or anything, other than herself. Oh I'm quite sure she wouldn't have wanted me to give this baby to Mavis, but would she have looked after it herself? That's a joke, isn't it? She couldn't even look after us. So she'd be all in favour of an abortion, wouldn't she? Just to tidy it all away. Get rid of the mess and pretend it had never happened.' The taste in my mouth was as bitter as the words that spewed out of it.

My dad stared straight back at me, but he was composed.

'You judge your mother too harshly, Hannah. She wasn't a bad person; she had her own problems, problems that weren't her fault. As for me, I've done so many things wrong, things I can never do anything to put right. So who am I to decide for you? For the first time in my life I can't make a decision. I can't make you abort this baby, I'm not even going to try. But if you want to, I'll arrange it; it can be organised in a matter of days.'

My anger dispelled in an instant. It hadn't even been warranted. My father had already decided to let me decide. Had Mavis begged or pleaded or reasoned? Or had she simply told him what to do? It seemed out of character for my father, a man so used to taking charge. And yet Mavis had seemed so confident that she could 'sort my father out'. It was almost like she had some kind of hold over him. Is that why she had stayed for all those years? Or was I just being melodramatic, dreaming up stories from thin air? In the end it hardly mattered; he was going to let me go ahead and have the baby.

And so it was all agreed. My father and Mavis came to an arrangement. He would pay the difference between what Mavis could get for selling her workman's cottage and the cost of something more suitable for her and the baby. He'd also pay Mavis a regular allowance from now on, to cover the cost of bringing up the child. It was a whole area I hadn't even given consideration to. The practicalities of the situation, the fact that somebody would actually have to pay for this baby's upbringing had never even crossed my mind. That's how naive I was when I decide to make Mavis the gift of a child.

Cat's reaction, when she arrived home a month later, could have been predicted. She was furious with Jean-Christophe for his contraceptive ineptitude, but when she heard what had been agreed, she walked out the house with the suit-case she'd not yet had time to unpack after Paris, and didn't come back for an entire week. She made one call to say she was safe and staying with a friend and that was all we heard from her until she decided to come home again.

'It's like a pact with the devil,' she hissed at me on her return, without even bothering to say hello. 'I never want to talk about your pregnancy, or this creature, ever again. I don't want to see it when it's born or know anything about it, ever. Not ever, do you understand? And when you've had it, we'll pretend you haven't and get on with our lives again. All right?'

What could I say? 'All right,' I replied. And we never did talk about it again. For the next few months Cat virtually disappeared from my life, not bothering to tell me what she was getting up to and with whom, not sharing any of the intimacies we'd so enjoyed in Paris. It always seemed to be like this with Cat. One minute we were the best of friends, the next we were sworn enemies. I missed her more now that we were back sharing the same house than I had when she was away in Paris. Friends at a distance was better than adversaries at close range.

Despite the dramas of my life, I sat my O Levels and passed all nine, all with top grades. It was decided that I would take a year off from school, then enrol in college to do my A Levels, after the baby was born. In the meantime, until such time as my bump became impossible to disguise, I could go and help my dad in the factory. Then, just at the last moment, in what was to be my last week working for him – I dreaded the thought of the three months before the baby was due with nothing to do and nothing other than the terrifying prospect of labour to look forward to – my dad had a change of heart. He said I could carry on working for him as long as I wanted, and damn the gossipmongers.

'The girls can say what they like, it's nobody's business but our own.'

Unsurprisingly the girls had already worked out for themselves that I was pregnant. Enough of them had experienced teenage pregnancies of their own to spot the signals, and not to castigate or judge me for making a mistake that could happen to anyone. What they couldn't understand was why I wasn't getting rid of it.

Once it was all out in the open, it became a favourite topic on the factory floor. All I'd say was that I couldn't go through with an abortion because it just felt wrong and that the adoption had been arranged and the baby would go to a good home.

'You're a braver girl than I'd be in your position,' said Sandy, the polka-dot queen.

'My dad chucked me out when he found out I was up the duff,' said Chrissie who, according to my dad, was his very best machinist.

'It was my stepdad wot made me pregnant,' said Bel casually, and a collective gasp went round the room.

'What happened?' asked Chrissie, as everyone downed tools and sat open-mouthed.

'I had an abo of course, and my mum threw him out, didn't she? Best result I could have hoped for, I suppose, as he was bound to get started on my little sister soon enough. I mean, what was the point of accusing him of rape and dragging 'im off to court? The judge would've said I was asking for it. That's what they always say if you wear a short skirt and like going down the pub. Which I do.'

'It's all about men, isn't it?' grumbled Chrissie. 'They've got all the power. It's men who rape, men who get you pregnant and go swanning off as if it was nothing to do with them, men in the courts who decide if you were asking for it and men who own the factories and pay your wages.

Your dad is a one-off, Hannah,' said Chrissie, looking at me, 'but it's still him what has the power.'

These girls, some not so much older than me, seemed so savvy in comparison. In a way I envied them both their common sense and their camaraderie. As for power, male power, it was something I'd never thought about before. They were right of course. Working in the factory during my pregnancy, sharing so many things with Chrissie and Sandy and Bel and the rest of them, planted all sorts of possibilities in my mind. One day, I thought, when all this was out of the way, I'd like to have some power of my own. After university, maybe I could even start my own business, and not just give the girls who worked for me a decent wage, but let them share the profits as well. And let the ones with kids work the hours they wanted.

Making new friends, daydreaming about the faraway future when I would become a successful entrepreneur, is probably what saved me during those difficult months.

'What about your dad, then, Hannah? How did he react?' asked Sandy.

I was on sewing-machine duty only because one of the girls was off sick. Although I enjoyed my regular despatch and back-office work, the factory floor was best of all.

'He just went along with what I said I wanted to do. I was amazed really. I thought he'd go crazy.'

'You don't know how lucky you are,' said Chrissie. 'I'd count your blessings if I were you.'

I was feeling pretty *un*lucky at the time, but I could see what Chrissie meant. It would be so easy to bleat on about being motherless, sixteen and pregnant and with a sister who, having loved me for about five minutes, could barely bring herself to talk to me. Or I could count my blessings as Chrissie suggested. So I started counting them. For a start, in the absence of my sister's support, I had the girls at work, and I had Janet, ever-loyal Janet, and Janet's mum, who treated me as one of her family. And Mavis of course. And my dad. That was five blessings just for starters.

We became so much closer at that time, my dad and I, driving to and from the factory together, five days a week, him telling me about every aspect of the business. About buying materials and profit margins and returns policy and what makes a good salesman and stock-taking and book-keeping. I found every aspect of it fascinating. Compared to some of those girls in the factory I came to realise I was probably very lucky indeed. I sensibly kept quiet about the private hospital my dad had lined up, the allowance he was going to pay Mavis for bringing up his daughter's illegitimate child, the flat he was going to finance. For these girls, getting pregnant in such circumstances would be like winning the Pools. With all that back-up they'd probably want to keep their babies and bring them up themselves.

'If you tell yourself something is true often enough,' Janet had said to me once, 'eventually, no matter how ridiculous it is, you can start to believe it.' That, I guess, is what I did. As my belly grew I convinced myself that I was lucky. I even began to believe I'd planned the whole thing, that I'd done it for Mavis.

Not everyone was as kind as the girls from the factory. From having spent most of my life to date feeling invisible, I now felt like an exhibit in a freak show. Neighbours and local shopkeepers had stopped nodding their good mornings or good afternoons at me, and muttered inaudibly at my bump instead. Girls from my old school greeted me quite normally as I waddled by the bus stop where they were waiting for the 240, but as soon as I'd passed them the giggling and snorting would begin.

A couple of boys from the upper sixth form cycled by one day when I was seven months pregnant and having a day off work for a hospital visit, screeching their brakes to a halt when they saw me. One of them was an acne-infested moron called Keith, who had endlessly pestered me to go out with him the previous year, and each time I'd come up with an increasingly elaborate excuse. Eventually he gave up, and by way of revenge had gone round the school telling everyone I was a slag. When he stopped his bike he eyed my belly and smiled slyly, 'Hi there, Hannah.'

On the off-chance he was just being friendly I replied, 'Hi there, how're you doing?'

'Who'd have thought?' he said, ignoring me now and addressing his friend. 'From Little Miss Stuck-Up to Fat Miss Fuck-Up.' Keith thought he was hilarious, and so did his mate. 'And I always thought you were the type to like it doggy-style,' he continued, smirking and turning back to me again, '– but a little birdie, Janet I think it was, told me you prefer it froggy-style.'

My face burned with humiliation and I waddled on as fast as I could while they cracked up behind me. There was no way Janet would ever say such a thing, I was sure of that. At first Janet had thought I was mad to keep the baby, but once I'd explained myself she just accepted it and appointed herself as my personal bodyguard. If Janet had been at my side when those bully-boys cycled up, she'd have probably tried to punch them on the nose. Apart from the factory and round to Janet's, I went out as little as possible.

Mavis wanted me to go shopping with her to buy all the stuff for the baby, but I couldn't bear the thought of watching Mavis going gooey over baby clothes and cots and prams. I refused to do anything that would connect me to this baby, or make me feel this baby was mine. For the majority of my check-ups at the hospital Mavis accompanied me, and if she couldn't make it because of work, Janet's mum came instead. But Mavis was there the time I had the scan. I turned my face from the monitor and refused to look at the image on the screen. When the radiographer offered me a Polaroid, I said, 'Mavis, you take it. It's yours, not mine.' Once the baby was out, I told myself, once it was in Mavis's charge, then I might be able to acknowledge its existence. Mavis would have become a mother, and I would be back to being me.

In the meantime I grew big and round and the baby kicked and somersaulted and my breasts grew sore and my legs ached, but not once did I feel an emotional connection to or even curiosity about this child inside me.

In biology lessons at school, when we'd learned about the female reproductive system, our teacher had told us about fibroids, which are benign growths in the muscular wall of the uterus. They can be as small as pea or as large as a melon. Some days I pictured a tiny pea inside me morphing slowly into a large melon. A melon I could cope with.

Mavis was with me throughout the labour. It hurt like hell until the epidural kicked in, but I was saved the agony of the last stages of labour. As soon as the cord had been cut and the baby cleaned up I insisted: 'Give her the baby. Let Mavis hold it.'

'It's a him,' said the midwife. I hadn't even asked.

Mavis took him in her arms. 'My little miracle,' she said. I lay on the bed, numb, not just in the area that had been anaesthetised by the epidural, but every bit of my body and my brain.

'My little man. My own little man,' she said, over and over. 'Isn't he the handsomest baby you've ever seen?' The staff in the delivery room nodded indulgently.

'Come on now, Hannah, don't you want to hold the baby?' said the midwife who had tended me, but who had not been filled in on the background.

'I told you, it's hers not mine.'

'It's just the shock,' she continued relentlessly, 'it happens sometimes. But holding the baby will help. As soon as you hold it, everything will change.'

'Leave me alone, please just leave me alone,' I pleaded. I closed my eyes. It was over. I'd done what I'd set out to do. Mavis had her baby and I would get my life back.

The three days in the hospital passed in a haze. Because it was a private room, and because Mavis would be taking the baby home with her, and because I refused to feed Frank myself, somehow the authorities had been persuaded to let Mavis sleep with me in the room, propped up in the armchair by my bed.

On the third day, Mavis and Frank left the hospital together in a taxi. I packed my small bag and waited for my father to collect me.

When I got home, Cat opened the door and held her arms out to me.

'Welcome back to the land of the living,' she said. 'Now we can start to have some fun together.'

She treated me as though my pregnancy had never existed. She didn't ask about the baby or what the labour was like. But she was back to being kind and loving and I was grateful.

It was six months before I could bring myself to visit Mavis and Frank in their cosy, newly built, two-bedroom flat with its communal garden complete with play area. I'd never seen Mavis look so happy. Frank was gurgling, smiling and content. He had J-C's brilliant-blue almond-shaped eyes, but in all other respects he resembled neither of us. Apart from the eyes, there was nothing about this baby to suggest a connection with me. He and Mavis were such an item, so clearly enamoured of one another, that I could hold Frank in my arms and feel nothing but pleasure that he had a happy home with a loving parent to care for him.

Mavis got a baby and I got my life back.

Chapter Fourteen

When you experience early loss – in my case first Mavis, then my mother – I think that you're always on the lookout for things to go wrong. It doesn't mean you can't be optimistic about your life, but there's this bit of you held in reserve – that's the bit you'll need to help you survive if the worst happens, the reason why even in your moments of greatest happiness you keep something back.

The five years between giving birth to Frank and meeting David at the beginning of the uni autumn term in October 1977 passed, as so many years in people's lives do, without major incident. There were neither head-dizzying highs nor stomach-thudding lows. Life was neither miserable nor ecstatic, but it became pleasurable for its take-no-chances predictability.

At a time when almost everyone around me was experimenting wildly – with drink, drugs, their sexuality, their clothes, their tastes in music – I was content to sit on the sidelines. I aspired only to the bland, the boring, the dependable. I took comfort in routine, in being on time for school, on never bunking off lessons, on having a drink but never getting drunk, of going out with boys, but never more than three times because then they'd expect sex, and they weren't going to get it, not from me.

If most teenagers felt the need to test their limits, I needed – or at least felt I needed – to do exactly the opposite. As long as everything remained calm, on an even keel, at a not too elevated level, even if it were to blow apart in an instant, the fall would not be so great.

No one at the sixth-form college I attended for my A Level studies knew about me having had a baby and most of my old school friends, with the exception of Janet, had drifted away, so I was saved having to explain myself. I made new girlfriends. We discovered wine bars, the cool new alternative to the beer-and-sweat-soaked male environment of the pub. Wine bars were a symbol of sophistication and liberation, places we could go to in gaggles, order a bottle of house red and chat for hours, places where we weren't under scrutiny for being on our own without male company. I never drank more than a single glass of wine in an evening.

My new friends didn't find me boring – I suppose a dead mother and a sister who was at fashion school but already made her own whacky clothes, which would sell as fast as she could make them from a stall in Camden Market on Saturday mornings, lent me an air of glamour. I helped Cat out on the stall most weekends and was able to prime my friends about what was coming into stock, so they could be the first to get there when the stall opened and snap up the best new designs at a discount price.

More critical than the low-key glamour that they ascribed to me was their conviction that my drabness was a pose. I encouraged them in this wholeheartedly, until it became a badge of honour.

'I'm glad to be grey,' I announced at Bubbles, a wine bar in a basement off Carnaby Street. I was stone-cold sober. I'd timed my announcement for when my girlfriends had already started their second bottle.

'Glad to be grey?' Trish eyed me sceptically. 'What are you on about?'

'Well, consider this. You all regard yourselves as cutting-edge and cool. But how can you be, if you're exactly the same as one another? You all drink. I don't. You all smoke dope and cigarettes. I don't. You have sex on the second date. I gave up sex when I was sixteen.'

'You did what?'

'I gave it up when I was sixteen.'

Trish looked at Nadia who looked at Cleo, and all three looked impressed. I realised I was on to something, something that could work to my advantage.

'I know all about drugs because my mother was an alcoholic and a junkie—'

'Wow!' said Trish.

'You're too right wow!' said Nadia. 'The only thing my mother snorts is Vick's when she has a cold.'

'– so you see,' I continued, 'I really don't need to go there. The way I look at it is that I am about the only true individual, the only one of us who's brave enough to be her own person.' I sensed I was only just within my safety margin. If I weren't very careful I could get myself black-listed by my new-found friends. It was important not to flatter myself too much or over-criticise them. I could see I was making an impact. They looked as spellbound as the under-sevens at a pantomime.

'The joys of grey. It's like a whole new philosophy. The antidote to the Beat Generation and the Swinging Sixties, the exact opposite of everything you guys believe in. It's not about dissing what you do, it's an alternative point of view. A new school of thought. I've even got a name for it: Grey Matters.'

'Bring it on, Hannah. Bring it on,' said Trish.

'OK, it works like this. Grey Matters because it involves the brain, you have to really think about it to get it; Grey also because everyone agrees that to be Grey is to be boring, and my philosophy questions the validity of this belief; and Matters, a play on matter, because it does matter, it's important. We could even start our own club, and you could be the first members.'

They were drunk, I wasn't. I was talking mostly tosh, but that night my reputation was forged.

We never did start a club – it all sounded too . . . grey, I suppose – but somehow I'd managed to convince my new friends that I was less the boring conformist, more the quirky iconoclast. I became a kind of mascot, their oddball, eccentric, incredibly normal friend. The one who'd tasted the forbidden and now had turned her back on it with cynical, world-weary eyes.

About the fact that I had turned into a bit of a boy-magnet, there was little I could do. My hair fell in a dark shiny mane to my shoulders when I bothered to straighten it, and in feminine curls when I didn't, and my inky eyes and slightly olive complexion, like my dad's, gave me an exotic, almost Mediterranean look. I used to feel so invisible, but not any more. It was really only Cat these days who could reduce me to my Mouse-like former self. I was more a glossy black olive than the lump of tofu I once imagined I resembled. It was ironic really. When I'd wanted to be noticed, I was invisible; now I wanted to be invisible, I seemed to fill people's vision, especially that of boys.

English boys often mistook me for Greek or Italian or Spanish. I think they also found my reticence more of a challenge than that posed by my up-for-anything friends. They regarded me as a tease, but they were wrong. I wasn't playing hard to get. I was impossible to get.

Where I got lucky was that my girl-gang became very protective of me. When word started to get around that I would never go beyond three dates, and that I was a bit of a frigid bitch, the kind who jumps a mile if you so much as try to put your hand on her tits, Trish and Nadia and Cleo, with my consent, started to whisper of a mysterious and dark past, of something that had happened that had turned me from a sex kitten into a born-again virgin. My reputation, far from being sullied, was enhanced. There was no shortage of boys determined that they would be the one to reawaken the Sleeping Beauty.

I took A Levels in English, History and Economics and got the grades to win me a place to study English at a northern university.

It struck me how much easier I found it to settle into life away from home than so many of my fellow freshers. The still mainly middle-class kids who went to university back then had come straight from living in a protected environment. They relished their freedom after a while, but in those first few weeks I could sense they missed home almost as much as a seven-year-old being shipped off to boarding school might. I'd come from home, but home hadn't been a sanctuary since Mavis left. There were too many shadows lurking in that house of my childhood, and being away from it suited me.

I didn't think my Grey Matters ruse would work at university level, and I was bored with it anyway by then, so I concentrated on developing other skills that would keep me out of trouble. It was my first business venture, not designed to make a profit, purely to cover costs.

The food at university was crap. Everyone seemed to live on baked beans, Mars bars and crisps. The girls went on the Pill and blew up like balloons. The boys began to lay down the stores of beer and chips that in future years would turn their bellies into footballs. No one knew how to cook, nor could they be bothered to learn.

I, on the other hand, had baked with Mavis from the age of three, and had sat patiently watching her make the simple, homely dishes at which she excelled. Armed with Jocasta Innes's *Paupers Cookbook* and a *Good Housekeeping* cookery manual I became a hostess with the mostest, cramming six or eight of us at a time around the small Formica table in the communal kitchen of our hall of residence. My beef casserole with olives was legendary; my onion, bacon and potato hotpot a masterpiece. Some of my fellow students had never tasted garlic until I came along.

What I'd do was pin a day and a time up on the main noticeboard in the entry to halls, and the first to put their names on the list would be invited to eat if they showed up. There were always drop-outs so even if someone didn't get to the top of the list they might appear on the off-chance and win a coveted place around my dinner table. The bill would be the cost of the ingredients divided by the number of people attending, all of whom were expected to bring along their own booze. It worked out hardly more expensive than the canteen, where the food was barely edible.

Now I had a new nickname: Hanny Haddock, after the far more illustrious Fanny Cradock. Yet again I managed to side-step relationships, drinking and drug-taking, but I had friends and fans, and I was content. Cooking was an effective diversion. I loved my subject, too, and found writing essays more of a pleasure than a bore.

Whenever Cat came to stay on a blow-up mattress on the floor in my cramped quarters she caused a minor sensation. By this time Cat was a punk, the classiest punk anyone had ever seen, dressed in bondage trousers made from Savile Row suiting material and ripped T-shirts in silk, held together with diamanté-encrusted safety-pins. Her Doc Martens were so shiny you could see your face in them. She wore her hair in a blonde bob with a fringe dyed shocking pink. The effect was startling, but not too alarming. Cat was a style punk, attracted to its aesthetic rather than its anarchic philosophy. She was willing to try anything once, but not washing was not an option.

'God, you guys are in need of help, fashionwise,' she told my friends on one visit as they tucked into home-made pâté and French baguettes oozing garlicky butter. 'You need to know that flinging a stripey college scarf round your neck is not a sign of fashion rebellion. What I'm going to do for you is organise a coach party and take you to Sex on the King's Road.'

My friends looked at her blankly. Who was this fabulous creature, this incredibly extrovert older sister of conservative, mild-mannered Hannah?

'You must know who Malcolm McLaren and Vivienne Westwood are.' The group nodded, although they might have been lying. 'Sex, or Seditionaries as it's now called, is the hippest, most happening store. You have heard of the Sex Pistols, haven't you? Please tell me that you have, otherwise I shall die of shame to be seated in your company.'

They lapped her up.

'I was in the front row at the Roundhouse,' she told her electrified audience as we dug into a main course of chilli con carne. 'The Stranglers came on and the first thing Hugh Cornwell did was spit at the audience. A great gob of it landed right here,' she said, pointing at her shoulder blade. Not a good look.' My friends roared with laughter. I could never emulate Cat, but I could bask in her reflected glory.

The university boys weren't really Cat's scene, not whacky or creative enough, and almost all sartorial nightmares. But she did concede that there were more straight boys at my uni than there were to be found amongst the students at art school, especially on the fashion course. And I'm sure that was what kept her coming back weekend after weekend, as soon as she'd finished on the stall, rather than the privilege of spending time with me. Half the boys I knew had slept with Cat by the time I graduated.

She'd grade them according to a good-in-bed rating. Very few got a First. Most barely achieved a Pass. If you added together my cooking and Cat's sex-kittenish ways, we were practically one perfect person.

'Good food and good sex,' Cat laughed, 'they're the only two things men want women for. And for us, it's the perfect division of roles. Me and my blow jobs, you and your blow torch.'

Cat thought it hilarious that I'd invested in a blow torch for making crème brûlée, but I had a reputation to keep up. Soon even some of the lecturers – 'lecherers more like it' according to Cat – started turning up to our soirees. Cat thought there was something incredibly sexy about men in threadbare beige-corduroy jackets with leather patches on the elbows and pipes peeking out their pockets. I found them mostly a bit creepy, especially since I knew they nearly all had wives who were quite capable of cooking for them. I would have put up an undergraduates-only notice, but Cat dissuaded me. Thank God for Cat.

It was the beginning of my third year, my second year of living out of halls, sharing a ragged Edwardian house that must have once been quite grand, with two other girls and three guys. The paint was peeling off the walls, odd windows around the house were boarded up because the landlords couldn't be bothered to replace them, and it smelled of damp. But the absentee owners' neglect was also to our advantage. They were so laissez-faire and lazy that they hadn't even bothered to sub-divide the rooms so as to cram in more students. As a result we had a huge bedroom each and a dining room which could seat twelve comfortably. I found a couple of old school-refectory tables at a sale of junk – thanks to Mavis I knew how to haggle for a bargain – and picked up an assortment of mismatched chairs. A bolt of cloth and some candles in old Chianti bottles, and my swish new restaurant was born.

It was a Saturday, Cat had come for the weekend and I was planning one of my dinner parties. It was mostly regulars but I noticed a couple of new names on the list, which these days was pinned up in college on a board to the side of the students' union bar.

I felt more comfortable with people I already knew, and Cat had already had her pick of my usual stalwarts, so I placed one of the new recruits, whose name was David, next to her. Seating plans were an important ingredient on such occasions.

The menu was French onion soup, followed by rabbit pie cooked with bacon, apple, onions and prunes, and with my famous blow-torch brûlée to finish.

My guest were arriving, each armed with a bottle of wine or maybe a six-pack of beer. One by one, after they'd come into the kitchen to announce themselves, I told them to go off into the sitting room and help themselves to drink and peanuts. I was still rolling pastry for the pie, and some of my curls, which had flopped out of the elastic band I'd tied them back with, were flecked with flour. I was always a messy cook, and each time I tried to brush my hair from my face with the back of my arm, I succeeded only in sprinkling more of it with flour. I heard a little tap on the kitchen door.

'It's open,' I shouted, not even bothering to look up.

'Hmm . . .' I heard.

'Come on in, I've almost finished this . . .'

'Mind if I watch?'

'No, do.' The voice was unfamiliar, but I had other things on my mind.

The pastry was going well. It was the right size and the right shape. I dipped my fingers into a small bowl of water on the table and moistened the rim of the dish. Then I cut an approximately one-inch strip from the edge of the pastry and positioned it around the dish's perimeter, pinching it firmly into place. Slowly, carefully, I rolled the pastry again, this time loosely back around the rolling pin so I could lift it from the board and up and over the Pyrex dish in which the rest of the pie ingredients were resting, waiting to be popped into the oven. It was a delicate manoeuvre to get the pastry into position without it tearing or collapsing, and to ensure it was centred and didn't have to be adjusted after it had been laid over the dish, making a split in the dough almost inevitable. I always held my breath at this point. Slowly I lifted the pastry above the dish as much as I dared, lowered enough of it to cover one end, then calmly unfurled the rest. *Voilà!* I stood back to admire my handiwork and once more tried to tame away the curls from my face.

'*Bravissimo!*' declared a deep and rich male voice, with a hint of laughter at its edge.

I turned to face a broad grin and smiley green eyes behind round, rimless John Lennon spectacles.

I did a little curtsey, conscious of the flour and of pinking up slightly, a combination of the effort of concentration and sudden shyness.

'*Sehr, sehr, gemutlich*,' he said, walking towards me with an outstretched hand and a perfect German accent.

'Sare what?' I asked, wiping my hands on my navy-and-white-striped chef's pinafore.

'It's German. *Sehr*, meaning very. *Gemutlich* means warm, congenial, friendly. It sums up a particular kind of welcoming atmosphere, and there isn't an English equivalent. I'm David, by the way.'

'And I'm just the hired help,' I replied. 'My name is Hannah.'

I took David's outstretched hand and he lowered and raised his head a fraction, in a barely perceptible bow.

'Are you German?' I asked.

'No, not even a bit German. But I've studied German as well as French, and I've lived in both places, so sometimes I just finding myself speaking all three languages at once.'

'Well, pleased to meet you, wherever you're from. And what are you doing here?'

'I'm lecturing. It's a temporary thing before I launch myself as an entrepreneur.'

A lecturer or a lecherer, I wondered, and found myself smiling, more to myself than to him.

'Where do I put these?'

He started to remove items from a plastic carrier bag. First a bunch of brilliant orange roses, then a box of chocolates wrapped in gold paper, and then a bottle of red wine.

'My goodness, you're generous,' I said. 'No one has ever bought flowers or chocolates to one of my dinners, let alone both. And the wine as well! Really, it's too much.'

David smiled again. 'If your cooking is as good as everyone says, it's the least you deserve. It isn't exactly the epicurean centre of the universe in these parts.'

'Did you say you wanted to be an entrepreneur?'

'Yes, one day soon, once I get a decent idea for a change.'

'Me, too,' I replied.

'You want to open a restaurant?'

'No way,' I laughed. 'As a hobby it's fun, as a business . . . absolutely not.'

'Well, maybe we should become partners.'

'Well, maybe we should. . . .' Who was he, this David? And why had he already made such an impact?

'Look,' I said, suddenly a little awkward, 'I still have a lot to do, so why don't you go next door and get yourself a drink? Once dinner's on the table, I'll be able to join in the fun.'

As soon as David was gone I popped the pie in the oven. And then I did something quite out of character. First I sneaked into the dining room and swapped the seating plan around so that David would be placed next to me. Then I went upstairs and got changed from jeans and a T-shirt into a pretty floral dress. Next I sorted out my hair and applied some lipstick and mascara. As I stroked the mascara wand against my lashes, over and over again, in tiny, repetitive motions, I was reminded of my mother, and quickly replaced the wand in its case. Why was I making such an effort for this David? I knew nothing at all about him. And yet for the first time, the first time since J-C, the first time since Frank . . . I wanted to look my best. Here was a man I was quite sure I didn't want Cat to get her claws into. At least not until I'd got to know him. Not until I was quite sure that I didn't want. . . . I dismissed further thoughts from my mind. It was time to mash the potatoes.

That evening David wrapped himself around me like a second skin. For all the attention either of us paid to anyone else we could have been quite alone together. After about twenty minutes in his company I wished we had been. At one point, when everyone had finished their soup, Cat, seated at the other end of the table, banged on it with her knife and fork.

'Compliments to the chef,' she shouted, 'but where the fuck is our second course?'

I started slightly, shifting my gaze reluctantly from David to Cat. I had completely forgotten where I was.

'Oh my God, the pie! I forgot about the pie.'

Everyone laughed, then good-humouredly joined in with Cat, banging on the table with their knives and forks, demanding the main course.

I wanted to shrug it off, to laugh along with everyone else, but I felt flustered and too much the focus of attention. I laughed, but the note was forced, off-key. David must have noticed.

'My fault entirely, for commandeering you,' he said, as I jumped up and made a frantic dash for the kitchen.

'Pass the bowls, everyone, up here to the end of the table,' I heard David call behind me. Thoughtful, I thought. And authoritative, too. I liked the way he told everyone to pass the bowls, rather than waiting for me to do all the work, which is what my lazy guests usually did.

Why couldn't I concentrate?

Pie, potatoes, sprouts, the dinner would be ruined if I didn't rescue it right away . . .

But there had been something about the fair hairs on David's forearms that I couldn't get out of my mind. They had been exposed by the rolled-up sleeves of his shirt, and just looking at them had made me think of how it might feel to brush my lips gently against what I could see would be their silky slipperiness, at odds with the muscled solidity of the forearms themselves.

Burned pie and soggy sprouts . . . not a good combination. So why I was stopping myself again, hovering in front of the oven, to remember the way his glasses steamed up from the soup, and that slightly myopic softness of his eyes when he removed them to wipe away the condensation. Eyelids that were kissable, eyelashes that were . . .

The oven. The pie. Open the door, for heaven's sake . . . I could hear his laugh travelling from the other room, quite distinct from the laughter of the others. It was the kind of full-throttle laugh you could lose yourself in, not a laugh-at-you sort of laugh, but a fully-inclusive, laugh-at-life sort of laugh.

And quite suddenly there was only one thing that mattered to me. And that was the pie. It couldn't be just any pie. This pie, of all the pies I'd ever baked, this pie had to be the best. It had to be perfect. It was essential that the pastry was meltingly light. The filling so richly flavoursome that whenever the words rabbit and pie were mentioned in the future, at any point in their lives, everyone in the room would remember the pie that Hannah Saunders, aka Hanny Haddock, that girl from uni, the one who could cook, had made on this particular night.

I crouched down and opened the oven door, eyes closed, not daring to look. I was enveloped in heat. I sniffed. No, it didn't smell burned, it smelled of the promise of good things, of comfort and contentment. In this pie lay the key to my future, I was convinced of it. I opened my eyes. It sat there on the oven shelf. My own creation, golden and gleaming. The perfect pie. My salvation.

I heard footsteps behind me and the sound of spoons and chinking china as bowls were placed in the sink.

'Well?' said David.

'It's perfect,' I smiled happily, turning towards him.

'That was my impression, too,' he said, scanning me from head to toe and back again.

'Now what can I do to help?'

'Can you mash?' I asked.

'I can try.'

'OK, so go mash. It's important to get rid of most of the lumps first, before you add anything.'

'Oh I just assumed you sloshed in the milk and butter and then mashed.'

'Well, you could, but then you'd never get rid of the lumps.'

David was bashing away like a labourer on a building site, and I found myself gazing at his forearms again.

'This is hard work,' said David, who had clearly never mashed a potato in his life, but was approaching the task with a level of enthusiasm and gusto that I thought might translate to other areas of his life as well.

'Who, by the way, was that pink-fringed crazy person? The one who seemed so at ease with telling you what to do.'

'Oh that's Cat, my sister . . .'

'Your sister! I would never have guessed in a million years. Do you always jump when she says jump?'

'I suppose I do,' I chuckled. 'But it's not like that . . .'

'Like what?'

'Well, Cat is just Cat. She's dynamic and creative and exciting and mercurial and difficult and mesmerising and . . .'

'So you're quite keen on her, then.'

'More than that . . . but it's complicated.'

'And does she appreciate you as much as you appreciate her?'

'Look, it's complicated. It would take for ever to explain . . .'

'Well, I've got for ever if you have . . .'

'Maybe another time. Pass me the colander for the Brussels sprouts, would you?'

Later that evening, Cat cornered me.

'So who's the good-looking guy you've been glued to all evening? Why did you swap places?'

'I—'

'Yes, you did, don't try to deny it.'

'Oh he's not your type at all,' I said, too quickly. 'He's very business school. Very straight. So after I'd met him in the kitchen . . .'

'Yeah, yeah, yeah. But you know something? He'd be worth a go. Maybe I could put a few kinks in him, maybe I could make him a bit more bendy and a bit less straight.'

'Cat . . .' I said.

'Cat what?'

'Please don't . . .'

Cat threw back her head and clapped her hands together gleefully.

'I was only testing you. Testing to see if you were still a pillar of salt. I do believe we're finally on the road to recovery. I shan't go near him, I swear. He's one hundred per cent yours, but if he ever hurts my little Mouse, if he ever upsets her in any way, he'll have me to contend with.'

'Oh Cat, you're not to worry, let's not even go there. I met him only two hours ago and so far all we've had is a polite conversation.'

Cat raised her eyebrows and smirked theatrically before marching off to claim her quarry in the shape of a corduroy-jacketed philosophy professor.

David stayed and helped with the washing-up. I was all heated up on the inside. At one point I straightened up from scrubbing the pots in the sink and lifted the curls at the back of my head to allow some air to freshen the perspiration-sodden back of my neck.

'I am *so* hot,' I said, tiredness beginning to overtake me.

'Don't move!' said David. 'Stay exactly as you are.'

I stood, mid-action, my arm frozen in position as the breeze from the open window began to cool me. David was right behind me and I could feel his breath closing in on the back of my neck, and then his lips resting lightly on my skin. I gasped slightly as tiny tingly sensations, like the mildest of electric shocks, sparked around the back of my head and down my spine.

'You smell so good,' he said, burrowing his nose into my hair as I let it fall.

'Garlic, sweat and onions most likely,' I replied, feeling fluttery and shy and fiery all at once.

I swung round and we kissed, deeply, hungrily and greedily, like people who'd been starved of kisses for too long. Which I certainly had. When we eventually pulled away, he asked quietly, 'Please, Hannah, may I stay?'

I put my index finger to his lips and smiled.

'You may stay, but not tonight. I need time. Quite a bit of time maybe. It's complicated.'

'You've said that three times tonight. That it's complicated. But you're right, it's too fast. I'm sorry, I couldn't help . . . It's just that . . .'

'I know exactly what it is,' I replied gently, 'but I need you to wait.'

'As long as it takes,' said David, back in command of himself. 'Would you like to go for a walk with me tomorrow?'

'I have an essay to finish for Monday, but I can do it in the evening. A walk would be lovely.'

'I'll see you in the morning, then, about eleven?'

'See you in the morning.'

But still he didn't make a move to go.

'Goodnight, David. And thank you for all your help.'

'Goodnight, my new friend. I'm so glad I was placed next to you rather than your crazy sister.'

'A lucky coincidence,' I replied.

'Yes, quite a coincidence,' he said, eyeing me quizzically. 'It's just that when you were in the kitchen Cat mentioned that she had been supposed to sit next to me and I just wondered if you'd . . .'

'Goodnight, David,' I repeated, this time more firmly, trying to keep a straight face.

Before I fell asleep, naked under the bedclothes, I ran my hands over my body, just to see if it could still feel anything. I touched my breasts, my torso, my hips, my thighs, between my legs. I touched the place from which Frank, Mavis's baby, had been delivered into the world. Frank, no longer Mavis's baby, but Mavis's little boy, just started school, almost five years old and 'as bright as a button, as bright as you', Mavis had said.

For the first time in nearly years, I touched myself and felt my body slowly stirring back to life. I think I can do this. With David, if he gives me time, I really think I can . . .

Chapter Fifteen

David did give me the time I needed. I suppose I wasn't so much a born-again virgin as an original virgin in all but name. One quick act of penetration with J-C, over almost before it had begun, and then a pregnancy and a birth, didn't really qualify as sexual experience. I wasn't taking any chances this time. Just as soon as I knew that David and I would have sex – weeks before we actually did – I put myself on the Pill.

David says he fell in love with me the first moment he saw me.

'You were rolling pastry as though your life depended on it,' he told me, as we lay in each other's arms after making love for the first time. 'It was something to do with the fact that even though you knew someone was standing there your focus was one hundred per cent. It was a kind of passion you were putting into that act of pastry-making. And it told me that you had the capacity for passion.'

'Gosh, and I thought I was just trying to get dinner on the table. Passionate is not an adjective I'd ever have used to describe myself. Not until now, that is.' I snuggled in closer to David, the hairs on his chest tickling my nostrils and making me sneeze.

'*Gesundheit!*'

'Excuse me?'

'It means bless you. But you've interrupted my flow. There was something else about watching you at your pastry-making. It made me feel like a voyeur. Like I was watching you perform an act of personal intimacy, almost like you were bathing or undressing—'

'Pervert.'

'—and then, when you brushed your curls from your face, getting flour on your skin and in your hair, I wanted to grab you, and make love to you, right there on the kitchen floor.'

David had unchained me, set me free after years in shackles. My limbs felt loose and lissom. Like water flowing freely downstream in a river. I wanted to wrap every bit of me around every bit of David. I no longer needed to put passion into pastry.

'And I fell in love with you when you started lifting chocolates and wine and flowers out of a plastic bag like Mary Poppins pulling surprises from her Gladstone. It was so uncool and unswanky that I knew you just had to be a genuine good guy. And you weren't even that bad-looking!'

'Can I make love to you again?' asked David. 'Now. Or would you rather have a cup of tea?'

'I'd rather get the sex out of the way first, if you don't mind,' I laughed. 'Then we can move on to the bit I'm really looking forward to.'

It was so easy, so natural with David, not just the sex, but that, too. I gave myself to him and he reciprocated. I told him all about my mother and father, about Mavis and my relationship with Cat, about Cat and her relationship with Mavis. About Mavis and her little boy, Frank. About everything, almost.

'You're very g-i-b,' said David when we'd made love a second time and were enjoying our post-coital cups of tea, sitting decorously, propped up side by side, with cushions and wall for support, like Rock Hudson and Doris Day in *Pillow Talk*. Except, of course, that we were naked.

'What's g-i-b? I don't speak German, you know that . . .'

'Good in bed, dummy.'

'Lack of practice must make perfect, then,' I replied.

'Come on, Hannah, I know you're not a virgin.'

'Does one act of penetration lasting less than one minute count?'

'Only technically, I suppose.' David grimaced. 'You don't make it sound very attractive. It reminds me of business studies. Market penetration and all that.'

'Well, it wasn't especially attractive, as you put it,' I replied, putting my cup and saucer back on the bedside table. 'To be truthful I can barely remember it, and certainly not what it felt like.'

'Then you're just a natural.'

'Guess I must be.'

'So how come you only did it with this one guy once and then never again until me?'

I was only just beginning to learn the art of intimacy. I hadn't realised that this was what new lovers did, picking and probing, peeling away the layers of defence, intent on reaching so deep inside the other person that they would eventually merge. It felt risky and dangerous and not at all what I'd intended, but it was also irresistible . . .

'Well, he was in Paris, so I never saw him again.' Could I, dare I, tell him? 'And I . . . well, I didn't meet anyone else I even fancied until you came along.'

'I'm flattered of course, but surely in all that time . . .' I started to shiver.

'Hannah, are you cold?'

I shook my head, but I was trembling. I reached over again to the cup sitting on the bedside table, but my hands were so shaky that the cup vibrated against the saucer and I couldn't pick it up.

'What is it, Hannah? Come on, tell me.'

'If I tell you that will be it. Over. *Finito*. Before it's properly even begun. And I don't think I could bear that.'

'Hannah, you're cuckoo. I don't care how many lovers you've had before me – what do you take me for, an old-fashioned, caveman type? We live in modern times. What matters is that we're here together now. That we've found one another.'

'But you don't understand . . .'

'No of course I don't understand. How can I understand something if I don't even know what it is I'm supposed to understand?'

'David, will you forgive me?'

'For what? I don't know what you're talking about. Hannah, you've got to tell me. What is it?'

I realised at that moment that if I couldn't tell David the truth, if I held anything at all back from him, that it wouldn't work. That our relationship would be worthless.

That the guilt, my guilt, would destroy us. If I loved him I had no choice but to tell him the truth. And if he loved me, then surely he would understand. But it seemed too soon, our relationship still too tentative, too fragile to take chances with. Yet now the thing I didn't dare to say hovered between us, almost out there, darkly hinted at, and I couldn't brush it back under the bedclothes.

'David,' I began hesitantly, 'you know what I said about only having had sex once before. That's all true.'

I was looking straight ahead, not at him. We were still sitting side by side in bed, each bare to the waist, the rest of our bodies covered by the flimsy sheets. Before, I hadn't cared about being naked, now I pulled up the sheet to cover me.

David reached over and framed my chin between his thumb and forefinger, turning my face towards him.

'You can always look me in the face,' he said gently. 'Whatever you have to say, you can always say it to my face.'

My throat constricted. I felt as though I might choke. 'Well . . . then I discovered I was pregnant.'

David looked almost relieved.

'But Hannah, that could happen to anyone. Didn't the bastard use a condom? Was it a big deal, having an abortion? Is that what still upsets you?'

'I didn't have an abortion.'

David furrowed his eyebrows.

'You mean you lost the baby? You had a miscarriage? That must have been just as hard.'

'No, David, you're not getting it. I didn't have an abortion and I didn't have a miscarriage. I had a baby.'

'A baby?'

'Yes, a real live baby. A child. A boy.'

'Jesus! That's not what . . . not what . . . It's the last thing I'd . . .'

'Exactly. Now you know why I didn't want to say anything.'

David's gaze didn't leave me for a moment. His eyes continued to look directly into mine. 'So this kid, this son of yours . . . I can barely believe you have a kid, it seems so unreal . . . where is he now? What happened to him? Did you have him adopted?'

This son of *yours*. What happened to *him*? He was personalising it. Making out it belonged to me. I never did this. The baby was an *it*, never a *mine*. As soon as Mavis signed the adoption papers it became a *he* or a *him*, belonging to *her*. Before Mavis named him Frank, he was an it.

'No. Well, yes. I gave the baby to Mavis and she adopted him. His name is Frank. I told you about Frank. Frank belongs to Mavis. And he's not to know. Not ever. Do you see? Do you see why it won't work between us?'

I was starting to cry.

'Shush, Hannah. Shush.' David turned his whole body towards me and wrapped his arms around me so tightly I could hardly breathe. He stroked my head, over and over and over. Just like Mavis used to do when I was upset, so many years ago.

'Hannah, it's all right. I don't mind. Really I don't. It's a bit of a shock, a big shock, I suppose, but I admire you for being brave enough to have the baby. And then to give him to someone who would care for him when you couldn't. Hannah, don't you believe me when I say I love you?'

'But I'm not lovable, David,' I sniffed. 'And the reason I'm not lovable is that I didn't love the people I was supposed to love. I didn't love my mother. And I didn't love Frank.'

'We can't always choose who to love,' he said tenderly.

'Why is that you seem so much older, wiser and more sorted than me? Like you've got it all worked out. I don't have anything worked out. I'm angry and guilty and scared and . . . you could do so much better than me.'

'That's for me to judge, not you. And I'm not sorted, I'm just lucky. No skeletons in my cupboard. Two parents who love one another and an older sister who thinks the sun shines out of my backside. My only problem is that I expect everyone else to love me as they do. And I expect you to love me most of all.'

'And I do, David. You have no idea how much I do.'

David was continuing to hug me to him, still stroking my hair, talking to me now over my shoulder.

'You say you're not lovable, but your mother didn't make herself lovable to you. She didn't earn your love. And Frank? You did the right thing. You gave him to Mavis, and Mavis presumably loves him.'

I drew back to look at him again, conscious of my red eyes, my mascara-streaked face, my matted hair, terrified that I would appear unattractive to the man I loved, that I would lose him. Now David would see the truth. I was ugly on the outside, and ugly on the inside, too.

'Can't we choose who to love? Are you sure about that? Don't we have a duty to love certain people? Like our mothers and our children.'

'No, not if they don't deserve it. Well, it's different with a child of course. But with Frank you were so young. You might have been with him like your mother was with you, and what good would that have done him? Isn't he going to be happier this way? You see him, don't you? Does he seem happy?'

'Yes, I think so. He's sunny and funny and . . . yes, I think he is probably very happy.'

'None of this matters to me, Hannah, except in so far as it matters to you. I've fallen madly, wildly, over-the-top-ly in love with you and there's nothing you can do to stop it.'

My head collapsed back against the pillow. 'Thank you, David,' I said to the space in front of me. I had nothing more to add for the moment. I was silenced by love, humbled by the enormity of what was happening to me, overwhelmed by relief and gratitude that a man such as David could want me just as I was.

'You're very welcome, Hannah. But now I know everything there is to know, do you mind if I cut the lovey-dovey crap? I'm beginning to sound like a Mills & Boon hero and it's not exactly my style. What I'd really like to do right now, if you don't object, is fuck you senseless.' He loomed over me, licked his lips greedily, self-mocking, his smile mopping up what was left of my tears, evaporating them.

'Be my guest,' I giggled, as he deftly dived under the bedclothes and clutching hold of my hips in the palms of his hands slid me down the bed. I closed my eyes. I allowed David to kiss every part of me. I opened my legs to allow

David's kisses to reach between my thighs, his tongue to caress the places no one's tongue had touched before, to lead me to places I hadn't known existed.

David had said he wanted to fuck me senseless. My last thought before the waves of orgasm washed through me was that senseless was what I wanted more than anything in the world to be.

After that we were together almost all of the time. I was a changed person. I felt light and graceful and unburdened. I started to have these wonderful dreams in which I could fly, like a bird but in human form. I'd take off from the top of the Tower of London or Waterloo Bridge or Alexandra Palace, it was always a different location, and always night time, but my flight path was invariably over London with the lights twinkling below and then on to the countryside beyond, and then over great oceans, and then up and up to the stars and the planets. I'd wake up, smiling, but not wanting the dream to end, and then I'd turn to see David next to me, or feel his limbs entwined with mine, and think: I haven't woken up, the dream is still continuing. As I stirred David, too, would open his eyes. Without his glasses he could barely see a thing. That was another thing I loved about him – that special look of myopic vulnerability that cloaked his face when he'd just woken up, and not yet reached for his glasses, a certain sweet softness about his translucent, jade-green eyes. David was such a self-possessed man, and I was in awe and admiring of his easy way with the world, but David without his glasses filled me with a special tenderness. It was an image that in the future, when he was gone, I would conjure up over and over and over to reignite my memories.

The summer after my graduation I called Mavis and told her I'd met someone I wanted her to meet.

'I just know you'll love him.'

'Well, if you do, I'm sure I will, too . . .' And then she hesitated. 'He . . . he doesn't know about . . . he doesn't know, does he?'

'Yes, he does. I had to trust him.'

'But we agreed to tell no one. That was our arrangement. You promised . . .'

'Please, Mavis, don't be angry. This is different. I couldn't have a relationship with David unless it was an honest one. And he understands, he really does . . .'

'But if Frank were ever to find out . . .'

'He won't, I promise . . .'

'But the more people who know . . . You didn't have to, Hannah, not so soon, how can you be sure this will last? And then the next time you meet someone you'll tell them, too, and . . .'

I could hear fear rather anger in Mavis's voice.

'Mavis, you really mustn't worry. Perhaps I shouldn't have said anything so soon, but I couldn't help myself and I knew, I just knew, that David wasn't going to be some short-lived affair. And when you meet him, you'll realise it, too, I know you will. You'll love him, just as I do . . .'

'Well, I suppose you know what you're doing . . .' said Mavis, still sounding less than convinced.

'The sooner you meet him the better, I think. Now how's Frank?' I wanted to move onto safer territory.

'Turning into quite a little bruiser. He got sent out of class last week for reciting a rude poem, in which he rhymed kangaroo with poo. Lord knows where he picked it up.'

Mavis and I sniggered in unison.

'Did I tell you we've been invited to share this cottage in Cornwall for a week in July?' she continued. 'By parents of this kid Frank's become quite attached to. Very middle class they are, more your sort of people than mine. But I think they think we're quite useful to have along as we only take up one room between the two of us. And as a single-parent family we're a bit of a novelty. A few years ago everyone would have been ashamed to have anything to do with us, now everyone seems to think it's trendy to have a single mum as a mate.'

Mavis was back to her usual, upbeat self. 'Don't be so cynical,' I laughed. 'Has it ever occurred to you they might just enjoy your company? And if not yours, Frank's . . .'

'Well, I've decided to go as it won't cost much and Frank's never been to the seaside. Anyway what I was thinking is, why don't you and David come for a few days and find yourselves a B & B nearby? Frank will be over the moon if Auntie Hannah's in the area . . .'

'That's a wonderful idea. I'll put it to David.'

'Has he met your father yet?'

'No, but that's next on my list.'

'Still knocking off the under-age Lolitas, is he?'

'C'mon, Mavis, he's not quite that bad. They're not literally under age. Frankly I can't see what they see in him.'

'Well, he always could charm the young birds off the trees . . .'

'Lovely to talk to you, Mavis. A big hug for Frank from me. And I'll let you know about Cornwall.'

It was easy to say 'a big hug for Frank from me', far harder to give Frank a hug when I saw him. A quick peck on the top of his head was about the most I could manage, the most I dared do.

Mavis and David hit it off instantly, as I felt sure they would. David quizzed Mavis endlessly about her second favourite subject – me as a child. I was rather grateful to have been pipped to the top spot by the arrival of Frank, because Mavis going on and on about me had become quite tedious over the years. But for the few days we were all together, Mavis reverted to her former number-one topic. While David and Mavis went for long walks together on the beach, I played with Frank and his friend Harry, or chatted to Harry's parents, or just lazed on a deckchair under the pale English sun and read a book.

I found myself surreptitiously examining Frank for signs of me, signs that he really was my son, but I couldn't see any. He was an absolute extrovert. He spoke like Mavis and had even started picking up some of her expressions. One morning we met at the café and I noticed he was wearing mismatched socks.

'Who got you dressed this morning?' I laughed.

'Me, all by myself,' he said proudly.

'Did you put on different colour socks on purpose?' I

asked, pointing to one blue and one red one. 'They're very handsome-looking.'

He looked down, and looked back at me.

'I look like the dog's breakfast, don't I?' and he laughed heartily, even more pleased with himself.

'You do indeed,' I replied. 'You and your mum are a very special pair,' I replied.

'You mean a right pair,' he said with total seriousness. And I laughed again, at this delightful boy who was and wasn't mine.

'He's a great kid,' David said to me later, when we were back in our B & B, sitting on top of the candlewick bedspread in our cosy little attic room with its exposed wooden beams and wallpaper covered with primroses. 'How do you feel when you see him?'

'Detached. Disorientated. Happy that he's OK. Happy for Mavis. Weird. Yes, mostly what I feel is weird.'

'Well, it's a weird situation so I guess weird is about right. That Mavis worships the ground you walk on. As do I.'

'Do you like her?'

'I think she's smart and courageous and proof that a formal education doesn't mean a damn. And we do share one thing that's very precious.'

'You're very soppy for a man.'

'Fancy a quickie?'

'How quick?'

'Let's see if I can make you come in three minutes.'

'It's not a race, you know.'

'I know, but it would be a personal record, and make me

feel like a hero. And then later, after dinner, we can slow things down a bit.'

And so we made love, for perhaps the hundredth, thousandth or millionth time, and when I came David let out a cheer and checked his watch. 'Two minutes, fifty-nine seconds,' he shouted. 'I get the gold medal.'

After dinner we made love again, slowly and voluptuously, with the swish-swish of the sea against the shore as the seductive soundtrack to our explorations.

People spend their lives striving for happiness, so much so that they miss the moments, the pure moments when joy rushes in then rushes off again. But it's the moments that matter, they're as much as we deserve, certainly as much as we should expect. We have no right to happiness, but we do have a duty to notice it when it comes our way. This is what I was thinking when we finally drifted off to sleep as the sun, far to the east, was just beginning to rise.

Sometimes my dad liked to put people through these little tests. He said it was his way of measuring someone's mettle, of sorting the men from the boys, the players from the pretenders. The old ashtray routine was one of his favourites. Whenever Cat brought a boy back to the house for the first time, he'd be subjected to the ashtray routine and, depending on his response, Dad would pronounce him worthy or not of Cat's favours. It didn't matter much to Cat either way, since she never stayed interested in one boy for very long anyway, but my dad and Cat did collude with one another and analyse the results afterwards in forensic detail.

Since I never had a boyfriend to bring home before David, it had been one less thing to die of embarrassment over. The thought of having a boyfriend of mine bumping into a girlfriend of my dad's, who in all likelihood would have been younger than my boyfriend, would have been enough in itself to put me off bringing anyone back to the house. That plus the ashtray routine was a double deterrent. Add in my own antipathy to boys in general following the birth of Frank, and I assumed I'd avoided humiliation-by-ashtray for good.

When I announced I was bringing David home with me after graduation, and that he'd be staying for the weekend, ashtrays were far from my mind. In any case, David was a man of twenty-eight, and my father should have thought to treat him as an equal.

Carmen answered the door when I rang the bell. She had stayed, after Cat had left home and I'd gone to university, out of loyalty to my 'poor father with dead wife'.

'*Su padre* in leebing roon,' she announced, kissing me on both cheeks and then eyeing David with suspicion.

He put his hand out to her, but she gave a little shake of her head and put her hands determinedly in her apron pocket.

'Is good to meet you,' she said.

'Good to meet you, too,' said David, smiling first at her then at me.

We dropped our coats and bags at the foot of the stairs.

'Come on, David,' I said, grabbing his hand. 'He'll be charming, I'm sure.'

troductions went smoothly enough.

'Black Label?' my dad asked. Test Number One of a real man: does he drink whisky in general and Black Label in particular?

'Yes, please. Neat, preferably.' I hadn't even primed him! This was going well. We sat down to talk. My father lit himself a cigarette.

'Do you smoke, David?'

'Just occasionally. But I do like a cigarette if I'm having a whisky.'

'Man after my own heart. Here, have one of these,' said my dad gruffly, proffering his Benson & Hedges.

And then he did it. He sat in his leather armchair, reached towards the coffee table for the rectangular, bone-china ashtray with the pheasant design on it and balanced the ashtray casually on top of his head.

My eyes shot from my dad to David, who was in the middle of running through his CV – background, education, etc. – in response to my dad's barrage of questions. David didn't even blink. He took a sip of his whisky, replaced the tumbler on the table and then drew deeply on the cigarette.

'Mmm,' he murmured appreciatively. He watched as my dad, looking straight at him, flicked the ash expertly above his head into the ashtray. Then, having taken a second drag, David examined his cigarette, got up and walked over to where my dad was sitting.

Without saying a word, he flicked the ash from his cigarette into the ashtray on top of my father's head, then turned away and returned to his seat, carrying on the conversation, not missing a beat, as though nothing out of the ordinary had occurred.

David had won. He'd won the game and he'd won my father's respect.

I do think Maurice regarded David as an equal, but they didn't exactly get along. My father never forgave him for his 'wimpy' MBA or his failure to ask my dad for a job in his business.

'If Maurice is too proud to ask for my help,' said David, when my dad's business started to go belly up, 'I'm not going to embarrass him by offering it. But what does he think he's doing, trying to design all the dresses himself, as well as not even considering manufacturing abroad?'

They were both too proud in a way. Perhaps it was their similarities as much as their differences that attracted me to David.

David and Cat were great friends at first. Cat called him Mr Straight Guy. 'How's Mr Straight Guy?' she'd ask when she rang. Or, to David's face, 'Hey Mr Straight Guy, how're you doing? Been ironing your jeans lately?'

David, to his credit, never ironed his jeans, and Cat knew it, but she was right about David's lack of cool. It was one of the things I loved about him. He didn't need to put on airs and graces, to seek refuge in the latest fashions or puff himself up to impress. I noticed he laughed so much more when he was with Cat than when he was with me. Cat made everyone laugh, I'd always known that, but when Cat made David laugh, I felt a sharp stab of jealousy. It reminded me of when even my mother was moved to tears of laughter by Cat's antics, and the way my dad used to clutch his stomach from laughing so much.

We'd spent the evening with Cat in a wine bar. I'd known David for almost three years by that point, so I should have grown used to his regard for Cat's humour as second only to that of Woody Allen. Cat had a 'late date' with some mystery man and rushed off at around 10.30, so David and I were heading home.

'You were quiet tonight, my love,' David said, putting an arm around me and drawing me close to him as we walked down the street.

'Boring old Hannah, quiet as a mouse.' I said it softly, almost to myself. And then, in a feeble attempt to seek reassurance, more loudly I said: 'Maybe you'd be better off with Cat than you would with me.'

'Ha, ha. Are you nuts? She may be hilarious, but a girl like Cat you can only take in very small doses – like for half an hour, once a month.'

'But I'm so dull compared to her.'

David stopped walking, turned towards me and grabbed me by both shoulders. 'Never, ever say that to me again,' he said angrily, shaking me roughly. It was the first time David had ever raised his voice to me.

'I'm sorry.' *Soon he'll stop loving me, I know it. I don't deserve him.* These were thoughts that ran through my mind.

'And don't be sorry when you've nothing to be sorry for. I know all about your fucked-up childhood, Hannah . . .' He was shouting and passers-by were looking at us in that way they do when they wonder if the girl is in danger but don't really want to get involved.

'Please, David. They can all hear.'

'I don't give a damn who hears. But it's you who needs to listen. I know it was ghastly being you in that dysfunctional family of yours, and I know you've been through traumas in your short life that I can barely imagine, but you've got to know this – and you've got to believe it: I love you now and for ever.'

He was silent for a moment, as if to allow his words to sink in. When he spoke again his voice was softer, and tender. 'Your earnestness is one of the things I love about you, Hannah. Serious, clever, adorable Hannah. And I love your tentative smile that sometimes looks as though it's asking for permission to spread from your mouth to your eyes to light up your beautiful face. And even your quietness I love, because your thoughts are as precious as your words, and I respect them even if I can't share them or enter into your private world.'

Just to nod my understanding was an effort. I was light-headed and weary with relief.

'You and I, my girl,' said David as he hugged me close again and we continued to walk, 'are going to build an empire together and at the same time I'm going to protect you and look after you. Cat makes me laugh, but it's you who makes me happy, and that's what's important.'

'David,' I said tentatively, 'I think I have an idea. I've been going over and over it in my head and I think it might just be the idea we're looking for.'

'Are you going to share it with me, then, or am I expected to guess?'

'Knickers,' I said.

'Knickers?'

'Yes, but not just any old knickers. Knickers for a new generation. Sexy knickers, bras, slips and even suspender belts.'

'Like Ann Summers, you mean?'

'No not like that at all. I'm thinking expensive, sophisticated, the sheeniest of satins, the most slippery of silks. And all by mail order. Quiet and discreet.'

'Quiet and discreet? Like its founder and chief exec?'

For once it seemed like a genuine compliment.

'So are you thinking the kind of stuff men might buy for their mistresses?' David asked, his interest definitely sparked. 'Or for their wives as desperate last-minute Christmas presents?'

'As secondary customers, yes, but as core customers definitely not. Didn't you know that sisters are doing it for themselves these days?' I felt restored, alive again.

'Right now the only knickers I'm interested in getting into are yours.'

Simultaneously we broke into a run. Five minutes later we were outside the door of our house, panting and sweating.

'First we make love,' said David, his breath coming in short gasps, 'and then we make our first million. How does that sound?'

'Good,' I panted back. By the time we'd climbed the stairs to the third floor, where our flat was located, we'd already removed half our clothes. In the heat of the moment I forgot to take my Pill. That same night I conceived Melissa. This time it was an event I greeted with undiluted joy.

Chapter Sixteen

My belly and my pride swelled in equal measure.

'My sister, the genius,' Cat declared, when I offered up my underwear idea and a job for her as designer-in-chief. Still nothing could send my spirits soaring as much as a word of praise from Cat.

She was dressed like a pantomime pirate in homage to the New Romantics style, which had replaced punk in her affections. It occurred to me that she was possibly getting a little too old for swooping up street fashion before it went mainstream, but that was Cat, and she carried it off with panache. The men in her life at this juncture were of a New Romantic bent as well, favouring masses of make-up and sticky, spiky Spandau Ballet hair. They all hung out at a club called Blitz in Covent Garden where the weekend scene had expanded to mid-week club nights and even the guys wore royal-blue satin ruffled shirts and layered strings of pearls under heavily brocaded jackets. I was glad that although David's look was more Jermyn Street than Regency Buck, he was totally non-judgemental. Nor was he at all uncomfortable with the androgynous girl/boy characters Cat introduced us to. We certainly looked incongruous as a foursome in the pub – David in his polo shirts, me in low-key tailored trousers and shirt, Cat and her beau of the week bejewelled and frilled, with matching maquillage.

Since her graduation Cat had taken jobs in Milan and in Paris, working in the design studios of some of the biggest names in the business, and she'd learned a lot about detail and technique, but in typical Cat fashion she'd too often spoken her mind when her opinion hadn't been canvassed, and twice been fired. She was beginning to get a name for herself, more for her bolshie behaviour than her unquestionable design talent.

She had recognised the importance of street fashion early on, and had worked hard to persuade her bosses that they should be taking their lead from the kids, but the design houses for which she laboured were just too conservative to accept this street-up mentality. It was the Brit mavericks such as Zandra Rhodes and Vivienne Westwood who were ahead of their times, not the labels that filled the shops of Via Montenapoleone or Rue du Faubourg St Honore.

'This is exactly what I need,' trilled Cat excitedly. 'And fuck the lot of them,' she added with a self-satisfied flourish, grabbing her burgundy-velvet tricorn pirate hat from the arm of the sofa, planting it on her head and doing a yo-ho-ho dance of delight, crossing her arms and kicking her long, bendy-tube legs like a drunken sailor.

'The Armanis of this world can roll off the assembly line as many taupe trouser suits as they like. Me? I will achieve greatness by designing for women's inner vamp! I shall hand in my notice tomorrow.'

'Hang on there, Cat,' said David, 'not so fast.'

I understood David's initial reluctance at having Cat join the family firm, but if I'd advertised for a designer, and five hundred applicants had responded, I still wouldn't have found a more suitable person than Cat as far as her design abilities were concerned. Her personality was something we'd have to deal with; I'd been dealing with it all my life.

'We can't afford to pay you a salary just yet,' continued David, 'so my advice to you would be to stick with the day job and do a little moonlighting with us until we've got things going.'

Advice, however good, was never something that held much sway with Cat. 'You can forget that,' said Cat indignantly. 'I'm resigning and that's the end of it. I'm going to start up a stall at Camden again with my own designs, my first Eleanor Collection, and I can probably sign on and get some dole at the same time. You won't have to pay me for the time being, but my mind's made up.'

The House of Hannah was launched by David, Cat and me over a bottle of plonk and a large dish of lasagne in the cramped living room of our rented third-floor flat. I had wondered if Cat would baulk at the name, House of Hannah, but she didn't.

'This is the plan,' I told Cat. And for once she didn't interrupt me. 'We take three of your designs and get them made up as samples. Designed By Cat will, of course, appear on every label.'

Cat beamed.

'You look like the Cat that got the cream,' I said.

'Well, that's what I am, Miss Mouse,' she grinned back at me. 'You know you always were my favourite sister.'

You see, I wanted to say to David, we're grown-ups now. We can make it work.

'Dad has come up trumps,' I continued. 'He's given us some great contacts for making up early samples even though he thinks the whole idea is totally barking. Naturally he's livid with David because for some unaccountable reason he blames him entirely for allowing it to happen.'

Now it was David's turn to beam. 'You cannot imagine the pleasure I will get from proving him wrong.'

'In the meantime, David is sourcing factories, and not just in the UK.'

I noticed Cat was beginning to fidget.

'You're not getting bored already, are you?' I unintentionally snapped. Please, God, I thought, do not let this be the shape of things to come. David shot me a look, as if to say, *I told you so.*

'Noooh, darling, not at all. Just go easy on the detail, would you? And pass the wine.'

I'd started and was determined to finish. 'Once we've got the samples, you, Cat, will need to sort out a photographer and arrange a shoot.'

'Cool, yes, no probs, much more my bag than factories. Luckily we get these wannabe photographers turning up at work all the time, begging to borrow clothes for test shoots. I've even worked with some of them, and I've got a whole Filofax of contacts.'

No change there, then; as long as it was about Cat, Cat was interested.

'Then we test the market,' I continued. 'My idea is to go to one of the big glossies – *Cosmo* is the obvious choice, all those working girls as readers – and get them to run one of your designs as a special offer. That way we effectively get a free page of advertising. If they don't buy the special-offer idea we'll have to pay for the advert ourselves. By which time David and I will have persuaded the bank to give us a whopping loan based on our brilliant business plan.'

'Too much information,' said Cat, slumping back against the side of the sofa from her position on the floor and yawning without even attempting to cover her mouth. 'You look after the business and I'll blow your mind with my first designs.'

Which is exactly what Cat did. The designs were a knock-out. Three sets of boned, push-up bras, bikini pants and suspender belts in three colourways – sultry black, classy ivory and completely off-the-wall orange with shocking-pink lace. Cat had drawn the underwear as still lifes, from back and front, so you could see every detail, and again on deliciously curvy models to show how they might look when worn. Fabric swatches were pinned to the mood boards to complete the effect.

'Just wait till I show this to the bank manager,' said a clearly delighted David. 'Oh Hannah, we're going to have fun with this.'

The bank manager turned out to be one Hazel Arnote. It was incredibly rare to meet a female bank manager in the early 1980s. She was a pioneer, and despite the obligatory navy skirt suit and sensibly low-heeled courts she had a real spark about her.

'Did you know that three out of four women wear Marks

& Spencer knickers?' she asked us as she peered at Cat's sketches. 'I read it in the FT.'

'No, we didn't know that, did we, David?' I spluttered, looking at David for support. I wasn't sure if we were supposed to be impressed or horrified by that statistic, and I didn't want to get my reaction wrong and put her off.

'Dreadfully dull of us, don't you think?' she smiled, breaking the ice.

'Dreadfully,' agreed David.

I explained my theory about inner sex sirens and David talked her through the business plan.

'Congratulations, by the way,' said Hazel.

'Thank you,' said David. 'The business is in its infancy, but I'm sure it will go far.'

'Oh I didn't mean that. I meant the baby. Hannah, I can see you're pregnant.'

I'd worn black to disguise my bump. I'd thought a bank manager would be put off by a co-habiting couple starting a business when one half of the couple was several months pregnant.

'Oh you noticed,' I said, looking down at my stomach. 'It won't make a difference, you know, it won't make a difference to my dedication to the business.'

'I didn't think for a minute it would,' said Hazel reassuringly. 'Believe me,' she said, 'if and when I meet a decent man, and if and when I have a baby, it's not going to stop me climbing up the greasy pole. In fact I'm rather on the lookout for a house husband, so if you know of any suitable candidates . . .'

This Hazel was a miracle. Not only was she a woman,

she was a human being first, and a bank manager second. On that same day Hazel unofficially sanctioned the loan we needed to get started. She explained it couldn't be made official until the paperwork was completed and all the channels gone through. Hazel became not just our business angel, but our friend, and one of our most loyal customers.

'Put me down for the orange/pink combo,' she winked at me, as we left her office. 'Oh, and I'm a 36C.'

'Who'd have thought – 36C?' said David, as we stepped out into the sunlight.

'What was that Cat said about me being a genius?' I smirked, linking my arm through David's. At that moment my baby gave me the most enormous kick and I cried out, winded by the suddenness of it.

'Yes, little treasure,' I laughed, stroking my budding belly, 'and I'm sure you're going to be a genius, too.'

The samples were made, the shoot arranged. The idea was to book a lingerie model to wear the underwear and then photograph her draped suggestively around a tailor's dummy swathed in a pinstriped suit. The message was ambiguous, and a touch ironic. Was the suit, covered with tailor's chalk marks, intended for a man and therefore the model set for seduction? Or was the suit being made-to-measure for the model herself, and the model a business-woman in alternative guise?

Cosmopolitan loved the pictures, and agreed to run an offer, but when they quizzed David about suppliers he was overcome with honesty and admitted that, er, he didn't have one just yet. They said they were unable to take the risk of upsetting readers if deliveries couldn't be made as promised.

So he booked an ad instead. The advertising department weren't quite so concerned with our credentials, as long as we paid what was owing. In any case, David reckoned we had time on our side as the magazine wouldn't come out for another three months and the readers had to allow twenty-eight days for delivery from ordering. He was confident he'd find a manufacturer to make up a small amount of stock in time for when the magazine went on the newsstands.

The 'offers executive', as she was called, was kind enough to give us some advice. 'This is pretty expensive stuff compared to what we usually run, so don't expect to sell in huge quantities. Think two hundred sets and you won't be too disappointed,' she told us.

In the event we sold two thousand sets and the magazine kicked itself for not partnering us.

I was seven months pregnant when the edition in which the offer featured went on sale. We had planned to send out all the orders ourselves. Our success was nearly our undoing. There was no way that by ourselves we could carefully package in tissue paper tied with ribbon two thousand sets of underwear, let alone box them up and despatch them with only our ten-foot-square living room tripling up as warehouse, office and soon-to-be baby's nursery. By the time we'd got a mail-order fulfilment house to take on the task, most of our profits were eaten up, but it didn't matter. We were on the road.

We made all sorts of decisions early on that held us in good stead through boom times and leaner patches. Unlike my

dad, we decided we never wanted to own our manufacturing, because although it would work out well when the
factory could be used to full capacity, in slow times you'd
be stuck with massive overheads and idle machinery.
David was adamant that we needed to have the flexibility
to switch between Turkey and the Far East, India and
Morocco, as appropriate to our needs. Neither did we want
to go the retail route. After our success selling off-the-page
in *Cosmopolitan* we produced a tiny catalogue, and took
classified ads in the back pages across a whole raft of
magazines. Then we got some publicity in the *Sun* which
elicited 15,000 brochure requests and masses more orders.

Within six months we had taken on a small serviced
office and a year down the line we'd rented our first
warehouse in a business park off the M1. It measured
1,200 square feet and we wondered how we'd ever fill it. A
year after that we needed to double our capacity.

It was a golden time of elation and exhaustion. Business
boomed. We'd positioned ourselves in the market as
classier than Ann Summers, more affordable than Janet
Reger. From a public-relations point of view, we focused
on the idea that we were the career girl's secret weapon. As
the paperwork piled up, David became convinced that
within a few years our mail-order systems would need to be
computerised. With his Harvard background he looked to
the States, where he said mail order was ten to twelve years
ahead of the UK game. It was David's business acumen
that transformed us from what otherwise might have been
a cottage industry into a successful business. He didn't live
to see House of Hannah become one of the UK's first

successful online shopping retailers, but it was his move to early computerisation, buying in mail-order software from America, that enabled us to switch seamlessly to the internet in the late 1990s.

With Melissa still a babe in arms we took out an enormous mortgage on a white stucco Victorian house in Belsize Park that was in dire need of renovation. Cat bought herself a flat. While all the magazines queued up to feature Cat's flat with its outrageous boudoir of a bedroom, like something dreamed up by an eighteenth-century courtesan, David and I quietly transformed our magnificent wreck into a comfortable, family home.

With our different personalities and skills David, Cat and I were – almost – a dream team. It was a good thing that Cat practically fell into a coma whenever things like stock-taking, systems, profit and loss were mentioned. It meant that we could get on with our job while she got on with hers. The only times she and David came to blows were when one of her designs costed out at more than we thought our customers would be willing to pay. Cat thought compromise was a dirty word and would go into a great sulk whenever she had to modify a design to bring the price down. She'd flounce around for days if either David or I said she'd have to use a slightly cheaper fabric or simplify her design. Eventually she'd march in with a modified version of the original, all smiles and excitement, as if it had been her idea to change it all along. And we'd all be the best of friends again.

The press adored Cat, partly because she was a fashion one-off rather than a victim, but also because she could always be relied on to say something controversial and cutting about the fashion industry. 'More trash than dash' was her favourite dismissal of our rivals in the underwear business.

While Cat played the journalists with all the skill of a Hollywood diva, I looked after everything behind the scenes, trained the office staff and the girls who took the telephone orders, drew up procedures for dealing with complaints and returns, interviewed new staff when necessary, wrote all the marketing materials, handled production glitches, ordered in labels and packaging.

Just as Dad had been wrong when he predicted disaster for our business venture, he had been wrong to predict that working together every day would destroy my relationship with David. We slipped easily and naturally into our respective roles, and always listened to each other's opinions. If one or other of us felt strongly about something, we'd usually work our way around to some kind of accord. And if not, the one with the most experience in that particular area would be allowed to hold sway. Another advantage was that working together afforded us far greater flexibility than working separately. If ever I needed to take a day off because the nanny was unwell, I didn't have to ask permission, and if I was snowed under and David relatively free at the time, it would be him rather than me who stayed at home. And then there was the Cat-effect. Having Cat to sometimes rail against was a perfect foil for our relationship, reminding us of how united we were as a couple, and how lucky we were to have one another.

'Do you think we're getting smug?' I asked David, as we spooned together under the crisp sheets, my eyes struggling not to close right away. It had been a great day. David had spent it going through our figures, and they were even better than he'd been predicting. We'd celebrated with champagne, scrambled eggs and smoked salmon for supper. Melissa, who was two and a half by this time, and already a delightfully opinionated little dynamo, barking orders in staccato, half-formed sentences, had been allowed to stay up while we drank our pre-supper champagne. She'd laughed and laughed when David had let the cork to pop dramatically and shoot right up to the ceiling before falling down and landing in a pot plant. I had let her dip a finger in the bubbles as they formed at the top of my glass, and watched her eyes pucker as she sucked on it. 'Fizzy finger,' she said, smiling happily, wriggling in my arms. 'More fizzy finger,' she demanded as I took my first sip.

'What's wrong with smug?' David asked. 'If there's anyone who deserves a bit of smug, my sweet, it's you.'

The last thing I felt as I fell asleep were David's lips, pressed gently against the back of my head, a little patch of warm air seeping into my scalp and suffusing it with a sense of well-being that spread all along my body, from my head to my toes.

On the same day as I discovered I was pregnant again, I got a call from a magazine called *Better Business*, to tell me that the House of Hannah had been short-listed for their Business of the Year Awards.

It was the morning of the award ceremony itself that I had an ultrasound scan.

'Do you want to know the sex?' the doctor asked.

I looked at David, who was with me. He shrugged. 'I just want to know the baby is OK, the sex is irrelevant.'

'I think I would like to know,' I said hesitantly, though not for any particular reason I was aware of.

'Fine by me,' said David happily.

The radiologist spread some sticky gunk on my exposed stomach and moved the ultrasound wand back and forth across my belly.

'Most definitely a boy,' he said cheerfully, pointing at the screen. 'And a healthy one, too.'

A boy! I gasped at what looked back at me from the screen by the bed. Instead of a grainy picture of a baby, an image of another child gazed directly at me. It was unmistakable. It was Frank. Frank in close-up, a serious little face with angry, accusing eyes. I blinked in shock and turned my head away.

'It's a boy, sweetheart,' said David. 'One of each. You don't get better than that.'

'I . . . I . . . I can't quite make it out,' I said shakily, 'but yes, it couldn't be better.' Hot, salty tears of regret, that David might have mistaken for joy, sprang to my eyes. I shook my head, trying to dislodge the image of Frank from my mind. When I looked back at the screen the image was once again the blurry outline of a baby foetus floating in its watery sac. How does the mind play these tricks, I asked myself.

*   *   *

Later, over coffee, in the ballroom of the Savoy hotel, with its ornate cornices and *trompe l'oeil* clouds scuttling across the ceiling, the magazine publisher made his announcement. A cheer went up around the room. Cat and David prodded me from either side.

'For goodness sake, Hannah, get up. You've won!' screeched Cat.

I hadn't even been listening. I'd been thinking about the mirage I'd seen on the screen. Rising from my seat as if in a trance I walked towards the stage at one end of the hotel ballroom. I smiled at the publisher as I accepted my award, a bird made of glass, of no obvious symbolic significance and propped up on a highly polished wooden base.

'Would you like to say something?' asked the publisher.

I immediately felt a lump in my throat, but of course I had to say something.

I moved to the microphone. I touched my belly.

'I can't begin to tell you how honoured I am to receive this award, especially as the House of Hannah is so young a company. But this award doesn't belong to just me. It belongs to my beloved partner, both in life and in business, and my beloved sister as well. We like to think of ourselves as the holy trinity of knickers.' There was a polite buzz of laughter. 'House of Hannah may have been my idea but without the two of them it would have remained just that. An idea without a platform. Thank you, David, thank you, Cat. And my thanks to *Better Business* for this fabulous recognition of our endeavours.'

I looked over to where Cat and David were sitting. It was

a trick of the light of course, but for an instant I could have sworn that sandwiched between the two of them, on the chair I'd just vacated, sat a small, unsmiling boy, slow hand-clapping, over and over, sending out a private message of chastisement quite at odds with the enthusiastic applause that filled the rest of the room.

Somehow I had sailed through Melissa's pregnancy, barely making a connection between the little girl growing inside me and Frank. But with Charlie on the way, Frank began to fill my thoughts.

For the first time I asked myself directly: How could you have done this? How could you have given away your own son?

I shared none of this with David. Not because I thought he wouldn't sympathise, but because I knew he would try to reason me out of it. He'd tell me, as he'd done often before, that I was too young at the time to be a mother, and that I'd made Mavis happy, and that she was a terrific mother, and that Frank was thriving. All of this I knew, but still I chewed it over and over. It was something I needed to do privately and without someone else coming up with excuses for me. I'd never before kept my thoughts secret from David, and it felt like disloyalty.

Rather than being preoccupied with the baby forming in my belly, I became fixated on Frank's well-being.

'You're very busy with the phone calls all of a sudden,' said Mavis. 'You've rung three times this week. Not that I'm complaining. But is something up?' Mavis could always tell when something was up with me, but even if I'd wanted to I couldn't have explained. I couldn't even have explained it to myself.

'Three times? Surely not. It must be the hormones making me forgetful. Anyway, how's Frank?'

'Pretty much the same as yesterday,' laughed Mavis.

'So he's going to have to wear uniform, is he?' I said, ignoring her sarcasm. Frank was coming up for twelve and to Mavis's delight he'd got into grammar school.

'Yes, and he's furious. Says the stripey blazer makes him look like a poof. He's going through a very anti-poof phase at the moment.'

'Well, at least they'll all look like poofs, as Frank so quaintly calls them.'

'And how are you?' asked Mavis.

'Tired. Tired and happy. I'm having a boy. We decided to find out the sex.'

'A boy,' said Mavis thoughtfully. 'A boy. Is that what this is all about?'

'What all what's about?' I replied, trying to sound innocent.

'It's not surprising, you know.'

'Sorry?'

'It's not surprising that you're feeling a bit odd, knowing it's a boy an' all. I understand these things, you know.'

'Oh Mavis,' I sighed, 'you understand everything it seems. I wish I did.'

'You made a decision twelve years ago,' said Mavis, 'and you've got to live with that decision. Believe me, I know just how hard it is, but you've got to get on with it.

No point in upsetting the apple cart now. It wouldn't help anyone.'

I was stunned that Mavis thought I might reveal our secret. 'Mavis, you know I'd never do that, it's just that. . . .'

'Just what?'

'I suppose the truth is . . .' Somehow Mavis's comforting, reassuring voice was enabling me to find at least some of the words. 'The truth is that I keep thinking about this boy growing inside me and muddling him up in my mind with. . . . I know it will be different when he's born. I'm happy about everything, I really am. I'm happy about you, and about the fact that you have Frank, and that you're happy, and he's happy. And I'm happy about David and Melissa and this new baby. And the business is doing brilliantly. So everything's great, and at least seven times a day I find myself sitting in a puddle of tears.'

'What are you doing Saturday, luv?'

'Taking Melissa riding in the morning, dropping her at a party in the afternoon, then working on some marketing plans before I go and pick her up again.'

'Drop it all,' Mavis ordered. 'Let David do the running around, and hold the marketing nonsense until Monday. Frank's going to a football day camp on Saturday so I'm free as a bird. You and I are going to get together and have a long chat, we are. I'll be at Liverpool Street by eleven o'clock. You can come and pick me up if you really want to.'

'Oh Mavis, I'd love that. Just to talk, you and me, it would be wonderful.'

If David had come into my life to save me from myself, Mavis had appeared all those years ago – like a guardian angel – to save me from my mother. Our roots, like those of California's giant redwood trees, had become entwined. The strength of our relationship lay not in the depth of our roots, which, as for those redwoods, was unimportant, but in the way those roots grew outwards to meet, mingle and sustain one another.

When Charlie was born, things changed again. One look at the adorable creature who was a pint-sized replica of his dad, and I was smitten. My confusion about Frank went into hibernation.

Just as Cat and I were like creatures from different planets, Melissa and Charlie were opposite in almost every way. I found myself giving them their own labels, just as Cat and I had been given. It's wrong, all my life I'd hated being labelled, but it's what we do, I thought. Fiery, forthright Melissa; dreamy, gentle Charlie. But at least, unlike my parents, I kept these labels to myself. Also I valued my children's differences, didn't brandish the strength of one to show the other in a lesser light. Charlie's gentleness seemed as commendable as Melissa's go-get-em approach to life, although I did worry that Charlie would have a tougher time in the modern world than Melissa, that his qualities wouldn't be as readily recognised.

I had it all. The partner, the kids, the success. Of course it couldn't last. It felt right for other people's lives, but somehow not for mine. The night David died I was shocked, heartbroken, terrified and bewildered. Was I surprised? No, I don't think I was . . . But I coped. I really did. And I went on coping. Right up until the day of Melissa's wedding, when a shadowy figure at the back of the ballroom, and a single, sneering look from my sister, stripped me of all the protective layers I'd built around myself over two decades, so that I became little Mouse again, a small child the colour of tofu, growing tinier and tinier until I eventually disappeared. The wedding guests turned to one another in shock, champagne glasses, knives and forks suspended, frozen, in mid-air. A split-second freeze-frame of time and then . . . pandemonium.

PART THREE

Chapter Seventeen

2007

A private doctor has been called by the club, someone used to dealing discreetly with tired and emotional celebrity members who prefer not to be caught vomiting in the gutter by the paparazzi or snapped zoning out on the pavement after a night of over-indulgence.

I passed out only momentarily. I came round after a glass of water, but I was in no fit state to continue with the wedding speech. I could stand, just about, but I couldn't speak. My voice. Completely gone. It has happened again, I thought, almost dispassionately. So I was led gently by Stefan and Charlie out of the ballroom as guests gawped and speculated and accepted large refills of *premier cru* and top-ups of champagne to help them deal with this unexpected turn of events. Stefan and Charlie called for the lift and together we went up to the fourth floor and one of the club's vacant guest bedrooms, where I now lie, still in my wedding finery, surrounded by the significant *dramatis personae* of my life.

At first the doctor suspected a minor stroke. 'No, no, it happens sometimes,' said my dad. 'Even as a kid she used to lose her voice if something upset her. We always thought she was just doing it to get attention . . . But as far as I'm aware it hasn't happened for years.'

'If you wouldn't mind,' says the doctor, turning to address the gathering crowd, 'I'd like a little privacy so I can examine the patient. Or one of you can stay behind to fill me in, if the patient doesn't mind.'

'I'll stay,' says my sister before anyone else gets the chance. She's still clutching a glass of champagne and she swigs back what's left of it in a single, noisy gulp before placing the glass on the dressing table. 'She'll be all right, won't she, doctor?' She looks at the doctor beseechingly, like a hungry Labrador, as he withdraws a stethoscope from his leather medicine bag. Cat twists her long arms over one another, intertwining her fingers, palms facing, like a gawky, menopausal adolescent.

'Let's just take a look first, shall we, before coming to any conclusions,' he says.

I feel utterly lifeless, drained of blood. Sinking, shrinking, dissolving into the bedclothes. The doctor takes my pulse, listens to my chest, tests my reflexes and examines my tongue and throat. He removes a portable blood-pressure kit from his case.

'So it's a wedding, is it?' he says.

'Yes, that was the bride who left the room just now. You know, the one in the wedding dress,' says Cat. The doctor smiles distractedly, failing to rise to my sister's sarcasm.

'Is she all right?' she asks again, more agitated. 'Shouldn't we call an ambulance? Surely we should do *something*.' An hour back she hated me, now she's terrified there might be something seriously the matter. She's determined not to let me out of her sight, to demonstrate how close we are, to be with me all the way. I fleetingly wonder if she blames herself. But introspection has never been Cat's strong suit.

'I *am* doing something actually,' says the doctor, starting to get a little agitated himself. 'Her blood pressure is on the low side, and her pulse unusually slow – although a slow pulse is usually a good sign. Apart from that and her inability to speak there are no other discernible physical symptoms. It could have been hot in the room, or low blood sugar combined with an attack of wedding-speech nerves. It's the voice, or rather lack of it, that troubles me. I've not come across this kind of response before . . . Are you sure you can't speak, dear?' the doctor asks me.

'Yes,' I barely whisper.

Cat has opened the door and everyone's filtering back into the room.

'Has she been under a lot of stress lately?' the doctor asks of no one in particular.

'She needs a good long holiday. All she does is work,' says my father, coming to sit at my bedside. He's being characteristically positive, but his head hangs low and he moves it slowly from side to side, as though he's disagreeing with his own suggestion of a cure.

'No she doesn't need a holiday, she needs a man. She's never even been on a date since David died.' Cat, now standing rather unsteadily at the foot of the bed, and looking more giraffe-like than ever from my prone position, thinks a good sex life is the cure for all ills. The doctor looks bemused, as though Cat is speaking in a foreign language.

'David?' he says.

I know just what my mother would have said if she'd still been alive. '*Too much. She never had the right help.*' For my mother salvation always did seem to lie in more staff and doing as little as possible yourself. Not that it saved her. My poor mother. Always a victim of her anxieties and her indolence. Which came first, I wonder hazily, the indolence or the anxiety. I've spent my entire life trying not to be like her. As long as I kept busy, as long as I had a purpose, I always thought, I wouldn't succumb as she had done. And now . . .?

'Poor Mum, all alone, with no me and no Charlie. I told her she should have had a life before, so she'd have one after, after we both left.' Melissa, whose wedding I have entirely ruined. I look at the bride through misty eyes. My darling girl, just a few minutes ago resplendent and shimmering, her face now a pallid mask of fear. How did I manage to cause such a bloody mess? I'm a coper. At least I always have been until now. And if I was going to fall to pieces, surely I could have held off until after the wedding. I feel my eyes closing.

'Mmm,' says the doctor, 'sounds a lot like nervous exhaustion to me.'

'That's a bit of a catch-all term, isn't it?' says my father sharply. My eyes are closed so I can't see his face, but his voice says it all. The doctor's words are reminding him of Eleanor. Like mother, like . . . No, not that, I think.

The doctor sighs, but doesn't respond.

I need to get up. Back to the wedding. I open my eyes and lift my head a few inches, but it falls back again against the pillow.

Melissa's wedding day. It was all so perfect. And now I've ruined it. For Melissa, for Stefan, for everyone.

'Maybe I should think about moving back in.' Kind, sensitive, worried Charlie has spoken. The boy I've always tried to protect. And now he wants to protect *me*.

'No, Charlie,' replies Melissa firmly, 'you need a life, too.' Good old Melissa. Tough and tender, how I adore her. She comes over to the bed and takes my limp hand in hers.

'She never even grieved for 'im. Not properly.'

Everyone turns to stare at the voice in the doorway. Mavis is standing there, outside the group as always, peripheral – and yet somehow critical – to the main event. They all have an opinion. No one, least of all me, has an answer. I can't speak, so I can't even apologise. I can't imagine ever getting up from this bed again. Something tells me I am both physically and mentally wrecked. A river run dry. I've come to a halt. A full stop. A brick wall. And it's going to take more than a shot of brandy, or even a holiday, to get my engine restarted.

'There's too many people in here. I'll take care of Hannah for a while, sit with her quietly while you lot get back to the party.' Mavis again. The one-woman cavalry coming to the rescue. 'And later, once we get 'er home, I can easily move in for a bit. I'm retired, aren't I? It's not like I've got a job to go to or a husband waiting for me to put his dinner on the table. And what with Frank working in Belgium I've got all the time in the world.' Nobody knows what to say. Nobody dares to protest. Not even Cat would want to make a scene while I'm lying here like this. They all look at me. I feebly raise the hand Melissa's clutching in Mavis's direction, to signal my assent, but it slumps straight back onto the bed.

'Come on, all of you,' says Mavis, still not quite in the room. A half-dozen pairs of eyes swivel back again towards the rotund figure in the doorway. 'I'm sure she'll be OK now. I know she'd want the party to carry on, so why don't I sit with 'er and make sure she has everything she needs? You do want the party to carry on, don't you, pet?'

I blink my assent.

'Are you sure, Mum? I don't give a monkey's for this wedding if you can't be part of it.'

I remove my hand from Melissa's grasp and put my hands together as if in prayer, scrunching my face as though pleading with her. 'Please,' I whisper.

'I think you're trying to tell me the show must go on.' There are tears forming at the edges of her eyes.

I nod again and close my eyes.

'The mother of the bride appears to have spoken,' says the doctor, who is finally beginning to get the hang of the relationships between the participants at this bizarre bed-side gathering. 'I think what she needs now is peace and quiet. And it would be an excellent idea if the lady in the doorway were to stay with her a while. Crisis over, I think,' I can hear the doctor saying, though my eyes are too heavy to open them again. 'I think the patient needs a good long rest, and I don't just mean for the rest of this evening. But we can discuss that another day, or you may wish to consult her regular GP. There's nothing more I can do for her at the moment.'

'I could stay,' my dad says.

'No, no,' says Cat. 'Why don't *I* stay? Otherwise I'm going to have to dance with that goofball I'm sitting next to. A sex god he isn't, Melissa. Where did you dig him up?' Everyone laughs. Laugh-a-minute Cat. Tongue-tied Hannah. You need a Cat in a crisis to give people a chance to calm down. Cause a crisis. Calm a crisis. Life with Cat could never be dull.

'That goofball you're referring to has just dreamed up a brilliant new quiz show that's going to net him two million quid, and he could prove very useful to me and Stefan down the line. That's why he's here. I know he doesn't have a personality as such, but you're the kind of person who makes other people feel they're interesting,' says Melissa. 'That's why I put you next to him.'

'Come on, the lot of you. Go off and have some fun.' Mavis seems unaccountably to have taken charge.

'OK, Mum,' says Melissa, 'we'll pop back soon. You, too, Cat, you're coming with us.'

Something's troubling me. The speech. It needs to be read. I'm struggling to get up, but it requires too much strength.

'What is it, Hannah?' asks Cat. 'Are you trying to tell us something?'

I open my mouth and point a finger inside.

'You want to say something.'

'Yes,' I mouth.

'Here, write it down.' Cat hurries round from the foot of the bed and hands me the notepad and pencil from the bedside table.

I write the word SPEECH in shaky capitals.

'It's out of the question, Hannah. You can't even sit up properly and you can't speak.'

She picks up the sheaf of cards next to the notebook, which Stefan or Charlie must have rescued when they fell from my hands before I fainted.

'Well, I suppose. . . .'

She scans the individual cards, shuffling them back into the right order.

'Well, I suppose someone could read it for you, if that's what you'd like.'

My mouth forms a 'Please.'

'But you know me and reading. I'm not much better than when I was eight. On the other hand, I suppose if you haven't used too many long words . . .'

Cat ruffles her short spiky hair. Confident Cat is suddenly perplexed. It's a big deal asking Cat to read my speech, and from her expression I can see she's not sure she's up to the job. There's a look of panic in her eyes and I sense she's close to tears. The same tears of frustration she shed as a little girl when the simplest storybook defeated her and she'd throw it to the ground with a dismissive, 'Oh these books are so boring. I hate stupid books.'

'I just don't know,' she says. 'I don't want to make a fool of myself. I don't want to spoil what I'm sure is your wonderful speech. It doesn't seem right.'

YOU CAN DO IT, I write on the pad. FOR MELISSA. FOR ME.

'Oh fuck it. I'll do it. I'll go to the cloakroom and practise it a few times and then I'll do it. I'll have another glass of champagne and I'll do it. You've really got me by the short and curlies, haven't you, little Mouse?' She leans over and kisses my cheek. 'What is this anyway? A wedding or a wake? Time to get back into the party spirit.'

I manage a whispered thank you and then close my eyes again.

Their footsteps are retreating. And then it's just me and Mavis. Mavis tucking a blanket around me. Mavis sitting on the side of the bed. Mavis stroking my brow. I am a child again, back in that golden time before Mavis was sent away.

My eyes remain closed, but the tears still trickle out between my upper and lower lids and slide slowly down my face.

'There, there, pet. Mavis will make sure you're all right. Mavis will look after you.'

But even Mavis wasn't going to be able to magic me back to health. When they carted me home I kind of collapsed all over again. Mavis must have undressed me because when I awoke the next morning, as light was beginning to filter through the blinds, I was wearing my cream satin pyjamas. I tried to get out of bed and got as far as sitting on the edge of it, feet resting on the floor, and that was it. I just sat there and cried for I don't know how long. An hour maybe. And when there were no tears left I just stared at the wall. At some point I felt the urge to go to the toilet and shuffled into the en-suite bathroom to relieve myself. Washing my hands afterwards I caught sight in the mirror of my red-veined, puffy eyes and knotted hair and shrugged. I shuffled back to bed, got into it and lay looking up at the ceiling. When Mavis walked in bearing tea and toast and cheerfulness I simply shook my head. Nothing Mavis said could persuade me to eat or drink.

'Melissa got off on time,' said Mavis, plumping my pillows for me and smiling. But when I looked at her eyes they were tight and strained-looking and ringed with shadows. I wondered if she'd slept at all. 'She rang from the hotel this morning, then again from the airport. She was ready to cancel the entire honeymoon, but I told her you'd never forgive yourself if she did that.'

I nodded dumbly. I didn't seem to have any cogent thoughts of my own so whatever Mavis came up with would have to do.

'I told her you were still sleeping and she wasn't to worry and that your voice would come back of its own accord, even if it took a while. She asked me to stay as long as it took and I told her I had no intention of moving anywhere until you were completely better. She's only going to Sorrento for five days. It would have been crazy of her to cancel.'

Crazy, yes, it would have been crazy. In the meantime, it was me who was feeling crazy. Crazy and confused. What do I do now, I thought. What am I supposed to do now? Get up? Get dressed? Go to the office? Get dressed, that would be a start. But where is all my stuff? What am I supposed to wear? How do I actually get my clothes on? It all seemed so complicated. Like something I'd never attempted before.

Crazy. Yes, that's it, I thought. So this is what it means when people say, 'She finally snapped.' Or 'She's having a nervous breakdown.' I've always hated those expressions. Twigs snap, not people. Nerves don't break down when you're anxious; when your nerves are screwed you get MS or Motor Neurone Disease. But now I'm beginning to understand it. This is what it feels like. I do seem to have somehow snapped, broken, fallen apart, body and soul and maybe nerves as well. Is this what my mother felt like? Is this how she felt all those years? And if so, why? And why, now, me too?

Dr Samuel J Frankel is small and stooped and avuncular. His head rests on his shoulders with no visible evidence of a neck. He scrutinises me over the top of his reading glasses, and writes his observations in tiny, slightly quavery hand-writing. His hands are covered in small liver spots. They make me think of a pointillist painting by Georges Seurat.

I am sitting in his office in the psychiatric hospital that has become my temporary home. The day after the wedding I had simply wept and stared and refused to eat. The doctor, my regular GP, who has tended us all for so long he'd even known David before he was killed, took a quick look at me and declared I needed more help than he knew how to give.

'The best thing would be to check her into a private clinic where she will receive round-the-clock care, complete rest, counselling and medication as required,' he told Mavis.

'But I could see to her just as well, doctor. I don't want

them stuffing her up with pills. That's what they did with her . . . with Mrs Saunders – and it didn't help her none.'

'It's Mavis, isn't it? You're an old friend of the family, I believe.'

'I suppose. But it's Hannah I know best. Hannah's the one I—'

'Well, I don't want to interrupt you, Mavis,' said the doctor, interrupting her, 'but I think the children are the ones who should be consulted, don't you? And perhaps her sister and her father?'

'If you say so. I suppose it's not up to me. But Melissa's on her honeymoon, and I know Hannah wouldn't want to upset her any more than she has been already. So you can talk to Charlie. But I wouldn't bother with Cat . . .'

'Cat's Hannah's sister, isn't she? Why shouldn't I ask her?'

'Because she'll just create a scene and get everyone into a panic. It's her speciality.'

The doctor turned to me.

'Hannah, as an old family friend as well as your GP, I really do think you need help. Will you trust me on this? It will take only a few hours to organise a room in the clinic, and someone can call the insurance company for you.'

I shrug. I'm indifferent.

'What's it like there, doctor?' asked Mavis. 'She's not mad, you know. I don't want her mixing with a bunch of nutters in straitjackets. It would do her head in even more.'

The doctor smiled, ruefully. 'No one is suggesting that Hannah is mad, Mavis, she's one of the sanest people I've ever met. So you needn't worry on that score. Where I'm sending Hannah is more like a hotel than an asylum. The kind of place you have in your mind thankfully doesn't exist any more. Try to think of it more as a health farm with doctors and nurses on tap.'

But of course it isn't really like a health farm. Sitting in Dr Frankel's office I'm struck by how quickly one becomes institutionalised. I've been here a fortnight now, and I've taken up shuffling and smoking. Nearly all the patients smoke, even the ones – like me – who were non-smokers before they came in. Since so many of the inmates have problems with drugs and alcohol, I suppose the powers-that-be thought that a smoking ban might finish them off altogether.

I suspect that it's costing my insurance company several hundred quid a night to keep me in this place, so the sparseness of my bruised-peach room, my single cell, with its locked windows, surprises me. It took me a while to work out where the tiny holes in my duvet, outlined with a thin ring of brown, came from. Then I got it. Cigarette burns. This is the kind of game people with psychiatric disorders, or loonies, play. Stabbing their duvets with the cigarettes they're not supposed to smoke in their bedrooms, only in the shared living room down the corridor. I'm not being disparaging when I used the word loonies. It's used by the patients all the time to describe themselves. The doctors and nurses would never call the patients that, or certainly not to their faces. But the patients wear their self-imposed loony label almost as a badge of pride. 'We loonies' they say, as though we are all members of an exclusive sect.

I still don't say anything. I'm an unusual case. But my

psychiatrist has been looking me up, referring to academic papers and conferring with colleagues.

'You're suffering from what we in the trade call a conversion disorder,' he told me. 'A conversion disorder is a specific kind of mental disorder whose central feature is symptoms which affect the patient's senses or voluntary movements. These symptoms are suggestive of a neurological or general medical disease or condition, but with no physiological base. We've had you checked out by an ear, nose and throat specialist so we know your larynx is in good working order . . . no polyps or nodules, no structural pathology as such, nothing untoward.'

This is supposed to reassure me. But I never did think there was something physically wrong with me. It's happened too often before and my voice has always come back. When I was little it scared me terribly. But this time around, I don't fear that I'll never be able to speak again. What I mind is this incredible black hole I'm in, this desperate need to get back to my life but at the same time sensing the utter pointlessness of it all. But this one thing, the silence, this inability to explain myself, this avoidance of being expected to explain myself or to justify my actions feels almost like a blessing.

'Generally I would expect my patient to do most of the talking,' says Dr Frankel, 'but under the circumstances that's not possible and I get to hold centre stage. Are you interested at all in Freud, my dear?'

I nod.

'There was a famous case. The case of Dora. In fact her real name was Ida Bauer and she went to see Freud around 1900 when she was eighteen years old. Dora's symptoms included depression, fainting spells and a loss of voice. She came from a typically upper-middle-class family. Her father was a dominating figure and her mother was obsessed with order and cleanliness. "Housewife psychosis" was the term used at the time.'

SOUNDS FAMILIAR! I scribble this on my notepad and pass it to my myopic doctor. My mother had been obsessed with housework, or rather getting other people to do the housework for her.

'Dora claimed that a friend of her father's, Herr K, had made sexual advances towards her. To cut a very long story short, Freud determines – based on the information Dora provides and the interpretation of two of her dreams – that rather than being disgusted by Herr K, Dora is secretly in love with him. Her loss of voice occurs when Herr K is away from home on business and when she can have only written rather than verbal contact with him. Freud was never able to cure Dora because she left treatment after a few weeks and didn't return.'

Why is Dr Frankel telling me all this? I've been taking antidepressants for two weeks now, and although I'm crying less – a kind of numbness has overtaken me – I sometimes find it hard to think clearly. Maybe I'm missing his point. Dr Frankel seems determined to carry on.

'It was one of the first seriously documented studies of what psychiatrists came to call hysterical aphonia. And by aphonia, I mean loss of voice of the kind from which you are suffering. You are not suffering mutism. Your cough is normal and you can just about whisper, which is not a great deal of help to me as I am growing increasingly deaf.'

A little joke from the good doctor, but I'm still not sure what Dr Frankel is trying to tell me.

'You look bemused, my dear, and I'm sorry if that is the case. I suppose I'm just trying to illustrate a point. Dora's loss of voice was psychological – whether it related to abuse or repressed desires, it was most certainly a response to trauma. The voice, we now understand, is an excellent barometer of mental and psychological stability. Fear, depression, anger, anxiety, unresolved conflicts can all, as they did for Dora, lead to loss of voice. It's not common, but interestingly it is far more common in women than it is in men, and has given rise to a great deal of feminist debate. In essence I want to assure you that we'll get to the bottom of it.'

I'm really not sure I want to get to the bottom of it. A couple more weeks here, get the pills to kick in even further, and a holiday abroad – *alone* – and hopefully I'll be back to normal.

Therapy is pretty useless because I can only whisper inaudibly in answer to the doctor's gentle promptings, and whispering is somehow exhausting and doesn't allow me to convey properly what I'm feeling. So I go to yoga in the basement, join silently in the group therapy sessions to see if there's anything I can learn from the rest of the inmates, and pray that no one comes to visit me.

Charlie and Melissa popping by – just so they can reassure themselves I'm still alive – I can just about handle, as long as they don't stay too long. All I really want to say to them is, 'I'm sorry. Sorry for letting you down. Sorry for being such a fool. Sorry for being so weak. Sorry for being such a burden. Sorry. Sorry. Sorry.'

After the first couple of days, during which time my dad and Cat appeared, alongside the kids, to be aiming for a twenty-four-hour vigil, I signified to Dr Frankel that I'd really be happier if my father and Cat didn't come at all for the time being. Mavis, thank goodness, had gone home to Chelmsford, there not being much point in her living in my house without me there, especially when I'd requested such infrequent visiting.

I have a room on the ground floor. 'Quieter than some of the other floors,' Dr Frankel assures me. I've been kept apart from the anorexics who have a floor to themselves, and the addicts who likewise have a floor of their own, and those on suicide watch who have guards posted outside their doors. In the dining room, however, I can observe them all. The depressives whom electric-shock treatment has made ravenous and who pile mountains of food from the buffet onto their plates, and the human skeletons who chase lettuce leaves – under staff supervision – around theirs. What am I doing here?

'I'm feeling particularly aggressive today,' barked a moley, masculine-looking, middle-aged woman the other day, as I pulled out a chair at a communal table and attempted to put my plate of chicken and salad down next to hers. 'Would you mind if I stabbed you?' she asked, a malicious grin that reminded me of Cherie Blair forming as she lifted the knife from her plate and raised it above shoulder height. I shook my head vigorously as she and the others at the table laughed in unison, and moved off as quickly as a shuffler can, leaving my plate where I'd placed it. My heart was hammering at my chest and it was some seconds before I dared to glance over my shoulder. Thank God the mad knife woman had lost interest me and was happily slashing at a piece of cold lamb. Determined not to leave the dining room where I assumed there was a certain safety in numbers, I returned, shaken, to the buffet, took a new plate, and scanned the room for an unoccupied table.

This was my home and it was beginning to feel like normal. People who shuffled. People who wailed. People who threatened to pull a knife and people with the saddest stories of abuse and violence and bad parenting and unbearable loss. What right, I asked myself over and over, did I have to be here? Yes, David died – too soon, much too soon; my mother, so long gone and a loss quite subsumed by the one which followed – but I had a life, two gorgeous kids, a positively blooming business, a business which, according to Cat, was continuing to bloom in my absence. I should be all right. I shouldn't be bothering the doctors or my family or even myself with this nonsense.

Dr Frankel knew all about my mother's suicide from Cat and my dad. They must have all been fearful I'd follow in her footsteps. But I harboured no fantasies of killing myself. I'd always seen my mother's suicide as an act of cruelty as much as desperation, and even in my darkest hours I knew I couldn't do that to my children. For a while I felt I'd welcome death with open arms, but it would have to come to me, rather than have me go chasing after it.

Chapter Eighteen

Since I couldn't speak, Dr Frankel suggested it would be a good idea if I wrote instead. He asked me to scribble down my thoughts and feelings as they occurred to me, and also to write about my life, anything I thought might be significant. I did as he asked, more to clarify things for him than for me. I knew the circumstances of my life well enough already. My negative thoughts were all to do with how weak and useless I felt. My overriding feelings were of guilt and shame. I'd let everyone down, including myself.

On the wall just behind Dr Frankel's head there was a badly executed watercolour. I found myself staring at it over and over and I couldn't work out why. It was deeply sentimental, the kind of painting you couldn't pay me to hang in my home. In the foreground was a river, with clear water running over glassy pebbles. In the distance were snow-peaked mountains and great waterfalls gushing down between the lower pine-covered slopes. It must have been spring. A man and a boy sat together on the grassy bank, fishing.

I wrote in my notebook: *Tell me about the painting*. I tore off the piece of paper and handed it to Dr Frankel. He smiled at me.

'And I thought you had just come up with something really significant, the breakthrough I've been waiting for. The painting's dreadful, isn't it?' Dr Frankel swivelled his chair round to look at it and snorted. 'I was in Zermatt one summer for a conference,' he continued, as he turned his chair back towards me, 'and there was an artist plying his wares in the square. I'd been rather anxious to find something to take home for my wife as a gift, and it was my last half-hour before I had to pack to catch my plane. The artist, an old chap, looked as though he could do with some patronage . . . or at least a decent meal. I paid far more than it was worth. My wife, lady of taste that she is, refused to have it in the house. So I was forced to hang it in my office. Does it offend you, too?'

I smiled back, shaking my head. Of course. Switzerland. It had been niggling me for a fortnight, every time I'd been in Dr Frankel's office. Switzerland.

I scribbled on my pad. *Switzerland might be more important than you think*. And again I tore off and handed Dr Frankel the paper.

That evening, sitting disconsolately on top of my duvet, waiting for my one allotted sleeping pill to take effect – it had become impossible to fall asleep naturally with my mind so full of jumbled thoughts – I ran through the whole scenario in my head. The night I'd made the extraordinary discovery that I'd been born in Switzerland, a discovery quite eclipsed by the knowledge that I was pregnant. The funny feeling I'd got that my dad hadn't been telling me the whole story. Not that it wasn't plausible, more that I found it curious no one had thought to mention it. Well, my mum never spoke to me much about anything, so it wasn't especially odd that she'd never brought it up, and my dad, he was always so busy and distracted. But Mavis, Mavis and I had always talked about everything, hadn't we?

I couldn't recall exactly what had happened when I went to see Mavis to tell her that I'd got pregnant in Paris. Didn't I ask her then? Thirty-five years ago! How the hell was I supposed to conjure it up? It must have seemed a minor detail compared to the far greater drama of my unwanted pregnancy. But I did have this sense of something to do with Switzerland passing between us. A hazy recollection of Mavis telling me pretty much the same story as my dad, of their stories corroborating each other and therefore there having been nothing more to add. That would have been reason enough to forget all about it. My mother had simply gone for her health and Mavis had gone, too, because my mother needed help and Mavis was the only option at the time.

Nevertheless, looking back, it surprised me that Switzerland had slipped quite so completely from everyone's agendas. Had it been deliberate? And then there was the business of the grandparents. After I was born they never again came to visit, and we never went there either. It was the very last time my mother saw her parents.

Why couldn't I get Switzerland out of my head? It was becoming something of an obsession. Was it part of my illness to fixate on minor matters, irrelevancies, in order to distract myself from the very real issue of how I was going to manage my life after leaving this place? Had the illness blotted out parts of my memory, but not others?

While I continued to churn Switzerland over and over in my mind, I became aware that something I'd always held to be true was in fact nothing of the sort. Mavis and I didn't talk about everything as I'd automatically assumed. How naive of me to think that we had. I knew almost nothing about Mavis's life before she came into mine. What we talked about was our everyday lives together, and far more about my preoccupations than hers. I'd been a child, she could easily have manipulated things, led the conversation down certain paths and avoided going down others.

There was a simple enough way to deal with this. I'd write Mavis a letter, asking her about it, saying I needed a recap on Switzerland. And then afterwards I could file it away in its rightful place in my past . . .

It had been over a week since I'd sent the letter and there'd been no word back from Mavis. During my session with Dr Frankel he said something that took me by surprise.

'I had a call from your friend Mavis.' He knew a bit about Mavis from one of the pen portraits I'd written for him about my friends and family, so he was also aware of the fact that she had adopted Frank. 'She says she'd like to come and have a chat with me.'

Why you, not me? I wrote on my notepad.

'She wouldn't say. But I did tell her I'd have to ask your permission first as you're my patient. I guess she may think she has some insight into what's going on with you, something that might help.'

I wondered again why she hadn't replied to my letter. *When's she coming?* I wrote.

'Next Wednesday we've tentatively agreed, depending on your approval. And now, my dear, we need to discuss your departure from here. I very much wish that we'd made more progress than we have, but your mood does seem to have stabilised somewhat, thanks in part to the pills, in part to the enforced rest. I'm reluctant to have you leave while you still have no voice, but you seem so convinced that it will return of its own accord that I'm inclined to believe you. In fact I'm inclined to think that your silence is a psychological defence mechanism that you have more control over than you're willing to acknowledge. That your voice will return when you're ready to talk. On the other hand I would very much like to do something more to help you. Would you at least consider hypnotherapy as an outpatient? There's someone here I can highly recommend.'

'Possibly,' I mouthed exaggeratedly, so the doctor would be able to understand.

'What I'm hoping,' he continued, 'is that you will come back and see me on a regular basis when you're talking again. We've barely scratched the surface in our one-way exchanges.'

Poor Dr Frankel, I thought. He wants so much to help me, I *will* come back when my voice returns. For reasons I couldn't explain I didn't want Dr Frankel to feel he'd failed with me in the way I'd failed with myself.

I'd thought that I would be thrilled to be 'let out of the madhouse', 'given time off for good behaviour', 'released on parole', as patients departing the clinic tended to describe it. But instead of relief I felt a flurry of fear. I may have needed to have all responsibilities taken away from me, but how was I ever going to take them on again? I still felt so incompetent, depleted.

Dr Frankel thought the explanation for my breakdown was relatively straightforward. 'You have suffered a good deal of trauma in your life, my dear. To lose a mother to suicide when you are a child, and partner to an accident when you are young and in love is a double tragedy. Not only did you then have to take on the responsibility of raising your children alone, you had to take on all the responsibilities your partner had taken care of in your joint business. And there's another loss that you have failed to properly acknowledge, and that is the loss of your first child. Of Frank. You've been denying the pain of that for two decades. It had to come out somehow.'

The doctor, kind-hearted though he was, hadn't really come up with anything different to explain my current situation than anyone else had – including Cat, my dad, my kids and Mavis. I kept thinking: So I've been in denial, so what? If denial is what's kept me going this long, why should it let me down now? And of course I'd grieved. I just hadn't gone around flagellating myself in public all the time. The only thing that mattered was finding the strength to get back on my feet and carry on. A task that seemed quite impossible. I loved my own home, it was my sanctuary, but now, for the first time, the thought of returning to it was infinitely scary.

I literally didn't know what day of the week it was, so when there was a knock on my door, and Mavis's face peered round the edge of it, I realised it must already be Wednesday. Two more days and I'd be going home.

I made my way around the bed from the armchair in which I'd been sitting and gave Mavis a hug.

Mavis, I noticed, looked in a worse state than me. She'd lost tons of weight and her eyes were hollow. A moment later Dr Frankel appeared.

'May I join you?' he asked.

I took Mavis's coat and she and I perched on the bed. As Dr Frankel sat himself down in the armchair opposite us, I instinctively took Mavis's hand and pulled it across to my lap.

'Mavis and I have had a good long chat, haven't we?' he said in his most soothing, sympathetic, just the right side of patronising tone.

'Yes, doctor,' replied an unusually subdued Mavis.

'Mavis has told me quite a story, a story that she's been keeping to herself for a very long time now. She wanted my advice as to whether it might be a good time to share this story with you, but she didn't want to do anything that might "set you back" as she put it. Have I got that right, Mavis?'

There were tears in Mavis's eyes. I wasn't sure I'd ever seen tears in Mavis's eyes before.

'All your life,' she said, her voice quaking from the effort of holding herself in check, 'from the second you were born, I've only wanted to do what's right for you. You do believe that, don't you, Hannah?'

What could this be all about? I squeezed Mavis's hand to reassure her.

'That painting of mine,' said Dr Frankel, 'the one my wife had the good sense to reject, has paid for itself many times over.'

So this was what it was all about. Mavis had come to talk to me about Switzerland.

'I believe,' Dr Frankel continued, 'that what Mavis is about to say to you is very important indeed. I'm happy to revise your departure date from the clinic if you feel you need more time to digest things. And now I'm going to leave the two of you to talk in private.'

Dr Frankel sprang from his chair, unusually agile for a man who must have been in his seventies. 'I don't wish to embarrass you in any way,' he said, extending a hand towards Mavis, 'but I have to say it's been an absolute honour to meet you.'

Mavis was clearly in no mood for praise, but she managed to mumble a gruff 'Thank you,' as the doctor shook her hand then made his way out of the room.

Mavis and I were alone. My stomach had filled with a thousand tiny, tickly ants, climbing all over one another in a frenzy of activity.

'I'm all hot and bothered,' said Mavis. She was fluttery, flustered, not like Mavis at all. 'My train was late so I had to get a taxi from the station – cost an absolute bloody fortune – and then when I did get here fifteen minutes late your Dr

Frankel wasn't even ready to see me, so I could have taken the bus and saved the money after all. And then, once I was in his office, he kept me going for over an hour and . . . and . . .'

She'd completely lost track of herself. 'Just pour me a glass of water, would you, pet? I'm parched.'

Poor Mavis. What could it be about my letter, about Switzerland, that would throw her into such panic? I poured some water from a plastic jug on the table next to the armchair into a plastic cup. Glass wasn't allowed in the bedrooms. You could do yourself a lot of damage with a shard of glass.

Mavis took several gulps, sighed loudly and wiped a bead of sweat from her brow.

'I hope that doctor knows what he's doing. What I'm about to say might result in us both ending up in the loony bin.' She stopped, took a short, sharp intake of breath, shocked at her own words. 'Oh I didn't mean that, Hannah, about the loony bin, I mean. I know it's not like that here.'

Mavis was desperately playing for time. Because I had no voice I couldn't offer any words of encouragement. I touched her arm gently, willing her to begin. Mavis closed her eyes, breathed in again through her nose, more slowly this time, then seemed to hold her breath for several seconds before exhaling even more slowly through her mouth. She was anchoring herself. She was ready.

It's hard to know where to start. It was like this, you see. When I first went to work for your mum and dad I

*didn't realise what a state she was in. I suppose if I'd
known I wouldn't have taken it on. I mean I wasn't
qualified or anything. I could clean all right, and I could
cook well enough; all the basics weren't a problem, but I
wasn't a nurse and I didn't want to be.*

*Your mum was in a right state when Cat was born,
or at least she was when I moved in and Cat was
around six months old. When I went for the interview
your dad took me aside after and said her health wasn't
strong, that she wasn't ill as such, but just not strong.*

*Post-natal depression I suppose you'd call it today.
The birth was dreadful, I was told. She had this really
long labour, and was torn to pieces down there,
according to Dot, who seemed to know all the gossip.*

*Your dad was all right. Truth is, I fell for him right
away. He was so handsome, so clever, and he could
really make me laugh. He was the only reason I stayed
in the beginning.*

*I know I should have felt sorry for your mum, and I
did in a way, but I kept thinking she didn't have
anything to moan about. She had a husband half the
women in England would kill for, more money than
sense, a healthy kid and a bloody great house with
servants running around after her. It was hard to
sympathise, I can tell you. Maybe if she'd been a bit less
sorry for herself, I could have felt more sorry for her. I
can see now she wouldn't have killed herself unless she'd
been really depressed, but at the time all I saw was how
spoiled she was. She never stopped looking in the mirror
to admire the view. I didn't know anything about*

depression being a real illness and all that, I thought it was more about your attitude to life, about getting on with it. I still do in some ways. If anyone was going to be depressed, I kept thinking, it ought to have been me, not her.

It began to eat me up. I began to hate her. And then I began to have these stupid fantasies that your dad would fall in love with me and leave her. Fat chance, eh?

Mavis laughed in a way that was both wry and regretful. I wasn't sure if I wanted to hear what was coming. I'd already learned more about Mavis in a few minutes than I'd known in a lifetime. Maybe I should stop her, I thought, before it was too late. But it already was too late. Mavis seemed to have found a way to start, and she and Dr Frankel had decided it was the right thing to do, and she wasn't going to stop until she'd given me every gruelling detail.

I'd been there about eighteen months, maybe more like twenty. Cat was two and a bit, and quite a handful. Your mother wasn't changing for the better.

I was sitting in the morning room one night, listening to the wireless. I'd finished the washing-up and there was a story I wanted to listen to. I'd heard the stairs creaking a while before so I thought your parents had gone to bed. And then your father appeared.

He always did like a whisky, your dad, but I'd never seen him drunk. I'm not even sure he was drunk that night, a bit tipsy, maybe, but not slurring his words or stumbling about all over the place.

'Mind if I join you?' he asked.

'Be my guest,' I remember replying, feeling for just one instant less like a servant and more like the lady of the house.

He sat with me at the table and started chatting, for the first time asking me all sorts of things about my family, my childhood, my hopes for the future. I was in heaven, I can tell you. And that was it. We must have talked for about an hour and then he went to bed.

I was beginning to feel not just nervous but nauseous. There was an inevitability about where this story was heading that I had never before considered even as a possibility.

After that his little visits became quite regular and I started to look forward to them. I knew I was nothing to look at — no one was anything to look at compared to Eleanor bloody Saunders — but I tried to take a bit more trouble with my appearance. I tried on some of her ladyship's make-up once when she was out — it had become a bit of a joke between Dot and me to refer to her as 'her ladyship' behind her back — but I looked ridiculous and wiped it all off again. Except for a bit of lipstick — I got into the habit of that. It's not something I'm proud of, but I stole one of her lipsticks, it was this lovely, creamy peach colour. Maybe I thought that your mum's looks would rub off on me along with her lipstick. She never even noticed, she had so much stuff.

You have to remember, I was only nineteen. I'd had

no education, and not much life. I loved your dad's harmless little visits.

And then one night when your dad came into the morning room he seemed really upset. He sat at the table, put his head in his hands and said, 'What am I going to do, Mavis? What am I going to do?'

And then he started to tell me. He told me that he had no relationship with his wife, but he couldn't leave her because she'd fall apart. That she refused to have sex with him ever again because the thought of having another baby was more than she could bear. And that she couldn't even stand for him to touch her. He said she shrank from him, and it made him feel like he was some kind of monstrous brute if he ever went near her. I can tell you, my heart went out to him. 'I don't think you're a brute,' I said. 'I think you're the kindest man I've ever met.'

Mavis had barely paused for breath. I touched a finger to her mouth, to shush her, then went to pour her another glass of water. So my parents had a sexless marriage, my father wanted to leave her but couldn't, and Mavis was in love with him. It made sense, it really did. I knew my parents' marriage was a cold one and I'd always felt that Mavis had a soft spot for my dad. What I hadn't realised was the depth of feelings all round. My father's unhappiness, Mavis's unrequited passion, my mother's post-natal depression. But hang on, what about me? If my parents' marriage was sexless, what had happened to change it? If my mother refused to have another child, what had happened to . . . I felt slightly faint. I had to grab the edge of the bed to stop myself from keeling over. I looked at Mavis and she continued.

All the time your dad was opening up to me about his failed marriage, I was having these fantasies about how I was going to rescue him. I wasn't completely sexually inexperienced. I'd had this boyfriend on the farm when I was sixteen, and we'd had it off a few times in the barn, so I did know a bit what it was all about. I can't believe what came over me really, but I just wanted your dad so much, I wanted to make him feel good about himself, I wanted him to fall in love with me. So I seduced him. Know-nothing Mavis, plain old Mavis, a ruddy-cheeked, farm-hand's girl from Essex, seduced the handsome army major, Maurice Saunders, her very own Clark Gable dreamboat come true. I just went right ahead and did it, without fear, without embarrassment. And he let me. I took him by the hand and indicated for him to quietly come upstairs with me. He followed, meek as a lamb. We made love in my room. Well, that's what I'd call it. We never even took our clothes off. It was up with my dress, down with my knickers. He was that frustrated it was all over in minutes. Making love is what I called it because I fancied I was in love with him. He might have called it something else.

Afterwards, I said, 'Thank you, Mr Saunders.' And he replied, 'No, Mavis, it's you I should thank. But it's a terrible thing we've done and we must never, ever do it again.' I was prepared to carry on, right under your mother's nose, but your dad wouldn't hear of it.

> *And just like you, Hannah, I got pregnant when I didn't mean to. And just like you I gave my child away to a family I thought would be able to give her a better start in life than I could give her. I was frightened, I can tell you: to be a single mum with no money was no joke in those days, and a backstreet abortion was even worse. But for a while I held all the cards, because there could have been a scandal, I could have caused an almighty stink . . . And then you were born and I no longer held the cards – the only thing that mattered was that you were properly cared for, and given all the advantages a girl like Cat would have. I should have left so much sooner, but I couldn't. I hope that you can forgive me, Hannah, because there is nothing so precious in the world to me as you.*

If I hadn't already been speechless Mavis's words would have rendered me so. As it was, they had the opposite effect.

The inside of my head was a supernova, a spectacular explosion of energy and light.

'So . . . so . . . that's why you and my moth—' I'd found my voice. I started again. 'So that's why you both went to . . .' I hesitated. 'Hello, Mu— Mum.' I tried the words for size . . . they seemed to fit, but there was a crack in my voice. I tried something else. 'Mavis. Mavis, my mother.' And then, in little more than a whisper, as though the words themselves needed to be handled with the utmost care, like a newborn child: 'So you are my mother. How very, very extraordinary.'

I paused, giving the words time to float around the room, up to the ceiling, down to the floor, into the corners, to fill every crevice, to seep into the fabric of the curtains, to percolate the paint on the walls, to establish themselves as real before finally settling back on the duvet, between me and Mavis. Between me and my mother.

'I think I know what happened. You went to Switzerland and had me there, and my mother – no, not my mother, I mean Eleanor – brought me back as her own. It had all been decided before. You gave me to her and my dad, so they could be the perfect family, but without my mo— Eleanor . . . having to make or have a baby.'

Mavis nodded. She looked so small, so frightened.

Then quite suddenly everything was clear, as though a fine layer of skin, like a cataract, had been peeled back from my eyes to bring the whole world into sharper focus. 'But don't you see, Mavis, it makes no difference. Don't you see how crazy and at the same time obvious this all is? You've always been my mother, Mavis. Even before I knew, I knew. Even if it hadn't been biologically true, it would have been true enough. All my life it was true enough. It doesn't matter that I only know now, that only now it's fact for me, because in some way I've always known.'

'Are you ashamed to have me as your mother?' asked Mavis, looking at her lap.

'And are you mad? Ashamed? How could I be ashamed of you? Without you I am nothing.'

I stopped again to take in the enormity of what I'd been told.

'Frank!' I gasped.

Mavis was still looking at her lap. 'Well, some might say that the next best thing to being brought up by your mother is to be brought up by your grandmother. Keeping it in the family an' all.' Her voice was neutral, as though she needed my response before knowing the right inflection to give her words.

And others, I thought, might say that the sins of the fathers shall be visited upon the sons . . .

My moment of clarity clouded. I must be hallucinating. My son had been brought up by his grandmother! By my mother! And I hadn't known. This was a surreal, drug-induced delusion. What did it all mean? What would be the consequences? For me, for Frank, for my kids and for Cat? Would Mavis and I still have to keep it all a secret? Would there be more lies? More cover-ups? What about my dad? I could see this was only the beginning and there were a thousand more questions I needed to ask, a hundred more mines to be cleared. And then another image flitted fleetingly in front of my eyes, and my breath caught again. Eleanor. Eleanor looking at herself in the mirror. Not to confirm how beautiful she was. No, not that at all. But to confirm that she existed. Villainess and victim both.

'Let's try to be rational,' I said, not feeling the least bit rational. 'Let's try to process this, a bit at a time. Finding out who your real mother is, after fifty years, is quite a bit to take in, you know.'

But for now there was nothing more that needed to be said. Silence, as I knew from experience, was often the only appropriate response. I looked at this woman I'd loved for fifty years, this woman who must have suffered so much to give me up, and I wept. But this time I cried not just tears of pain, but tears of release. And Mavis wept too.

And that's how Dr Frankel found us, hugging and weeping and laughing, and hugging again until our arms and our chests ached from so much hugging. Then, when he'd gone, we lay down together on the single bed, on top of the duvet cover that was pocked with cigarette burns, like a spattering of bullet holes from a machine-gun, in the psychiatric clinic where windows were made not to open and neither pills nor talking therapy had provided any kind of cure, but where healing had nevertheless tentatively begun thanks to a painting that a doctor's wife was too snobbish to hang on her wall. I was ready to go home.

Chapter Nineteen

No sooner had I got home, and been able to reassure my kids and Cat and my dad that I had re-entered the land of the living, than I decided to go away again. I had told them nothing. Only that my voice had returned as suddenly as it went, just as it had before.

There was so much I still needed to absorb, and I wanted to do it in seclusion. I couldn't just slot into my old life as though nothing had changed. I needed time to reflect, to plan, to think who else would need to know what I had learned. Now, more than ever, I needed, or rather wanted, David.

The business had been doing pretty well without me, although I'd never before given my staff the chance to prove themselves capable of running the show on their own. It had always been David's contention that as a leader you had to build the kind of team that could survive quite happily without the boss, but working demonically had been part of my survival strategy after David died, and handing over the reins hadn't been an option I was prepared to consider. But I had at least had the good sense to replace David right away, and I had known exactly who I needed to recruit to handle the company's finances. Hazel

Arnote, bank manager extraordinaire, 36C, with a pench-
ant for neon-bright knickers, was the woman I wanted. She
had been thrilled when I'd approached her and had offered
to make her Finance Director of the House of Hannah.
And she'd stayed with the company ever since.

It had been Hazel who nudged us into expansion from
underwear to sex toys. At first I'd been horrified.

'But it's all so sleazy, Hazel,' I'd argued. 'We're about
sexy good taste. It's what makes us unique.' What would
David have thought? I always asked myself this question
before coming to any big decisions.

'You've made exactly my point,' Hazel had countered.
'Sex toys are fun, but their image is understandably
dreadful. What we need to do is look at what sells –
handcuffs, vibrators, nurses's outfits, whatever – and in-
itiate our own classy versions of the same thing.'

'So what you're saying,' I replied carefully, 'is that if we
send out the vibrators in packaging that's the equivalent of
the Tiffany blue box, and if our nurse and schoolgirl outfits
are made in fabulous fabrics and really fit, we might
transform sex toys into the equivalent of luxury accessories.'

'You've got it,' she smiled.

'You really weren't brought into this world to be a
banker, were you?' I grinned.

Cat thought the whole thing was a hilarious wheeze and
was delighted to give it a go. I got the feeling the two of
them had been conferring long before Hazel came to me
with the idea. She and Hazel had hit it off right from the
start.

One Saturday morning – Hazel had already been with the company a couple of years by this time – I had decided to drop in on Cat unexpectedly with the kids and croissants. The kids adored Cat. She played dress-up games with them, chased them round her flat and sang and danced with them to blaring rock music. Age had increased neither her inhibitions nor her sense of rhythm. I rang the buzzer and a tousle-haired temptress wearing a short, diaphanous nightdress opened the door. The nightdress was one of ours. The wearer was Hazel.

'Rumbled!' she said cheerily. 'Come on in, kids.'

Her casual welcome went some way towards mitigating the shock I'd had, seeing her almost naked – and clearly having stayed the night – in my sister's one-bedroom flat. There was no room for doubt. Cat and Hazel were lovers.

The kids, nine and six at the time, hadn't given the scenario a second thought; it was just a sleepover to them. I tried to stay casual as well, but it really had never once occurred to me that Cat might be gay. All those guys she'd gone through!

When Cat appeared from the shower, she was wearing jeans and a vest that didn't quite meet them, along with a belly-button stud and a look of defiance.

'So Hazel and I are an item, so what?' She glared at me.

'What's an item?' asked Charlie.

'It's a single thing in a collection of things,' I said desperately, trying to get off the subject. 'Like when you have a whole shopping list, for example, a tube of toothpaste might be one of the items you needed to buy.'

'So why are Cat and Hazel on a shopping list?' my son asked with the irrefutable logic of young children.

'Anyone for croissants?' interrupted Hazel.

Once Hazel and Cat had come out as lovers I better understood Cat's past promiscuity. She'd been looking for love, not just sex, all along, but in the wrong places. Her encounters with men had never felt quite right, so in a crazed mission to find the chemistry she craved, she'd become more and more profligate in offering her sexual favours. Not until she met Hazel had she really understood that she was a lesbian.

'We're just two girlie girls who've fallen in love,' Hazel explained to me when the kids had gone out to play in the communal garden at the back of Cat's flat. 'Well, I've always been bisexual, but your sister didn't have a clue she was gay until she met me. It hadn't occurred to her. Do you mind?'

'Well, I am a bit shocked, but I don't mind as such. What does concern me, hard-bitten businesswoman that I am, is how you two are going to work together if you ever split up. I also remember very well the conversation we had when we first met you at the bank. You seemed very keen on babies and house husbands at the time.'

'Well, the babies might not happen,' Hazel responded, a little frostily. 'But as far as Cat and I breaking up is concerned it would be no more difficult, as far as I can see, than it would have been if you and David had split up. Less, in fact. You two were equal partners, and a bad divorce would have ruined the business. I'm just a paid director with a few share options. Much easier to get rid of me.'

Cat and Hazel didn't split up. They screamed and shouted and hurled abuse at one another, they slammed doors and threatened to kill one another on a regular basis, but they were in it for the long haul.

My dad, when he found out, said, 'But Hazel, I've always fancied you for myself.'

'Thought I was too old for your tastes, Maurice,' Hazel replied flirtatiously, 'otherwise I would have saved myself for you, rather than your daughter.'

'It's not too late, you know,' he smirked.

My father was a complete enigma. You could never tell how he'd react. On another occasion, presented with the information that his daughter was a lesbian, he might have embarked on a homophobic rant. But on this particular day he seemed to regard the whole thing as an amusing interlude cooked up for his entertainment. That he seemed to approve of Hazel rather more than he had ever approved of David, on both a business and a personal level, was something I could never quite come to terms with. But I never asked him why. Like so many other things between us, it remained unspoken.

'Take yourself to the Caribbean, Mum. And if you do, I'll come, too. I'll even allow you to pay, just this once of course.' Melissa was clearly in love, looking luscious and content.

'I think I need to be alone, darling,' I replied, 'and you have a new husband to look after. You don't want to abandon him so soon.'

'What, for a week in the Caribbean? I'd be off like a shot.'

'Marriage twenty-first-century-style of course,' I said. 'But in any case, I had somewhere paler in mind.'

'Paler?'

'Yes, nothing too brightly blue or blazingly yellow. I'm thinking weak sun, bracing walks and lots of wind.'

'Cornwall's windy,' said Charlie. 'You could go for long, miserable, lonely walks and I could go surfing. Then we could meet in the pub for supper.'

'Thanks, Charlie, but you're working for House of Hannah now, remember. And that website you're re-designing is long overdue.'

'You're being very difficult,' said Cat. 'If you won't let your children take care of you, how about a girlie shopping trip to New York with me? Hazel will hold the fort while we're gone.'

The five of us, Hazel included, were having supper together in my kitchen. Everyone kept popping in on me, checking up to make sure I wasn't having a relapse.

'No cities. No shopping. And much as I love you all, no companion. I really do want to be alone.'

'So where are you thinking of, Mum?' asked Charlie. Charlie seemed changed since he'd started to take his work seriously. He seemed more sure of himself. And someone kept texting him throughout the meal and making him smile. Maybe there was a girl in the background. I hoped so.

'Skallerup Klit actually,' I said.

'Sounds like a busman's holiday to me,' laughed Cat. 'I thought clits would be the last thing you'd want to be thinking about at a time like this.'

We all groaned.

'Wash your mouth out with carbolic, the lot of you.' I

tried to sound convincingly cross, but a smile broke
through my voice.

I hadn't really forgiven Cat. I was sure it was Cat who
had been the trigger for my collapse at Melissa's wedding.
The way she'd verbally attacked me outside the club before
the ceremony for having invited Mavis. The look of sheer
contempt she'd thrown me as I was about to begin my
speech. Cat, stealer of tongues. But of course it couldn't
have been entirely Cat's fault; it was an accumulation of
things that went way back. I knew that, but I was still angry.

'So come on, then,' said Hazel, 'tell us where in the
world this Skallerwhatsit Clit place is, and how on earth
you came across it.'

'For your information it's Klit with a K, not a C. I'd been
idling on the internet, thinking Scandinavia might suit my
mood. And I came across this perfect little cottage for rent,
just a couple of hundred yards from the beach. Skallerup
Klit is in north-west Denmark, right on the North Sea. I'm
thinking of flying to Arhus, hiring a car, and holing up for a
couple of weeks. It all sounds incredibly civilised. You
know what the Danes are like, with their mod cons and
tasteful design. It has a sauna, indoor swimming pool with
wave machine, solar panels and a wood-burning stove. It
sounds perfect.'

'Not to me, it doesn't,' said Cat. 'It's a million miles from
anywhere.'

'Nor me,' said Melissa. 'You'll have no one to talk to.'

'Exactly,' I replied.

Only Charlie, somewhat lamely, said, 'Well, I don't
mind a bit of herring every now and again.'

'Well, that's it, then,' I said. 'Settled.'

'How are you going to light a fire, Mum?' Charlie asked. I loved the way he always looked out for me.

'You're going to teach me before I go.'

I was going to have to tell them the truth, wasn't I? Charlie and Melissa were both going to have to be told who their real grandmother was. And that they had a stepbrother, whose name was Frank. But what about Cat? If I were to tell Cat I'd lose her altogether. No more sister, no more House of Hannah. But how would it be possible to tell the kids and Frank and speak to my dad, and for Cat not to find out? And would Frank hate me as well when he discovered the truth? And would he despise his adoptive mother for lying to him? It wasn't just a can of worms, it was a giant vat. No wonder I needed to go away to clear my head. Nothing was what it seemed any more. Not since Mavis's bombshell. There was so much joy in what I knew now to be the truth. Mavis was my mother. But new anxieties and anguish too. About the past and about the future.

When they'd all gone after supper I went straight back onto the internet, and booked my flight, my car and my house beside the beach.

It was early September. Only the holiday stragglers were left and it looked like my solitude was secured. I'd stocked up on provisions at a roadside supermarket en route from Arhus, and the drive had been straightforward enough across flat countryside that was sparsely populated, the ubiquitous red Danish flag with its white cross flapping outside many of the farmsteads and houses. Brown cows, green fields. Tidy, I thought. Just as I'd hoped.

The house was as advertised. A simple wooden structure with a black tiled roof and an underside painted white, large double-height windows facing towards the sea to let in the light. It had a spacious, open-plan design with split-level living and eating areas, both spotlessly clean and free of clutter, and a well-equipped kitchen. The slender lines of the light birch dining table and chairs, the pale wood floors and the large black-leather sofa with chrome trim had a modern simplicity that suited me. There was nothing in this house to evoke the past, either mine or that of previous inhabitants. I'd chosen well.

There were days when the wind and the rain whipped my face and the waves lashed the shore and the North Sea frothed and foamed and raged. I wrapped up in layers and wellies and waterproofs and walked along the beach barely able to stand my ground, clambering awkwardly over boulders and groynes. I'd return to the house and light the wood-burning stove, and wrap myself in a blanket until I felt warm again. On other days it was so mild I could strip down to a T-shirt. People would emerge as if from no-where, throwing balls for dogs, holding small children aloft on their shoulders, running and laughing in the dunes, distributing bread for the birds. On days like these, and when the tide retreated, the wet sand glistened and sparkled – pink the shade of rose quartz, blue like aqua-marines and lavender, like the palest of amethysts.

I walked to Lonstrup, an hour or so along the beach, a small hamlet with a lighthouse that seemed to be slowly submerging into the dunes, and where the fishermen pulled their vessels up onto the beach after a morning's fishing. Sometimes I would stop for something to eat in the village, or pop into one of its many galleries displaying glass and ceramics and the work of local artists.

No one spoke to me, other than to say *god dag*, good day, as we passed on the beach. I was grateful to be ignored. In the evenings I would cook myself a simple meal, sweat it out in the sauna and then float weightlessly in the pool. A week passed like this.

My response to the discovery that Mavis was my mother surprised me almost as much as the discovery itself. Instead of regretting the wasted years, the years that we could have, should have, spent together, I comforted myself with the thought that all along I'd effectively been a good daughter to her. Just as she'd been a good mother to me. And I had given her the gift of Frank, a son, or rather grandson, and she'd been happy. Knowing all along that he was her grandson, a true blood relative, had perhaps made her even happier than I could have imagined. I didn't blame Mavis – how could I? What she had done, I had done, though the circumstances were more difficult by far for her than they were for me. In the seventeen years that elapsed between Mavis giving birth to me and me giving birth to Frank, so much had changed. The world had moved on. Single mothers weren't the pariahs they had been in 1956.

When I thought of my father I felt sad and angry in turn. He should have known better than to take advantage of Mavis, even if it had been she who'd led him on, been the seductress rather than a victim. He had so much power compared to Mavis. On the other hand, a man duty-bound to a fragile wife who couldn't cope with life and spurned him sexually? How was a healthy, virile man, in his prime, supposed to deal with that? But if Eleanor had been close to breakdown before I came into the picture, what must have been the effect of me on her frangible psyche? Was it anything other than wanton cruelty to saddle her with me, the messy result of a furtive fuck under her own roof?

She did try in a way. She was never exactly unkind. She did what she could, which wasn't much, but neither was it nothing. It wasn't as though she'd even chosen to adopt me; I was foisted upon her to avoid a scandal and to foster the sham ideal of the nuclear family. Maybe she'd have favoured Cat over me even if she'd given birth to both of us. Cat had so much more going for her than I did as a child. She wasn't a dull little swot, she was bursting with life and sunshine. As much fun as I was solemn.

Slowly, Hannah, slowly, I reminded myself. Rome wasn't built in a day, and my life wouldn't be rebuilt in a day either.

My Lonstrup local, equivalent of the village pub with its long bar, solid wooden tables and chairs and smoky atmosphere, was empty, except for a few regulars. I was even beginning to think of myself as a regular.

It wasn't the first time I'd spotted him. He had a craggy, weatherworn face, the deep tan contrasting with the wild white hair and bushy beard, making him look startlingly alive and bright. Pushing sixty, I thought, but his body looked younger – upright, solid, lean. I wasn't sure why I'd even noticed. Mostly I ignored men I didn't already know, and they ignored me.

At first I thought he was a fisherman. He wore a cream, cable fisherman's sweater, blue jeans and light suede Timberland boots with crenellated rubber soles. But the boots gave him away. They were barely scuffed.

We'd several times made eye contact. It was only polite. But on this occasion he got up from his table and walked to mine.

'English?' he asked.

'Yes, I'm English,' I replied, and realised they were the first words I'd spoken since I'd arrived, other than to order food or drink in a restaurant or buy provisions in a shop. I'd spoken to the kids and the office a couple of times as well, but face-to-face talking contact: none.

'Olav Pedersen. Pleased to make your acquaintance.'

I smiled at his formal English, word perfect as it was.

'Please may I join you? Or is that maybe too much liberty?'

'No, it would be fine,' I said, pleased to have the company. 'My name is Hannah.'

It was hot in the room. Before he sat down Olav Pedersen crossed his arms over his torso, clutched the hem of his sweater and pulled it over his head. The faded blue T-shirt he was wearing underneath rose up with his arms and revealed a few inches of firm belly, covered with a smattering of light hair, and strong forearms and biceps, as tanned as his face.

I felt myself redden, and I turned away before he could notice me staring at his taut, masculine stomach.

'What are you drinking?' he asked.

'Well, I was about to have something to eat. *Smorrerbrod* probably, they do such good open sandwiches here. And I guess a lager.'

'I'll order you the best Denmark has to offer, and it won't be Carlsberg,' said Olav, laughing throatily at his little joke. 'Something light, crisp and delicious, and not what you call a cliché.'

'I'm in your hands,' I replied. I was feeling almost skittish.

'So what are you doing here all alone?' he asked. 'I must assume you are alone as you are always by yourself.'

'I needed a break,' I said lightly. 'I've not been too well. And I wanted to come somewhere I'd never been before, somewhere I could grow strong again.'

'And has your mission succeeded?'

'It's beginning to,' I smiled. 'The walking is wonderful. And the light. At least the light when it's not raining. And the air. Yes, I think it's working very well indeed. But what about you? Are you from these parts?'

'My home and my business are in Copenhagen, but I have a summerhouse, not far from here, in Skallerup Klit.'

'Then we must be neighbours,' I replied.

'Indeed we must,' said Olav, and something about the way he said it suggested to me that he already knew, before I'd spoken.

'Are you alone as well?'

'My three kids were here in August, the eldest boy with his wife and two little children of his own, and I joined them at the end of the month. There were seven of us in a house big enough for four. Now they're gone, but I'm holding out for a few more days. I love my family but I also love it when they go away and leave me alone.'

'That's how I feel, too. Sometimes my children treat me like a child, rather than the other way around.'

'So you, too, have a family?'

'Yes, two adults. A boy and a girl. My daughter, who's twenty-five, recently got married.'

'And your husband?'

'No husband.'

'No husband ever? Or no husband now?'

'He died.'

'I'm sorry indeed. So many questions I ask you. I intrude your privacy.'

'Invade, I think you mean. But I don't mind. He's been dead for twenty years, a very long time.'

Olav shook his head.

'But you are a lovely woman. I knew that right away. Why are you not married again? I do not understand.'

'You do not understand,' I smiled, kindly I hoped, 'because you are a man. Because you think a woman cannot survive without a man. But I'm all right like this. I have my business and my children and my friends, and mostly it's enough.'

'Mostly?' said Olav thoughtfully. 'So tell me about your business.'

So I told Olav about my business and when I said 'House of Hannah' a kind of gurgling sound emitted from the back of his throat.

'This I do not believe.'

'And why not?' I asked, amused and intrigued.

'My wife left me because of you.'

'She did what?'

'She caught me looking at your website. I had decided to buy her some beautiful underwear for her birthday. It was five years ago now. She came into the room and saw me looking at the pictures of women in their underwear and made the assumption that I was buying underwear for my mistress.'

'I can't believe what I'm hearing. The coincidence of it.' A bit of me wanted to laugh, but I was also shocked.

'She entered the room just as I was double-clicking on an image of a woman in a black suspender belt and stockings and she started screaming at me like I was pervert. "You have mistress," she said. "You have mistress. Who is your mistress?" After that she stopped trusting me, and six months later she announced she was leaving me for her tennis coach. And you, Mrs House of Hannah, are to blame. For ruining my life.'

I can't say he looked like a man whose life was ruined, his eyes were twinkling as he told me, but maybe he was telling the truth.

'There's no need to look so upset, she was already having the affair with her tennis coach. She just decided to use the underwear as excuse. I'd stopped loving her long before. The underwear was desperate measure to renew our relationship.'

'And according to my customers it often works. Especially once they've added in a sex toy for good measure.'

And then we both started to laugh at the absurdity of it all, the outrageous coincidence, the randomness of things.

After lunch we walked back together along the beach. The sky was clouding over, but I was unbothered. When we reached my turn-off from the beach, Olav turned with me.

'I'm over there,' I pointed.

'And I'm over there,' said Olav, pointing just a few hundred yards to the right.

'Seeing as we're neighbours, would you like to come for dinner?' The words just slipped out, before I'd had a chance to think about what I was saying.

'When did you have in mind?'

'Any time really. Tonight?'

Olav smiled. His face was preternaturally lined. In a few years it would resemble a road map. But you could trust a road map better than your instinct, and I felt inclined to trust him.

'Tonight it is. Eight o'clock?'

I nodded and turned away towards the house.

I had four hours until eight o'clock. First I sat in the sauna, then I had my customary float in the pool. After that I showered and washed my hair, changed into a clean pair of jeans and a fresh sweater. I didn't have much left in the way of provisions, so pasta with a fresh tomato sauce and some salad would have to suffice. I wasn't setting out to impress Olav with my culinary skills, I just wanted to spend a pleasant evening with him. He'd seen me wind-blown, without make-up, looking every bit my age, but he obviously liked my company, too. But I did apply some make-up, some tinted moisturiser, mascara, a little lipstick and blusher. I wasn't at all on edge about Olaf's visit, I was looking forward to it.

I did keep checking myself in the mirror though, far more than was my custom. *Admit it, Hannah*, I said aloud, the fourth time I'd scrutinised my reflection, *you fancy him*. It was a feeling so unfamiliar that I barely recognised it.

Olav arrived with a bottle of wine, wearing a different sweater from the one he'd had on earlier. He removed his boots in the porch, and joined me barefoot, turning up the cuffs of his jeans to stop them trailing on the floor. I've always had a thing for men's ankle bones. His feet looked much younger than his face.

We ate and drank and talked and I learned that Olav was a furniture designer with his own store in Copenhagen, selling mostly one-offs, but also simpler pieces that were manufactured.

'Copenhagen is a beautiful city, you must come and visit me there,' he said.

'I'd love to,' I replied, 'I don't know Denmark at all, apart from this very spot we're in, and neither have I visited anywhere else in Scandinavia.'

Olav talked about his children and encouraged me to talk about mine. I liked the fact that he was so involved as a father and grandfather. He also talked about his love of his work, carving wood into works of art. I told him about the cupboards, the cupboards in my parents' bedroom that I'd so loved as a small child, and shoe trees, made of cedar.

'I can smell the cedar now,' I said, 'as fragrant as the pine wood burning in the stove.'

'Do you mind growing older?' he asked.

'Not really,' I replied. 'What women of my age mostly feel is the loss of their beauty, the fact that they may no longer be sexually attractive. After David I wasn't much interested in either men or how I looked, so I'm not much affected by ageing in that sense. I don't mean I didn't want to look good, to stay in good shape and wear stylish clothes, but I never measured myself in terms of whether men did – or didn't – find me attractive.'

'You are an unusual woman.'

'After David died I couldn't think about the future. Only about surviving day to day. Another reason why I don't dwell on ageing.'

'In my head I am still a young man,' said Olav, 'but next year I will be sixty and, how you say it, a Chelsea Pensioner.'

'Old Age Pensioner,' I laughed. 'That's what we used to call people over sixty. But we're very PC in England these days and now the over-sixties are Senior Citizens.'

'What is PC?'

'Politically correct,' I replied, pouring more wine into both our glasses.

The candle flickered on the table and the pine wood scented the air. After dinner, Olav sat on the sofa, with his feet up, crossing his hands behind his head, half lying back against the cushions and sighing contentedly.

'You're a lovely woman,' he said, looking at the ceiling rather than at me. I was curled with my legs tucked beneath me on the armchair opposite.

'That's the second time you've told me that today.'

'And I shall say it quite a few times more if you don't mind,' said Olav, turning his head towards me.

He patted the sofa next to him.

'Would you come and sit beside me?'

I didn't even hesitate. He was still laid out, relaxed, sure of himself, sure of me. I went over and sat on the sofa, looking down at his face. I began to trace my fingers over it. Over the lines on his forehead, across his cheeks, feeling the bristles on his chin.

'I suppose they must tickle the person you kiss,' I said.

'Try it and see,' Olav suggested.

So I did. I kissed Olav like a woman possessed. Like a woman who hadn't made love to a man for twenty years. But I hadn't forgotten how, only how it felt. And it felt good. Afterwards, as we lay naked in each other's arms, he said it again.

'You are a lovely woman.'

'And you're a lovely man. You can stay the night if you'd like.'

Olav stayed, and when I woke at dawn and turned towards him, for a split second I thought it was David lying in the bed next to me. But it wasn't David, it was Olav, and that was fine.

I'd always been aware of the irony of being a sex magnate with no sex life of my own. But my punters didn't know that and neither did the media. They'd got wind of Hazel and Cat though, and for a time the newspapers – in particular the *Sun* and the *News of the World* – had a field day. It didn't last because once Cat and Hazel came out publicly and declared they had nothing to hide, the press had nothing more to unearth. It occurred to me that my celibacy would probably have caused even more of a stir than Cat and Hazel's girl-on-girl romps. Fortunately they never found me interesting enough to investigate.

I was lying in bed with Olav, silently reminiscing about my twenty years of celibacy, when I heard a car rumbling towards the house. Who can that be, I wondered. The bed was so close to the window that if I sat up and peeked behind the blind I could press my face right up against the window. Yes, it was a small car, and it was stopping right outside the house.

By the time I'd managed to get out of bed and slip on a dressing gown, there was a loud banging at the door.

'Coming!' I yelled, smoothing down my hair, licking my finger and rubbing it under my eyes to remove any lurking mascara stains from last night's activities, when my cleanse, tone and moisturise routine had been the last thing on my mind.

I opened the door and came face to face with my worst nightmare.

It was Cat.

'God, you look a mess,' she said. 'Lucky I got here in time.'

'Jesus, Cat, why didn't you tell me you were coming? And what do you mean by "in time"?'

'Before you did anything stupid.'

'I wasn't planning on doing anything stupid.'

'Well, never mind that, I wanted to surprise you. Aren't you going to get out the bunting?'

At that moment Olav walked naked out of my bedroom and crossed the corridor right in Cat's sightline.

'No wonder you didn't want any visitors,' shrieked Cat, turning round and stomping back towards the car. 'You've been deceiving us all along.'

'Please, Cat,' I pleaded, 'just calm down and I'll explain everything. Why would I deceive anybody? I don't have anything to hide.' Nothing to hide! That was rich, coming from me. There was plenty I'd been hiding from Cat, but a secret lover wasn't it.

She turned back towards me. 'Well, seeing as I've just flown halfway across the world and driven across the whole of this godforsaken country to rescue my poor little sister, I suppose I'm going to have to stay for a while. But your explanation had better be a good one. We all thought you were about to top yourself. If I'd known you'd sneaked off to fuck a Viking I really wouldn't have bothered.'

'Oh for heaven's sake, Cat, just come in, would you? Any in any case, he's not a Viking, he's a Norse god.'

It was all so ridiculous. Life veered wildy from pathos to bathos and back again, with tragedy, comedy and farce thrown in for good measure. I started laughing, and once I started I couldn't stop.

'There's a spare room over there,' I spluttered, 'where you can put your stuff. I'll put on the kettle and my friend will put on some clothes. I can explain everything. Olav,' I called, 'there's someone I'd like you to meet.'

Chapter Twenty

Once I'd been able to explain everything to Cat, she calmed down. The sweet, sticky Danish pastries and strong black coffee seemed to mellow her mood. But Cat's presence had quite the opposite effect on me. I became jittery and distracted.

I'd been looking forward to a few days of no-strings-attached sex and companionship with my Norse god, before he went off back to Copenhagen and me to London. He'd awoken something in me and I felt renewed, a good ten years younger than when I'd left home. Our affair, short-lived as it was likely to be, felt like a gift. And now, unfairly, it was being wrenched away from me again by the sister who first stole my tongue and now had arrived to steal my little parcel of pleasure. She hadn't known, of course, but as always Cat had reduced me to the position of the put-upon child, the child whose older sister had been placed on this earth expressly to snatch all good things from her sister's grasp.

Olav sensed my change of mood and prepared to leave.

'We'll talk later,' he said, giving me no sense of when – or if – we might actually meet again. 'You're lovely,' he whispered reassuringly in my ear when I followed him to the front door, with Cat still hovering behind, like a centurion at the gate.

Cat's arrival confronted me once again with stark reality. A reality I had wished to put on hold, if only for a few blissful days more. I was face to face with the dreadful dilemma of whether or not to tell her the truth. Not knowing whether telling her would mean I'd lose her for ever. And I couldn't afford to lose her. She meant too much to me, not just to the business, but to me. I'd lost too many people already. Cat, despite everything, was my sister. She looked out for me. Even now. A trip to a windswept house on the North Sea was her idea of hell. But she'd come. And when she joked that they all thought I'd top myself, there must have been an element of seriousness in what she said. That she cared I couldn't doubt. Perhaps we were destined to forever be Cat and Mouse. Why couldn't I just accept it?

I persuaded Cat to go walking with me. Her clothes were flimsy and unsuitable. It gave me an excuse to go to Olav's house and see if he had any spare weatherproof clothing left by his family.

He looked delighted to see me.

'You and your sister are not such good friends, I think,' he said, ushering me in.

'It's a very, very long story,' I said. 'We are so different, Cat and I, but there's a lot of loyalty there as well.'

'When she goes you will tell me about it.'

'The problem is, I fear she won't go before you do. I had been so looking forward—'

Olav bending in to kiss me cut off my words mid-sentence, and I felt instantly aroused. But now was not the time for making love. I broke away.

'I'm so sorry, Olav. We can't do this, not now.'

'It's OK, Hannah, I understand. But I do not like your sister for taking you away from me when I have only just found you.'

'Me neither,' I sighed.

'You know that if we have no chance to be together here I will follow you to England. Not right away, but soon, when the exhibition season is over.'

'Or I could come back at Christmas,' I said, amazed at my forwardness with a man I'd just met.

'Then we have a deal. And I will try to be patient.'

I took Olav's spare waterproofs and trudged reluctantly back to the house where Cat was waiting and, I suspected, hoping that I'd failed to find anything suitable for her to wear so she could be excused the walk.

I had no plan at all.

We talked first of the business.

'How's it going?' I asked.

'Hazel says we're raking it in.'

'That's good,' I smiled. 'You know, I've been thinking . . .' Actually I hadn't been thinking at all about what I was about to say, but the thought that had just popped into my head sounded so right to me that I needed to express it immediately.

'So what else is new?' said Cat. 'Do you ever stop thinking, even for one second?'

'Last night, I didn't think last night. When I made love to Olav for the first time.'

'And you met him when . . .?'

'Yesterday lunchtime to be precise.'

Cat flung her arms around me and gave me a hug.

'My goodness, little Mouse, a spontaneous fuck after all these years. I'm impressed.'

'I thought you were furious.'

'That was when I thought you'd been plotting and planning behind our backs. No, this is seriously good news. How about if you have him back again tonight and I'll put in my earplugs?'

'I shall give that some serious thought,' I laughed. Cat and I were getting along just fine. 'Now that thought I was having . . .'

'Come on, then, spit it out.'

'Maybe it's time for me to sell the business, move on, do something different.'

'You're kidding me, surely. *You! Sell the business!* But since David died it's been your life. What would you do?'

'I don't know, I'll think of something. It's only a thought at this stage. Hazel could do an MBO, and maybe Charlie could get more involved.'

'Well, actually I've been thinking, too,' said Cat. 'I'm pretty pissed off with knickers. I need a new challenge. In fact I've had this offer . . .'

So that's why Cat's here, I thought. All that talk about being worried about me was nonsense. She's come to tell me she's leaving.

'I didn't think you'd come all this way just to check up on your little sister. There had to be an ulterior motive. Of course there did . . .' I couldn't help myself, all the anger was welling up and any second now I was going to say something I'd really regret.

The wind and sea were roaring around us, and a storm was brewing. We had to shout to make ourselves heard.

'Don't be so bloody uptight, Hannah. You've said yourself you might want out, so why shouldn't I want out as well?'

'Do you remember Switzerland, Cat?' I had nothing to lose. She was going to leave anyway, regardless of whether or not I sold the business. I could get my revenge on Cat at last.

'Do I remember where? It's this wind . . . I can't hear you properly.'

'Look . . . over there . . . behind those rocks . . . we can shelter there.'

'What did you say?'

I grabbed Cat's arms roughly and dragged her with me towards the rocks.

'Duck down here,' I ordered and we crouched together as the sky grew blacker. Now we were partly sheltered, and could hear one another speak.

'Do you remember Switzerland?' I said coldly.

I turned to look at Cat. She stared back into my eyes, unsmiling.

Cat hesitated.

'No, I didn't think you would,' I continued.

'But I do remember Switzerland,' said Cat.

'B-b-but, you couldn't. You were only three.' This wasn't going the way I expected.

'Don't tell me what I can remember and what I can't. I don't remember it all, but I remember some of it. Images, voices, that sort of thing. You're the one who can't remember it, you were just being born.'

I gulped. So Cat knew I'd been born in Switzerland. But why had we never discussed it?

'I don't get it, Cat,' I said, suddenly quite close to tears. 'Why did no one ever talk about it? Why did you never talk about it?'

Cat turned away from me now, and stared out towards the dunes.

'I couldn't. I was sworn to secrecy.'

'By whom?'

'By myself.'

'By yourself! You're not making any sense.'

'What do *you* know about Switzerland?' Cat asked, turning back to me again.

'Everything,' I said.

'And when did you find out?'

'Just a few weeks ago. In the clinic, when Mavis came to see me.'

Cat wrapped her arms around her eyes to avoid looking at me. Hunched against the wind, her back against the boulders, unable to bear my seeing her.

'You've got to talk to me, Cat. You've got to . . .'

Cat still didn't move. I reached over and tried to pull her arms from her face.

'Leave me alone. For fuck's sake leave me alone,' she screeched, her arms now flailing in the air, her eyes red and wild. 'If you know, you know, why do we have to talk about it . . .'

'Know what?' I asked, incredulous that Cat could know

what I knew. Even if she remembered Switzerland, she couldn't know . . .

'Know what?' I asked again. She had to say the words herself before I could be sure.

'That Mavis is your mother.'

I felt I'd been hit by an earthquake.

'You know *that*? You know that Mavis is my mother? When did you find out? It's impossible.'

Cat was trembling now, heaving, out of control.

'I've always known, Hannah, from even before you were born. Mavis was so fat, so fat I thought she'd burst like a balloon. I wanted her to burst. I wanted to stick a pin in her, she was always so horrible to me. Grandma and Grandpa talked about it all the time when we were in Switzerland with them. I heard them, I used to hide behind the door and listen. When they said, "Mummy's had a little girl," I knew they were lying. I just knew. She never even got fat. But because I was so small they thought they could tell me any old thing and I'd believe it. Maybe I did believe it, sort of, at first, but when we got back home, I knew you must belong to Mavis. I'd go into the nursery and it would always be Mavis, not Eleanor, who was holding you in her arms. "My baby, my baby." She said it over and over and over until I wanted to hit her.'

'But Cat, why did you never say anything to anyone for all these years?'

'You don't get it, do you, Hannah?' said Cat.

'No, I'm afraid I don't.'

'The only thing that mattered to me was that you were my sister, that I could keep you for me, that no one would take you away.'

'You thought someone would take me away?'

'Of course I did. I thought Mavis would just pack her bags and take you with her.'

'Is that why you hated her?'

'It was mutual. We hated each other, but for different reasons. She hated me because she thought I had it easy, because they preferred me to you. I hated her because she was your mother, and I thought she could do what she wanted with you.'

'What about the bruises? Those bruises you said Mavis inflicted on you. When she finally got fired. Did she or did you?'

'I did, of course. I had to get rid of her, I had to. I couldn't bear it a minute more. I knew it was a risk, that she might try to take you with her, but I also knew she'd always put you first, and I was desperate. And the risk paid off. She went and I kept you.'

'But you never even seemed to like me.'

'I didn't for quite a few years. I thought you were a wimp. But you were my sister and I thought we belonged together.'

'And when I had Frank?'

'Every time something happened to bring you closer to Mavis, I thought I'd lose you. That's why I was so angry about Frank, that's why I had nothing to do with it. I could picture the three of you together, all cosy and comfortable, and I couldn't stand it.'

'And when Mavis turned up at Melissa's wedding?'

'Same thing. It was always the same thing. I was jealous. She was always a threat, a threat I couldn't eliminate.'

Nothing in my life was as it seemed. Every time Cat was cruel, every time she'd snatched my tongue, every time she'd slighted me, put me down, disappointed me, was because she loved me and couldn't bear to lose me.

I believed her entirely. Of all the people I'd ever known it had been Cat, in her own curious way, who had been the most loyal of all. Even Mavis, my mother, had let me go. But not Cat. She'd hung on, whatever it took. We may have had different mothers, but what we shared had little to do with blood.

I was fifty-one years old and everything seemed possible. I could talk to my father and the kids . . . or not. I could even talk to Frank, though I couldn't predict his reaction. I could sell the business or not. Cat could leave the business or not. I could fall in love with Olav, or just in like. But I could fall in love with someone. Even that was possible now.

For fifty years I'd had a sister who cared, who lashed out at me not because she didn't care, but because she cared too much.

'Come on, Cat,' I said, taking her damp cold hand and pulling her up from behind the boulder. 'I've had enough of this awful weather.'

And we walked back along the sand. Two middle-aged women, head to toe in waterproofs, the taller one with her arm wrapped tightly round the smaller of the two. The smaller one with her head resting against the shoulder of her older sister as they faced the elements. Together. One thing I knew for sure. Cat had given me back my tongue. I'd found my voice. And it was highly unlikely that I'd ever lose it again.

Acknowledgments

This book is dedicated to Susan Graff, the only person to whom I dare show my work in its early stages. A hard taskmaster, she'd chain me to the keyboard if she could. I trust her judgment and am grateful for her honesty. Everyone needs a Susan Graff as a sister, I'm the one who got lucky.

I would like to thank my agent Jonny Geller for backing me every step of the way and for believing in something I didn't know I had.

Grateful thanks, too, to Sue Fletcher for so enthusiastically putting me into print – and for keeping me there. Kerry Hood is my kind of colleague – full of good ideas and equally good fun. Thanks also to Katie Davison. I am indebted to Clare Parkinson for her meticulous editing and Swati Gamble for her graciousness in dealing with my queries and requests. My thanks also to Doug Kean, Alice Lutyens, Tally Garner and Carol Jackson at Curtis Brown and everyone in sales and marketing at Hodder.

Rachel Black helped me find my singing voice, though there's a very long way to go on that score. Judy Lever and Vivien Pringle were generous with their time and insider info. Nadia, Gabrielle, Celia, Adrienne, Rivkie,

Sue, Evelyn – the women I rely on for so much. And Ask Dave – he knows why.

Gladys Ewers shaped my life and this book in ways she never could have imagined. She will always live in my memory.